THE
GRAND MAGE'S
PET

THE
GRAND MAGE'S
PET

T.D. WILLIAMS

Printed in the United States of America

First Edition, January 2022

ISBN: 979-8-9876097-0-5 (paperback)

ISBN: 979-8-9876097-2-9 (ebook)

Chapter 1

Five.

Issi forced a breath through grit teeth. The cloth came away bloody. She cursed quietly as she added it to the pile of stained silk gathering on her table.

Her candle flickered as it worked to beat back darkness. The room was alive with the dancing of shadows and the glint of gold that scattered at the edge of her vision.

Six.

The bleeding didn't seem to be slowing. She eyed her master as he snored quietly on her bed, clad only in a button up with a blanket draped over his chest. He clutched at the fabric as some nightmare or other took him.

Even from where she sat, on the other side of the small metal room he'd gifted her, she could smell the magic that settled across his skin. Sunbaked soil and the sparks she'd once noted at the metalsmith's. And stupidly, the scent of it was comforting, the fact that she felt *anything* at all was comforting.

Seven.

The knife he'd used to carve her sat on the dresser; the tip dyed ruddy. Her blood splattered across her sheets. They'd need cleaning.

Replacing.

Eight.

There were a thousand things she'd rather be doing. There were papers that were supposed to go out, and the newest batch of medical reports had come in, and she'd really like the world to stop swaying—

She sighed, planting her feet firmly on the floor as she pressed harder against the wound.

Nine.

Her master groaned from the bed. The frame creaked as he rolled over to give her a fantastic view of his ass. His back.

The very exposed side of his neck, beneath which an artery ran.

Her eyes ticked to the knife by his bedside. One moment. One infinitely small, fraction of a tick and gods above she could be done with it.

She'd be hung, of course. High treason called for nothing less.

Her pulse skittered. She frowned, counting the cloths before her.

Twelve.

Fuck.

One of these days, he was going to kill her. The old maids used to take bets on how long she'd last.

Turned out she was sturdier than anyone had anticipated.

Thirteen.

She breathed and set the last cloth against the table. Her fingers flicked through her drawer and reached for another. She bound the wound the best she could. She was running out of headscarves.

Her master cried out in his sleep as her alchemy clock launched four puffs of cherry red smoke into the air.

It was time to get up.

Issi ambled to her wardrobe, picking out a drab grey dress from an array of pompously ruffled and lowcut gowns. The only splash of color coming from the amethyst dyed threads that formed the raven of her master's insignia on the gown's breast.

Dressing was a slow, painful process. The ground acted as if it were set atop the godsdamned sea, and her fingers fumbled with the many buttons that cinched up to her neck.

She tugged at the fabric, until it lay flat. The mirror mounted against the not-bars of her cage showed a very tired reflection. Issi attempted a spin and nearly pitched into the wall.

She sank to her knees and waited for the ground to still.

Pain was still better than the alternative. Fear was better than the alternative, hells, death was better than the alternative.

She breathed in the smell of magic and felt the world around her vibrant and brutal and *real*. The light from the candle played across the floors, the fabric was soft against skin, the wounds on her spine formed a steady painful ache. She could smell the wax from the candle, and the burning of the wick, and her blood, and the soap the maids used for her gowns.

Yes, this was certainly better than feeling nothing at all.

She moved slowly, straightening to her full too short height, and tried again with the mirror. The dress hid the bandages, and the silver that'd started to snake along her skin.

Still, she covered what she could of the silver with make-up.

She wasn't sure what to do about her hair. Her master had ruined it, but she couldn't raise her arms above her head without the risk of reopening the wound.

Again.

She'd woken in a puddle of her own blood. Not as unusual an occurrence as she would have liked, but, still, distinctly unpleasant.

Maybe it was the smell of it that had ignited her master's dreams. Surely, he'd smelled plenty during the subjugation of Repren.

She digested the thought and decided to keep a cloth on hand. It'd be petty, but a few nightmares wouldn't kill him. Gods knew it was a better alternative to slitting his throat.

Tempting as it was.

Her sheets really would be ruined then.

She fixed her gown and set her canvas by the single window she'd been granted. It looked to the garden her master tended.

Once upon a time, it'd been filled with neatly filed plants that gave fruits and vegetables, and organized swaths of herbs. She started to sketch the overgrown mess that spanned beneath her now.

Wild, without the careful hands of the gardeners to keep it controlled.

He wanted her to draw people, not plants. Years ago, once he'd realized she'd a knack for it, he'd ordered her to draw portraits, and maids, and guards. It'd been a parlor trick to show off to the court ladies, *the Pet who could draw.*

Her teeth ground together at the memory. An ache ran up her left hand, tracing along the crinkles and pocks in her skin that'd never quite forgotten the fire that'd bitten into it. *Gloves,* she'd need gloves for the day as well.

She worked on a patch of golden bell-shaped flowers, hells, it didn't matter that she couldn't *see* them. She'd painted the same thing yesterday, and the day before, and the flowers would never do something as interesting as walk away.

The patch expanded as she summoned oval-leaved vines, and the small, gnarled bodies of the wide petalled flowers that smelled of sweets in summer and disappointment nearly every other time of the year.

Her mind wandered, she'd drawn the gardens so often, she suspected she could accurately track the rate of the overgrowth. Not that that was the type of experiment she found to be titillating, but it was *something* to do during the hours she wasn't allowed to read or write.

She'd moved to the palace wall by the time her master began to stir. She ignored the groaning of her bed as he shifted about and the quiet curses he spat when he realized where he'd woken up.

He hated waking behind the not-bars of her cage nearly as much as she did. Disguise them all he want as flowers and meadow grasses, a prison was a prison was a prison.

Issi'd yet to find someone who enjoyed waking up in one.

To be fair, she didn't meet a lot of people these days. Maybe she'd get lucky if she cast her net a bit wider.

"There's blood," he commented.

Issi squinted in the early morning sunlight that tumbled through her window. "There is, it's mine."

"There's a lot of it."

How would the king ever survive without him?

"It was hard to stop the bleeding, master. I apologize for the mess." She stood, faced him, and bowed. The world swayed drunkenly to the right. She locked her legs and focused on the floor until it steadied.

She wondered absently if her sister had to put up with this. Their mother had never adjusted well to the beatings. The twins were almost the age to be sold off too. How long would it take them? A moon? A year?

"—Issi?"

She blinked. "I'm sorry, I was days away. Could you repeat the question?"

"Stand."

She straightened slowly and plastered a warm smile on her face. Her master closed the distance between them.

Hot earth and metal sparks.

His hand cupped her cheek, and she breathed deeply as he tilted her head towards him. The world seemed to sharpen with the smell. She melted against his palm.

"What were you drawing?"

"Plants, the golden sanguinary is doing well," she lied. It was dying a slow and painful death by the window because the concubine's shadblow had finally grown enough to blot out the sun it'd been languishing in.

He kissed her forehead. "Are you not bored of plants? I can get you a model."

Again, her hand ached, she clenched it to remind it that life would be easier if it didn't insist on being an ass.

She pretended to consider his offer. Issi was, indeed, very bored of plants. She could draw them from every angle in every state of germination, and she could tell him which parents had fathered which seeds.

But that didn't mean she'd like to draw people again.

"Master." She reached up. Her hands ran through the soft curls of his hair as she grinned. "I love drawing them. Would you like another sketch?"

She felt him shudder.

He had an entire drawer filled with the damned things. She'd made sure it was the same stupid flower every time.

"No," he replied. He tried to keep his expression warm, but that stressed look had started about his eyes and mouth.

He hesitated. "I don't enjoy disciplining you."

Rage ignited in the pit of her stomach. "I know. It won't happen again."

He nodded.

It'd been a stupid thing: she'd been trying to ask for an oil lantern. Well, "ask" was a bit too direct. She'd been trying to circle about getting around to having him *offer* her an oil lamp, when she'd made the mistake of warning him against casting *light* and set him off.

And now her sheets were covered in blood.

It didn't take much these days.

"Does it hurt?"

She held out, the answer on the tip of her tongue, a compulsive need to respond that would soon cinch her throat shut and stop her breathing until it was let out.

One heartbeat.

Two.

Three—

It wasn't a smart game to play while suffering from blood loss. "No." Her record was one hundred, but she couldn't remember how that one had ended.

Obviously, she had lived, which was a bit of a pity.

The Grand Mage smiled. "Good."

He kissed her, and Issi fought the revulsion that turned her stomach. His fingers wound through her hair and his free hand pushed her flush against him. She forced down her disgust, as she busied herself with the technicals of the response.

He wanted warm and playful.

He wanted love and comfort.

He wanted the lie.

And it was Issi's job to make it feel real.

He broke away, his breath painting the air between them. "Tell me," he ordered.

Issi ignored the urge to retch and gave him a playful smirk. "Tell you what, Sir Grand Mage?"

He grinned.

Gods how she wanted to break his nose. She should have run the knife through the skin of his throat when she'd the chance.

But rage was important.

Hatred was important.

Because it wasn't *nothing*.

She swallowed the bile that bit her throat and kissed his cheek. "I love you."

Chapter 2

The muffled whispers of the maids were almost musical. An incessant twittering that reminded Issi of the birds that lived in the orchard she'd grown near.

Like the birds, the maids sang the same songs over and over.

Gossip about the Athijan nobles, the youngest prince's latest tryst, the last zealot hung in the market square, the newest treat at the bakery. Rumors, secrets, promises, the maids picked them up like sweets from all over the palace.

Her master had fired most of the private maids moons ago, the new ones rotated through in batches of five. Issi had *hoped* that meant they'd gain a little more variety in their set of interests, but all that had changed was the timbre of their voices and her ability to track their names.

A maid with green eyes played absently with Issi's door, swinging large metal flowers to and fro, "The Athijans are a very tall people, don't you think?"

Issi contemplated the merits of banging her head against her table.

"They are, aren't they? I just saw one in the atrium. Very tall."

Dear gods above, anything but this. "Why do you think they're here?"

The women paused at her interjection. New maids always did, like they were surprised she could speak, or maybe at how she sounded. The words tumbled from her mouth in Qashan fair enough, but she didn't *sound* Qashan.

She held onto vowels too long, swallowed the wrong set of consonants which twisted the jagged tones of their language into something else entirely. Egrean, which was the joke of it.

A Chousalian with an Egrean accent, living in Qasha. She supposed it was enough to give anyone pause.

The disgust that crossed their faces felt a bit unfair, but she was used to that too.

The one on the right, a quiet woman with a propensity for shrinking away whenever someone so much as sneezed out of turn spoke up, "Well…miss Anders, they're diplomats and it's almost time for the King's Dinner, so I suppose they're here to watch."

That was true enough, but it didn't really answer the question. The King's Dinner was a biannual affair, used to establish who had risen ranks or fallen out of favor in the rapidly changing landscape that passed for the king's court.

However, it was usually an internal affair and from the rumors that circled, they didn't seem to be doing anything at all. If it was information they wanted, they certainly didn't have to stay in the castle year-round to get it.

"And why are they watching?"

The maid shared a look of concern with her green-eyed companion. "Well, it's not our place to worry about such things."

Issi bit back a retort, *everyone* in the palace was trying to figure out precisely what they were doing there.

She wasn't the only one bored within the walls.

"Well, this is nice and clean," the green-eyed maid stepped in, though what *this* was, was beyond Issi. The woman had feigned swiping at the doorframe, before she offered Issi a lackluster bow. "If you'll excuse us, we've other things that need doing."

They didn't wait for her dismissal. The title was in name only after all.

At least she wouldn't have to listen to how *tall* the visitors were for the next bell.

She counted down the moments on her alchemy clock as she tore the sheets off her bed, revealing that the mattress underneath had stained too. She folded the fabric, setting it in a heap before promptly running out of things to do.

Maybe scaring the maids off had been a bad idea after all. She paced around her cage, and then out of her cage to pace the rest of the room before going back inside.

The knock at her door was almost cathartic.

"Ner!" Issi's face lit and the maid's darkened as she looked her over.

"You're not planning to—"

"Oh, but I am." Issi swiped a few of the bloody scarves off her table and stuffed them hurriedly into her pocket. Gods, what was a reasonable number for her to have bled through? Was five too much?

"You look tired." The smell of breakfast trailed after the maid as she walked through the room. Warm flatbreads with a spiced cimmeona jam and an assortment of fruit rattled on the breakfast tray she carried. Issi's stomach twisted. Was she supposed to eat or not when she lost this much blood?

Issi moved the rest of the clothes to make room for the maid to set down her burden. "I *am* tired," she said, shaking one of her scarves. The pattern had been obscured by a dark stain that'd gone well on its way to brown. "Busy night."

Ner frowned, honey-colored eyes showing disapproval. "Again?"

Issi dipped her finger into the jam, her eyes widening at the sweetness of it. *Sugar.* That was what she wanted.

"Issi, how bad was it?" the maid prompted. Issi pointed her chin to the pile she'd collected while spreading jam over bread.

The maid tutted, counting the scarves and noting the size of the stain on her sheets. "Are you feeling alright?"

Issi had just stuffed the entirety of the flatbread into her mouth, as if the near decade of etiquette lessons hadn't taught her a damned thing. She chewed quickly, covering her mouth with her unscarred hand as soon as speaking became feasible. "Sorry...hungry, just very, very...hungry."

"Well, you've got an appetite." The maid smiled and reached to touch Issi's head.

Issi lurched back and unbalanced herself, she had just enough time to curse before she banged into the not-bars and the world snuffed out for a fraction of a heartbeat. In the darkness something called her. Or it felt like something. When she opened her eyes, the maid loomed over her, pulling the dirtied fabric from Issi's pocket.

Her painted lips pursed to form butterfly wings as she shook out the fabric. "Really? Is this how we're going to do this today?"

The world swam, rocking side to side like it fancied itself on a pendulum. Issi blinked trying to think past the pain that turned her thoughts to ash. She gasped and said the first words that came to mind, "You were to stopping me." She frowned, that was wrong. "Going to stop me."

"Because what you were planning was stupid."

Issi struggled to sit up. The maid watched her, but blessedly, decided against offering a hand.

Ner's frowned deepened as she counted the stained scarves, "Did he send for a healer?"

"I'm *bored,* Ner. I was only going to borrow a couple of bells," she complained. "Two at the most."

"That's a no then."

"I even waited for you so I could eat first. Do you know what the other maids were prattling on about? They said the Athijans were *tall,*" outrage forced Issi's voice into peaks. "It was going to be their entire conversation, I could *feel* it. They would have filled an entire bell just comparing their heights to other *less tall* things until they managed to get the proportions just right."

"And you're off again." The maid set to gathering the copious amount of stained fabric.

"I'm not asking for a lot, Ner, but a nice piece of actual gossip would have been lovely."

"Finish your breakfast. I'll bring more water, you need fluids," she said, as she started through the cage's doorway.

"I *need* you to be adventurous," Issi groused, as she tore into the fruit.

The young maid didn't justify that with a response. Issi tapped her fingers against the table contemplating how much of a lecture would await her if she up and left *anyway.*

She felt along the seam of her sleeves until her fingers brushed against something hard just a bit bigger than the nail on her small finger. She bit back a yelp of excitement. Ner hadn't found this one yet. A few moments of graceless flailing resulted in a small wooden tablet depositing itself neatly into her open palm.

The front was covered in painstakingly carved notches and lines while the rear was a red brown color that closely matched that of the stained scarves the maid had hurried off with.

Issi ran her hands through her hair trying to detangle what she could without raising her arms above her neck. She gathered unruly strands and bound them together with a ribbon from her wardrobe and studied herself in the mirror.

The meal had done wonders. She felt...not quite alive, but well on her way to it. She looked mildly unkempt, but no more than was to be expected if someone lived a life for purposes other than preening and looking pretty.

Her alchemy clock informed her it was a half-bell before nine. Her master wasn't fond of mid-morning or lunch visits so that meant she usually had this time to herself. Full bells dedicated to not going mad with the conversations from the maids, or drawing the same stupid set of flowers, or doing the same embroidery, or practicing the dozens of pieces waiting to be brought to life on her violin.

And, about two or three times a moon, sneaking out of her master's wing.

It'd been easier when there were students about. The entire wing had been livelier, and nobody questioned the existence of a student leaving in the middle of the day.

Now, things were a bit more precarious.

She slipped on a pair of plain slippers and nudged the door to her room open, peeking through the crack. Ner was nowhere in sight. She went back into her cage and retrieved a sketchbook and a dainty bag of charcoal.

Summoning an air of propriety was the most difficult part.

Issi left her cage and hurried down the hall, passing the green-eyed maid and her mousy companion who spared her the barest glances before returning to their work. From the edges of their whispers, it seemed they were trying to determine if the Athijans were better measured in hands, like horses, or in terms of the giant stones that formed the supports for the palace's outer wall.

The stairwell she paused before was an awkward twisting structure better used by children and mice than a person of even Issi's stature, much less the servants it was intended for. Issi ignored the way the walls pressed in around her and forced her way to the ground floor. The stairway deposited her between the door to the garden and another corridor that'd lead her straight to a myriad of halls, one of which led outside her master's suite.

She stopped in the garden first.

It was worse up close.

From her window she could force everything into order, see which greenery belonged to which plant and haphazardly map the structure. Now all she knew was that there was a branch in her face, and another branch that nearly struck her after she cleared the first.

There wasn't much need for hiding her things. She lay them at the base of a gnarled tree and trusted that no one had been this far in the garden for nearly half a year. That, and the fact that nobody had found the box filled with small copper pieces she'd simply placed near the wall some moons ago.

She took six small plated coins from the box and slid them into her pocket before pulling out the marked wooden tablet.

She pressed her thumb against the carved surface. The air filled with the scent of spices, and aggerlon oranges. The world snapped into focus as her skin disappeared beneath a layer of olive tone that along with a handful of minor alterations would make her appear passably Qashan.

A hiss escaped between her teeth as she tied the pendant around her neck and tucked it between her breasts.

A creak dragged Issi's gaze upwards.

She backed hurriedly towards the building as Ner thrust open the window to her room. Through the leaves of an overgrown shrub Issi spied the maid's form tipping through the opening. Her grey uniform billowed against the blue of the sky.

"Issi, you better be down there, or I swear on the honor of—"

Well, that was going nowhere good. Issi slipped back through the doorway before the rest of Ner's promise made itself apparent.

It was a blessedly quick walk to the front of the wing. Issi stopped just short of bursting through the doors, startling the guards on duty.

"Kings, Del." The one on the right recovered faster. "I thought something was wrong."

Issi smiled and worked to slow her breathing. Sometimes it felt like Ner was better at sniffing her out than the royal dogs. "Oh, I would never dream of making you work."

Nalav straightened, according to some of the maids, he was a handsome man. Issi supposed she could see it. He had a confidence about him and a deceptively delicate face. It was almost a shame that that confidence came from a rather interesting gambling habit that had him forever dipping into the pockets of his companions for that last scrap of copper.

Almost.

His colleague, on the other hand, Issi didn't recognize.

Another guard change.

"You know her?" the new guard, a woman with close cropped hair, spoke up.

Nalav grinned and wrapped an arm around his companion's neck, his free hand gesturing grandly to Issi. "This is Del, the last of the Grand Mage's students."

Issi offered a shallow bow. "It's a pleasure to meet you, miss—?"

"Ari, you can call me Ari," she muttered, studying Issi skeptically. "I didn't hear about you."

Obviously.

Issi frowned. "Don't tell me you believe the rumors about the Grand Mage dismissing all the students."

A blush brought out the smattering of freckles that danced across the woman's cheeks. "Well, that is—"

Issi laughed, "That'd be insane, he still needs an assistant, you know?"

The blush deepened. "Well, of…of course. It's just you weren't mentioned."

Nalav let the woman go his grin tugging higher on the right side as he fought back laughter. "Do you really you'll learn everything from a morning briefing?"

Ari's eyes darted to the floor. Issi felt a pang of pity, but this was what made Nalav so very perfect. And a godsawful gambler.

He never questioned convenience.

Issi's existence made *sense.* Her master's sudden dismissal of all the students and gardeners and maids had been concerning at best. If he'd kept even a single student, just for assistant work, well that painted a nicer picture. It meant he hadn't completely lost it in the face of illness.

And that was more than enough for Nalav to stop thinking about it. He convinced nearly everyone else to do the same.

"To be young," he scoffed. "Del has been here forever."

Some days, it really felt that way. "I'm off for breakfast, do you want anything?"

"I couldn't—" Ari began.

"I saw the Northern Tribeswoman bringing cimmeona jam," Nalav interrupted. "Could you get your hands on that?"

Issi shifted. "Well, that's a bit..."

"Come on," he prodded, "A small jar?"

She pursed her lips, glancing nervously at the door. "I'll get what I can."

She hurried away with a wave before her luck ran out.

The servant's corridor swallowed her. The only light came from the smokeless blue flame provided every dozen paces or so by torches of mage's fire.

She gave them wide berth, mage's fire, for the most part, was smokeless and heatless, but that didn't mean it wouldn't burn if someone was dumb enough to thrust their hand into it.

And Issi had already proven herself more than capable of that particular flavor of stupidity.

The halls populated the further she moved from her master's wing. Servants joined her, first in a smattering, then in a crowd that eventually became so big that when the traffic bottlenecked near the kitchens she was forced to a standstill, broken every few moments by an awkward and desperate shuffling that somehow got her to the door.

Thank Ose's blue skies.

Issi loved the kitchens for two reasons. The first being that they were absolutely brimming with magic, and runes. They reminded her of her master's wing when things had been going...well, certainly not great, but *better*. There'd been fewer beatings, better conversations to eavesdrop on, and more opportunities to sneak away.

But mostly, it had *felt* of magic. From morning to night, she could *feel* the enchantments the students worked on singing through the air. Spells that wrangled magic into neat little runes to make things light up, or move, or bloom, had surrounded her and set the world right, brightening the color of the skies and sharpening corners.

It made things feel *real*.

The kitchens were, given a world where the best outcome was denied, a reasonable, if pale, facsimile.

She was rushed through a crowd of frenzied individuals, who were busy shouting orders at the chefs and poor kitchen boys forced to weave in and out of the throng. This close to the King's Dinner, the castle was filled with guests, and nobody had thought that staggering orders might have been a good idea.

Issi tried to ignore the press of bodies against her as she scanned the cooking stations for a head of short black curls.

"Where are you looking?"

The voice sounded in her ear. Issi spun, the world tried and failed to keep up with her. "Don't *do* that."

And here was the second reason she loved going to the kitchens. A kitchen boy towered over her by nearly a head and a half, his attention flickered to the crowd that had started to split around them. "You're the one standing in the middle of a whirlwind and looking dour about it." His smile was pure mischief, even as his brows lowered, "I thought you liked crowds."

"I like people," she corrected. The crowd had always been a bit...*much*.

"Is there a difference?"

"Of course, there's a difference Ardein," she muttered, darkly. He waited a moment, and then, sensing she had no intention of elaborating, turned and carved a path to one of the corners of the kitchens, blessedly far from the great fire that served to power all the runes in the area. It was hard to get the smell of it out of her clothes.

And Ner got very angry whenever Issi returned from places she shouldn't have gone, *smelling* of places she shouldn't have gone.

Ardein produced a ladle and sunk it into a pot warming on an engraved tablet the size of Issi's torso. Or that was what he'd intended to do.

The liquid proved too viscous for his attempt to succeed. He ended up rocking the ladle back and forth, muttering under his breath, until it finally slipped beneath the surface.

With his free hand, he gestured for her to take a seat. "Are you ready?"

"To die?"

The cook frowned. "The thickness is new, but I only left it for a tick so it shouldn't be anything serious."

Issi studied the pot's contents skeptically. It looked like something an evil mage would force children to drink in fairy stories.

"Are you sure?"

His eyes, a warm brown, grew warmer still as his smile widened. "I'm never sure about anything, but you haven't died yet."

"That's promising."

The cook pulled at the ladle with a disturbing amount of effort that did little to speed the process along. It released with an uncomfortably loud *pop*.

"Are you sure you don't want to try it first?" Issi tried.

Ardein shook his head. "I haven't been able to taste anything for the last few days."

"Another experiment?"

"Please." He rolled his eyes and waved the ladle about. Issi could not help but notice that the liquid in the spoon never once seemed interested in sloshing around. "Experimenting is for mages and alchemists...I was just...trying something different."

"The very definition of experimenting."

"Shut up, Del, I'm trying to be dramatic," he snapped at her, playfully, "Besides, I have your payment."

Issi sat up straighter. "Really?"

He held the ladle in front of her face. "You don't have to act surprised."

"Oranges aren't the easiest to come by," she pointed out. "I haven't seen a proper vendor *ever*."

"Who said I got these from a *proper* vendor?"

"These?"

He shook the ladle again. Issi took it into her hand and sent a silent prayer to Naya.

May she not come to retrieve her soul just yet.

She put her lips to the spoon and very nearly wished the goddess had chosen to kill her instead. As with all of Ardein's experiments, it was impressively awful. Sweet and salty, overpowering and bland.

"So?"

Tears filled her eyes. The texture was some impossibly thick consistency that stuck to the roof of her mouth and teeth.

"It's...badly...badding...awfulling," she struggled a moment, "Ardein...I don't think Qashan *has* words to explain how badly this is."

He arched a brow. "Badly?"

"Bad, how *bad*, it is."

"You haven't spit it out yet, that's an improvement."

Issi's tongue worked to pry the monstrosity from her back teeth. "I can't. I think it's bonded to my mouth."

"Oh." Realization lurched across his features. "Oh, you weren't kidding. Wait."

He produced another ladle, this one filled with water. Issi emptied it in less than a beat. "What *was* that?"

He looked at her sheepishly, as he removed the concoction from the heating plate. "Soup."

"Soup?" she parroted blankly.

"Del, there's no need to—"

"Explain to me how." She stood to get a better look at the liquid, it was so dark it was nearly black. She'd never seen a plant or anything short of a very exotic edible ink manage quite that shade. He moved her out of the way.

"It *was* beef and a few greens."

"*A few greens*?" she echoed. There was nothing green about it, and if she'd tasted anything that could have been identified as meat, she'd walk herself to the gallows.

He set the atrocity on a low rack for cooling and produced an orange seemingly from thin air. Not magic, but a very clever sleight of hand that made it feel astoundingly close.

She plucked the orange from his palm, her nails breaking through its skin. The smell of citrus reached her nose and for the first time in ages she smiled simply because she wanted to.

"There we are," Ardein muttered. "I knew you were looking a little peaked."

"I haven't been sleeping well."

His eyes lit with curiosity. "Is the Grand Mage working you again?"

Issi's hands slowed. "...in a fashion."

"What's he have you doing this time?"

"Oh...well..." She shifted, uncomfortably. She didn't enjoy lying to Ardein, he was the first friend she'd made who hadn't been ordered to like her. "Keeping up with the reports, writing, experiments. The usual."

Ardein pulled another giant pot from beneath the table and stared down at it curiously, likely trying to figure out the next abomination he was going to slap together. For all the time she'd been in the kitchens, Issi'd never seen him successfully cook anything. How he managed to keep his job was another mystery she intended to figure out, right after putting together where he kept buying the oranges.

"You're as vague as ever, Del," he grumbled.

Issi swept the peel pieces into a pile before splitting the fruit between her hands, "You ask too much."

He let out a sharp laugh. Issi flinched crushing her second breakfast. She let out a curse and licked where the juice threatened to spill out of her palm.

"Sorry," he added, quickly.

"It's nothing, just surprised me." She forced a laugh and tried to convince her hands to still. Laughter from Ardein wasn't a dangerous thing.

Laughter from Ardein wasn't a dangerous thing.

Ner was right, she was far too tired for this. She pulled off a piece of the orange and popped it into her mouth.

"How is it?" the cook asked.

"Still not right, it's not..." She paused, searching for the word, "acidic enough? It's sweeter than the last one though."

He frowned. "I could have sworn that would be the one."

"It's fine, I don't understand what you find so fascinating about this, it tastes alright." She ate another piece.

"But it's not what you want," he continued. He dumped an entire bundle of greens into the pot without even trimming the roots. "I bet you'll smile, *really* smile, if I find it. Maybe I'll even get a genuine laugh, *imagine that.*"

She glared at him. "Ha."

"There you are."

Issi knew rude gestures for a multitude of cultures, but none could be achieved with the pulpy remains of an orange in her palms.

Issi relaxed. "Do you want some?" She shook the remnants in his direction. He made a face.

"Really, Del?"

She shrugged. "It's supposed to be shared."

"No."

A tired laugh escaped her and Ardein arched his brows. "That was pathetic, I'm not counting it."

"Do whatever you want," she sighed, laying across his table. The magic from the tablet smelled of winter flowers.

"Del, that's all I ever do." He dropped something black into the pot, as if to prove the point.

Issi watched him work and felt time slip by. It was nice in the kitchens in a way it wasn't anywhere else.

Chapter 3

Issi woke with a start.

The kitchen stood empty. The hearth fire had long burned out, no embers, no cooling coals. There was nothing to be seen other than row after row of clean and empty workstations.

Her master would have noticed she'd been missing. Her mind nearly stopped. Denial fogged her thoughts as desperation tried to paint the scenario in brighter strokes. Maybe he'd been called out, or Ner had been able to cover for her, or—

A sob scraped her throat.

Nydelissi.

Her name sounded dulcetly behind her. The voice tilted the vowels in a way she hadn't heard since she'd left Egrean soil.

Like it actually knew how to pronounce her name.

Issi tried to turn. It was like moving through honey, every motion heavy and slow and dull. From the corner of her eye, she made out a girl. She was younger than Issi with a halo of hair that'd been convinced into a fat braid that'd been twisted to rest atop her head like a crown. Her skin was the color of burnt cedar. Near the color of Issi's skin, her mother's, her sibling's.

Issi had never seen another Chousalian before.

Her mouth opened the language ready to tumble from her lips. She wasn't sure what she was meant to say, or how any of this was possible, but maybe she'd be able to stop feeling quite so alone.

Something touched her back, brushing against fresh cuts and weary nerves. She whimpered, opening her eyes.

"Del?" Ardein's face hovered above her. She leaned away trying to gain some distance and nearly tipped the chair.

"Del." The cook rushed to steady her.

"Don't," her voice wavered. From the position of the sun, it seemed she'd only dozed for a bell, maybe two. The kitchens were still noisy with orders. "I'm fine. I just...you were right there and...uhm..."

He produced a handkerchief and held it out for her. "You're crying."

She nodded and ignored his offering, favoring her sleeve.

"Do you—"

"No, I'm..." Embarrassment set her face on fire, she forced a smile. "...do you, by any chance, have cimmeaon jam?"

The cook frowned and gave a minute shake of his head.

"Alright, that's fine," she sniffled, and shook herself. "I was supposed to bring some with me."

Her hands shook so badly, the coppers bounced twice before landing on the table. Ardein looked from the coins back to her, worry softening his face.

"I don't need your—"

She shook her head. "Ardein, don't, I...if you could just taking, *take*, the fucking money, that'd be great."

For a moment, the boy did nothing at all. Issi waited, feeling like she was a tick from falling to pieces. She stifled a hiccup, blinking quickly to keep more tears from falling.

At last, he nodded, slipping the coins into his palm. Issi ignored the way he tracked her as she left. She made a point not to meet his gaze. If she didn't see it, she could keep pretending she hadn't royally screwed up. She stopped at the first station out of his line of sight and asked after Nalav's bribe.

She visited five before she managed to trade three coppers and the promise of a heating enchantment for a jar small enough to fit in her palm.

She cursed the guard under her breath as her fingers wrapped around the glass.

The servant's corridor was still packed. She hovered by the edge as people hurried by. Her heart thrummed painfully against her ribs as she clutched at the jar of amber colored jam.

She could do it. All she had to do was slip into the throng of workers brushing against each other, touching her when she wasn't meant to be touched, while fending off blood scented memories and successfully keeping herself from collapsing into a sobbing mess.

Simple.

Her legs nearly tangled as she backed away.

Issi left through the main entrance instead, following the hall's twists and turns through a series of connecting rooms that didn't feel at all like they should as high ornate ceilings shrank and gave way to plain stone, which later turned to ruined murals.

The patterning was largely due to the odd manner in which Kothen Palace had been built. Its first expansion had elected to build *over* the original structure, connecting the old with the new through a series of hallways and integrated rooms. The second had done something similar, as had the third, the fourth, and the fifth, resulting in a mishmash of forgotten corridors and indecisive halls that spoke through eras.

The rooms eventually spat her into the main atrium, a large glass domed structure that rained sunlight through slabs of colored glass. The patterns it cast along the floor were nonsensical, but if Issi squinted just right, she could find where mages had thinned glass and changed its color to erase what had once depicted the gods atop their spired towers.

Still, hard as the king had tried, some of the room's original purpose remained untouched. The atrium had been a room of worship, a place where everyone was equal. There was no servant's corridor here. Everyone walked beneath the ruined pictures of gods with equal standing, nobles and servants, merchants and children all milled beneath its colorful sky.

Issi hurried through, catching sight of the Athijans before they turned down another corridor. They *were* tall, but they were also graceful, and odd, and severe looking.

Their faces scrunched like they'd eaten something unbearably sour.

A near suicidal urge to follow them tugged at her, but she made do with staring longingly at where they'd disappeared before slipping into the servant's corridor on the other side.

The tunnels spread before her like many fingered hand, branching off into long forgotten paths that led to neglected rooms and hiding places. Issi followed the lights, passing quickly from the glow of one torch to the next.

She tossed Nalav his godsdamned jam before retrieving her things and removing her enchantment in the gardens.

Issi slunk into her ornate prison and collapsed on the bed feeling the heavy bone dragging weariness that came from making a fool of oneself in front of friend and stranger alike.

She'd been trying to be normal.

Waking up panicked, crying, and shaking was not *normal*.

Was it?

She didn't respond when she heard a knock on the door, and she didn't move when she heard the delicate footsteps that crossed the room to reach her cage.

If Ner planned on giving her a dressing down, she'd have to do it to Issi's prone figure.

"Issi?"

She bolted upright, ignoring the pain in her back as she scrambled to her feet. "Master. I'm so, so, sorry. If I'd—, I should have—, I mean."

"Shut up."

Her mouth snapped shut. Fear from the dream ran down her spine and threatened to buckle her legs. He was going to ask where she'd been. She glanced at her notebook. Would he believe she'd gone to the gardens?

"Strip."

The order was unexpected, and it took her mind a beat to catch up. Issi straightened and studied the Grand Mage wearily. Her hands trembled as she worked the buttons. Her breath hitched as everything tumbled from her fingers.

"I'm sorry, I just—."

The Grand Mage's lips all but disappeared as his expression pulled in annoyance. "Shut up."

Run.

Issi forced herself still as he approached her.

Run.

She clasped her hands behind her back to stop the shaking and forced a smile. He unbuttoned her to her waist and spun her, stripping the fabric from her shoulders.

His finger ran along her makeshift bandage. "Did you do this?"

Issi nodded, and the Grand Mage sighed as he worked to pull the fabric away. She bit her lip to keep from making noise as dry blood peeled from her skin.

"This is going to need stitches," he grumbled. He spun her back around.

She stared at him baffled.

The sight of him bent over and annoyed as his fingers worked to thread the buttons through their holes was completely foreign.

He didn't do things like this.

He released her and started towards the door. "Follow."

She did.

The Grand Mage's wing more closely resembled a museum than a proper living space. It was cluttered with knickknacks and baubles and large spanning tapestries. Every few steps there was a statue, or shiny on display to be fawned over and forgotten. Issi was forever trying not to feel like another collectible.

Her master stood before a set of heavy wooden doors. Gifts from Repren before the war had wiped them from the maps. She hurried to open them, letting the Grand Mage through before following on his heels. The room smelled of hot earth and metal, oranges, and perfume.

A dozen or so empty desks sat in the center, while books and cabinets lined the walls, beneath high arching windows. Extra shelves dotted the floors to cram more tomes, reports, and experiments. Fire crackled happily on a pile of logs in the hearth on the far wall.

Her master pointed to one of the desks. "Sit."

She crossed the room quickly, trying not to feel exposed. There was an emptiness to it during the day that she couldn't articulate. She wove her fingers together as she perched on the table's edge.

She tried to breathe past the panic fluttering in her chest. By the time he returned, she'd worked herself into a frenzy.

"Can you unbutton your dress?"

Issi nodded and in moments had the garment undone. The Grand Mage's eyes swept over her, taking in the brands that crossed her torso and the scars that traversed everywhere else.

"Does it hurt?" he breathed.

Issi stiffened, her body wanting to answer.

Her master tutted behind her. "I should have phrased that better." A finger tapped the center of her spine. "Out with it."

"No," she panted. Her shoulders rose and fell as she sucked at the air.

"How much does it hurt?"

She hesitated, searching for a safe response. "A—, master it...I'm fine. It's fine."

Issi gasped as pain forced the world dim. She pitched forward, the only thing that kept her from tumbling onto the floor was her master's arm. Her teeth gnashed together, narrowly missing her tongue.

Breathe.

She willed the room into focus.

"I didn't ask if it was fine," he muttered. The Grand Mage pulled his fingers from the wound and righted her.

"Sorry." For what, she wasn't exactly sure, but she felt like she should say...something, anything, to beat back how *empty* the room felt. "It hurts...very much."

He muttered disapprovingly. A soft pop sounded behind her. The scent of rot and the bright high noted smell she associated with the turning of plants reached her nose. She twisted to get a better view.

"Face forward."

She complied and tried not to flinch as his fingers painted over her wounds.

"I told her to bring something better smelling," he grumbled.

The tension in her shoulders eased as the poultice numbed the pain. A sigh of relief escaped her.

"I couldn't get a proper healer to patch you. They're cutting me off." He laughed, darkly. The sound of it set her heart thrumming like an Egrean engine as she recalled how the last healer howled when the Grand Mage struck him. "I'm not dead yet."

She tensed as a needle broke her skin.

"Hold still," his voice rang hollow. "It's been a while."

Issi narrowly stopped herself from asking what he meant by *a while*.

The current Grand Mage had made a name for himself by designing a few very nasty enchantments and having a hand in the creation of the Transfer, a large, hulking machine that could send letters across vast distances in a matter of moments. But before all that, he'd been a boy in a particularly bloody war where mages had served the frontlines.

She imagined he'd done a lot of patching.

He didn't speak as he worked, his movements rigid. She felt the needle shaking between his fingers.

There was a lot of work to be done.

By the end, a heap of bloody gauze had been added to the table and she felt stiff from sitting still for so long. The ring of metal as scissors cut thread was musical.

She yawned. The world had long gone soft at the edges. A shiver shook her despite the fire that still snapped away behind her.

"To your rooms," the Grand Mage ordered, wearily. He dropped the needle into a shallow porcelain bowl.

Issi leapt down, gripping the edge of the table as the world pitched.

"Your rooms," he repeated.

"Yes master, and..." She frowned, this felt all sorts of wrong. "Thank you."

Surprise shifted his features. His dull green eyes widened a moment before a blush touched his cheeks. Then it was gone, like a curtain had pulled across his face. He started brushing the gauze into a bin. "Yes, you're very welcome for fixing a problem I caused."

Ah, that was right, wasn't it?

She nodded faintly and tottered to her cage to find her sheets cleaned and any trace of the night before wiped away as if it'd never happened. She flopped gracelessly onto her bed.

For the first time in ages, she sank into oblivion and woke only after the sun had risen.

Chapter 4

Issi woke to the birdsong that sounded from the gardens beneath her window. The chitters, chirps and warbling cries formed a melody that kindly informed her that she'd overslept. She burrowed beneath her covers trying to catch the tail end of a dream.

It'd been a sweet thing about a forest somewhere outside the Grand Mage's reach. *She'd* been somewhere beyond his reach. That idea had been too intoxicating to let go.

She sat up, ignoring how her back complained. Exhaustion tried to coax her back beneath the covers with whispered promises of warmth and rest.

Ner found her staring blearily at a scrubbed stain on the carpet. "Seems like he got you a healer, hmm?"

Issi's stomach rumbled as the smell of breakfast filled her cage.

"Come on." The maid set the tray on the table. "I know it's hard, but you've got to get up."

Issi nodded drowsily, fighting a yawn. "I'm up?" That didn't sound right, had that been Egrean? Gods, she couldn't remember the last time she'd slept the night through. Her eyelids fluttered.

The maid smiled, letting her hand brush against Issi's arm. Issi was suddenly *very* awake. She pulled away as if she'd been burned. Her heart set a panicked drumbeat between her temples.

"*Now* you're awake."

Issi glared at her. "I hope your laundry stains."

Ner gasped, her hands flying to her mouth in mock horror. "Oh, the cruelty. Issi, dear, whatever will you threaten me with next?" She wiggled her nine fingers, the last, the thumb on her left hand, ended in a stump.

Issi swallowed an old argument. The maid lifted a brush from the vanity and Issi braced herself as it ran through her hair.

"I wish you wouldn't be so flagrant about it," she breathed, "Ner, please—"

The maid didn't stop. "Issi, what I do is my business."

She caught Ner's reflection in the vanity's mirror. The woman stood completely at ease; her eyes trained on the top of Issi's head.

Issi's attention darted to the door, expecting the Grand Mage to burst through and—

She squeezed her eyes shut.

"You're going to have to breathe," the maid sighed. She set the first pin in Issi's hair.

"I can finish on my own."

Ner's skepticism tried to bore a hole through her skull. "Raise your arms, then."

Issi tried, a hiss escaped through her clinched teeth before she guided her arms carefully to her sides. "I'll look subpar, that's fine," she grumbled, "He hardly notices."

"If I were doing this for *him*, I'd have left it loose," Ner answered, pointedly, "But the annoying child I used to care for, hated having hair in her face. I don't think she ever got used to it."

A blush warmed Issi's cheeks, "I don't—"

"Just say thank you."

"I...I can't repay you, Ner," Issi answered, softly.

The maid tugged at a patch of hair. "I didn't ask you to *repay* me, I asked you to *thank* me."

Issi toyed with the fabric of her dress. She hadn't bothered to change out of yesterday's uniform.

"Come on," the maid prompted, warmly.

"Thank you, Ner," Issi muttered. It wasn't enough, if she had the power her master had, she'd give Ner everything her heart desired, make-up, dresses, books, enchantments, weapons. *Anything.*

Ner finished pinning and tipped Issi's head up, so she caught her reflection. "There, pretty as a summer sunset."

Issi rolled her eyes. Maybe if she could wield her beauty like the noblewomen in the courts, she'd care for it more. As it was, the way she looked only served to remind her of her mother and siblings.

At least half of it did. The grey eye she'd apparently inherited from her father ruined the effect on the left side.

"Can you dress yourself?" the maid asked.

"Of course." Issi poured as much disgust into the statement as she could manage. Ner nodded and they both pretended there hadn't been times Issi had broken into tears at the mere sight of buttons and lace.

"Then I've spent too long pampering you," Ner teased, "What are you going to do today?"

Issi squinted at her. "Get dressed and eat? Try not to go mad with boredom?"

"And?" Ner prompted.

"And...what? I don't think there's anything on the schedule."

The maid's lips twitched downward. "You're to pick out three pieces."

Dread filled Issi's stomach. "For what?" It'd been two moons since her master had received any sort of private invitation, and three years since Issi had been allowed to leave the wing, but she prayed that *that* had somehow changed in the last twenty-six bells.

"The King's Dinner," the maid answered, patiently, "You're going."

Issi bit her lip. "Am I?"

"I know it's difficult, but he needs you."

He *needed* her. Issi's hands passed absently over the brands that crossed her torso. "I know."

"So today, you'll dress, eat, pick out your pieces and rest." The maid ticked off the chores on her uninjured hand. "How's that sound?"

Issi didn't respond.

Ner's face clouded. "Are you worried about what to play?"

It didn't matter what she chose. Issi could pick the best pieces, play them perfectly, be pretty and witty and *charming*, but none of that would matter because the Grand Mage would find something. Her eyes might linger too long on some lord or lady, or maybe she'd laugh for a beat too long, or bow slightly too low or too high, and he'd hold onto to that mistake, let it fester in his mind and beat it out of her later that evening. Or worse, he'd find nothing, and use that perfection as a reason to lock her in her rooms and take what little freedom she had left.

As he'd done after the last King's Dinner she'd attended.

Issi took a breath and held it. Four beats in, hold, four beats out. She shook her head and offered the maid a small, nervous smile. "I know precisely the pieces I want to choose."

Ner studied her for a moment, looking displeased.

"Don't do anything stupid," she warned. Issi's hands clenched in her lap.

"Get dressed, we don't know when he'll be needing you."

"Thank you for breakfast."

"Don't string it out," the maid continued, as she stepped across the cage's threshold, "He wants your decision by midday."

Issi glanced at her alchemy clock and found the hands had frozen a few ticks before second bell. She hadn't wound it.

It gave a small metallic rattle as she grabbed it, splitting its casing with ease. The exposed gears attempted to move before promptly giving up. What a stupid, stubborn contraption. Mechanical in a land starved of metal when a single rune would have had the same effect.

And it wouldn't ever need to be wound.

Issi shut her eyes and imagined hurling the damned thing at her wall. The edges of its casing dug into her fingers until it creaked a protest.

She let the contraption drop into her lap.

It had been the first gift the Grand Mage had given her. Mechanical because it'd been Egrean in origin, to remind her of her home. He thought she'd miss it.

Not the people she'd left behind, of course, Ose's skies forbid she pine for her siblings and her mother, but the nation that housed them and caged them was something she was permitted to look at with longing.

Her hand ached.

For a beat she recalled the sketches he had tossed into the workroom hearth, the way the faces she'd drawn had gaped and screamed as the flames ate at them. Her mama, her sisters, her brother, had begged for her to save them and she'd been desperate enough to plunge her hand into the blaze.

Mage's fire wasn't hot, and it didn't smoke. But it burned well enough.

Issi flexed her fingers, banishing the memory. She grabbed the dainty rose handled key tucked into the case's home and wound the mechanism, watching balefully as the gears started ticking.

She closed it and set it on her nightstand. The Grand Mage was far more likely to see that the clock had stopped, than notice it was a few bells behind.

Issi began going through the motions of her routine, she dressed, covered her silver markings with a mixture of pastes, and tugged on a pair of gloves to hide the scarred skin of her left hand.

If she looked in the mirror, she'd find none of the scars her master had left on her body. Every outfit she had, had been tailored for that exact purpose, plunging necklines that missed the edges of burned skin, ruffles that obscured scar tissue, swaths of sheer fabric that were just enough to hide what lay beneath while giving an impression of shape. The gloves held similar meaning.

He didn't like to look at the brands, the scars, the carvings. She wondered at times if the memories haunted him, the way they haunted her. If he ever caught himself talking about how he didn't wish to hurt her and gag on the irony of his actions.

She shook her head, dislodging the thoughts.

Atop her wardrobe sat a thick pile of papers gone yellow with age. She pulled her dining chair to its side, climbed it and through much wincing and cursing managed to grab the stack. Her stomach growled as the smell of baked fruit and fresh bread filled her room with single-minded determination.

She flipped past pages of dancing notes, her eyes scanning titles that'd been scribbled out and replaced with pictures. A snake for the *serpent's lament,* a house for *the traveler's return*, a dancing couple for the *midnight waltz*, and so on.

The first two she picked at random before searching through the rest. She stopped on a sheet with a tree crawling up its side, *The Sailor's Tale* sat in neat script beneath the scribbles. Her finger traced the drawing as she stepped onto the floor.

It looked like a child had been given free reign with a quill and played across the papers. Every few notes there was an accidental, or the need for her hand to climb the instrument's neck, or a slur that very much stretched the realm of possibility. But despite all that, if someone could somehow coax the piece together, it sang.

She breathed. She could imagine it, the song rising softly in the stillness after battles, a dulcet melody meant to carry the souls of the dead along Ipheoth's roots of mercy to Naya's gates. *Grant them forgiveness for the sins they've committed*, the words remained untouched at the bottom of the paper.

The king of Qasha would absolutely loathe it.

Chapter 5

Issi pressed her enchantment to her forehead. The wood ground into her skin as she crouched low in her master's garden.

To leave so soon after her last trip was idiocy at its finest.

And yet she did nothing to stop the smell of oranges and spices that leapt into the air. Or the magic that dusted itself across her skin. A sigh escaped her as the world focused for the first time in days.

The Grand Mage was panicking, ever since that night she'd dared to sleep through, he'd been on edge. Too worried to cast, and hesitant to activate enchantments. The world had bled dull from the lack of magic.

Issi woke that morning to echoes of nothing pressing against her. Even the panic that realization summoned had been a cold, distant thing. Her heart hadn't even had the decency react.

She let out a shuddering breath. Tears burned her eyes.

"A short break," her voice caught itself in overgrown branches and weeds. Somewhere, far above, she heard birdsong. Her ears strained for the sounds of the Grand Mage's rage or Ner's searching call.

There was nothing, Issi forced her shoulders down.

Relax.

She did a very poor job of it.

The servant's corridor welcomed her with its blue light. She worked her way through it quickly, nodding a brief hello to the guards. She was terrified that if she stayed too long, or tried so much as a proper greeting, she'd burst into tears.

She didn't even know what she was doing or where she was going to go. She'd just been struck by the need to *leave*.

Issi slipped down an increasingly complicated series of halls, some dark as pitch and others warm and blue. Only one held a window, which the servants kept spotless. She suspected it was the *only* window the vast network of corridors had claimed. It looked out towards one of the courtyards though which of the nine it was, she didn't know.

The scents of summer fresh blueberries and hearth fire stopped her in her tracks. The entire corridor was aglow with it.

Had she been searching for magic? She hadn't been thinking of it, she'd even been avoiding the kitchens, rather than face Ardein and his questions about her last visit.

But now that it was there, it was all she could focus on. She found herself wandering in circles running her hands along the stone surface of the tunnel walls until her fingers brushed over a brick that was not quite brick.

When she tapped it, it echoed.

Hollow.

Issi straightened and peered down the hall. A torch sent shadows scattering along the walls, but this was one of the emptier corridors.

She crouched and ran her hand along the surface, her fingers dipping into grooves and elaborate lines. Issi squinted. A rune?

How anyone had even gotten the magic to stay bound for that long without regularly bathing the brick in herbs and oils was beyond her. But there were no signs of scrubbing, or the gentle circles needed to get long standing castings to settle.

It *felt* abandoned.

She pressed her thumb against it and felt the old magic attached to it rouse sluggishly as her will urged it into motion. From the smell of it, whoever had crafted this enchantment had loved rainstorms and old paper. Behind her, a torch sputtered and died. Whatever extra energy the rune needed, it drew from her, setting her teeth chattering.

The wall groaned as it swung open. A giant door on hidden hinges. The opening was just wide enough for her to see another corridor lay on the other side.

More magic snaked through the opening. Blueberry and hearth fire fought cimmeaon jam and wet soil, Issi pressed against the door, her shoes digging into the ground as she forced herself forward. It protested as she coaxed it wide enough to let her through.

The new corridor was dark and Issi warmed up by ramming her shoulder against the door until it lay flush against the wall. Precisely as she'd found it.

The hall she found herself in was extremely narrow, her arms brushed against both walls without her trying. She navigated by feel, there seemed to be no branches, and going backward led her to a dead end.

Issi yelped as she tripped on a patch of raised floor.

She crouched, her hands searched for the rise only to find it followed by another, and another.

She hesitated, her ears straining for the sound of stone grinding against stone, or footsteps.

Issi didn't *like* casting in this manner, it was more common for the Erbosians and, more importantly, if she was *ever* caught with her illusion enchantment she could always lie and say that she'd coerced it off an old student.

Casting directly was riskier. Unless someone was hiding behind a wall nearby when she got caught and felt like being very kind, it would be a quick trip to the gallows.

Still, she wanted to *see*. So, she borrowed magic from the small well that ran beneath the castle walls, using herself as a conduit to pull it to the surface.

As she moved a pale thread of off white trailed her hands.

She bound the magic in quick moving arcs, drawing runes in the air and locking them temporarily with her will. Every limit she placed set the air smelling of oranges and spices. When she finished, she ran her hand through the center, the smoke collapsed into a small bright orb of light that pulled heat from her core.

In its glow she made out a narrow set of steps. They climbed well over her head and disappeared somewhere above the ceiling.

Where exactly was she? Kothen palace had always been a bit of a mess, but she'd never heard of *hidden* doors. Forgotten? Yes. Inconvenient? Sure. But secreted away behind runes? Well, that was something else entirely.

She went up.

The steps let off in a small room.

It seemed to be a closet of some sort that had been converted into a napping area. A thin mattress was folded in a corner beside a stack of chairs set before a door.

A wave of disappointment doused her casting, plunging the room into darkness.

Issi groped through shadows, bumping into the chairs and pushing them to the side. She pressed her ear to the door. If nothing else, it seemed no one was on the other side.

She felt for the doorknob and opened it. A groan built in her throat.

It was another corridor.

Light and noise spilled in from the end. Issi shuffled towards it, wary of attracting attention.

As she got closer, it became clear that the sound was coming from below. She found herself on a balcony. Spread beneath her was the vast dining hall in which the King's Dinner would take place.

It smelled wildly of magic. Issi's heart thrummed as she took in the sight of it, climbing ceilings supported by marble pillars atop which bloomed flowers so delicate they looked real. Warm as it was, the windows had been taken down, so the hall opened to the palace's primary courtyard. Jewels tumbled in dainty strands from the ceilings and sparkled like the night sky. The stage had been cleaned and was now lit by lanterns whose cloth bellies had been filled with mage's fire. Small contraptions that, at this distance, were little more than smudges against the light danced through the air. One of the servants did something and the bits of darkness moved in unison, their delighted laughter echoed off the walls.

"I didn't expect to see you here."

Issi turned and let out a helpless high-pitched laugh. "Why?"

The cook lowered his brows. "Well, I've only ever seen you in the kitchens."

She blinked, that wasn't what she'd meant. "Why are *you* here?"

"To watch the decorating," he answered, as he joined her by the railing. He peered over the side. "You?"

Somewhere Issi couldn't see, she was sure Mihr-Did, god of tricksters and thieves, was laughing at her. There was no good answer to that question. She followed his gaze to the patterned flower the tiles made across the floor.

"The...uhm, the same."

His disbelief settled across her shoulders. "Mhmm, how did you get here, Del? The doors are locked and guarded."

She blurted the first answer that came to mind, "Secret."

Ardein barked a laugh, that sent Issi's heart beating frantically against her ribcage. "Del, really? That's what you're going with?"

She gave him a curt nod. "How'd you get in then?"

He grinned. His tongue peeked through the gap between his front teeth. "Secret."

They were both liars then. Issi giggled at the absurdity of it all and Ardein sprung towards her. She cringed away.

"You laughed." His eyes sparkled with excitement. For a moment, in the light, the warm brown almost seemed blue. "*That* was genuine laughter, right?"

Issi glanced around for somewhere she could step back, but short of taking a leap over the railing, she was trapped.

"Uhm...Ardein...I need."

"What was it? I didn't think it was that funny," he pressed.

Blood tinted the air. It wasn't there, it couldn't be, but she *smelled* it. The bright scents of copper and salt bit at her nostrils. "*Ardein,* please step back."

Her ears stopped. Like the world had swallowed all sound and left nothing but ringing behind. She watched nervously as his lips moved but the meaning of the noise he made was lost to her.

"*Ardein,*" she tried. She couldn't hear herself, couldn't make the sound out over the high-pitched wailing that pressed against her ears. All she knew was that it didn't seem to slow him.

Maybe the words hadn't made it past her tongue or had died somewhere in her throat.

She watched in disbelief as a fist made contact with his face. *Her fist,* though surely, she had to be wrong. The pain that buzzed along her knuckles belonged to her, but the fist couldn't possibly—

His eyes widened in surprise. The blow hadn't landed *well,* the last person Issi'd ever hit had been her sister, and she'd been a child. The step back he took was more from shock than pain.

Space. She wanted to dart for it, but her feet rooted to the floor.

The cook ran his hand along the curve of his cheek, it'd already started to go a bit red. His lips moved.

He frowned and said something else.

He wasn't the Grand Mage, and she wasn't his Pet.

Ardein was a friend, or as close as she could get. Guilt lay like a stone in the pit of her belly.

She'd *hit* him.

"Del?" His voice broke through.

She studied his face, looking for any of the little ticks that appeared on her master's when he was going to fly into a rage. But all she saw was annoyance that was vastly outweighed by genuine concern.

Issi found it in herself to nod. Once, a sharp jerky motion that hurt her neck. She needed to slow her breathing.

The cook sighed, "Did I scare you?"

"I didn't want you to get hurt."

His face stretched as his eyebrows arched. "So...you punched me?"

"Yes."

He let the silence linger like he was waiting for her to add something else, when she didn't, he sighed. His hand ran along his jaw.

She'd hit him.

"I'm not going to pretend to understand you, Del, but it's nice that I found you. I guess." he was very careful about keeping out of arm's reach.

"I'm, I'm sorry," the words left like they'd been squashed and stuck together in her mouth. "I never meaning to—, meant, it just, I was so, I didn't want what happened to Ner to—." Her mouth snapped shut.

Ardein smiled. "I think that's the most I've ever heard you say at once."

"I'm so sorry." Her throat burned. "I *hit* you. I don't want to be that kind of person, you didn't—."

"Del," he interjected, "I wanted to tell you that there was someone looking to hire a mage."

Issi blinked. "You can't be serious, this isn't the time. I just struck—"

"There's no such thing as *a right time*." He rolled his eyes. "And since you hit me and feel guilty about it, you can make it up to me by considering the offer."

Issi was nearly convinced she'd heard wrong.

She couldn't even begin to tell him all the things that made his suggestion impossible. "I'm sorry, but I can't—"

He clutched dramatically at his face. "Oh, ouch, it really stings, Del."

She sighed. The tension in her shoulders eased. "I'll *think* about it Ardein, but I'm working with the *Grand Mage*. I can't see anyone matching the status of that."

"Status isn't everything," he pointed out, "He'd be a nicer boss."

She stilled for a beat, she didn't like how it felt like he was seeing straight through her. "I've been nothing but a mess the last two times we've met, huh?"

He smirked.

Issi blushed, gods above. "Things have just been...getting harder. He's ill, so I have to do what he can't. That's all."

"But Del—."

"That's all it is. He's not a cruel teacher." She didn't remember him being so, but she'd only heard his lessons when she'd been feeling brave enough to press her ear against the doors of his workrooms.

He'd seemed almost kind at points.

Ardein let out a frustrated breath. "Think about it, you'd still get to work for a noble—"

"That doesn't matter," she interrupted. "Do you expect me to work on petty enchantments or, or, stupid trinkets for small-minded people. Till land? Bring back dying crops? Ardein, I've written papers on that. I've set new protocols. I am indirectly responsible for at least half of this year's harvest."

The cook looked at her with disappointment. "So, you want the clout?"

"What would you do to get the entire world to listen to what you have to say?"

It'd started slowly of course. The Grand Mage had been busy, and he'd had so many students. She'd already taught herself the enchantments. Scoured even the oldest tomes. She'd been better than his prized students.

It'd taken her three moons to get his handwriting just right. Her heart had almost burst through her chest the first time she'd slipped a paper bearing his hand into one of his files.

He'd been confused, but he hadn't questioned it.

After all, he'd been busy. And the theories had proven helpful enough. Inventive enough. After a few moons, he'd simply accepted he'd become more scattered than he once was.

And how clever people had begun to think him.

"Del..." Ardein's brows lowered, he picked his next words very carefully, "What if I could promise something similar?"

Her chin ticked upwards in defiance. "I'd call you a liar."

His face collapsed into a mask of annoyance. "Think about it."

She couldn't. She wasn't Del, the Grand Mage's last student, who could do whatever she damn well pleased. She was Issi, the girl with tracking brands running across her belly, and even if she cut through another one, her blood had sunk into her mattress. Her master could track her in other ways.

And then he'd brand her again.

"I'll think about it Ardein," she assured him, "But I promise, I'm perfectly happy with the work I'm doing, even if it's running me a bit thin. I'm useful."

"But what if you could be more than a tool?"

If Issi could be more than an object to be kept pretty and ignorant and caged, she'd have surely figured out how to do so by now.

"I have to go back," she muttered.

He didn't look like he believed her in the least.

Chapter 6

What if you could be more than a tool?

Issi groaned and tried to focus on the medical reports. They'd been coming in quicker and in larger batches, but they all said the same thing. The mage's illness showed no sign of slowing. She'd been staring at it for bells, a headache had already worked its way beneath her temples. Words swam before her, meaningless.

Three moons, that was the longest most people survived. And Qasha was hemorrhaging mages.

"Issi."

She looked up from the piles of papers she'd spread across an open patch of floor. Her master towered above her, his face contorted in disgust. "Tea."

She stared at him blankly. The words from the reports whirled between her ears, death dates, confirmations of drownings, stabbings, and poisonings.

"The tea," he insisted.

It still felt unnatural, having him present as she read and crafted castings. Either one of those things would be enough for him to turn her over, have her hung, but he simply watched her with distaste. His eyes started tracking along the ceiling as he waited for her response.

Tea.

"Yes." She set the report down and stood. "Sorry, I forgot."

The Grand Mage gave her a stiff smile. "This is your idea. Do better with the execution."

She bit back a retort. Eight moons she'd kept this fool alive, going on nine. She'd shattered every godsdamned survival record there was.

They both knew it wasn't enough.

Issi pulled on a raven shaped handle and picked four cups, two tins, and two kettles, from the deep bellied drawer. She set them all on top of the table before grabbing a pitcher and filled the kettles absently. Her thumb pressed against the stamped enchantment on the vessel's handle, awakening the magic locked within them. It raised curiously beneath her before she used her will to set the water boiling.

Opening the tins released the sweet scents of earth, and flowers. She set leaves inside the strainer and waited. Her fingers drummed against the table as she counted in her head and tried not to think of how low one of the tins had been running. She'd order more, but the herbs were Chousalian and nothing that went into Chousal returned these days.

Steam dusted beneath her eyes as she filled two cups with a brown bitter liquid and the last two with a sweet-scented tea.

"Master?" She turned to find he'd wandered off to go staring at a corner of the ceiling. His eyes tracing the molding.

She waited, hoping he'd come to himself. After it became clear that wasn't going to happen, she grabbed two cups and approached him carefully. Her shoes sounded loudly as she desperately tried to make enough noise to keep from startling him.

She called him again.

The Grand Mage didn't move even when she was close enough for the soft smelling oils the maids delivered to keep his skin soft and smooth to reach her nose. She sniffed searching for the familiar tint of his magic and found nothing.

She tapped him gently with one of the mugs. "Master?"

The Grand Mage flinched but his attention stayed above her. His expression was full of the love and adoration he imagined he'd been giving her all these years. She looked away. It'd been easier to accept her treatment when she'd thought her master incapable of such soft emotions.

But he wasn't. He just hadn't been willing to give that sort of tenderness to her.

"Master, your tea is ready." She clinked the cups together. The high ring of them finally dragged his attention from the heavens.

He looked at her, distracted. "Is there any way to make this taste better?"

She raised the cup in her left hand. "You have the tea."

He frowned before snatching the vessel in her right hand and emptying it with clear distaste. She nearly dropped it when he shoved it in her face and grabbed for the tea which he finished next.

The Grand Mage focused pointedly on dredges at the bottom of the cup.

"They're still here," he murmured.

Issi didn't bother asking what. His face brightened unwillingly as his gaze drifted to the table beside him. He dropped the cup. Issi dove for it barely saving it from dashing to pieces against the floor. Pain rainbowed behind her eyes, her breath coming shallow as she waited for the throbbing in her back to subside.

Her lips almost formed a prayer for Ipheoth, goddess of mercy, before she forced them together. Issi deserved a great many things, but mercy wasn't one of them.

She took a shuddering breath, thanked the gods that the cup had the good fortune to stay in one piece, and made her way to her feet. Her legs shook as she forced them into service, making them carry her to the basin for dirty dishes the maids would pick up in the morning.

Gods she hurt. Her headache had doubled as if in sympathy for her body.

She sighed, finally making it back to her own cups grimacing at the dark brown liquid staring up at her. She pinched her nose and drank it as fast as she could.

Somehow, it'd turned out gritty. The art of setting leaves in hot water was lost to her. She dragged the second cup back to her patch of floor, settling between the reports.

An array of noble seals surrounded her; an assortment of colors, beasts, and weapons begging to be addressed. She picked one at random and broke the wax absently, shattering the enchantment that kept it closed and dry. The papers that spilled from it might as well have caught fire for all the good they did her.

She finished her cup and set it to the side. The reports all followed the same pattern, a strange mark appeared on a mage's body, followed by vivid dreams, hallucinations, and death. She frowned moving the papers around. The mark went down to the bone, dyeing muscles and scraps of vein with strands of silver. Even the removal of limbs only resulted in the marks reappearance in a more vital location. That was it, the sickness was brutal and simple.

Well, the sickness was, the deaths themselves were fascinating.

Starving despite the insistence of friends and family that the victim had been eating regularly, deaths from trauma that almost looked like a carriage strike on individuals who hadn't left their homes in days, people who drowned on dry land.

Half the papers turned out useless, they started clinical but rapidly turned into fanciful things obsessing over visions and dreams. Interesting, but nothing more.

And the deaths had worn a hole in Qasha's army, while small-town mages near the epicenter were becoming scarce, causing a host of domestic problems.

They needed a cure.

Issi ruffled her hair. Her head pounded. So far, she could only delay the inevitable. It was still coming.

The Grand Mage was going to die.

What if you could be more than a tool?

Issi cursed, wishing Ardein had kept his well-meaning mouth shut. If she could leave, she'd have done it.

Her hand ran over her stomach.

It wasn't anything as simple as donning an enchantment and skipping off palace grounds. She picked up a report from one of Jadan's territories smaller lords and sighed at the broken Qashan scrawled across the page. The reeducation of the Reprenians was slow going, spoken language had gone a lot faster, but many of their survivors hadn't been able to read in the first place, having preferred passing their histories down in song.

She flinched, curling into a ball as something shattered.

Another crash sounded in the far corner. She unfurled herself.

He was getting worse.

She let out a curse. Her master saw birds, blue birds, *blue as the clear summer skies*, he'd once whispered to her. In the beginning he could ignore them, focus despite their existence, but as time wore on, they'd started tugging at his attention. It had started small, his eyes would skip to them and back to his work, he'd cock his head at times to better hear their chirping. Now it appeared to be a compulsion.

He trailed after invisible birds like a lost child. It was better when the sun marched across the sky, though she caught his eyes ticking at times. It was night when the illness really showed itself.

And Issi had no idea why.

She found the Grand Mage with his shoulder shoved through the shelves of a bookcase. The crash she'd heard had been a bauble leaping for freedom only to find that gravity had determined to shatter it. From the amount of gold, it had been expensive.

"Master," she called, gently.

He pulled his arm back like something had burned him. "Issi..." His eyes skipped to the shards scattered across the floor. "You should have stopped me."

Rage tore at her throat. He was being ridiculous, and he knew it. She swallowed her pride and gave him a short bow. "I'm sorry."

Pain blossomed across her right cheek as her head snapped to the left. Her ear rang. The headache she'd been nursing spiked viciously. The Grand Mage's hand returned to his side.

Breathe.

She dropped lower, tasting blood. "I'm truly sorry, master. It won't happen again."

"My well-being is your primary concern," he growled.

"Of course, master." Her back ached. Her skin still stung and warmed where he'd struck her.

"Stand."

She complied, shoving down reluctance. She flinched when his hand brushed against her cheek.

"I'm all you have, Issi." he forced her gaze to match his. "Without me, you won't last. People will find out what you are and what you can do, and they will not be as kind. They'll cut off your hands and they'll hang you in the market square as they did with your teacher."

The hanging would be a mercy.

If it was just that, she wouldn't have *cared*.

It was what happened before that sent her pulse skittering. It was the loss of her hands, the loss of her *magic*, that terrified her. She'd not be able to carve, or weave enchantments and it'd take ages for her to teach herself to cast any other way.

In the interim, the world would bleed color until it felt far and unreal. She'd stop *feeling*. There'd be no fear when she walked up the steps to the gallows, no sadness, *nothing*.

She'd be questioning if she was alive at all by then.

"I'm sorry," she repeated. A tear trickled down her cheek.

His fist dug into her stomach. Her legs gave as the breath was driven from her lungs. She collapsed to the floor, gasping. She was crying in earnest now.

Run.

There was nowhere she could go that he wouldn't follow.

"Does it hurt?"

She refused to answer.

Fear and anger mixed in her stomach and gods, she was torn between throwing up that awful tea and breathing. The answer burned on her tongue. Her master loomed above her as she tried to haul in air. She swallowed and focused on digging her nails into the stone floor.

What if you could be more than a tool?

What would she be if she'd been born anyone else? As a child she'd held some distant dream of being loved, but even she knew that this was something else.

"Does it hurt?" he repeated. She watched his foot swing back and had a beat to brace herself before the blow to her ribs sent her sprawling. Whatever air she'd managed to haul into her lungs, was lost. Everything hurt, her back, her stomach, her arms, her head.

All she had to do was answer. It wasn't hard, she'd just have to let the word she'd caged behind her teeth leave as it so obviously wanted to do.

Her throat sealed as a series of scars on her inner thigh chilled.

She fell silent.

Choking was a very quiet affair so long as she didn't insist on thrashing about. Her heartbeat was loud in her ears. He kicked her again, but no sound escaped her. Her lungs began to scream. Each beat of her heart was thunder in her skull.

Her vision started to darken near the edges.

What if you could be more than a tool?

What else in Naya's hells was there?

"No," she sobbed. Her throat spasmed and she set to coughing and sputtering.

The Grand Mage had off and disappeared. Likely chasing after those damned birds. Issi rolled onto her back, trying to convince her lungs to take in air.

She was fine. She was fine. She was fine.

She wiped her tears on her sleeve as she pieced together a haphazard list of chores. The experiments needed tending and she still had to finish cleaning up the reports. Her breath rattled uncomfortably in her chest. Go to the gardens and pick herbs for a few oils.

Her fingers probed her cheek. There'd be swelling.

Issi almost started crying again. No amount of make-up would be able to hide what he'd done. She sat gingerly cradling her aching head. It was so close to the King's dinner.

Gods, she was so tired.

Chapter 7

"It's noticeable," Ner tutted.

Issi winced as the maid dabbed at her cheek. Ner moved the brush to the palette hidden in the array of pastes, perfumes, and oils she'd lined across Issi's vanity, muttering her discontent. The maid had already claimed she'd finished, gone to line Issi's eyes with kohl and declared that she wasn't satisfied as she took the brush again.

"It's fine," Issi argued. Her reflection was pretty enough. The Grand Mage enjoyed showing how Chousalian Issi was, so he'd ordered Ner to go for a "traditional Chousalian feel" when specifying her make-up. This had resulted in Issi's dark lined eyes and a smattering of gold dots travelling along her cheekbones and across her brow. A few Chousalian letters spelled in white ink just beneath her hairline, if she cared to put them together it read *tree, tree, tree, tret, tree.*

As far as Issi was concerned the slight rising of the skin just beneath her right eye was nearly unnoticeable. Besides, with the gown she was wearing, people were hardly meant to look at her face.

"It's not, 'fine'," Ner insisted, she pressed at Issi's cheek with renewed vigor. "This is the King's Dinner, not some lady's tea party."

Issi wished it was. She'd give anything to spend the evening grimacing over tea while ladies probed her for news of the Grand Mage's decline.

The maid clicked her tongue and gestured towards Issi's lips. Issi's eyes darted to the palette she was studying.

Curiosity loosened her tongue, "Which color?" she asked, then blushed as the maid gave her a knowing look.

"Same as always/" Ner gestured to an autumnal red. "It compliments your skin."

Issi leaned towards her. Her mind whirled quietly with marigold yellows, sunset oranges, poppy reds, rose pinks, deep violets, starless night blacks, glittering golds, and sky blues.

If she had the chance to decide what she'd wear herself, what color would she pick?

Ner frowned as Issi's forehead wrinkled. "None of that."

Maybe she'd ignore the palette altogether, buy one of her own. Something simpler. But the color—

"*Issi*," the maid snapped.

Maybe she'd decide not to wear make-up at all.

Ner flicked her forehead. Thoughts of colors disintegrated in favor of the maid's honey-shaded eyes.

"What's got you thinking?"

Issi fidgeted. She'd been seated for bells as Ner organized her hair into hundreds of neat braids that had to be coaxed into staying by wax and fire.

"...who do you think I would've been if I'd been born anyone else?"

The maid stiffened, the stump on her left hand ticked nervously. "You were born *you*, Issi."

That was where the conversation was meant to stop. Issi felt the edges of Ner's reluctance the same way she felt for her master's moods. But there was something about this she couldn't let go.

Her heart skipped as she broke past Ner's quiet barrier. "Yes, but what if I hadn't been? Do you think I could have been a musician, or a dancer..." She swallowed and searched the maid's face. "A mage?"

"Issi," Ner's voice rang with disapproval. Issi quailed at the sound of it. She shouldn't have pressed.

"You have an important purpose *here*. The Grand Mage would be lost without you. He loves you, so stop these silly thoughts."

Issi looked at her hands running her thumb over the scars. Silly, yes, it was silly.

She winced as Ardein's words continued to circle in her head, *what if you could be more than a tool?*

She didn't have the papers to be a mage, and even if she could arrange for them, she knew nothing about living outside the palace walls. Even the coins she'd hidden in the garden were a mystery to her, just trinkets she'd collected and thrown about because that seemed like something she was meant to do.

Ner continued painting Issi's lips in silence. When she finished, she leaned back and gave a small, satisfied smile, her eyes warm with motherly affection. "So very pretty. You'll be the talk of the dinner."

Issi tried to smile in return. Butterflies circled in her stomach. She'd be talked about regardless. If it wasn't her status, it would be her dress, or her heritage, or her make-up.

Ner handed her a pair of gloves and Issi donned them obediently before ticking her chin up to meet her reflection in the mirror.

Issi watched as the maid set a leather collar around her throat. Gold embossing flashed in the evening light denoting Issi's status as a Pet belonging to a high noble. The crow stamped into the side informed people of precisely whom.

The maid worked quietly with the lacing that ran up the back, her fingers working deftly, until she fumbled with the knot.

"Now, don't go all quiet on me," Ner prompted, "We're almost done, aren't you excited?"

What if you could be more than a tool?

Gods, why couldn't she just stop? The idea was infuriating, it stuck like jam to the inside of her skull and refused to quiet. She wasn't a child anymore, there was no point playing pretend with ideas that could never take root. She might as well be wondering what she'd do if she could pluck stars from Ose's skies.

Issi sighed. Her face crumpled. "Ner, it's been years since I've left the wing in any official capacity."

"You'll be fine," she hummed. "It's not something you'd forget."

But she wanted to, the eyes, the whispers, the plastered smile that made her cheeks ache. She'd spend the whole night balancing her master's need to show her off with his desire to monopolize her. Everything would be so much easier if she could just stay inside and curl into one of the Grand Mage's fat-pillowed chairs.

"Cheer up, there'll be delicious food," the maid tried, "And dancing." When that failed to get a reaction, she grinned playfully and tugged at one of the braids framing Issi's face. "If you're quick, maybe you can try some of the wine."

Issi's lips quirked at the idea. She'd spent years hearing the whispers of maids and watching what she could of the festivals from the window. To say she wasn't, at least the smallest bit curious, was like denying the seasons.

Maybe she could at least *taste* what they'd been talking about.

The door opened, and Ner let the braid fall back before scurrying to the far corner of the cage. Issi mourned the loss of her even as she struggled to understand why the

Grand Mage had come into the cage rather than wait for Ner to escort her to the wing's main hall.

"Good evening, master." Issi stood and dropped into a curtesy, trying to make sense of his mood. He seemed…wound, the sides of his eyes crinkled with stress.

His attention flickered across her face before shifting to Ner.

Issi tried not to follow his gaze and failed. She shoved the betrayal she felt at the reverence that blossomed across Ner's face somewhere she couldn't reach. The maid had always looked at the Grand Mage like she was seeing a god. She'd worn the same beatific expression the day he relieved her of her thumb.

Even as Issi screamed and wailed for him to stop.

"Was there nothing to be done about the swelling?" he asked.

The maid's voice wavered, she spoke carefully as if raising a prayer, "I'm afraid not."

Ner flushed as his attention lingered, her hands tugging fitfully at her servant's greys.

"You did well."

She beamed, "Thank you, sir."

"You're dismissed."

She was still grinning as she hurried away, offering Issi a wink as she slipped over the threshold.

The Grand Mage hummed tunelessly as his fingers probed the skin on Issi's cheek. His eyes raked down her body. He liked putting her in tight things that clung to her like spider's silk with necklines that plunged between her breasts.

He smirked, satisfied. "Does it hurt?"

"No."

He kissed her briefly on the lips. "You look beautiful."

Pride flared in Issi's chest. Even after all this time, some small part of her reveled in his attention and yearned for more, pursuing a kindness that didn't exist. She forced a smile. "I *am* beautiful. You look well yourself."

"Now, I know you're lying." He pulled away from her skin. She drifted after him, searching for magic where there was none. He let out a soft laugh and her limbs locked.

"That's my girl," his voice was deep and sweet. Almost as if he really cared. Her stomach soured as he tucked a braid behind her ear. "Where's your violin?"

Move.

She stared at him with wide eyes, as if she'd been caught in some sort of trap. He wasn't hurting her. She searched his face. His eyes were kind. Was that enough?

Move.

Her hand curled around air.

Her violin. She swallowed nervously and forced her thoughts to form through the panic raging between her ears.

"I, uhm, I haven't gotten it?"

The Grand Mage frowned his hand dropping to his side. "The escort's waiting."

Escort?

What in Naya's hells did they need an escort for?

She crossed the room as quickly as her dress would allow, retrieving her instrument before returning to the Grand Mage's outstretched hand. He stepped closer to her at the last moment, wrapping his arms around her waist. He lifted her easily, spinning her once before setting her down.

It'd all happened so quickly all Issi could do was stare.

He smiled at her confusion and pressed his lips against her forehead before holding her at arm's length. "I love you, Issi."

And she honestly believed he thought that was the truth. "I love you too, sir Grand Mage."

His eyes lit and he kissed her deeply as he guided her through the doorway.

The escort straightened abruptly from where he'd been readying to poke at a moving statuette. His ears reddened and his gaze dropped to the floor as the Grand Mage pressed Issi against the wall. Her master's hand had started to wind its way beneath her skirt when the young man, boy really, gave a polite cough.

The Grand Mage nipped at Issi's lip and backed away reluctantly as Issi tried her best to appear as if she wasn't desperate to breathe. Or retch. A wave of nausea hit her so hard it made her dizzy.

The escort brushed self-consciously at his tunic, flashing the insignia that crossed his front. A snake winding around a scepter.

It was good to see that the Zeilid family had continued to think highly of itself during Issi's impromptu exile.

"Good morn—, evening," the boy flushed as his voice cracked. He began anew, "Good evening, Sir Niao and…miss…" He trailed off uncertainly as his eyes landed on Issi's collar.

"Anders," her master supplied shortly.

The boy fidgeted, his eyes raking over Issi's form. "Miss Anders." he returned his attention to the Grand Mage. "Will we be leaving?"

"An escort is hardly necessary," the Grand Mage drawled.

The boy quailed, his eyes darting for the exit. "I—, I, was sent here to…uhm…escort you to the dinner."

"The one half-way across the palace?"

"Uh…yes, that. That one." His eyes shifted back to Issi's collar. "Are—, are you sure? I mean, do you really want—, that is…your attendance is required, but—"

The Grand Mage cut him off, "She's performing."

The escort tugged at his tunic again before dropping into a shallow bow. "My apologies."

"If he's going to send you over, you should have been better prepared."

The boy paled. "It…it was my mistake. I'll make sure it doesn't happen again."

Her master straightened, shifting his full attention to the boy at last. "There will be more of you?"

The child nodded. "I heard that, you'll get an escort to every event…needing your appearance until, that is—"

"I die?"

The boy flinched and looked to the floor like he wished for it to swallow him. His answer came soft, "Until you *retire*."

"So, I'm retiring now?"

The escort shifted, his face gaining an unhealthy pallor.

"Master, do you think I'll need to set up soon?" Issi asked. There wasn't much she could do. She couldn't accept Ardein's offer, she couldn't be mage, and she'd never survive alone outside the palace. But sparing a child?

She could at least try.

The Grand Mage glanced at her and relaxed. "Yes…yes, you will."

He kissed her cheek, brushing a stray braid that'd tumbled between her eyes. The boy stilled, his eyes wide, like he hadn't thought her master capable of such tenderness.

She stiffened as the Grand Mage's hand slid down her arm. He pulled her until she pressed against him. The rapid, *thrumthrumthrum* of his heart echoed through her body.

The hand that held her trembled.

Her forehead crinkled as she pressed her hand over his. A dozen explanations shifted past her.

The Grand Mage couldn't be afraid.

He didn't get scared.

Issi forgot all about the escort and the King's Dinner and her stupid little performance. She pulled away from her master, just far enough to see his face in earnest. The *thrumthrumthrum* continued to drive against her as she took in the wild look about his eyes and the slight tremble in his lips. *No, no, no, no.*

Lord Gadna Niao, the Grand Mage of Qasha, did not get scared.

Her mouth opened before she'd decided what to say, "You'll be perfect."

His eyes searched hers, with a desperation that only served to compound her unease. "Is that right?"

Her heart hammered, matching his beat for beat as she nodded. Ose willing, the fear that'd settled in his eyes would disappear.

He snapped at the escort, "Don't you have a job to do?"

Issi stared at the boy as if he'd ghosted through the room. Did he see the way her master looked? Could he tell? Or was it only her who felt like the sun and moon had switched places in the skies and wondered if the ground beneath them was still solid?

The escort's cheeks warmed, and he avoided her gaze. "Yes, Grand Mage, uh, sir, we'll be on our way then?"

Her master nodded, his jaw tight. The hand that sat on her waist started to dig into her skin.

Trembling.

She stumbled as the Grand Mage's grip tightened. The muscle in his jaw bounced as he worked on grinding his teeth to stumps as they navigated the castle's vast halls.

Large marble pillars manifested as they neared the ballroom, their white structures spun into giant trees with emerald leaves. Small birds hid in their branches, their feathers crafted from azurite and lapis winked in the evening light. Issi had always wondered if they were the reason for the Grand Mage's fixation. She glanced at her master and felt her worry renew itself.

His eyes pinned to the floor. He looked more like a child being dragged about than the most powerful mage in Qasha. What had happened? What had changed? Surely, it wasn't the existence of the *child* before them that'd set him acting this way.

Was it?

Their escort stopped before a large stone archway. The ballroom doors were held open by a series of royal guards who looked straight through them as if Issi and her master were little more than air.

The boy bowed, muttering a hurried farewell before rushing down a servant's corridor.

The Grand Mage started towards the archway. Issi thought of her mother's tales of animals pulled into men, as she watched him roll back his shoulders and become someone else entirely.

But the fear was still there.

She turned away.

Somehow the ballroom was even grander than when she'd left it. Sunlight streamed between the pillars catching in brightly colored fabrics that waved in the breeze coming off the Copros. Small cloth lanterns drifted through the air; the flames they contained sent light bouncing off the jewels suspended from the ceilings. A large blue flag boasting the royal insignia hung in the center of it all, and everyone who was anyone in all of Qasha seemed to be somewhere beneath it. The floors were absolutely covered in the soft pastel colors of nobles more in tune with the fashion of the courts. They looked dainty and prim, like flowers tentatively reaching for the skies.

From somewhere, a voice boomed, "Announcing mage Gadna Niao."

The entire room seemed to fall silent. Only the gentle coaxing notes of a ballad played through the air. No *Grand*. Just mage.

His mouth opened in a small "o" of surprise. Issi hoped she'd heard wrong, and failing that, that someone had made some sort of error.

No correction came.

She searched for something to say. Anything to comfort him and help drive away that damned fear that'd flared in his eyes again. No words came to mind.

He'd fallen faster than either of them had anticipated. That was all.

"It's...it's just two bells, master," her words rang hollow.

He closed his mouth and forced a smile that didn't reach his eyes. "Two bells," he echoed.

She knew from the moment they entered the crowd that it'd feel a lot longer. The whispers were deafening, and the silence that fell as they neared was worse.

Her master clung to her like he feared getting swept away. His nails dug into her ribs as he squared his shoulders and set a smile on his face that was too sharp to be sincere. He spoke to the first couple who had the misfortune of making eye contact.

Lord and lady Lry, to their credit, only looked as if they'd run if they were given the opportunity and both proved reasonably bad at crafting one. Issi did her best not to wrinkle her nose at the smell of them. Half of their wardrobe had been poorly enchanted, making a cacophony of mismatched scents.

She hated the way their eyes kept drifting to her collar.

If she hadn't worn it, if her master had chosen a looser gown, if she'd been less Egrean, *less Chousalian*, maybe they would have stopped looking at her with so much venom. Her master didn't seem to notice, but Issi read their hatred in the draw of lord Lry's lip when he caught her eye, or how the lady moved closer to her husband whenever Issi addressed her.

But Issi's smile never faltered. Every quiet slight and soft insinuation that she was not meant to be there only served to confirm what she already knew.

She hated everything about the King's Dinner.

It took the couple fifteen ticks and what Issi suspected was most of their combined imagination to come up with the half-decent excuse of *oh, we haven't seen lord Ruail for a while, we really must greet him.*

Her master stared blankly at the space they left behind until it filled with someone new. During the fourth conversation, Issi concluded that the only thing nobles hated more than getting caught with a fallen member, was missing a good bit of gossip.

That and they wanted what most people desired. To be flattered and complimented. Made to feel clever, and smart, and beautiful. They drifted towards her without seeming to realize it, called by the promise of easy accolades.

They didn't like her, but they wanted what she had to offer.

As the bell wore on, Issi turned it into a dance, carving their empty promises between the delicate notes of a nocturne. Reaching shameless platitudes as the music swelled and searching for clever insults when the notes bounced about. Her cheeks went stiff from the smile that had stitched itself onto her lips, her eyes refused to identify anything more than bright blots on a cream-colored background.

That is, until the pastels started to move in odd patterns.

Issi blinked, forcing the world into focus. A man with sky-colored eyes seemed to be leading a small parade of nobles around the room. Her eyes ticked after him. It was almost a funnier version of how nobles responded to *her*.

She checked, but there was no collar on his neck. He didn't cower or bow.

A compliment died on her lips as she tried to piece together what she was seeing.

The lady before her coughed delicately. She was a tall thin woman, with deep beautiful eyes and a pastel green dress that cinched neatly around her waist. Issi blinked up at her trying to recall what nonsense she'd been about to say. Something about the pendant hanging at the hollow of the woman's neck?

The sky-eyed man seemed to be making a round about the room. His baffling little group flitting around him like bees bumbling about a flower.

Issi started blathering about the cut of the necklace's gem, tossing out random phrases about how it complemented the woman's eyes and how clever she was to match it just so. And just as the woman had begun to smile and regale Issi with tales about the craftsman, Issi looked to see where the blue-eyed man had gone and caught his eye.

She braced for the warmth to drain from his expression, but his face lit up as if he'd been searching for her. Issi's thoughts tangled.

The woman coughed again.

"Oh, I'm sorry, that sounds absolutely lovely," she began, her attention spitting between the woman before her and the sky-eyed man who seemed to be coming closer. "It seems you've a bit of a cough though, were you aware that," Issi launched into the most boring lecture she could manage as she tried to figure out what in Naya's hells was going on.

The sky-eyed man was still heading towards her.

The woman grunted her frustration and stormed off all flowing skirts and indignation. The Grand Mage let out a sigh of relief. His grip on Issi's waist loosened until he saw where she was looking.

His arm became a vice as his teeth ground together. She tapped at his hand hoping he'd realize he was driving the air from her lungs.

The man approached with his not quite entourage. He didn't spare the mage a passing glance.

"What happened to your face?" his voice was soft and deep. Quiet. She'd thought thunder and had gotten summer rain.

Her mouth opened, but her voice had skittered off. She managed to smile as her master answered for her.

There was an accident in the workroom.

Issi's smile went brittle. She nodded.

"I don't recall asking you, Gadna," the sky-eyed man's tone left little room for argument. The Grand Mage was crushing her. Issi squirmed trying to buy herself breathing room. The man still hadn't *looked* at her master. His head had tilted to face him, but his eyes had never left hers. "I was speaking to…excuse me, may I have your name?"

She hesitated and glanced at the Grand Mage hoping for some direction. He might as well have died on the spot for all the help he provided.

"It's, ah, Nydelissi Anders," she pronounced it carefully, *nuh-ee-del-es-ee,* and waited passively as he butchered it. "I also go by Issi."

He smiled warmly before parroting her.

The nobles nearby were still dancing around him. There was so much movement Issi had a hard time knowing where to look, they leaned towards the man like flowers to sunlight. But there was a desperation to their fluttering that she'd never commanded and didn't recognize.

The man either didn't notice or didn't care.

"—Issi?"

She blinked. "I'm sorry, I was…distracted."

"I asked if you were excited to perform."

"Oh, yes, of course." the blood drained from her face, as she remembered the piece she'd chosen.

He chuckled and the crowd drew closer. Flowers to sun, moths to flame, nobles to—

Royalty.

He was a royal.

Which one? She glanced at the Grand Mage, why hadn't he warned her?

Was there a way to buy back the deference she'd denied him? Pushing the sky-eyed man out of the way to grind her forehead into the ground felt like it would defeat the point.

She swallowed a string of curses as her gaze dropped to his shoes.

"I thought I'd have longer before you figured it out," he breathed, "You're as quick as the rumors suggest."

Rumors? Her ears heated. She was hardly important enough for stories about her to reach him.

She dropped into the deepest bow she could manage with the Grand Mage trying to collapse her middle. "I'm sorry, I meant no disrespect, my prince."

"What was it that gave me away? Was it the insignia?"

Her eyes darted to his breast. The king's insignia had been obscured by a small purple broach fashioned into something that vaguely resembled a lizard. Or possibly a long-tailed child. She almost laughed, *what was that?*

"Your eyes, my prince," she lied. She'd seen the king up close twice, she should have recognized them instantly. "They're very...pretty."

"Pretty?" amusement tilted the word as he echoed it back. Issi nodded, realizing her mistake too late. The Grand Mage straightened.

The prince grabbed her hand and spun her out of her master's grip. Issi stilled, a rabbit in an open field. He was warm, smelling of ink and flowers, he held her gently, his hand a whisper against her waist like he feared she'd break.

Maybe she would.

She stole a glance at her master. He looked like he wanted to be angry, his face had certainly gone through all the motions, his brows lowered, his teeth bared, and a bell ago, she might have cowered. But now?

Her brows drew low. "He's still scared."

The prince laughed; his chest rattled with it. The sound set her heart thrumming.

"Gadna? He's always scared."

Issi shook her head.

"He's never—"

The prince was far too close. Space. She stole a step, then two.

Her hand stayed in his for a beat longer than what was proper.

A panicked squeak scratched at her throat, as his lips pressed to the back of her glove.

Gods above, there were simpler ways to kill her. Quicker ones.

How was she supposed to respond? Smile? Thank him?

"I'm flattered," she croaked. She fought to keep her expression warm, as the Grand Mage's arm circled her waist. Was there anything else she could add? Her hand fisted, crumpling the paper the prince had slipped into her palm.

His answer was something kind, she couldn't parse above the sound of her blood in her ears. He settled, looking like he expected the conversation to last.

Etiquette be damned.

"My prince—" Issi winced, as the prince halted midsentence. If the lack of decorum bothered him, he was too well-bred to show it. She continued hurriedly, "If I may be so bold as to request to be excused. I have a performance soon and I need to—"

The Grand Mage's arm made a decent attempt at breaking her in two.

"Ah, of course," the prince answered easily, Issi dared a glance at his face. He looked almost...apologetic.

She didn't wait for him to repeat himself. She gave a short bow before extricating herself from the Grand Mage's grip and nearly running away.

The far wall was a welcome oasis, brimming with wallflowers, quiet gossipers, and nosy servants.

Had anyone noticed?

Had her *master*?

Issi bit her lip, crumpling the paper in her hand. She'd never spoken to any of the princes before, Naya's hells, she'd never even *seen* them. What had she done to gain his interest?

Gods, what did she know of them? The eldest was supposed to wear the successor's headdress, and the second prince had been working with the guard, the one she'd met was too thin for that, wasn't he? That left the youngest.

Tiremalv. She frowned. The rumors were that he was a palace tart. Was that all that had been about?

She studied the idea with unease. The note could be some lewd picture, a crude invitation with a time and a date? Pets weren't meant to read so it would have to be something rudimentary. She sighed, fighting the urge to ruffle her hair.

He was a prince for gods' sake. He could simply order the Grand Mage to lend her to him.

The way his gaze had settled over her replayed in her head. It had been a long time since she'd felt *seen*. Her fingers fluttered against her cheek. She'd thought Ner had done a well enough job.

Issi stopped at the foot of the stage. The band was in the middle of playing a soft, dreamy piece that was popular in the capital. Fat bellied lanterns skimmed the floor casting warm lights over the players. The small specks she'd seen the day before had resolved themselves into hundreds of gently glowing flowers that drifted through the air.

She set her case down by one of the pillars before she removed her gloves and secreted the paper into the fabric's palm. Her fingers flexed in the cool evening air.

The dips and scarring on her left hand couldn't be hidden by pastes alone, she felt more herself at the sight of it.

She waved at the band to announce her presence before sneaking behind the platform. The waters of the Copros ran clear on this side of the island, she sat and dangled her feet above it, letting her shoes rest just above the surface.

A stolen moment. The air here was sweet and devoid of the heady honeyed wine that permeated everything beneath the ballroom's dome.

One bell.

That's all she needed to do. She watched quietly as a ship sailed its way across the river and tried not to think of the punishment she was going to receive if she returned to the wing.

Her hand warmed where the prince had kissed her. If only she'd been faster to pull away, but what choice had she had?

She started as footsteps neared. Issi scrambled to her feet looking at the waters and the reeds in the distance. Gods if only escape were that easy. Her back pressed against the stage as she shuffled around the lip.

"You," a voice breathed.

Issi froze, her blood turning to ice. She recognized his tone, though she wished she didn't. It was too early. Her legs threatened to buckle.

"Slaves and whores are meant to bow, not sneak away," the king of Qasha drawled. He took a drag from a long-stemmed pipe, the smoke that poured from his mouth was sickly sweet. "And here I thought I'd found a place to relax."

Issi lowered herself and pressed her forehead into the marble. "My apologies, my King," she muttered.

"Why are you here?" his speech slurred at the edges. She dared a glance and found him looking down at her with glassy eyes.

"I...uhm..." Her throat ran dry, she tried to come up with an excuse. "I thought the water was pretty?"

He stepped closer. "Sit up."

Issi complied, fixing her gaze on the king's chest. He'd once been a strong person, leading armies on the frontlines of bloody battles. But time had thinned him, hollowed his eyes and sunken his cheeks. Despite the effort his clothes made to drape and hang across him, his chest looked delicate, like it had been crafted from sticks and twine.

"You look just like her," he muttered, dispassionately. "How many times have you tried to die?"

She frowned, her forehead crinkling. "I...I don't understand."

"Of course, you do," he said. He reached down and grabbed a handful of her braids and let them run through his fingers. She shivered and shook her head.

"I don't, my king, I'm sorry," the words were lead on her tongue. She didn't mean any of it, the apologies, his title, she'd tried to die more times than she cared to count. But she found herself shrinking beneath his gaze, flattening as if trying to blend with the ground.

Here was the man who was single handedly responsible for the destruction of her homeland, the reason her mother had fled and sold her freedom, the reason Issi had ever met the Grand Mage at all.

She'd say nearly anything to get away from him.

He frowned and straightened, his eyes matched his son's, a brilliant, unending blue.

"What would you have done?" he asked. "If your so-called gods had failed you? How would you stop them from ruining everything they touched?"

He took another drag from his pipe, holding the smoke in his chest before releasing it into the air. His shoulders relaxed, and Issi wished that his death would mean anything, anything at all. But Chousal was gone and killing him wouldn't serve to bring it back. It wouldn't touch the quiet ache she held for a place she'd never known. She wouldn't even feel better for it.

Issi answered passively, "I am just a Pet, I can't understand the decisions you had to make."

He let out a hacking cough. "If a religion is a disease and there's no cure, how do you stop the spread, little heretic?"

Her heart nearly stopped, she scarcely dared to breathe. He couldn't know, she made no shrines, spoke no prayers, everything she held of the gods fit between her ears. Her voice refused to come, she gaped a few times in vain before giving up.

The king grinned. "Don't worry, *you*, I won't let die. I like you where you are, bound and chained," her heart sank, as his laughter turned to coughing. He looked past her, to the river, towards red-rooved houses that marked the outer ring of the capital. Issi knew it to be the direction of Chousal, where his wife had died so many years ago. She'd stared that way hopelessly for bells hoping to make out some village peak or building, a sign that the nation might still breathe when everyone thought it dead.

The king continued wistfully, "it's a worse fate than death really."

Vengeance hadn't stayed his heart either. Destroying two countries and banishing the gods hadn't ushered a single breath into his wife's lungs. These days he dulled the world with heady smoke until the ache he felt drifted away. Even as it sapped the strength from his bones.

"I like you where you are too," she admitted with some childish defiance.

The king's face shifted in surprise, an unexpectedly infectious grin warmed his lips. "I see, I see." He took another drag holding the smoke inside his chest as if it were air and he was desperate not to drown. "I guess you're right, aren't you? A fate worse than death," he muttered.

He cocked his head to the side, his gaze distant. "You should leave, it's your turn to play."

Issi blinked. Her ears strained, only the murmurs of conversation reached her above the quiet lapping of water.

"Run along." He shooed her, as one might an insect or a child.

Her legs shook as she made her way to her feet, the king let her by with a simpering smile. The guard who hovered outside their hiding place spared her an uninterested glance.

Her hands trembled as she grabbed her violin, setting her shoulder rest. She made her way onto the stage. The light from the lanterns painted everything in soft, dreamy hues. The stage's carpet swallowed her footsteps. The magic that ran beneath it smelled of sweet summer blossoms and would send any sound she'd make to even the furthest reaches of the room.

She'd prepared an introductory speech, two pieces to please the people who'd killed hers. But she couldn't remember any of it. She stared out above the crowd completely blank.

There was only one thing she really wanted to play.

But she'd chosen it with the faint hope that the king might deem it treasonous and have her hung for playing it. After all, it would have been a notable performance in front of the court, and he'd have to keep his reputation.

She hadn't realized how much she had hoped it might work.

Issi sniffled wincing as the sound traveled across the room. A few heads turned her way. Her cheeks were fire as she bowed and brought her instrument beneath her chin. The first note of *The Sailor's Tale* rang out.

The melody unwound slow and somber, she could imagine it as it must have been raising above abandoned battle fields, sung through the air by passerby over the bodies of the dead. A song of mourning.

Looking out at the sea of nobles, she doubted many of them would recognize it. So many had purchased their safety, fled to their homes tucked away in the country sides where mail was slow, and news was slower. But they knew something was wrong.

Those who did remember stood stock still. Too afraid to move in recognition of a song that wasn't meant to exist.

The melody picked up. In all honesty *The Sailor's Tale* was a mess of a piece. Filled with accidentals and shifts and double stops that rang dissonantly and if given the chance, would gladly sink into a smattering of discordant wails. It was a piece that needed tending and a gentle hand, to calm it when it railed and give it space when it exalted.

If someone could coax it together, the piece sang.

The room flickered, as her mind pulled her through time to when her hands were smaller, and she'd struggled to keep her violin upright. She remembered the way the kind eyes of her violin teacher had lit up when he'd given her the piece. He'd spoken excitedly about it, telling her the safe retelling of the story that went along with it. Until a necklace had tumbled from the nestled safety of his shirt.

It had been a simple thing, with a cord of carefully tended leather and a pendant at its center. A small depiction of Ipheoth's tree had hung before her.

In that instant, she'd wanted to tell him everything, that she still worshipped in her own ways, that she didn't think he was wrong, that she thought the gods remained to watch them, and that the king was being silly. But when she looked at him ready to breathe the biggest secret she'd left to tell, his eyes had been filled with fear.

Issi had turned away, let her gaze drift to her window, pretending she hadn't seen. And he'd tucked the beneath his shirt without a word.

The last she saw of him were the small quick twitches of his legs as the noose dug into his neck. The roar of the crowds still rang in her ears.

Even as she unspooled the piece, finishing somberly before the small crowd she'd managed to gather.

The king watched her from the front of the stage.

No soldiers climbed the stairs to grab her.

There was only silence. And then the king began to clap, and the ensuing applause roared between her ears.

The rest of the event passed in a blur of vapid conversation. Issi found herself flouncing about the edges of the aristocracy, flattering any low nobles who captured her as she searched for her master. Bowing deeply to the few middle and highborn nobles who gave her the time of day.

She found the Grand Mage looking miserable as he spoke to a mage brought from a province marked by a pale green scarf. Issi knew vaguely of him. He was a slightly substandard mage newly designated to work a small bit of land that'd once belonged to Repren. He'd visited once or twice before her master had dismissed his students, and his recent reports had left much to be desired.

Her master's face filled with relief when he saw her. The fear still sat deep in his eyes. She looked away.

The former Grand Mage gestured to his companion. "Issi, you know, Fyno."

She smiled and dropped into a bow. "I don't believe we've met."

The man in question, nodded, his eyes travelling down the neckline of her gown. He was lost instantly to the void between her breasts.

"I...uhm," the man began. He fidgeted, tried to change his focus, and failed. "It's a pleasure to make your acquaintance."

Likewise, the word shriveled in her throat. She managed a passable smile. Beside her, the Grand Mage stood straighter.

"You can look, there's no shame in it," he gestured towards her. "And she doesn't mind."

The lesser mage dropped any pretense. She felt him break her down into hips and breasts, his gaze lingering on curves and the slit that climbed up her thigh.

He did not notice the swelling on her face.

"She's very..." He caught himself and swallowed, dragging his gaze away. "I heard the piece she performed. She's very skilled."

The Grand Mage nodded sagely, sliding his finger along the opening in her skirt, widening the gap so most of her thigh flashed. Her hand clamped down on the fabric before he could do it again.

"Master," she began, quietly. "Isn't the sunset wonderful?"

The Grand Mage turned to one of the openings. The waters of the Copros had gone warm with the setting sun, and had begun reflecting reds, yellows, and oranges across the dome's ceiling. His face drained. "Ah, yes, it is. Fyno, feel free to send a letter detailing your requests."

"Yes, well, but—"

"We're leaving," the Grand Mage continued curtly, as he snatched Issi's hand. His grip was tight enough to leave her worrying after her bones. "I only came to make my presence known."

"Oh, I suppose—"

The young man was left speaking to the wind, as the Grand Mage whisked Issi around and started for the exit. He ignored the questioning look of his companions. His face had drawn, the color was slowly dripping away until he was the shade of dry soil.

The dinner itself hadn't even started.

He pressed her against the wall as soon as they'd entered his wing, kissing her desperately. His hand hiked her skirts, and she slammed the instinct to recoil.

She managed to convince him to his bed before he had her undressed. He checked the scars he'd carved into her as he muttered about. His words were empty promises and accusations. Love letters and threats tied together with strings of desperation.

He'd seen how she'd looked at the prince. He wanted to know how she'd managed to seduce him in so little time.

Her denials fell on deaf ears. She melted beneath his hands and forced her mind silent.

She lay awake beside him when he slept. The Grand Mage's bed was a ridiculous thing, so soft she felt like she was suffocating in a nest of sheets and covers. His ceiling had been enchanted to show the sky, currently a set of rose-colored clouds floated above them as the Grand Mage let out a soft snore.

When he slept, he really looked like nothing more than a boy. She reached out tentatively and let her fingers brush his cheek. She moved a lock of hair away from his face as her eyes traveled down his neck.

If he were gentler, would she have loved him?

She couldn't imagine it.

Once, he had smelled of magic and magic made the world feel *real*, and terrifying, and exciting. Now he smelled of sweat and sex and the perfumes he'd donned to attend a banquet where he'd been slighted by the man who's approval he craved more than anything in the world.

Her finger hovered above this throat. She imagined it was a blade and ticked it across his neck. He breathed softly against his stupidly soft pillows. She stayed beside him feeling time slip away as the room dyed from a golden rose to black.

The Grand Mage only stirred once.

She imagined killing him a thousand times over.

Issi sat up. Her stomach heaved. She doubled waiting for the nausea to pass before slipping from the bed and picking her clothes off the floor. She dragged herself to her cage. A small basin of water stood on her table with a washcloth folded neatly over its lip. Beside it sat a small, sweet bread wrapped in a handkerchief.

She felt a weary smile stamp her lips. Small miracles.

She could kiss Ner.

Issi washed thoroughly. She scrubbed at her skin until it went raw and angry before changing into a set of loose-fitting night clothes. The bread was gone before she really had the chance to taste it. She'd starved herself to fit into that damned dress.

The stone floor muffled her footsteps as she left her cage. Her violin was where she'd left it, by the front door. The case opened with a quiet click.

Her glove had nestled itself against the instrument's neck. She picked it up and flipped the fabric inside out. A scrap of parchment fell to the floor. Issi picked it up and unfolded it.

Read it.

A slew of bitter curses leapt from her lips as she hurried back to her room. She banged about looking for the fire-starter. Her hands shook as she slid the prongs across one another, their ends, tipped with flint and steel respectively, sent a spark that lit the candle's wick.

Soon as the damned thing caught, Issi dipped the paper into it. Flame crawled across it, until the parchment burned down to her fingers. She dropped what remained into her wash basin.

She cursed again pacing the length of her cage and drawing to a stop in front of her window. In the darkness the branches and leaves seemed a small forest.

She let out a breath. How could she have been so *stupid*?

She should have seen it from days away. A cook who was horrible at cleaning, a cook who had noble contacts, a cook who couldn't fucking *cook*.

The air filled with the lavender scent of her candle.

The letter, now little more than cinder, had been short.

Hello Del, meet me in the kitchens at your earliest convenience.

-Ardein.

And below that, because the bastard couldn't just leave well enough alone, he'd signed *Lesser known as Prince Tiremalv.*

Chapter 8

Issi fiddled with an enchantment. This one was designed to help pull the salt from the more thoroughly ruined fields of Repren. Or, at least, it was supposed to, her master's notes were nearly indecipherable, scratched out on corners of papers and wedged between pictures of beaks and wings.

The letters blurred as she sifted through the papers again. Maybe if she lit them on fire and scattered the ashes, whatever it spelled would prove more useful than the nonsense spread before her.

"Issi."

She flinched. The papers spilled from her hands and scattered across the tables.

"*Issi!*"

She squared her shoulders and bade her heart calm. "Yes, master?"

"You're useless, go to bed." She went rigid when his hand landed on her shoulder.

Fear clouded her thoughts. "I...uhm, I wanted to—" the rest of the sentence escaped her. When was the last time she'd slept? "Who will watch you if I sleep?"

"I didn't ask. Go to bed."

Issi swallowed a complaint and stood. "Of course," she said. Breathing was easier once he let her go. She hurried through the door, flinching as it slammed shut behind her.

The halls were dark. Her master hadn't thought to light the torches, so the only illumination came from the pools of moonlight that spilled through the windows that faced the garden. The claustrophobic stairwell that led her to the second floor was a starless sky.

Her cage wasn't a welcome sight.

She'd been avoiding it. These days, sleep brought nightmares, if it wasn't a beating, it was her family's portrait going up in flames, or her trying to accept the prince's offer only to find her mouth sewn shut.

And the forest.

It was waking from that one that she didn't like.

Her body ached for her to rest, but she forced herself before her vanity and carefully plucked the pins from her tresses. Large tumbles of hair, now freed, cascaded down her back in black velvet waves.

She braided it and tucked it beneath a silk scarf before spending a half bell deciding on her outfit for the next day and donning a night dress.

Her bed called her, and she was fast running out of excuses to ignore it. She still wasn't permitted to read outside the study, and violin practice would alert the mage to the fact that she was still awake.

She could try sneaking out, but "Del" appearing in the middle of the night would be hard to explain.

And her bed was soft.

She was asleep before her head hit the pillow.

Sunlight kissed her skin and pressed its warm body in dapples against her eyelids. Her chest rose and fell with a sigh. She almost wished for the smell of burning flesh and searing flames.

At least when she woke from that dream, she was grateful to be where she was.

Birds chirped high overhead. If she opened her eyes, she'd see their bright bodies flitting through the branches of long-limbed trees.

Even the clothes were pleasant. A pair of gods blessed trousers, and a shirt that didn't seek to press her breasts together and stop her from drawing air.

She sat up and ran her fingers through her hair until they caught in ringlets and curls. She laughed despite herself, delighted.

If she had the choice, this would be it, how she looked, how she dressed, how she'd *be*. She fell back into a bed of vines and twirled a leaf between her fingers.

"You're a weird one."

Issi bolted upright. She searched the woods and found nothing.

"Hello?" her voice shattered against the trees and scattered through the undergrowth. There was no response. "I'm sorry? Did I not start soon enough on the search for nothing?"

The forest was decidedly quiet.

The need to move niggled at her, the desire to seek out warmth and sweetness that would drive the sudden dryness from her mouth, hadn't yet grown insatiable, but it was there. She stood and started searching, but without knowing exactly what it was she was looking for, it felt useless.

She pried up rocks and studied the many legged creatures that clambered beneath them, she crossed small rivulets, and traversed meadows thick with flowers.

Nothing answered the yearning she felt.

"What are you looking for?"

Issi spun again, a shadow caught the edge of her vision, but when she turned to face it there was only forest. She ignored it and focused on finding a way to cross the river without getting completely soaked.

"What are you looking for?"

Issi threw her hands up in frustration. "I don't know."

"Why are you looking for it?"

She sighed, "It'll make me feel whole."

"Whole?"

"Yes, whole," Issi grumbled. She could try skipping across the rocks, but there was a jump she wasn't sure she'd manage.

"You look whole to me," the voice mumbled.

Issi paused. She was looking for a girl, or at least someone who *sounded* like a girl. There was nobody near her and no *body* anywhere. Stupid dream.

She leapt to the first rock. Her arms flailed as she caught her balance.

"And what'll you do if you find it?"

She fell. The water, it turned out, was cold enough to snatch the air from her lungs. She spat out a series of curses as she clambered to her feet.

"Are you ignoring me?"

At least that meant Issi didn't have to worry about leaping across. The river only came up to her calves. It didn't look to get much deeper and the current was very forgiving.

The grit was going to irk her.

"If you don't tell me why, I won't understand."

Issi sighed, the voice showed no intention of leaving her be. "I don't *know* what I'm looking for, or what I'll do when I find it. I just know that I'm getting closer."

"What does it look like?"

Issi reached the bank, her clothes dragged and stuck to her skin. Water splattered into the dirt as she wrung what she could from her shirt.

"I don't know that either. I just know that it'll taste...sweet."

"So, you're going to eat it?"

She wondered. "...I'm not sure."

"You seem awfully unsure of a lot of things."

Ipheoth grant her patience, "It's a *dream*, I don't think it needs to make sense."

"So, you spend all dream looking for something you'll never find?" the voice pressed curiously.

"What does it matter?" Issi snapped. This had been fun and games, but all the questions were beginning to grate.

"Because if you keep looking, you're going to die, and you won't even know why."

She carved a path between the trees, her voice dropped to a petulant whisper, "I'm dying anyway."

"You're only dying because you don't realize there's a choice," the voice replied, emphatically.

Issi paused, her feet drawing still. "Then how do I stop?"

"You're already whole. Stop looking, whatever it is they're offering isn't meant to complete you."

She let out a jagged peal of laughter as she turned towards the sun, it felt right, warm. Sweet? Her nose crinkled. That wasn't quite right, but had she been meant to follow it?

She nearly made it a full tick before her curiosity got the better of her. "Who are *they*?"

She could almost feel the voice *shrug*, "Not much of anything these days. Whispers, bedtime stories, legends, myths. I think your lot calls them gods."

Issi prickled, was it testing her devotion? "And *you*?"

"A fable, maybe? A prophecy? A girl? I'm not too sure anymore. I used to be called Tani, but things changed and changed and changed. I haven't talked to anyone in a very, very, long time."

"I must be *very fortunate*," Issi's words dripped sarcasm.

"You're not, I pity you," the voice answered, blandly, "Rua would have wanted to talk to you, so I figured I'd try, but you're not very nice, and talking is...hard."

"It seems like it's—"

Issi stopped, forgetting the conversation entirely. It was there, or at least part of whatever in Naya's hells she'd been looking for. On the other side of a meadow, the forest changed, the trees stretched until their limbs seemed to scrape the skies and the undergrowth all but disappeared. Flowers lined the edges in all sorts of shapes and colors.

It was there.

Whatever she was missing was somewhere in that forest.

Issi took off at a run. The grasses brushed against the fabric of her clothes, the sun beat down on her from above. The flowers were more beautiful the closer she got. She hadn't known colors could be so *vibrant*.

Just ten more steps.

Six more.

Two more.

One.

"I'm sorry," the voice was barely a whisper.

"No!" Issi woke abruptly the cry still scraping her throat. She'd screamed. Her cheeks reddened as a startled Ner hurried to her side. The sun outside her window had risen high enough to stop painting the skies anything other than a pale, sickly, blue.

Issi had to reset her alchemy clock.

"You almost gave me a heart attack," the maid squeaked. Her hand clutched at her chest.

"I'm...uhm..." Issi's attention drifted towards the window as she worked on convincing her fingers to release her covers. A vine curled through it, dripping in delicate white flowers.

"Ner," she began, slowly, "Is there a—, could you check my window?"

The maid studied her curiously, before she nodded. "Of course."

Ner peered through and around the glass. Issi watched intently as the maid's hand pressed against the vine, then went through it.

She blinked. It wasn't real.

"Everything seems to be in order." Ner swiped unnecessarily at the sill, gathering whatever imaginary dust she'd decided needed dealing with, "Was something wrong with it?"

Issi shook her head. "Uh...no, it was nothing." She plastered a warm smile on her face, "I just thought I saw something. That's all."

Chapter 9

As far as the prince's invitation was concerned, Issi's "earliest convenience" would come eight days later. In the time between, her mind curled around the memory of the note. It was a good distraction from the vines that had started to plague the corners of her vision.

She found herself searching for hidden meaning in the one sentence invitation.

There didn't seem to be any.

Had he wanted information on the Grand Mage's condition? He hadn't seemed interested in him at all. Besides, what did it matter these days? Her master had fallen from the king's favor and that sort of gossip wasn't worth writing a *letter* for.

She circled the kitchens a second time. There was no sign of him, and his workstation had been cleaned, or as close to clean as it ever got. When she asked about, she received only a series of apologies.

Maybe she'd taken too long, and he'd lost interest. Sometimes problems resolved themselves.

"Who are you looking for?"

"Don't," she whirled, stopping midsentence. Unlike her disguise, the prince's consisted mostly of well-applied make-up. The only magic worked to change the color of his eyes and to darken his hair from brown to black.

"Are you just going to stare? I worked very hard, to earn your curiosity." He acted as he normally did, comfortable and self-assured.

Her heart fluttered as she met his eyes and realized, uncomfortably, that she still adored him. It pissed her off. "Why are you such an ass?"

Surprise lurched across Ardein's face, replaced quickly by amusement.

Her irritation grew. Gods above, she was sure Mihr-Did was fucking with her.

The prince started towards his workstation.

"Issi was it?"

"Del," she corrected, shortly.

The prince arched his brows. "Okay…do you want to—?"

"What do you want?"

He looked at her, like he suspected she might have been joking. "Del, I've already told you, I want you to work for…well, me. I thought that'd be obvious."

Issi frowned, what in Naya's hells was he trying to accomplish? "What do you mean?"

"I. Want. You. To—"

Issi waved his response away. "No, that much was clear, but *what* do you mean by that?"

He looked at her like she'd gone slow, "Work for me?"

"I can't help you with that," she hissed, softly, her eyes darted about their surroundings searching for eavesdroppers. "I thought you'd have figured that out. If you want a Pet, you go through the proper channels. In case you haven't noticed, I don't exactly have an abundance of rights in your stupid country."

His face lit with understanding. "I don't want you as a Pet. I want you as a mage."

Any thought that'd been under the delusion of completing itself stopped. Issi's mind went as blank and empty as the cloudless skies outside.

"You've been writing the Grand Mage's reports for the last six moons," he continued, softly, "I'd like to hire you for a project."

His words turned to smoke between her ears. Issi found her head shaking.

"I—, no, you…you have the wrong person. I'm…I'm not what you thinking, *think* I—"

"Del, I don't think, I know." He reached for her arm. She was so stunned she hadn't thought to move it away. His thumb ran confidently across the hidden pocks and marks of her left hand, "Just how I know that the way you look is due to a very clever enchantment, leagues above anything Gadna could cobble together."

She pulled her hand away and clutched it to her chest.

"I begging—begged, I begged it off a student," she tried, "I just—, I wanted," her words tangled. What had she wanted? Where had all this been meant to go?

Her heartbeat was a thready hum between her ears. Was there a way out? Some way to convince him that he saw wrong, that he *knew* wrong?

"Let's finish this conversation elsewhere," she finished, softly.

"There are plenty of places in the royal wing—"

"Not there!" She started at the sound of her voice. It rang too loud. A few heads peeked up from their workstations. Their stares burned into her skin.

She forced her shoulders down and convinced air into her lungs. "I—, uhm, there's a place. I know a place where we can talk."

The prince paused, his eyes skipped over her face before he nodded. "If that will make you feel more comfortable."

"It would." She didn't think saying that his father was the thing of nightmares and she wanted nowhere near him, was a good way to keep the prince agreeable.

He gestured for her to lead the way.

Issi stuck to the main halls for as long as she dared, gathering her courage to ask him into the servant's corridors. He didn't hesitate when she finally succeeded.

Tiremalv didn't strike her as very prince-like. She'd imagined something closer to her master. Proud and unwilling to compromise. In many ways, it felt like she was still speaking with Ardein.

Except he knew more than Ardein had. And she felt moments from losing her breakfast from the nerves.

The prince hummed tunelessly, eyeing halls curiously as he trailed behind her.

He hesitated when she'd started down a branch too dark to see down. Her hand ran along the wall to guide her.

His humming stopped.

Issi slowed when she missed the sound of his footsteps. Her mouth opened, but what was there for her to say? Her throat ran dry as the silence between them grew heavy.

"That hall is very dark, Del," he said, at last.

She hadn't paid it much mind. Her eyes picked through the blackness. "Uhm, yes, it is?"

The prince's hand crawled to his belt. He made no attempt to move forward.

Lines of confusion appeared on her forehead. "If...if it was *not* dark, would you keep going?"

"Did you really think I'd follow you down a pitch-black hall?" he asked.

She shifted, searching for a response, "I'm sorry, it's, I didn't, I just didn't think royals were afraid of the dark. Can you cast light?"

The prince frowned and shook his head.

The torch twenty paces back was the obvious choice, but she wasn't fond of anything larger than a candle flame. She suspected that the prince had come armed, which meant he wasn't going to allow for anything that'd limit his movement. She couldn't fathom what he imagined she might do, but the lack of trust bothered her. *He'd* been the one who'd tricked *her* as if this was some little princeling game instead of her life on the line.

Her fingertips warmed and she cast as quickly as she could manage, wincing as the spell stole heat up to her elbow.

The ball of light illuminated the halls until they reached somewhere better populated and thus worth the hassle of keeping lit. She dispelled it absently and kept them going until she found what she was looking for.

Her hand pressed against rough lines of the false brick rousing the tired magic within it. The torch behind them went out shortly before a chill ran through her, setting her teeth chattering. The hidden door swung open.

The prince's eyes had gone wide, "Del, how did you find this?"

Issi shrugged, her hands already painting the air. It was only a beat before she had the light casting balancing in her palm. She walked through the doorway and waited for the prince to follow.

He didn't complain as he shadowed her up the narrow staircase. When they reached the room with the chairs and pallet, his expression filled with realization.

"This is how you—"

"How did you know it was me?" her words wavered, she hadn't been able to think of a way to convince him that he was wrong, not when he was so sure. And not when she wanted so desperately to be seen.

What if you could be more than a tool? The promise of it still echoed between her ears. Intoxicating.

When the prince didn't answer, she continued "The handwriting on the reports matched master's, I even used Qasha's stupid theories and systems, master's tone, I never pull information from non-Qashan mages, even *he* looks over my submissions and finds them satisfactory, so, how?"

A small frown tilted Ardein's lips. "Gadna knows?"

Issi fought the urge to roll her eyes. "Of course, he knows. I mean not about this," she gestured vaguely to herself, "But," the casting in her hand flared briefly, "*this*, yes, he knows all about this."

"And the reports?"

Her attention danced to the wall. Exactly how much did the prince know about the Grand Mage's condition? "He's been...preoccupied lately, but the reports still needed to go out on schedule." She continued, nervously, "He wanted to keep from falling out of the king's favor for as long as possible. I was the...obvious solution. Fat lot of good it did though."

"I was under the impression that he—"

"It's complicated," she interjected, impatiently. "How did you know it was *me*?"

The prince sighed. "The reports changed. You *tried* to copy his tone, but everything came out too...clever for Gadna."

He saw the confusion on her face and continued, "He wants to release enchantments as fast as possible to solve as many problems as possible but that makes his work boring. *Your* enchantments are never that simple."

"So, his designs changed a bit, I don't see how—"

The prince continued as if she hadn't spoken, "Around the same time the change occurred, rumors of the Grand Mage's last student visiting the kitchens started again. 'A pretty woman, a little cautious, Egrean accent,' I think is how they described you." His brows knit together before he waved the thought away. "Really, you're the type of person rumors are made for. I figured *the student* might have something to do with the change. Except...I couldn't find any record of her."

Issi worried her lip, the prince grinned in response. "You can figure out how the rest went," he said.

She shook her head, it'd been pure luck she'd even spoken to him at all, she'd just been searching for—

"Oranges," her voice rang thick with indignation, "Are you telling me you baited me with *fruit?*"

Like a common rat.

Joy danced in the prince's eyes when he nodded. "You only asked for one thing when you went on your little escapades. Oranges aren't very popular in Qasha, I'm afraid, but it made it very easy to get you to talk to me."

Issi took a deep breath. The prince's easy-going delight pressed against her as she gathered herself.

"That still didn't make it *me.*" She felt like a music box, repeating the same melody over and over.

"Well, no, but I started to suspect when I met you. *Smelled* you, your master orders some awfully expensive perfumes," he continued, "Which ruled out most of the servants because rumors about *that* would have spread like fire on kindling. That, and I had a dream."

"A *dream?*" Issi echoed, in disbelief.

The prince nodded, "I know how it sounds," he shrugged, "but it was right."

"How many people know?" she asked.

"Just me."

"*Why?*"

Confusion twisted his expression. "I don't know what you mean by that."

Issi wasn't entirely sure either. Did she want to know what he needed her for? Or did she want to know why he couldn't have found her earlier when any of this could have made the barest bit of difference?

She shook her head. "I can't help you with whatever it is you're doing."

"Del, you don't even know what I'm asking."

"I know I can't help you with it," she reiterated, "It doesn't matter what it is."

His nose scrunched in annoyance.

"Tell me why," he ordered. Issi stilled, something in her gave at the sound of the command. Maybe some part of her had hoped they could remain friends after all this.

She let the casting in her hand brighten, willing it to a warm orange that snuck tendrils into the far corners of the room. "I need the Grand Mage."

"What?"

"I need Gadna, and…he needs me," she mumbled. Ner had been taking care to remind her of that since Issi had expressed doubts. "I can't leave him."

"Del, are you *stupid*? You've been to the healer 10 times this year alone," he exclaimed, "he's abusive, and—"

"I *know*," Issi bristled. "I'm not *simple*. It's very fucking clear that he's abusive, princeling. You may have eyes watching me, but I've lived it for eight years. I *know* what he is. And I know that I can't. I can't leave him."

The prince let out a harsh laugh, "Do you *love* him?"

How could she explain how much she abhorred the man? How often had she imagined killing him only to freeze at the thought of a world without him? Were there even words in this awful growling tongue to describe the certainty that she wouldn't *exist* without him nearby?

"I can't leave him," she repeated, "I need him."

"Why?"

Because life without him was unimaginable, because the mere thought of his passing made the world dim, and her lungs want to collapse.

She swallowed. "Because, we're dying. I'm sorry that you've wasted your time, and I'm sorry that I can't help, but—"

"Dying?" the prince rolled the word like it was some exotic sweet.

Issi didn't respond, her hands toyed with the casting, dimming and brightening it nervously. Her demise and her escapades were the only secrets she'd ever managed to keep from the Grand Mage.

And now both were lying bare before her, ten moons that could be summed up in a single sentence, *I am Del, and I am dying.*

It was almost pathetic, except those secrets had brought her the closest to freedom she'd ever managed to get.

"How are you dying?"

"I thought it was obvious," Issi echoed his earlier declaration, her voice too raspy and soft to manage bravado. She smiled despite the failure because, gods, at least she'd *something* the prince hadn't known.

He didn't seem to find it as amusing as she did. She barked a laugh that rang high with desperation.

"I—"

"The Mage's Illness," she answered, dutifully, "I have two moons. There's no cure, at least, not one I've been able to find, though I suspect I've gotten pretty close."

The prince blinked as Issi pulled her sad wood carved enchantment from her breasts, letting it twirl as it tried to sort itself out. Her free hand wiped fastidiously at the make-up she used to hide the sprawling silver that marked her collarbone and had started to crawl up the side of her neck.

The prince's gaze didn't seem to know where to focus, dancing first across her skin, then her eyes, and the low-cut gown that had looked like student greys a moment ago, before finally landing on the mark.

He was completely silent.

Several beats passed before she found her voice, "I'm sorry to disappoint."

"I can work with that."

"What?"

The prince nodded as if agreeing with something. "Your dying? It's not a deal breaker."

Had he gone mad? "Prince, I don't think you understand what you're—"

"You don't understand what you *are*. Today I've seen you cast light in a way I didn't even think was possible. You're *fiddling* with it, changing colors and brightness like that doesn't fly in the face of logic!"

"The Northern Tribespeople do it all the time," she muttered, blankly. She'd read it in one of her master's older books, when scouring for a tome nobody would miss.

"But they don't cast like the Erbosians, they *dance*," he continued, excitedly. "And they can only change the casting so long as the dance continues, as soon as it stops, it's set."

She frowned. There was a lot about that that he was missing.

The prince's grin widened. "I still want you to work for me."

Issi sputtered, "Then why are you asking? If you want to own me, get my papers. This has nothing to do with me."

"Apparently having your papers doesn't mean I have your loyalty or your trust."

There was nothing to say about that. Having her papers meant owning her life, to be gifted with the right to do whatever he wanted, whenever he wanted, with no explanation needed. But that was all. He could demand her loyalty the way her master demanded her love, but the results would be the same.

He still wanted to use her.

What if you could be more than a tool? Did he not see the irony?

Issi stilled. "If you're asking, am I allowed to refuse...my prince?"

He spread his hands. "I suppose that's an option."

"Then I refuse."

His eyes went to flint. His lips formed a flat, hard, line of discontent. She half expected him to cross the room and strike her.

Instead, he closed his eyes and took a breath. When he opened them, for a tick in the light of her casting, they looked blue. She couldn't remember having seen Ardein in direct light before, except for that brief moment before the king's dinner.

"The offer stands, Del," he said, dismissing her.

She bowed and excused herself, leaving through the door they'd entered, taking the light casting with her. The third prince, surely, would do alright in the dark. After all, he was free to exit through the door to the ballroom if he so desired.

Chapter 10

Issi didn't sleep well for the next half moon. When she did manage to *fall* asleep, she didn't stay there long, waking abruptly whenever she even suspected she felt sunlight on her skin. The times she did dream, she woke to the prince's offer ringing in her ears.

The vines had gotten worse.

They started small, sitting at the edges of rooms, growing quietly on tables, snaking between baubles and trinkets. Then they started dumping flowers everywhere. Vines set to climbing chairs and the not bars of her cage, they used her easel as a trellis and cascaded petals into her paints.

For the most part, she managed to ignore them. But nights were...different.

Twice she'd caught herself following the tendrils out of the wing entirely.

Issi berated herself during her waking hours for not having paid enough attention to the reports. She'd thought they'd been exaggerating the importance of the delusions.

Or maybe, she'd thought she was better than all the fools who'd fallen prey to them. In her small, limited world, it'd seemed plausible.

She started sneaking the reports in her room. Scouring over them during the day, despite the danger, and shoving them hurriedly beneath her mattress when Ner came by with whatever food went with the time.

Sunlight hours filled with stories of cloud colored deer bleeding rose petals from knife-slashed throats, and soft burbling songs whispered from bodies of water. When exhaustion claimed her completely, her dreams filled with forests and green things, and shifting stealthily over the ground a bow in her hand.

She brewed stronger tea.

She searched the libraries again and again in hopes of finding out why a Chousalian remedy her mother once brewed to stave off fevers might do anything to beat back an illness that seemed otherwise unstoppable. But Qasha didn't *have* books that praised other magic systems. All she'd ever found on Chousal had regaled her with tales of savagery and the backwards way they'd run their country.

She reached dead end after dead end, the limits of everything she'd managed pressed against her. A new suffocating weight that she carried with her always.

Maybe that was why she didn't notice the Grand Mage had wandered off until she felt the humid, late-spring air lay thick hands on the back of her neck.

The windows in the workroom weren't supposed to open, some of the experiments being very particular about the temperature she kept their components. Issi looked towards the runes above the fireplace set to pull the heat towards the roof, but the magic beneath it hummed quietly. She stood up and muttered several bitter curses as she followed the smell of overgrown herbs and heat from her master's garden to an open window.

She checked to make sure the Grand Mage hadn't thread himself through to go for a night walk. None of the plants beneath the window had been crushed. She'd been about to set the paneling right, when movement caught her eye.

A shadow in the moonlight shifted along her lonely patch of palace wall. She blinked away inviting tendrils of green and watched in disbelief as the shadow traversed the black line of the roof.

She nearly thrust herself through the opening, squinting at the impossible angle. Three stories above her head, she saw the barest flutter of fabric. A flash of a hand. Her heart gave a nasty twist.

Issi raced through the room, nearly slipping in the mess her master's tea had made across the mosaiced floor.

She slammed into the doors that lead to the second story, forcing them open before taking the steps two at a time. She sprinted past a series of empty rooms that'd once housed dozens of students and healers. Her lungs burned.

When was the last time she'd run?

The ladder to the third floor had been drawn down. Issi scrambled up it, fighting through the insistence of greenery and memories of orange trees.

The third floor was filled with the remnants of experiments too dangerous to throw out and too expensive to burn.

A coating of dust covered every surface. It hadn't been cleaned for moons. That had been a chore belonging to the students who knew enough not to press mysterious marks and set things better left silent to ticking. She followed the clear patches the mage's feet had carved against the floor's dirty surface to a small open window, her breath leaving her in painful pants.

She spied him through the window, walking along the very edge of the roof paying no mind to the drop.

She wanted him to jump.

Under Ose's great skies, she wanted nothing more than for him to tumble downwards and die.

She still couldn't imagine a world without him, any more than she could conceive of a world with no sun. The idea of him simply being gone, made her stomach twist and her heart race.

But for a moment, she was almost willing to see it through.

The prince thought he'd seen something in her and made an offer, but there was nothing she could do. She wasn't what he thought he wanted, and as soon as he realized that he'd grow angry. The Grand Mage knew exactly what she was. His anger was familiar, his disappointment was something she'd grown accustomed to. She'd learned, over the years, to grow comfortable with it.

Because without Gadna, she was nothing.

And it was that thought that scared her lungs into working. She called him through the window, just loud enough to be heard above the wind and distance.

The Grand Mage stilled and turned, silhouetted against the night sky. He wasn't seeing her. His eyes tracked the heavens instead of falling to the window.

He smiled.

It made him look very young. He *was* very young, at least for a Grand Mage. He'd just reached thirty.

Issi forgot that most days. It felt like he should know more than she did, be more, be grander somehow, than a man who purchased love. But he wasn't and he had.

Some days it felt like that was more her fault than others.

She forced herself through the window. Humid air gathered around her, drawing sweat from her skin. Her legs shook, her knuckles paling as she gripped hard on the frame.

"Master," she shouted. She couldn't see if he'd heard her or cared.

It didn't look like he cared.

"Grand Mage."

Nothing.

"Gadna," her voice sang with desperation. She suspected it was the total lack of decorum that caught his attention in the end.

He glared at her. Issi felt her heart, which had already busied itself hammering against her ribs, try for an extra leap.

"I, uhm, could you come back inside?" She worked on prying her fingers from the window frame. "It's not safe up here."

He glanced off the rooftop, seeming to register the drop for the first time. He gawped a moment, before the annoyance in his face shifted to fear. "Why weren't you watching me?"

And there he was. The most powerful mage in all of Qasha, in his nightrobes, perched at the end of a roof, moments from tumbling to an unseemly demise.

Completely and utterly indignant.

This sad little man was the only reason she still existed.

She laughed.

It wasn't the proper titter, the high bell-like bullshit that he insisted on that she'd never once uttered with any sort of sincerity. He seemed surprised at the sound of it, harsh and stupid, spiked at the edges with honest joy.

"You are not to laugh at me," he snapped.

"That's the most lucid you've sounded in days," she gasped and snorted, which only made her laugh harder, "You're ridiculous."

He opened his mouth, surely to berate her. Call her a whore, or useless, or stupid, perhaps some less than imaginative combination of all three. But all it did was make him seem more childish than he already did, and Issi found herself caught in another fit of giggles. Her sides ached.

His eyes ticked away, following those damned birds.

Right, this was important.

Issi gasped, trying to gather herself, the world had run bright with tears. Her vision cleared in time to see her master totter on the roof's edge.

The fool was going to do it.

She released the frame, her legs carrying her too quickly to the drop. Her heart sank with the realization that she wasn't going fast enough.

He tipped forward slowly, like he was sure the ground would catch him. Like he was on a morning stroll to his gardens. She doubted he even noticed the roof ended. She launched herself forward trying to clear that last bit of distance. The tiles hit hard, driving air from her lungs as they dug into her stomach.

She forced her hand to clasp around his ankle. Her nails bit into his flesh.

She was dragged forward, roughly, her free hand grabbed at a decorative outcropping. The skin along her palm tore, as she caught. Her arms strained as she tried to still.

He was too heavy.

She was nothing without him. She needed him, nearby and unafraid, as he'd always been so she knew the world was as it was supposed to be.

The world could not go on without Grand Mage Gadna Niao.

She hissed as the outcropping ripped away the rest of the skin on her palm. She started sliding forward.

He was going to take her with him.

She clawed at whatever was in reach, the tiles, the stone. Nothing *stuck*.

There was only a beat to decide. Maybe one day, Ipheoth willing, she could convince herself that she actually thought she'd be able to reach him on the first floor and care for his wounds. Tell herself that she'd every intention to call a healer.

But truthfully, the moment her fingers snapped away from his ankle, the only thought that'd run through her head was, *fuck it, maybe he'll actually die.*

The Grand Mage plummeted, a cry startled from his throat before he hit the overgrown weeds with a series of rustles and cracks and crashed to the ground with a loud snap.

Her ears strained as her eyes tried to pick him out between swaths of green, both real and imaginary.

He was silent.

She scrambled back from the ledge, falling on her back. The ache of it was distant. She remembered her mother's tales of Ose, the god of sky and adventure. In the stars that danced distantly above her, she wondered if he was watching down on her from his spired tower.

The gods felt so distant in this damned country.

Issi wasn't sure how long she stayed there. But her body had grown sore and stiff by the time she decided to move. She'd all sorts of scrapes and bruises, her palm stung where her skin had ripped away, and she'd torn through patches of her dress.

All that time and the Grand Mage hadn't uttered a single groan. It'd been quiet but for the night song of insects.

Issi worked her way through the mage's wing, until she landed in the workroom. She'd never gotten around to closing the window. She pulled herself through it painfully, the strong scent of crushed herbs met her nose.

The garden pavers wound about, stopping beside specimen that'd once been trimmed and pretty but had now grown unkempt. Issi lingered by a few, wondering which enchantments she'd be using them to strengthen.

She found the blood first, thick and dark, in the moonlight. It spread slowly across the pavers, soaking into her slippers, threatening to pull the silk away from her skin.

She hardly noticed.

The Grand Mage lay beneath the broken arms of an elder tree. She ran towards him, there was too much blood. His skin was cool beneath her uninjured palm.

"Master," she spoke as if she were trying to wake him.

He did not respond.

There was too much blood.

She shook his shoulder, and his head lolled. Rolled. His eyes had already started to cloud. The only thing that'd kept his skull with the rest of his body was a patch of skin that'd been too stubborn tear. Blood still wept from the wound.

Issi stared at him blankly.

She needed to get her embroidery kit to sew him back together.

No, that was wrong. Stupid. There was too much blood. She'd need the medical supplies he'd used to patch her.

Her brows lowered, "No, that won't work." The sound of her voice, pure and eerily calm, made her jump.

But she was right. Sewing him back together wouldn't work.

Why?

Her mind was quiet. She poked at him.

The air was thick with the smell of copper and salt.

He'd make for a ripe corpse.

"You're dead, aren't you?" she asked, the words tumbled wrong. It took her a moment to realize she'd spoken in Egrean.

Longer still to realize why that didn't matter.

The idea of his death refused to solidify, instead bouncing through her thoughts and sending little waves that attempted to set her in motion.

His dying wasn't real, she was still there.

And the will was too.

What was it he'd done again? Granted her to his cousin in Athijan? They didn't let those with mage's mark over the border. They were afraid they'd make the illness spread faster despite all evidence to the contrary.

They'd slay her in the mountains.

She studied her master's unseeing eyes.

How much time could she steal? She'd need his resources if she even wanted a chance in Naya's hells of finding a cure. Chousalian herbs were both finite and expensive, and his private collection had been running low.

His body was going to be a problem.

Issi straddled over his head, her shoes sticky with his gore. Beneath the thick smell of his blood lay something far less pleasant. His bowels had loosened, the stench of him was something that'd never been covered in any of the books. She threaded her hands beneath his armpits and tried to pull.

He was heavier than her by far, the stress from the recent months having piled around his middle. She was rewarded with the slightest give. Five attempts and she was covered in his blood and breathless.

The body had only moved a pace or two from where she'd found it.

This wasn't going to work.

Issi wracked her brains. She didn't have the funds on hand to buy someone's silence.

Nobody would come down to the garden any time soon for maintenance. It'd truly belonged to her master, but if the smell got bad enough, the scent of turning meat and rancid bile was going to send someone exploring.

The body.

It was meat, right?

Issi left him there, smelling of turning flesh and blood. Her hands left ruddy prints on the windowsill as she pulled herself through. Her shoes tracked red in uneven streaks across the workroom floor. She washed her hands in a basin, registering neither the coldness of the water, nor how her master's blood painted the liquid an anemic pink.

She searched the library for kitchen enchantments. Most of the books were lousy, thick things, she couldn't force her way into understanding. It took her nearly a bell to find anything useful.

She flipped through pages of an old cooking tome, dismissing anything that'd run the body hot. The smell of burning meat would attract someone and the burning fat and bowels...there'd be no explaining that away.

Her eyes lit when she found the enchantment that the kitchens used for cold boxes. If she could slow the rotting, she could buy enough time to find a better solution.

Issi set the book on a worktable and took an engraving pen to a piece of practice wood.

Her hands shook, sending the lines wild. It took her four attempts to get the enchantment to work and three more to get it to work *well*. She tied it to the mage's fire roaring in the hearth, before rubbing elderberry seed oil into its crevices and feeling the magic lock.

Whenever she set it working, the flames went low, despite the fuel that fed it.

Hopefully the maids wouldn't think anything of it.

She went back to the window, her hands tracing the prints she'd left before as she vaulted through.

She found the Grand Mage more by smell than sight.

Time served only to make his position more inelegant. She pressed her thumb against the enchantment and prayed.

She wasn't sure whose realm hiding a corpse fell under, Ipheoth goddess of mercy, Mihr-Did, god of tricksters, or Naya, goddess of death, so she sent prayers to each of them in turn before she set the pendant atop his chest.

A few heartbeats passed and nothing happened.

She added a quick prayer to Hoten, god of luck.

She waited a few beats longer when ice started to spread tentative tendrils from beneath the wood. Fingers of cold stretched across his breast dripping down his torso, pulling the still wet blood into sharp crystalline angles. Her skin prickled as her breath clouded the air.

The smell became less pungent and Issi's legs attempted to fail.

Would this give her a day? Two? Maybe three, if she was very clever about it. She bit her lip running through spells she'd read about on those quiet nights she'd managed to sneak tomes from her master's library.

There was no time. She looked up at the skies and hopelessly wished for rain. Anything to wash the blood, and gore, and shit, into the soil or somewhere far away.

But the skies were clear.

She left what remained of the Grand Mage frosting over in the walkway and put herself through the window. She stripped, pulling her slippers away, and gathered the ruined cloth of her dress.

His blood had stained her skin.

Her stomach flipped. She nearly lost the tea she'd managed to drink. He was ubiquitous, bits of him tracked everywhere she'd been.

She tossed her clothes into the low flames of the fire. His blood made it catch faster than it'd any right to. Magic a fire all they wanted, there were reasons mages had been burned on pyres.

Issi dumped the remains of the water she'd been squirreling away for the extra cups of "tea" she'd taken to brewing throughout the day into a shallow basin. It barely filled half, though she'd retrieved two, and a handful of cloths used for wiping workstations.

She dipped a clean cloth into the water before scrubbing at the blood. It wasn't long before it'd run completely red and useless. The cloth landed with a wet thwack in the second basin before she picked a second. Six piled in the bowl's shallow belly by the time they'd finally stopped dyeing red. She fed them into the fire too.

She didn't feel any cleaner for it. The stench of her master had lodged in her nose. The clock above the hearth informed her it was nearing sixth bell.

The sun was beginning to brighten the sky.

A brief round about the room with what was left of her water and a few cloths took care of most of the blood, or, at least, smeared it into something unrecognizable. She was thorough with the windowsill, erasing her handprints completely as well as any memory of red.

It was a relief to close the window. She drew the curtains for good measure, but it turned out she needn't have worried, because nearly a beat later, she heard a raindrop strike the glass.

Followed quickly by another.

And another.

A downpour struck the building in waves. Issi stared at the window not quite trusting her ears. But when she dared to pull the fabric back to peek, she saw only water.

She sent a quick prayer to Ose and left the room to dress.

Chapter 11

"*Issi,*" Ner's voice rang out like a shot.

Issi started, her knife pulling from where it'd been moments from biting into her hand. "Shit," she muttered.

The maid hurried over, all grey skirts and worry. "Are you okay? Did you hurt yourself?" She clasped Issi's gloved hands in her own. Issi stared at her blankly, too tired for the panic that flared to make much of a difference.

She pulled herself free and studied her gloves.

"I'm fine, Ner...just tired."

"Well, the Grand Mage is out, why not get some rest?"

Issi glanced at her window. Rain still beat against the glass. It'd been going for bells now and had shown no signs of slowing or stopping.

At this rate, the island was going to flood, and the ships that ferried people in and out of the capital would soon dock to wait the weather out.

"Why don't you go home early?"

Ner blinked, a small frown appeared on her butterfly lips. "There're things to be done."

"The ferries aren't going to run for much longer," Issi pointed out, "And the Grand Mage isn't here. I'll be fine. You don't get this chance very often."

"Issi—"

"I'm worried, Ner," she interjected, "master doesn't...leave very often under such short notice. Or, he'd at least have told me beforehand instead of just leaving some vague letter about his departure that had to be read to me," her voice warbled, and she paused as if to collect herself, "This is new to me. I want to think he's really out there studying, as he said, but I can't help but worry that he's off somewhere doing something else...*someone else.*"

She fretted for a moment wondering if she'd been too dramatic. When she looked up, red spread beneath the soft brown of the maid's cheeks. Ner's jaw worked a few times before she managed to open it.

Issi let out a breathy laugh, her eyes tracing back towards the window where a vine had started to curl about the frame. "I'm sorry, that was vulgar. Just, please, I'd like to think this over without having the maids waltzing around and eyeing me with pity. Can you arrange that for me, Ner?"

The maid paused. It'd been years since Issi had truly asked her for anything. It was clear that Ner wanted things to go back to the way they had been, when Issi had confided in her, and told her stories. Before the Grand Mage had relieved Ner of her thumb and Issi had taken to keeping to herself and filling the quiet moments between them with idle chatter.

Maybe Ner hoped this was a step in the right direction.

"Okay," she answered, softly, "I can do that."

Issi smiled. "You're the best."

It wasn't long before the last maid sauntered out of the wing, whispering excitedly about how she intended to spend her unexpected evening off.

Issi waited half a bell before she left her cage and scurried through the halls.

She hesitated before the workroom. Part of her was afraid she'd somehow dreamed the whole thing up. That the Grand Mage would be in there, bent over a desk, or hidden in his library, wondering where the maids had gone.

She'd seen his body. She'd been covered in his blood...but her limbs still froze, and she had to talk herself into pushing the door open.

The workroom was empty.

There was no smell of heat and spark, just the faintest tinge of orange.

She checked the entire floor, just to be sure. There was no sign of the Grand Mage having been there, even the tea he'd spilled the night before had been cleaned away, and the faint bloodstains Issi hadn't been able to completely clear had been scrubbed to oblivion.

She approached the window and shoved it open.

The rain was bracing, cold, despite the late spring heat. Issi hissed as she worked her aching body through the frame.

She was soaked within beats. The plants beneath the window had been trampled, so, at least, climbing through had been real. As she neared the place she remembered leaving her master's body, her breath began to cloud. Her slippers stuck to a thin layer of ice.

The rain had done wonders at washing away the blood.

The Grand Mage was exactly where she had left him. A twisted, frozen, soaking mess. Her eyes filled with tears.

He was dead. And the world still spun. Time was moving forward, and she was still there.

Thank Ipheoth, it hadn't been a dream.

Issi shivered as she crouched beside the corpse. His skin had gone brittle, his eyelashes frozen over with a mixture of blood and ice.

She had no more luck moving him now than she had the night before. Her thoughts wandered vaguely to the practicalities of a shallow grave, but she wasn't convinced she'd be able to dig it in time.

And if people got nosy, or if a downpour like this ever happened again, or a maid so much as scuffed a slipper in the wrong spot, she'd be in trouble. She couldn't afford to waste time worrying about that.

Issi ran her fingers down the length of her master's arm, lingering quietly on his wrist, and grimaced.

Of all the things she was going to have to do, this felt the most like a sin.

She grasped his pointer finger with one hand and his palm in the other. The frost of him bit through her gloves. She shut her eyes, and whispered, "Ipheoth, grant me forgiveness for the sins I must commit."

The finger broke with a clean snap, right above his knuckle. The base of it was a jagged mixture of muscle and bone.

Her stomach twisted and she turned to keep from desecrating the corpse any further. She wiped her mouth on her sleeve and peeled off a glove before wrapping the digit in the fabric.

She swiped at the rain that dripped down her eyelids. It felt like she should *say* something, like she owed him some form of thanks or apology.

"You were an awful person," she muttered, "But..."

Was there anything to add to that?

Issi shifted on her feet, recalling those rare conversations they'd held late at night, the ones where he'd talk of his family, or the court, and twice very, very, quietly about the wars.

The fear she'd first identified at the king's dinner had been bright in his eyes then, too. She just hadn't known to look.

He'd been a child when he was thrust into a world of violence, coercion, and manipulation. He'd been abandoned, starved, made to watch his friends die, and somehow, against all odds had still managed to climb the ranks to Grand Mage. That didn't make what he'd done to her any better or forgivable, but she was beginning to understand why he might have done it.

And there was nothing more she had to say.

Ipheoth's blessing rested on her tongue. *Grant him forgiveness for the sins he's committed.* Maybe it'd been easier to speak over the nameless soldiers who'd only done as they were ordered.

But no one had ordered the Grand Mage to strike her.

No one had ordered him to carve her.

No one had made him touch her.

He'd done all that on his own.

She was supposed to trust the gods in times like these, believe they'd know better than to let his sins go uncleansed, that Naya in all her wisdom would punish him appropriately. But she couldn't.

The words were still warm on her tongue as she left him. She shivered as she pulled herself through the window and landed with a splash in the puddle that'd formed on the other side. Issi set her master's severed digit in a bowl before returning to her cage to change out of her sopping wet clothes and wring what she could from her hair.

A half-moon.

If everything fell into place, if she was clever enough, she could keep the Grand Mage's death a secret for a half-moon.

If she could get rid of the body.

For a chance to succeed, she needed twice that.

And she needed help.

She sorted through her closet, pushing aside her gaudier gowns, searching for something that might, if looked at sideways, pass for something current and fashionable.

She couldn't pay someone for their silence. Firstly, she'd have to know someone she was sure wouldn't feel enough patriotism to report his death, and secondly, more importantly, the Grand Mage hadn't kept much money on *hand*.

He'd dealt mostly with promissory notes that completed transactions directly through the king's treasury. It'd be traceable and if the body were found, that would be a much bigger problem.

She chose a gown that would fit a bit too tightly to conform to the modest standards of the courts, but it might pass if she tied a scarf about her waist to obscure her hips.

It was the best she was going to manage.

Issi ticked a dozen or so ill-conceived notions and ideas, circling the choice she knew she'd have to make. There was one person who had the power and knowledge she needed.

She put it off for as long as possible.

After changing out of her wet clothes, she returned to the workroom, prepared the paperwork, and started to read pages upon pages of medical reports, ignoring the symptom catalogues and focusing squarely on the hallucinations and delusions as she waited either for her master's finger to thaw, or night to fall.

Her eyelids grew heavy, the text on the page became nonsensical smears of ink. She dug her nails into her arm.

A soft shuffling sounded behind her.

Her heart leapt in her throat. For a brief, insane moment, she was convinced she'd turn to find the Grand

Mage standing behind her with his twisted neck, and the stump of his stolen finger weeping blood onto the floors.

Her breath came ragged. She wanted nothing more than to squeeze her eyes shut and pray he go away but that particular prayer had never worked.

She turned.

The Chousalian she'd dreamt of that day lifetimes ago in the kitchens stood before her. Vines gathered at the girl's feet and climbed up her legs. Issi reached out and pulled her hand back like she'd been burned.

The girl was warm and very, very, solid.

She grabbed for Issi's hand. Issi felt the heat from the girl's fingers, the roughness of her palms. She smelled of green things, like the Grand Mage's garden after it'd gone wild. Like the forest Issi wandered in her sleep.

The girl opened her mouth to speak. No voice came out, she frowned, tried again, her grip tightening until her nails dug into Issi's skin. She started to mouth words.

Issi woke with a puddle of drool clinging to her cheek. She wiped her mouth as she looked around for any sign of the Chousalian using enough magic to make the room feel seconds from blooming.

Her body vibrated with the memory of it.

There was nothing but the faint shadow cast by the dim glow from the mage's fire that danced in the hearth.

She scrubbed her palms over her face in frustration. *Right*, vivid dreams, another symptom to add to her ever-growing list. The memory of the girl's hands still wrapped around hers.

She ran slow. Whatever amount of sleep she'd stolen hadn't been enough and she *ached* all over. Her palm stung, her legs and torso were stiff with bruises, even her fingers hurt.

Not to mention the soreness from having sprinted for what she expected was the first time in nearly a decade.

She fussed with her dress until it lay right and picked up a sheathe of papers, and a forged lending charter, before she donned a pair of satin gloves that climbed to her elbows. Outside the sun had long set, not that it felt like it'd properly raised at all. The rain clouds had blot everything out.

Despite the stars she'd seen so clearly the night before.

She braced herself against the front door, she wanted to leave through the servant's exit, but the Grand Mage had never allowed that. She held her breath as she pushed against the paneling.

A sprawling green landscape sat behind the door. She studied the hills that rolled off into the distance and the trees that lined the horizon, before blinking them away to find the guards watching her with a mixture of curiosity and annoyance. There was no greenery in the hall, just rough stone and the light from the torch by the door.

Nalav's face showed more disgust than anything else.

Issi's heart sank. She lingered hoping he'd smile or crack a joke. He did neither, just turned back to his companion who was moments from bowing and forced him upright.

"Don't, she's just his whore." She winced, but what had she expected?

The soldier, this time a young man with wide eyes, looked at her uncomfortably, "But—"

"She won't say anything." Nalav turned to glare at her, "Right?"

She bit her lip to keep from responding.

He knew what Del sounded like. The illusion had done nothing to alter that. She offered him a hurried bow and rushed off with the quiet complaints of the younger guard sounding behind her.

The halls spat her into the atrium before guiding her through a series of mismatched rooms until Kothen palace's nonsensical layout left her before the soaring ceilings and brightly lit halls of the royal wing.

She felt the moment she crossed through, the magic that spilled across her skin was likely some sort of perimeter casting, the type used to secure the boundaries of war camps. She waited, her eyes taken by a tapestry that smelled of fruit tarts and summer warm evenings.

Since the illness and the wars, magic was very rarely used for art. Her master held some enchanted tapestries and statuettes, but nothing so grand as the one she was looking at.

It ran the length of the hall. A bright portrayal of a battle spanning meadow and forest. Battalions with proud banners waving in the wind were posted on either side. One leader, perched atop some beast Issi couldn't hope to name, raised their sword and hunkered down as their mount started forward at breakneck speed.

"Pardon me do you—, you need to go home."

Issi dragged her attention away as the first clashes began. She'd forgotten to breathe.

"I, uhm." She bowed, hurriedly, grasping tightly at the papers in her hand, "I having, I *have* been sent to meet the thir—, our Prince Tiremalv."

The royal guard was a smartly dressed woman. She stood a full head above Issi.

Her eyes rested on Issi's neck, "Where's your collar?"

Issi's free hand rushed up to feel for it. Her fingers brushed skin.

"Ah, I'm sorry, it was such short notice, we got a request from th—, our prince and the lending charter had to be drafted. It was all a bit of a...rush."

"Our prince *requested* you?"

"Uh, *yes*. Exactly."

The woman was unmoved. "He doesn't do that."

According to the rumors, he bedded all sorts. What was one more?

"He specifically requested my master send me," she tried.

"He doesn't accept Pets."

Issi's heart thrummed, she just needed to *see* him, but to come as Del was to invite people to look closer at what the Grand Mage was doing. Rumors from the kitchen and a few guards could be dismissed as idle gossip.

A royal guard was something else entirely.

"I have the form." She picked a paper from the pile, sparing it a glance before holding it to the woman who shook her head.

"Not my first time getting a forged charter," she explained. "Go home."

Issi swallowed. This was the only option that had a chance in Naya's hells of working. She could try to promise bind someone, but to do that to an unwilling soul...well that was a much bigger sin than breaking a finger off a corpse.

Issi forced as much righteous indignation into her voice as she could, "Don't you know who I am?"

The woman nodded, unimpressed. "You're the Grand Mage's Pet, Curly or something."

Issi didn't have to fake the outrage that crossed her face.

"I am not some common *dog*." Though to be given the rights of one would certainly have been a step in the right direction. "My *name* is Nydelissi Anders, and I serve the Grand Mage of Qasha." She tried to conceive of a way to look down her nose at the woman who towered above her at a dozen paces, "Are *you* willing to tell him why I've been turned away?"

The guard paused. Everyone knew of the Grand Mage's temper, the incident with the healer hadn't been the first time he'd sent someone to the infirmary. And rumor was Issi frequented quite often herself.

And she did.

"I—"

"He's in an awful mood. The Grand Mage doesn't just *lend* me. I am his most prized possession. Have you ever heard of me being lent out before? Do you think the Grand Mage would really send me here, if it wasn't a direct order from our royal family?"

The guard rocked on her feet. "And if you're lying and the prince didn't call for you, and your master sent you here as a bargaining chip?"

"He would *never*," Issi hissed.

The guard nodded, looking vaguely unnerved. "Alright, come on."

The woman turned neatly and started down the hall. Issi hurried behind her, trying to keep an air of confidence around her. But she started to lag, the façade falling away, as they passed more and more enchanted items.

Magic hung thick, painting the air with scents of favorite foods, and seasons, and places. She paused before a book that smelled of baked persimmon and flipped a page only to squeal as a striped four-legged monstrosity leapt at her from its pages.

The guard chuckled softly before telling her to hurry up.

Issi was left gawping like a child at every new rune and smell she encountered. Her fingers ran over the bases of moving statues that made her master's look like an ill-crafted trinket.

"So...you like magic?" the guard called from ahead.

Issi had paused by a sculpture of a young boy casting a net from a boat. The net flew out in an expanding arc that reminded her of misting rain.

"No," she lied, "It's too...hard for me to pick up. I just like watching the little people move. They're pretty."

The guard sighed as if Issi's answer disappointed her, though what the woman had wanted Issi to respond with remained a mystery. Pets weren't allowed to have interests in things like magic, or fighting, or strategy, or anything that could make them dangerous to their masters.

She did not try to make conversation again.

The halls shrank abruptly, wide marble expanses giving way to ancient stone that would be right at home in her master's wing if the hall hadn't been illuminated by light castings instead of mage's fire.

Even the door was a better dressed cousin of the one belonging to her master's corridor.

The guard coughed politely. "Are you going to knock?"

Issi felt the blood rush to her cheeks. "Of course, I will."

She reached for a golden snake shaped knocker and struck the door twice. The door reverberated the sound echoing down the hall before fading to nothing. She glanced at the guard whose eyes stayed trained on the wood. Moments passed and nothing happened.

She raised her hand to knock again when the door swung open.

A sleepy looking maid frowned first at Issi, then at the guard.

"What is this?" her voice was a sharp thing Issi associated with rigid instructors and rapped knuckles.

"A present for our prince, apparently," the guard answered, swiftly. She had the decency to keep from looking Issi over. The maid did not. Her eyes lingered on Issi's raised hand, which received a disapproving grunt, before drifting down the rest of her with an air of disappointment.

Issi shoved her hand behind her back, embarrassed.

"A Pet?" the maid asked, at last.

"Gadna's," the guard answered.

The maid's eyes widened a fraction before her jaw set. "I don't care who sent it, send it away, Tiremalv does not accept—"

"He asked for me specifically," Issi interjected, trying again for the lending charter. The maid snatched it.

"Forged charters," she scoffed, "I don't have time for this." The woman shook her head as she ripped the paper down the center and turned to the guard. "I told you I didn't want to see any more of them. They're vermin, take it home."

"I just—"

Issi watched in dismay as the maid took a step back and moved to shut the door. She was so *close*. He was in there, he had to be. If the wing really was the twin of her master's she knew how well the sound travelled within it.

The conversation was ten steps too far, and twice as quiet as it needed to be…assuming he wasn't out near the workroom. Before she could think about what she was doing, she drew air into her lungs.

"I am the Pet of the Grand Mage, you will *not* turn me away without letting me do my *job*," she shouted.

The guard jumped, her hand flying to the sword at her hip.

The maid narrowed her eyes. "So it speaks out of turn."

"Push me and you will see that I do *more* than speak," Issi continued, crisply, "I am tired of the lack of respect I've been shown since I got here, y—, *our* Prince, requested me specifically and I was sent *here*. If you have a problem with that take it to *your* master, not mine."

The maid wore an expression that would curdle milk/ "Take it back to Gadna."

"I am not an *it*," she railed, dramatically. She was almost having fun. After being forced to scurry about and bow, and apologize for existing for most of her life, this was a welcome change. If it weren't for the quiet voice in the back of her head insisting that this could only lead to her demise, she might have laughed.

She continued emphatically speaking absolute nonsense. Her tongue ran away from her, she might have called the maid a damned fucking twit, but she'd lost track of the conversation and the guard was doubled on the floor guffawing too hard to grab and drag her away.

It had to have been ticks. Issi was losing hope, maybe he wasn't there, and she'd have to draw her luck thin hoping to hide the Grand Mage's absence and her own as she sought him out in the kitchens some other day.

"Perenne," the prince's voice was thick with annoyance. "What's the matter and why—?" He drew to an abrupt halt. Amusement sparked across the remnants of Ardein's face. "Well, this looks fun."

The guard tried to gather herself, her laughter scattered between deep gasping breaths.

The prince smiled. "Hello, Issi."

Chapter 12

"My prince." Issi dropped into a hurried bow, bending at the waist. She didn't think she could pick herself up from the forehead grinding grovel that the situation demanded without making how hurt she was obvious.

"Stand," he issued the command absently.

Issi straightened and found herself looking into the unexpected blue of his eyes. She'd been so surprised to see him that she hadn't realized how *wrong* he smelled.

Her gaze dropped to the insignia on his chest.

Beneath the obvious tint of wine, was something sour and sickly. Issi nearly gagged. "I've come to respond to your invitation."

The prince paused and for a moment she wasn't sure she wasn't better off being dismissed. "Ah, your lending charter?"

The maid, Perenne, paled.

"Forgotten," Issi supplied, quickly. "The Grand Mage was more than pleased to help the royal family, but your request made him...distracted."

The prince reached forward and ran a finger along her neck. Her breath caught.

She nearly threw up.

"And your collar?"

She forced a smile. "Forgotten as well, I'm afraid."

He pulled her against him. She fought against the blind panic that nearly set her running down the hall. She was vaguely aware of the conversation the prince was holding beside her, and her own mumbled responses.

It would have been a blessing for the hall to fill with green, but she was stuck with the smell of wrongness and the cloying scent of blood, trying to fight the edges of a memory.

She wanted to scream, she felt it building in her throat.

Pets didn't yell, it did no good and served only to anger irate masters. She bit down.

The pain in her lip surprised her as did the small, steady rivulet of blood that dripped down her chin.

Her eyes focused and she let out a slew of curses as she leaned forward.

"Are you—?" The prince stopped when he saw her gloves staining. Blood puddled in her palm. "Ah...hmm, Perenne, you're dismissed for the evening."

"What?" the maid screeched, "My prince this is a—"

"That was not up for debate," he answered, calmly.

The maid looked like she was going to argue and Issi wondered if the woman was insane...or was it that some men did not fly into rages when questioned?

"Think of your *reputation*, my prince," she whispered and gestured grandly to the bloody mess Issi had become.

"I think we all know how my reputation fares," he chuckled, and Issi was reminded of the king's dinner as she felt it rumble in his chest. "Besides, the least I can do is get her patched up."

Perenne sighed and dropped into a bow. "Yes, my prince."

"And thank you for bringing her," he told the guard who had regained her composure some time when Issi hadn't been looking.

She performed a complicated salute. "It is my honor to serve."

The prince hauled Issi through the door before letting her go and running the lock.

The smell was worse inside. Issi's hands were overflowing, drops of red fell to the floor.

"Do you—"

"You have a Shattered in here. Why is there a Shattered in here?" They weren't allowed on the island, much less *in* the palace.

The prince paused, his smile vanishing. "You always surprise me, Del."

"Can...can you move it? It's making me," she tried to find the words that described what magic did when it went rancid, how it twisted her stomach and clawed at her as if begging to be fixed. She kept it short. "...I'm going to throw up."

Tiremalv arched his brows. "Well, how about we deal with the bleeding first?" He pressed a handkerchief in her hands, it soaked up enough blood to keep her from making much more of a mess. She peeled her gloves away and pressed the second one he provided to her face.

He studied her left hand.

"Did he do that?"

"Do what?"

The prince ran a tentative finger along the back of her palm. Issi pulled away.

"It was mostly me being stupid. I didn't need the sketchbook that badly, but I didn't realize that until it was too late."

The prince frowned. "And you want to stay with him?"

She offered a small smile, despite the ache in her lip. "If you think that's bad wait until you see the rest of me."

He seemed to find her comment more concerning than amusing.

"The Shattered, *please*," she pressed.

"There's no Shattered here."

Issi glared at him. "I'm going to need a bucket if you don't move it."

He frowned, his eyes drifting across her face before he nodded. "I was just about done with it anyway."

What business the Prince had with a Shattered she couldn't guess. They weren't supposed to be on the island because they were too easily manipulated, but they were very good at carrying out orders and being silent about it. It's what happened when magic went sour and devoured its host.

By the time the prince returned, Issi had gotten the bleeding to stop, and she'd done enough snooping to confirm that this really was the other side of the original castle. The layout mirrored the halls she'd wandered for the last eight years.

He looked paler than he had when he'd left, but otherwise unbothered.

"You smell awful," Issi supplied, backing towards the door.

He sniffed his arm.

"You smell like a Shattered," she clarified. Her stomach twisted.

The prince frowned. "And what does that smell like Del?"

"Broken magic."

He laughed just as Issi rushed to a bin.

"Oh...you weren't kidding."

Issi shook her head as her body shook with dry heaves. "I can't...they're wrong...turns my stomach."

"But you can *smell* them?"

Issi nodded and repeated, "Broken magic. Makes me nauseous."

"Can you...smell other magic too?"

"Can't you?"

The prince studied her with excitement. "Del, you have no *idea* how fascinating you are."

"Please do something about the smell," she pleaded. He frowned and disappeared into a room that would have housed a bathtub in her master's wing. He came back smelling of perfume. It didn't completely mask the scent of the Shattered, but it made it bearable.

Issi straightened, her nails digging into the bin. "I need your help."

"And what do I get in exchange?" he asked.

She handed him the papers she'd held beneath the forged charter. Her cheeks heated when she saw the state they were in. She'd gone and bled on them, and they'd been torn and crumpled.

The prince, for his part, plucked them from her fingers without any hesitation. He skimmed them, then tracked back and reread each one, slowly.

Issi watched him. He seemed content with reading her work, but she'd seen his eyes when he'd asked what he'd be getting in exchange. They'd been cold, like they'd been the day she'd refused his offer.

"This isn't what you've published."

She shook her head and made her way to her feet. "It's not."

There was no way it could have been. Qasha was a *proud* nation that only taught Qashan magic and Qashan discoveries. Most didn't even look at their neighbors and those who did had their papers buried quickly, the magic community labelling them as impure or flawed.

But applying the theories their neighbors had long since flushed out, had made Issi's designs what they were, small ingenious little creations that apparently did things Qashans thought impossible. She wasn't convinced that made her as valuable as the prince claimed she was, but she wasn't going to go out of her way to correct him.

He finished reading. A smile tugged at his cheeks.

"Do these enchantments work?"

"The ones I've been able to test have, the others should, though they probably need some tweaking."

"What do you want?"

Issi swallowed, she'd been trying to think of a way to put this delicately. "The Grand Mage leapt from a roof yesterday and I need to get rid of the body."

Tiremalv blinked. "Oh, is that all?"

Issi picked at the gauze that pressed against the ruined skin of her palm. "...no."

He laughed, setting her skin twitching, "*Kings, Del, I was joking. You're already asking—*"

"I need a quarter moon after that," she breathed, "I...I'll still need your help, but after that I'll give you..."

"*You?*" the prince asked.

Issi's heart twisted. She'd known going in what this would cost her. The prince didn't smile, there was no warmth in his eyes. No trace of Ardein in his posture nor the goofy man who'd slipped her a note.

It wasn't supposed to matter. She'd been born in a cage for gods' sakes, passed from one set of bars to another. What in Naya's hells did she know of freedom? She couldn't regret losing what she'd never known.

But when it came to answering, it was like her throat had sealed.

"I...uh," her voice was little more than a whisper, "I...yes. You can."

"Promise?" he asked.

Issi's stomach lurched, the smell of the Shattered seemed to surge. She hesitated.

Stall.

"Aren't you going to ask me what I need the time for?"

The prince shook his head. "You aren't going to come up with anything that will push me beyond where I'm willing to go."

Issi's fingers wove together, making a tapestry of pocked and torn skin. "What...what...if I'd asked you to kill him?"

"I'd have done it." He smirked, "If that's what it took to get you."

In that moment, the façade of the happy-go-lucky, sex-mad prince slipped, just a fraction. Issi swallowed uncomfortably and dropped her gaze to the floor. She didn't doubt that he'd do whatever he could to get what he wanted.

But he'd allowed her to refuse, he'd waited for her to come to him. Maybe that meant something.

"I'll...yes," she nodded, slowly, "A Promise, is it?"

"Precisely." The prince nodded, absently. "All I want is to ensure your loyalty. I don't need more Shattered. I need you while you can *cast*."

Issi shuddered and the prince chuckled holding his left hand for her to shake. She reached for him, wincing when their palms made contact. The prince was already muttering under his breath setting the room smelling of a thousand things.

Her forehead wrinkled. What was that supposed to mean? That he'd enjoyed a great many feasts? She picked out the high notes of candies like the ones she'd always wanted when she was younger, and honeyed meats, wines, and something softer. Perfume?

It was nothing like what he wore now, the scent too light and faint for the current trends in the courts.

Wispy tendrils of magic climbed up her arm as the prince's voice rose and fell hypnotically until he drew to a stop. Issi shivered as the magic snaked beneath her skin, *old* magic, heavier than the kind used for enchantments and Erbosian casting. He opened his eyes and almost seemed surprised that she'd stayed. "All I want is your loyalty. State your terms."

She nearly choked. "I...I get to choose?"

"I'm not a monster, Issi. In a quarter moon, you will be mine. So, in those ten days, what do you want?" His expression was kind. She thought briefly of the kitchens and the boy who'd produced oranges from thin air.

And she realized she wanted something a thousand times more than a cure.

"I want you to help me buy my family." His grip tightened. Issi couldn't help the way she shrank, trying to flatten herself to something small and inconsequential. Her voice fled and she hurried to find it. "I—, I have the money, or the Grand Mage does, but mas—, my old master, the one in Egrea, insists on meeting the people who buy from him. I...I think he likes the clout, but I need to find a way down there, and I need the Grand Mage to seem *alive* while I do it. And I need to set up somewhere for my family to go and...and learn, it's, they've lived on the orchard their entire lives, they need a skill, and they won't know the language here. Mama used to teach them but—" Issi cut herself off. He didn't need to know *that*. She tried to catch her breath as she gathered her courage to looked up.

The prince seemed as shocked as she felt. His eyes were wide expanses of summer sky. She hadn't spoken that much at once in *years*. The enchantment still twined around their wrists, binding them.

"I just need your help getting down to my old master's home and setting up a place for my family to adjust until they can stand on their own. I...I don't know anything about property owning, or how to buy homes, or even how to charter a ship, you see?" She searched his face for any understanding or pity and found only surprise with a hint of sorrow. "For that to work, I need you to keep it a secret that the Grand Mage is dead. And...and when I," no she still had a chance to find a cure, she just needed to put it off for ten days. She ignored the vines crawling at the edge of her vision, she could manage ten days, "*if* I die, could you...take care of them until they can take care of themselves?"

"Are you asking or are those the terms?" he asked gently.

"T-Those are my terms, help me hide the body, buy my family, and set up a safe home for them until they can live on their own."

The prince studied her for what felt like a full tick.

"I feel like I'm swindling you," he responded, quietly. Issi laughed.

"Prince, you're hiding a *body* for me and you're helping me buy my family." she couldn't think of anything she wanted more. "All in exchange for the loyalty of a Pet who's going to die in a few moons. You could have just purchased me."

He smiled at that, letting his grip slide up to her wrist, she followed suit feeling the old magic hum like a string pulled taut. "And I've said, you have no idea how much you're worth."

The spell bit down on her arm. She let out a whimper as the prince's hand bore down on hers. Magic surged beneath her skin before pooling around her wrist and cooling to a sleepy buzz.

Then it was over. He let go. A pale circlet of scar tissue had formed where his hand had been.

She studied it curiously, for all his cruelty, the Grand Mage had never forced Issi to make a Promise. This had been her first.

The prince stretched. "Come on, let's get rid of that body."

"Let's?" Issi echoed.

"Yes, let us, you and I, get rid of the body."

She wasn't sure what she'd expected, but she'd assumed the royals had some sort of protocol for this. The prince glanced at her.

"If it were anyone other than Gadna, I'd assign the duty to someone else, but with someone this important, the fewer people involved the better, mmm?"

Issi toed the carpet. "Will we need to leave the palace?"

"Of course, you don't leave corpses you don't want found right at your doorstep." The prince laughed, darkly, "They have a way of coming back to haunt you."

The more he spoke the more she wondered what the prince had actually been doing. She'd always assumed courting whoever he pleased and sneaking out to get roaring drunk in bars across the island had taken most of his time.

Though perhaps that explained his need to hide a body or two.

"Then I need a knife," she informed him.

The prince studied her.

Issi swallowed nervously. "Or a dagger. A sword could work too, but I'd need you to do it for me."

"Do what?"

She shrugged, "Cut through the brand."

The prince stilled, "The what?"

Issi tugged at her neckline and when the fabric refused to give, gathered her skirts and pointed with her free hand to the brands that crossed her stomach. Her finger lingered on the one furthest left.

"This one's still whole. I need to cut it, or I can't leave the palace without setting the whole wing clanging."

When she got no response, she looked away from the scarring and found the prince staring at her stomach with something close to horror.

"It's not as bad as it looks," she continued, quickly, "It, it was supposed to keep me in the wing, but I added a few ticks to connect it to the palace wards. Uh, *breaking* the brand was obvious, and he'd just do it again. So, the last time I tried altering it and he never noticed so...I could expand it to include the entire island, but he'd have noticed *that*. I can do it now if that would make you feel better, but I'll need to break it anyway if I'm going to go to Egrea or—"

"Del," the prince interrupted.

"Yes?" Thank the gods, she was going to ramble for an eternity if given the chance.

He moved stiffly. "I—, could you...how many enchantments has he branded you with?"

"Just the three. He found knives were more practical in the end."

The prince nodded, slowly. "What else did he do?"

She tilted her head to the side. "Does that matter? The ones that he carved are very difficult to break, but they don't do...," her voice gave after seeing the quiet rage that'd settled across his features.

She was in her undergarments before the prince, and he hadn't even asked her to strip. Issi blushed as she let the fabric go and dropped into a bow. "I'm sorry, I've been very forward. I'll use the scalpel in—"

"Del," the prince snapped.

She locked her legs so they wouldn't give out. "Yes?"

He sighed and when he spoke again his voice was softer, "Kings, straighten up. I didn't mean to scare you."

She stood and glanced at him. "You're not mad at me?"

"Why would I be—" He shook his head in frustration. "No, I'm not angry with you, Del. I'm mad at the Grand Mage."

Issi squinted, "Why?"

The prince's mouth dropped open. "Do you realize how many laws he broke?"

"Fifteen," she responded, quickly, "Seven of those are hanging offenses, but according to your laws, I am technically property. Nobody complains if you enchant a hairbrush."

"You are not a...alright, what do they do?"

"The brands around my torso were supposed to keep me from leaving the wing without him. The carving on my back...I'm not entirely sure. I haven't *seen* it. The ones on the outside of my legs control a set of responses, but I broke through most of them. The one on my inner thigh is the only one that really matters, I'm afraid I'll nick the artery. Uhm...ask me if anything hurts."

"Do they hurt? The scars?"

Issi held the answer behind her teeth, locking her jaw tight. The answer fluttered above her tongue. The prince studied her with confusion clear on his pretty face.

She grabbed his hand and held it beneath her nose. She opened her mouth and tried to form the word "yes", tried to breathe it to life, the way she could breathe magic into enchantments.

No sound came.

She furrowed her brow and tried harder. *Nothing.*

"No," the word came ragged in a gasp, she sputtered, stepping away from the prince as she dragged air into her lungs. "I can't answer that question any other way. I've tried. And if I'm stubborn enough, I'll black out, and presumably die. I think the Grand Mage had to slap me awake a few times to get the answer he needed. I'm not sure."

The prince looked at her as if she'd suggested he'd go about and start knifing infants.

Issi rubbed her arm, suddenly self-conscious, "I thought it'd be better to show you, that one's difficult to explain."

"Del, if he hadn't died, would you really have stayed with him?"

"Of course." When she saw the discomfort on his face she nearly laughed. "Princeling, I've lived this way for *years*. What were two or three more moons? Another dozen?"

"I offered you a way out."

She smiled. "And I couldn't take it. He needed me."

"You hated him."

Issi shrugged, and tried to hide her hands behind her back, like a child who'd stolen a sweet. "How I *feel* isn't important. As long as I pleased him and please you, I'll be alright."

The prince stilled, surprise dancing across his features, but whatever he'd meant to say, he let die on his lips.

Chapter 13

Issi shuffled awkwardly in the hall as the prince changed. Her gaze shifted restlessly to doorways that spilled varying amounts of light. Now that the Promise band circled her wrist and the initial panic had dulled to a constant thrum, she realized she didn't understand the third prince at all.

But she was very sure that he wasn't going to have her working on beauty enchantments, and kitchen stoves.

"What do you think?"

Issi turned. He'd changed into a uniform not unlike the one worn by the guard who'd brought her there. But instead of the blue claimed by the royal family, the trim was an earthen brown. The insignia that sat on his chest featured a sharp eared dog.

She didn't try to hide her shock, "Did you steal that from lady Surannie?"

He gave a weary smile. "I wouldn't dream of it, that woman terrifies me. It was her idea, actually, makes night visits easier. I wasn't really for it at first, but her husband hasn't complained."

Silver flashed as he slid a ring onto the little finger of his right hand. His hair darkened and shadow bloomed in the sky blue of his eyes, like soil upset at the bottom of a puddle, until they became the brown she'd loved so much.

When they caught the light, she spied eddies of blue. How had she never noticed?

"This enchantment is a mess," she muttered.

The prince winked. "Think you can fix it?"

Issi waited for him to realize she had gone far beyond coloring hair and eyes. After a few beats, he started *humming*, his attention drifting to the cuff of his sleeve.

She nodded. "Yes, yes I can."

Mischief sparked in his eyes. "I thought so, when can you have it by?"

"A bell, maybe two." Half that if he just wanted something *better* than what he had.

"Really? We'll get you on that later."

"Are you sure? I can have it done—"

"The body, Del."

Issi blinked, maybe it was because of all the magic she'd felt in the hall, and the way her mind felt clearer than it had in ages, but she'd been finding it hard to keep her thoughts in order.

She'd forgotten why she'd gone there in the first place, "How do we get out of here?"

The prince gestured for her to follow before starting down the hall. They passed half a dozen chambers, each singing with different flavors of magic.

Issi glanced into a room full of windows that looked at sunny skies and sand dunes and cities and mountains, playing quiet scenes that started and reset. One window was filled with people so pale they looked like they'd been crafted from moonlight.

Another room seemed to be entirely dedicated to the consumption of tea. Another still, was covered wall to wall in sheets of music, though there wasn't a single instrument in sight.

Then the rooms stopped, the corridor falling into a dull flat expanse of wall.

She'd never noticed it in her master's wing because it'd been covered with a tapestry.

The prince slowed in the center and pressed against the surface until a faint click sounded. The panel swung open. He glanced at her and smiled. "It's pretty cool, right?"

Issi found herself trying not to smile in return.

The guard on the other side of the door simplified the task significantly.

He was a monster of a man, even though he was nearly the size of the Grand Mage, he felt *bigger* somehow. Like the air he breathed held mass and reason. The look he gave her said he'd gladly use all that weight to suffocate her if given the chance.

The left half of his face twisted into a permanent sneer by the scar that climbed from his chin to just above his left eyebrow.

His glare sent the hair on Issi's neck standing on end.

"Thanae, be nice," the prince chided. The guard didn't stop and Issi swallowed before dropping into a bow.

The guard's frown deepened.

"Del? Please." The prince tugged, hard, on her collar, forcing her upright, "None of that. Thanae," the prince drew the name out and at last the guard's attention shifted away.

"Who is she?" the man's voice was the rumble before true thunder.

"This is Del, also known as Issi, also known as, pardon me, I'm going to absolutely butcher this, *Nydelissi*," he did, "The Grand Mage's Pet."

The guard's storm grey eyes flicked across her, he frowned when he noted her collarless state. "Did she come through the front?"

The prince shrugged. "If she did?"

Thanae lurched forward and Issi held her breath, waiting for the blow. It never came. Instead, the guard stood before the prince like an overgrown dog.

"My prince, think of your—"

"Shut up," the command was almost conversational, the guard's mouth shut with an audible snap, "You've been talking too much with Perenne."

"I'll be back before sunrise, and I dismissed my *nanny*," the prince supplied, as the guard pried himself from the corridor. "If you hear anyone inside, take care of them."

Thanae glanced to Issi again. His hand tightened on the pommel of his dagger. Gods, he made it look like a *toy*. Her stomach twisted.

If it came to a fight between them, there was no way she would win.

The guard sighed his hand relaxing before he bowed stiffly. "Yes, my prince."

Tiremalv grinned, as if he'd won some private battle. "Thank you."

The prince walked by his guard, Issi hesitated before scrambling after him. The hall smelled faintly of the Shattered, but whoever it had been was long gone.

She felt the guard's glare try to burn a hole in her skull.

After a tick, what remained of Ardein sighed, "Sorry, he's usually not so...well, he's always been overbearing. That's just—"

Issi stopped.

"Del?" The prince turned to face her, "Is something wrong?"

"Um, no, it's..." She forced her feet into motion, unsure if she wanted to tell him. The more he learned about how she lived the more he seemed to want to tell her how unfortunate she'd been. "It's nothing."

She just wasn't used to people apologizing to her with any sort of sincerity.

He set down the hall again. Issi learned quickly that silence made him uncomfortable. Every time it stretched for more than a tick, he made a noise of complaint or a quiet comment. In the end he hummed a waltz as his hand ran along the wall.

The corridor split and the prince stayed to the right, the echoes of Shattered disappeared completely. Issi lingered, trying to imagine where that hall let out when the prince called her, and she hurried ahead. Tiremalv pushed at another panel which dropped them just short of the atrium.

Muted colors danced across Issi's skin as she followed behind him, their footsteps echoing like the first drumbeats of the festival songs she sometimes caught through her window. The prince stopped short of cutting down a corridor.

"How do you usually get in?"

"Through the front. Unless I want to go outside, the exit leads past the guards."

He nodded and Issi pushed them forward at a quick pace. She didn't bother greeting the soldiers before nearly shoving the prince through the front door.

She was tempted to run the lock, but the Grand Mage, for all his paranoia, had never locked the doors.

"So," the prince looked about, his gaze falling along the cluttered walls and tables and bauble filled display cases. "Where is he?"

Issi swallowed, feeling blood climb her cheeks. She realized, abruptly, that they were alone. She'd never been the one to bring someone into her rooms before.

Embarrassment nipped at her as if all the trinkets and litter were hers.

Her finger ran along the new scar tracing her wrist. She had to trust him.

She led the prince to the corridor that went to the gardens. The door at the end opened to a downpour. The rain still showed no signs of stopping.

The prince stopped short of bumping into her and regarded the downpour with mild disinterest before turning his attention to her. "Is something wrong?"

Issi shook her head. Freezing rain pelted her skin as she took the prince along muddied paths, apologizing for the dripping of plants and overgrown patches.

He had the grace to ignore her, his attention grabbed by the swaths of green.

Issi shivered as the air chilled. The prince slowed as his breath clouded before him.

The Grand Mage was precisely where she'd left him.

What was there to say? She gestured awkwardly to the corpse. "Uh, this. This is him."

The prince snickered, "Is it?" He crouched, studying the body curiously. His hand traced her master's unmoving chest.

He mumbled something, the rain whisking away the sense of his words.

His fingers moved for the enchantment.

"Don't," Del's voice stopped him mid-reach, his fingers hovered just above the wood, "he'll thaw."

"What is this tied to?"

She wiped ineffectively at the water that'd started to drip down her face. "The fire in the workroom hearth."

"What else?"

Her brows knit together. "Nothing, that's all I had."

The prince frowned as he stood, brushing at imaginary dirt. "How do you get out of here without passing the guards?"

Issi pointed to the metal door built into the fence that fed off the palace wall. "That exit leads to the palace gardens, close to the eastern gate."

"Is it locked?"

"It's warded," she corrected, gesturing to the ornate loops spinning off the door. "But that's not a problem."

"The only issue is moving him, then?"

A laugh startled from her throat, "That's not the *only* issue. It's just the biggest."

The prince's lips twisted into a wry smile. "Any thoughts?"

She hesitated before muttering, "the wheelbarrow." She would have tried it herself the night before, but there was no way in Naya's hells she could have maneuvered the corpse into its belly.

The prince's smile grew into a grin. "You want to wheel the Grand Mage's corpse out like fertilizer?"

Her nose crinkled. "Do you have a better idea?"

"A few, but this seems like more fun."

"*Fun?*" Was this meant to be fun?

The prince regarded her the way children looked at promising toys. "Where is it?"

She gestured mutely to the shed in the garden's center. In the six moons since it'd been abandoned, the Grand Mage had allowed it to fall into disrepair. The prince let out a low whistle when he noticed the hints of rot gathering at the edges of the door.

The hinges squeaked in protest as he forced them into service.

The interior was dark, lit only by a light casting the size of a candle. The small tables that lined the walls were filled with long dead sprouts, while torn bags of fertilizer held sickly growing weeds and mosses, their rail thin bodies spilling down shelves.

There was no sign of the wheelbarrow.

Issi followed the prince inside.

Vines had snuck inside from the gaps around the door and windows, snaking through patches in the roof where sky had fallen through. They gathered in a corner where a shelf had collapsed, their green at odds with the sickness and death that surrounded them.

Issi grabbed for a leaf and frowned as her hand passed through it.

She blinked and the vines were gone, replaced by dirt and the very edge of a plank of wood. Its partner appeared a little to her left.

Her heart leapt. "I found it."

She didn't wait for the prince's response. She grabbed both handles and pulled. The shelf that'd collapsed into the structure's metal stomach groaned, digging desperate fingers along the wheelbarrow's surface.

The contraption broke free, sending Issi stumbling.

She slammed into something soft. It moved and she squealed letting the handles go. The wheelbarrow settled with a thud.

"Del, you could have asked for help," the prince hummed.

Issi scrambled away, her hand hovered at her breast like it would keep her heart from bailing. This was it. Her heart was going to give out before she accomplished anything.

She managed a nod and waved her hand towards her prize. The wheelbarrow had dented where the shelves had collapsed, but otherwise, it'd fared better than she'd expected.

"So, you think we should dump the body inside, cover it with a blanket and wheel it through town?" the prince asked.

Issi stared at him, trying to decide if he was serious.

"You'd be surprised the things you can get away with when you've the courage to try."

"Is...is this from experience or..." she petered out, unsure of how she wanted the sentence to end.

He flashed a grin. "What do you think, former Pet of the Grand Mage?"

Former bounced between her ears.

"I think, I'm not sure I want the answer to that."

The prince studied the wheelbarrow like it was a complex Egrean apparatus.

"You lift it by the handles until the wheel catches," she explained, as she moved to demonstrate, "Up and down."

He nodded, before gesturing for her to let him try. "It'll be a bit unwieldy when it's heavy won't it?"

Issi shrugged. She'd learned from watching the gardeners.

"Are you sure you don't want to use any of those other ideas you mentioned?" she muttered.

"I like this one." He dropped the handles. The wheelbarrow's supports banged against the ground, setting dents into the earthen floor.

"Prince...I..."

"Call me Ardein," he answered, lightly, as he grabbed the handles again, "or the disguise will have been for nothing."

"*Ardein*," she breathed, "You realize this isn't a game, right?"

Surprise tripped across his face, followed shortly by understanding, then delight. "Everything here is a game. You just haven't figured out how to play."

There was something deeply wrong with him.

He rolled his eyes. "Del, please. Don't go making that face. I don't need any more Shattered."

She bit her lip, flinching as the wound threatened to reopen. The magic living beneath her skin hummed dully.

They made their way back to her master's body. Together they struggled to get him into the wheelbarrow's belly even if it was a significantly less bloody endeavor than her first attempt.

The frozen mass of his head rolled near the wheelbarrow's edge, while his limbs were convinced into an ungainly pile.

Tiremalv looked the body over. "So, is there a blanket you want to use or...?"

Issi shook her head and pulled an enchantment from her pocket. It smelled faintly of the dogwood and yew oils she'd massaged into its surface to convince the magic to run along the paths she'd delineated. She placed it on her master's chest, and he disappeared. It wasn't precisely the invisibility told in legends, but it did reflect what was beneath him and the near vicinity.

So long as nobody looked too closely, it'd be passable. Issi hoped the rain would work to her advantage. It was too miserable to go looking for trouble. Her teeth started to chatter. She hadn't tied the enchantment to anything, so it stole the energy it needed from her.

The prince looked impressed. He started poking about the Grand Mage's body. "It's still here?"

Issi nodded before forcing open the window to her master's study and climbing through. She picked the first engraving pen she could find and hiked up her skirts.

She studied the brand briefly, before running the pen carefully over the bottom patch of the outer ring.

"You're not going to use anesthetic?" The prince leaned against the sill, seeming to relish how the water had stopped streaming into his eyes.

The pen tip dug deeper, until blood spilled from the wound, "An—, aneth," she fumbled, trying to make her tongue cooperate with the unnatural twist in the center, "*Anes-thetic?*" The moment the blade reached the end of the scar the magic woven beneath snapped like an overwound spring.

She sighed, grabbing a cloth from the table.

"Yes, anesthetic, so it doesn't hurt."

Was that the name of the paste the healers used when they patched her? "There's none here," she answered, "Or if there is, he's hidden it."

The prince frowned. "He should have some, enchantments need blood."

"It's usually just a drop," she explained, and pointed to the shallow bowl about the size of her closed fist that sat in the center of a desk. "At most, enough to fill that, but mages need to have a high pain tolerance. Or else they'd be useless in whatever stupid skirmish they're sent to next, so he doesn't keep any around."

"Stupid skirmish?" the prince echoed.

She hissed as she pressed down to staunch the bleeding. It wasn't necessary to deploy mages to quell the small gatherings of worshippers, and the smattering of whatever remained of the Reprenian resistance, but it helped the king control the narrative. Magic was once thought to have been gifted by the gods.

But that couldn't possibly be true with mages killing the clergy. If the gods held any true power, they would have saved their followers and the Reprenians.

Or so the story went.

"Yes, stupid, brutal, and unnecessary," she continued, as her free hand searched for another cloth and something to bind it to her skin.

"Tell me how you really feel."

Issi patched the wound and started pinching the fabric along her sleeve. "That's sarcasm?"

"Very much so."

She nodded and started digging through a hidden pocket, until a small enchantment deposited itself into her hand.

She eyed the clock, three bells. Could they really get rid of the body and return in that time?

Her skirts tumbled from her hands and she straightened despite the ache above her left hip.

"I'm ready," she announced. She felt anything but, but the Grand Mage had died, and she still drew breath. The world continued without Gadna in it with none the wiser.

Even though it felt like she'd lost a limb.

"*Del.*"

She started.

The prince studied her, a frown tugging at the sides of his mouth. "Come on. We're running out of time."

Three bells. She pressed the enchantment and felt the illusion pass over her skin before passing through the window.

He'd already dragged the apparently empty wheelbarrow to the garden door. Issi swallowed nervously as the rain danced along the illusion's edges, bouncing off a complicated mass of nothing.

"Do you really think this will work?" she asked.

The prince shrugged, "You're the one who killed him. I thought you might—"

"I didn't kill him," she corrected.

"Come on, Del, not even a little push? I could hardly blame you."

"I didn't," she repeated, venom welled beneath her words, "I *never* hurt him. I wanted to, but I *couldn't*."

Her chest heaved and her ears rang as her words bounced against the walls until they echoed out of existence. Her cheeks went to flame.

The silence that spanned between her and the prince was filled only by the determined dashing of droplets against the ground. She could feel his next question hanging above her, *had the Grand Mage stopped her from doing so?*

The air felt thick in her lungs.

She gave a slight bow. "Sorry for showing you something unsightly."

For once, it seemed the prince had no retort.

She turned on her heel and faced the door.

The ward her master had placed on it had been bypassed ages ago, likely by a student sneaking from the dormitories. The lines of the enchantment were crude, the gashes had been worn smooth and barely registered as she pressed against it. The magic tied to it was slow to respond. It fought her before lumbering reluctantly down the patterns it'd been given. Her teeth began to chatter in earnest as the door swung open. She held it long enough for the prince to pass through and winced as the door clanged shut behind them.

The gardens outside her master's area had all been tended. Warm colored flowers huddled together to escape the rain, while large, lush leaves seemed to beckon for more.

It was nearing summer. If things hadn't gone so spectacularly to shit, her master would have started making noise about going on a vacation he'd never take while trying to regale her with tales of exotic dances and foods and a language that when whispered breathed magic into the air.

The prince hit a stone and the contents of the wheelbarrow jostled with a decidedly harsh *thwack*, followed by a smaller bang that might have been her master's head.

Something about the sound was oddly cathartic.

The palace walls loomed before them. Large pillars of stone were separated by elegant patches of twisted metal that spelled pictures of Qashan history. As they approached, a shadow pulled away from the wall and slouched sloppily towards them.

"We—," Issi began.

The guard held up a hand to silence her. He yawned before nodding to the wheelbarrow, "What's going on with that?"

Issi's heart fluttered, she worked to still her jaw, stop the shivering. "Uhm...well, you see..." She glanced to the prince for aid, but he only offered a smile.

Loyalty. Gods what had she done?

The guard's hand waved dismissively. "I'm not looking for your life's story. Where are you going and why so late?"

Oh.

"The...duchess required a tincture from the Grand Mage, not all the materials were on hand and the apothecary wasn't willing to cooperate."

The guard nodded absently. "Sure. Papers?"

Papers.

She tapped at her dress pockets hoping for the crinkle of parchment. Nothing. When the guard finally looked at her, his breathing stalled. It was short, a fraction of a beat, she might have imagined it. The rain had pinned the fabric of her dress to her skin.

Was he anything like the Grand Mage?

"Ah," she let her voice hitch, as she looked up at him, "I'm so stupid."

"Is there a problem?"

"I'm sorry." She shook her head and swiped at her cheek. "I forgot the paperwork, would you believe it?"

"Well—"

"It's fine, we'll, ah, we'll just go back," she swallowed, as if she were holding back tears.

"Wait," the guard breathed. His eyes drifted down her figure before skipping back to her face. "What are you getting?"

"Moonbriar flowers," she bit her tongue. Of the hundreds of herbs she could have named, why had she chosen that one?

Behind her, she heard the prince's breath go uneven. He was holding in a laugh. She nearly spun. A question burned on her lips.

"How long?"

"No more than three bells," she supplied.

The guard let out a weary sigh and rubbed his eye. "I'll open the gates. Come back this way when you're done."

Issi nodded as the man turned and disappeared into an alcove. A moment later the gates swung open. The plaza that sat beyond it felt hopelessly far.

Her legs tried to root her to the spot. A nudge from the prince sent her stumbling.

Come on, he mouthed.

She followed half a step behind him. The palace gate soared over-head, large wrought iron bars that could slam and snap her in two like a twig. Her feet touched cobblestone and she froze. She expected the Grand Mage to stir, or a far-off clanging to sound.

Nothing happened.

There were only the sounds of rain and the bump-stutter rhythm of the wheelbarrow moving over the road.

She let out a breath and tried to walk like her brain wasn't aflame with a thousand new sensations and questions. Fear curled in her throat as the prince started south. This close to the palace, there was open ground marked by a smattering of stalls that'd be filled shortly after sunrise.

Issi'd never seen them so close, or so completely. They were larger than she'd thought, their fabric covers alive with embroidered slogans proclaiming goods of all flavors.

"*Del.*" The prince pointed his chin to a stall with a canopy spelling *Aror's.* Beneath the name it clarified in short, neat letters: *All sweets and goods, for the well proclaimed to the misunderstood.*

"Best Candy in the entire country."

Issi glanced at the prince and back to the stand. She wished it were open, she was sure, somehow, that it'd be alight with all sorts of magics and that the sweets displayed in the cases would dazzle her.

"Uhm..." She bit her cheek, trying to abandon ideas of piles of brightly colored candies. She wasn't a child to be mollified by promises of sweets.

"I won't punish curiosity, Del," the prince said, "Ask away."

The words came out in a rush, "What's it like when it's open?" *No*, that wasn't the question she was supposed to be asking. But soon as it left her lips, she realized she desperately wanted to know.

"The stand or the plaza?"

Issi's mouth opened. She couldn't fathom a plaza full of people. How many shops even fit there? Her cheeks heated. "I—, I don't know."

He smiled and the skin around his eyes crinkled, "It's nice enough. Crowded. At lunch the smell of roasted meat and fresh bread is enough to make your mouth water."

"Are there more stands?"

"Then there are now? Plenty." He nodded to the perimeter of the plaza. "They go all the way around in a ring and then there's another ring inside."

That had to make the King's Dinner seem small in comparison. Issi's heart rammed itself against her ribcage as she tried to imagine it.

Too many people.

"And moonbriar," she began, hesitantly, before petering out, unsure of how to continue.

"What about it?"

"You laughed when I mentioned it," she skirted.

He was studying her through the hair that'd plastered to his face, his lips quirking. "I didn't *laugh*."

"You wanted to."

"Because you listed something from a children's story."

There it was, she hurried ahead so she could walk backwards and look at him clearly. "How do you know that?"

"That it's from a children's story?"

She nodded so quickly, water droplets sprang from her hair. "Yes, it's *Chousalian*...and this is Qasha."

"And?"

"You don't *do* that here. You don't listen, you don't bring stories, you bring back golds and treasures and call them dirt because you can't be bothered to understand them."

The prince frowned and started down a street wide enough to accommodate two carriages side by side. The houses that lined it were grand structures stuck together like neatly decorated soldiers. They walked in the warm and hazy lights of streetlamps brightened by light castings.

"That's a very narrow way of seeing things, Del."

"Qasha's a narrow place," she answered, defiantly.

He didn't respond. She worried her lip as quiet wove between them. As they continued, the houses scrunched and huddled together, growing sickly and thin. The glass of their windows disappeared, and soon large, bosomed women and half-dressed men peered through the openings.

Some called down, offering prices and compliments. Others simply tracked them with their eyes. Long plumes of smoke drifted from cigarettes and sweet-scented pipes before being cut by the rain.

"There was a Chousalian merchant, once," the prince said, at last, "When I was younger. My father hated Chousalians so much, I'd wanted to see what kind of monsters they were."

A Chousalian merchant. The words clashed between her ears. She'd never heard of anyone older than ten having survived the wars, her mother and father being the exceptions.

"And?" she prompted.

The prince shook his head. "I'm just proving you right. I *wanted* a monster. I got a doddering old man whose cart smelled of funny herbs and boxes filled with what I'd assumed were trinkets. He wanted to tell me stories, and I listened a little before running off."

"Do you know where he is now?" She knew the answer, but she *had* to ask. She'd give nearly anything to find him.

"If he was smart, he left the country."

Issi nodded, and turned to walk forward, trying to ignore the wave of disappointment. She wrapped her arms around herself, trying to stop the shiver that ran through her.

There were other Chousalians. *She'd* never find them, but maybe her siblings would.

Maybe they could cobble together some sort of community, make some place where they could feel like they belonged.

Or was she wrong in thinking there was value to be had in something like that? They were Chousalian in blood only, they'd never even *seen* the country, just dreamed about it, heard about it, breathed life into its dying language to beg desserts off their mother.

"Del?"

The wheelbarrow had lodged itself into a narrow corner, Issi rounded the front and pushed the contraption back.

"Why were you so close to the edge?" she huffed.

"We're going down the alley," he answered.

Issi's eyes struggled with the darkness. The lamps this far down used true flame, and the rain had doused most of them. The street in question was little more than haphazard stone, and dirt. The houses that lined the sides were so close and poorly constructed, they leaned against one another in a drunken mass.

Rhythmic grunting sounded from one of the doorways.

"Down here?" she clarified.

The prince dragged the wheelbarrow through a graceless arc and started down the road. "Scared? I didn't think Pets were afraid of the dark."

She was afraid of everything, but most pressingly, getting stabbed in a narrow passageway when she'd finally acquired a reason to live.

It was awkward going, the alley reeked of sex and piss and alcohol despite the rain, and the prince hadn't mastered the wheelbarrow. The road itself turned sharply, with little warning, and the houses pressed so close at times, Issi worried they'd collapse and bury her alive.

Tiremalv stopped abruptly before what might have generously been dubbed a door, and realistically called a water rotted hunk of wood forced into service.

"Here we are," the prince began, jovially. He set his burden down and ignored the door entirely, cupping his hands before his mouth. "Ada!"

His voice rattled the air. Issi's breath caught, and she made herself very still and small.

A tick passed with no response. The prince grumbled before shouting again.

This time, a chorus of voices rained down. None of them were particularly kind and at least three contained threats of some kind. The prince laughed.

"There you are, Ada," he said, softly.

"D'ya know what time it is?" a voice of sand and ash sounded from the other side of the door.

The prince raised both his hands. "No watch I'm afraid, but if you're offering?"

The door swung open revealing a stocky man dirtier than anyone Issi'd ever laid eyes on. Even his beard was snarled and filled with stains of what she hoped was some type of soup.

He swayed unsteadily in the doorway. "What's it this time?"

The prince waved his arms grandly. "Something fun."

"You don' do *fun*."

"*Everything* I bother to do is fun," the prince insisted.

The old man went to shake his head, and ended bracing himself on the wall. "Just tell me."

"Ardein" went over to the wheelbarrow and groped across her master's nothingness before wrapping his fist around the enchantment. Warmth flooded Issi's body as the Grand Mage's corpse came into view.

Ada's eyes widened. "Oh...*fun.*"

The prince gave an enthusiastic nod.

"What'd he do? Paw at your new toy?" He glanced at Issi.

"Yes," the prince answered, easily, "That precisely. How did you know?"

"First time you brought someone." The man shrugged, and tottered over to the corpse. "The fucker's frozen solid?"

"Easy clean up."

"Never seen an enchantment this clean," he muttered. "What's it tied to?"

"If I wanted questions, I wouldn't be here, Ada," the prince supplied.

The man smiled, exposing a mouth of surprisingly perfect teeth. "Ain't that the truth. Bring it in, rain's colder than a witch's tit."

Ada held the door open, and Issi hurried by, nearly slipping in the sawdust that covered the floor. The interior seemed to be some sort of drinking den. It reeked of cheap spirits. A series of makeshift chairs carved homes across sawdust floors, and a single long table crafted of driftwood sat lined with stools on the far side.

The wheelbarrow's movement felt like a roar.

The prince's voice cut through the air. "How much is this going to cost me?"

"Ah, hundred gold?"

Both men had a hearty laugh. "10 silver," Ada corrected, "And I want that thing you used to hide him."

"This?" The prince sent the enchantment's wooden body bouncing down his knuckles. "I think it's worth hiding three bodies, don't you?"

Ada's eyes followed the piece blearily. "It's not perfect, Ardein."

"It's a damn sight better than what you've got."

Were they joking? It'd taken her two bells to carve it, and all it did was bend light.

The old man paused, rocking unsteadily on his feet. "And the freezing enchantment?"

The prince shook his head. The enchantment had unraveled as soon as they'd left the gardens when the distance between the mage's fire and the wooden chip had grown too large to sustain. He flashed the illusion piece across his knuckles before palming it. "Do we have a deal?"

Ada's eyes tried to focus on the corpse. "Who was he?"

"Questions, Ada, I don't like them," the prince restated.

The den dweller grumbled and chewed his cheek before giving a slow nod. "Sure, deal."

The prince stuck his hand forward and Ada's features bled into a disapproving frown. "There's no need for that."

"Ada, you get drunk, you talk."

The old man spat. Issi stifled a squeak of distress, but the prince barely glanced at the wet patch before returning his attention to Ada's filthy face.

The old man sighed and grabbed the prince's hand. He paled as the spell wove up his arm, though he didn't so much as peek at the tendrils of white.

"You won't speak of the events of tonight," the prince stated. "In exchange for this enchantment. Do we have a deal?"

Ada huffed, his breast moving like bellows. "Yes, we've a deal."

The spell bit down and Ada jerked away, flexing his fingers. His attention landed on Issi, setting her skin crawling.

"Take a seat." He gestured, vaguely, to a ramshackle chair. "You look like you're about to fall out."

She glanced at the prince who shrugged.

She sat gingerly atop the sturdiest chair she could find, listening to the men hammer out the details. They were going to sink him in the muddied waters of the river. Issi had no idea what happened to bodies in Qasha, but she doubted that was proper.

The conversation muffled as their voices lowered and what sounded like an argument ensued.

Her head bobbed.

She woke with a start. Confusion set within the mussiness of her head.

"Master?" the word echoed hollowly across the empty room. The events of the day came rushing back.

The rain had stopped.

Issi snuck to the pathetic excuse of a door and peered through one of the sizeable gaps around the edges. Water had gathered into the pits of the narrow road and set everything else shimmering in the light of the sister moons.

It was quiet. She could still smell smoke from unseen pipes. The air was cool and damp against her skin.

She was alone. The Grand Mage was nowhere to be seen.

When his corpse had been near, she'd felt more at ease. Without it, it felt like she'd return to the palace to him bent over his worktable.

Waiting.

She shut her eyes. She could still make the shape of him behind her eyelids. Was it really so easy for people to die? The Grand Mage had felt so permanent, even with the illness nipping at his heels.

Never once had she imagined she'd cobble together an actual life without him.

No prison, no gallows, no Athijan.

Her eyes opened and she looked to the Promise band. No prison with *bars* at least.

And ten days of freedom.

She flinched as the back door opened. Conversation bounced off the walls and the prince came into view. He looked hale despite what'd surely been rough work. Ada, by contrast, had paled considerably. His eyes flicked to Issi with a sober glint.

"Done," the prince announced. He gave her a playful bow, "He's gone."

She wasn't sure what she was meant to feel.

"Get out," Ada instructed, dully. His gaze stayed away from the prince and his hands trembled.

"Thank you for your service," the prince offered, warmly.

The old man's skin turned sickly, and he nodded a curt acknowledgement. "Get out."

Tiremalv grabbed the wheelbarrow and made for the door. Issi left on his heels.

"Poor Ada," the prince sighed, theatrically, "too clever by half."

"Is he really gone, ma—, the uhm, the Grand Mage?" the words felt like flame in her chest. They threatened to blister her lips as she spoke.

"Of course, he's gone. Keeping him around would be riskier than this," he gestured down the alley. "I'm not looking for trouble Del, not unless I make it."

She nodded vaguely.

They splashed their way through puddle laden streets. Fear sank in her stomach and set her heart fluttering as they neared the gates.

What if her master woke up?

What would she do if he was waiting and livid?

"What happened?" The gates sat open, the guard on the other side eyed the empty wheelbarrow curiously.

"I...uhm, it," she'd forgotten to arrange for the flowers.

"It didn't work out, we hit every apothecary on Kothen," the prince added, "it's out of season. What can we do?"

The guard gave a drowsy nod. "Ridiculous, the lot of them."

The prince laughed a bit too hard at that, but the guard let them pass without further question. They returned to the now corpse free garden and dumped the wheelbarrow in the center of the shed.

"Alright," the prince muttered, softly, "that's half of my Promise kept. I'll organize the rest later."

He started for the main garden. Issi regarded the doorway that led to her master's wing, and felt a tremor run through her.

"Pr—, Ardein." The prince stopped short, her face heated, and her voice had to be wrangled before it ran off somewhere stupid, "I, uhm...could you...I mean, I would like you to—"

"Del, spit it out," he snapped. She shrank.

It was such a stupid request.

"I...uhm, could you help me check the wing?" she asked softly.

"Speak up."

"Could you please help me check the wing?"

The prince narrowed his eyes. "What for?"

Here was the stupid bit. Her nails dug into her palms. "For...uh...him."

His expression twisted with incredulity. "The Grand Mage we just sank in the Copros?"

Issi nodded.

He sighed, "Del, it's late and you know that he's—"

"I know," she interrupted. Her hands fiddled with the enchantment around her neck, dispelling the illusion. "But, I can't, he was...too big, too much. He can't really be dead that easy, can he?"

The prince's brow furrowed. "He was just a man. People have died from far less."

"But they weren't *him.*"

"I'll arrange for a guard to watch over you from tomorrow on, would that help?"

He wasn't listening, or maybe he just didn't understand. Didn't care. Issi's vision began to blur with tears. She wrapped her arms around herself as if that could keep her from shattering.

"Yes, my prince," she lied, "That would be very helpful."

He nodded, looking pleased with himself. "Could you open the gate?"

Issi complied, watching him go for longer than was safe.

She stayed outside the wing, in the garden, shivering in her wet clothes for bells trying to gather the courage to go inside.

Ner found her there well after the sun had painted the skies blue.

"Again?" the maid tutted, "I'd thought you'd grown out of this."

Issi forced her lips into a smile and decided to put some faith in the prince's words. "The Grand Mage said he found someone better, and that he wanted to spend the night. I had a lot of thinking to do."

The maid's expression collapsed like wet bread. "Oh, Issi."

"I don't think he's coming back today either."

Chapter 14

Issi spent the morning searching through her master's rooms.

"There's nothing to find," she muttered. Her hand passed over his bed. The sheets were new and clean despite him not having slept there the night before. Stars flickered on the fabric between her fingers.

Her name drifted from the doorway.

Issi looked up. "Still no sign of him?"

Ner shook her head, her mouth puckering. "How about we get you something to eat?"

"I'm not hungry."

The maid was careful to make noise as she sidled up to Issi's side. "Come on," her voice was soft and inviting. Issi's heart skipped nervously in her chest.

"He loves you, you know, he's just...lost," Ner offered.

"Don't lie." Issi took a breath, she'd checked every room a dozen times over. Unless her master could use the magic of legends and fairy stories, he was gone.

Even if it didn't feel like it.

Ner looked at her with pity. "Are you—"

"I'm *fine*," she answered, shortly, "I'm just, I mean—"

"Don't cry." The maid froze, with her hands poised to cup Issi's face. If the Grand Mage was dead, could Issi have this much?

It was such a simple, quiet yearning. To be comforted by something more than empty promises. She flinched as the maid's fingers brushed her cheeks and ignored the memory that played behind her eyes. Issi clutched at Ner's hands, a small laugh bubbling in her throat. "Ner, you're so warm."

The maid furrowed her brows. "When's the last time you slept?"

"Why are you asking?"

The woman sighed, brushing at the tears that'd started tracking down Issi's face. "You look tired."

"I *am* tired."

Ner gave a sad smile and pressed gently at Issi's cheeks. "Come on, I got you something sweet to eat. Sweets for a broken heart, right?"

"Yes," Issi's voice broke. "I think I'd like that a lot."

She let Ner guide her to the cage. The plate the maid had left on the table was piled high with cakelets decorated with creams. A rainbow of fruits and honeyed breads sat fatly beside them. "Thank you, Ner."

Issi settled in her chair and picked quietly at her food until the maid left the room. The first bite was wonderfully sweet. Her stomach awakened and howled. She scarfed down the entire meal in ticks.

Even the drink was something sweet that nipped at and warmed the back of her throat.

The stress from the last few days settled around her shoulders pulling her downwards.

Could she really trust the prince?

He'd made a Promise, but had she missed something? Not been clear enough? How precise did a Promise have to be for it to stick?

There wasn't a lot of literature on old magic, the prices were considered too high to make it valuable, and nobles weren't fond of Promises. They preferred making do with papers and inks. Tie their names to things that could be torn in two and cast into flames with no repercussions.

For a noble to Shatter...

Issi shuddered to think *herself* as one, what would the royal family do if one of its sons started wandering about with eyes the color of a starless sky?

She'd leapt so readily at the chance to buy her family, and she'd been so shocked at the offer, she hadn't even thought of how wrong things could go. If the prince Shattered, would she be blamed? She shook her head and nearly pitched off the chair.

Sleep, the word whispered its way through her mind, warm with promise.

Fretting over a decision she couldn't unmake wouldn't get her anywhere.

And she *was* desperately tired. She'd barely had any sleep in the last three days.

She didn't make it to her bed.

Sunlight danced across her skin. She squeezed her eyes shut and willed herself awake.

"You don't sleep enough," the voice tutted.

The sunlight stayed. Issi tried again.

"I'm not letting you go that easy."

"This is a bad place for me to be," Issi breathed.

"If you toss a child into deep waters without teaching them to swim, they might drown," the girl's voice rose and fell as if she were reciting something. "You're drowning."

Issi risked a glance, her curiosity getting the better of her. The girl with the braided crown sat neatly beside her. She looked past Issi, seeming more interested in the line of trees that sat barely a footstep away.

"I'm not drowning."

"You obviously aren't swimming, you're not even treading," the girl sighed.

"Treading?"

The girl frowned. "Yes, treading."

When in Naya's hells would Issi have *ever* been allowed to submerge herself into anything deeper than a bathtub?

"Well, let's assume you're not insane," Issi hissed, "Is there any way to *stop*?"

"Stop looking," the girl answered, "What you think will make you whole will just as soon tear you to pieces."

Issi stilled. "You know what I'm looking for."

"Yes."

Desperation clawed at her throat, "What is it?"

"Not important," the girl snapped, "If I said it was a box of sticks, or a necklace, or a *dog*, it wouldn't matter. Nothing would change. You need to stop looking for it."

"Why?" Annoyance pricked Issi's skin. She could feel the need to search starting in her legs.

Finding whatever she was looking for *would* make her happy and whole and...it would fix her somehow. Whatever it was the Grand Mage had broken inside her would mend itself and—

"You're not broken," the girl railed, impatiently. She flopped into the vines spread beneath her. "There's *nothing* wrong with you. You're just hurt and you're confusing the two."

"You have no idea—"

"I am *older* than you," the girl interjected, "I know what you're chasing, and it makes *everyone* feel that way. I'm here to tell you that it's lying."

The girl's jaw sawed back and forth, her fingers tearing absently at the grass, setting the smell of green leaping into the air.

Issi rolled her eyes. This was just a dream. A dream where she got to wander somewhere looking as she liked, exploring what she wanted, and looking for whatever she desired.

And she wanted to feel whole.

The girl's fingers wrapped around Issi's wrist. "You'll drown."

Issi tried to shake her off. "It doesn't matter. None of this is real, right? You're just a piece of my imagination that's gone and gotten ideas of its own."

"You know that's not true."

What Issi knew was that she needed to leave. That the itching in her legs was growing unbearable and this odd, confusing girl was making everything far more unpleasant than it needed to be.

This had been her favorite dream at some point and now...

Why was she so sure that whatever she was looking for would save her?

"You need to know that you have a choice," the girl murmured.

Issi faltered at the tree line. One step, and she would be worlds closer to finding whatever she was looking for.

But the girl's words were starting to worm their way into her head.

Issi sighed. "I...," she winced, as her voice warbled, "I need you to let go of me...please."

"Are you going to run?"

"Would you stop me if I did?"

The girl pursed her lips. Her fingers peeled away. "...if you don't want to listen, I can't keep doing this. I'm tired, talking is so hard...and *finding* you...but Rua wouldn't want this for you, not when you don't know what you're doing."

Issi shook her legs against the ground, it felt like bugs were starting to trek along her skin. "So, why are you here?"

"I need to tell you something, but you keep running off and...I keep forgetting. Forgetting. I can show you," her expression filled with relief, "I can try to show you...if you let me."

"Show me?"

The girl nodded. "Yes...it's jumbled and...I can show you...but it's unclear, everything starts to get muddy when I try to focus. I'm supposed to be, not try. Trying's so hard." She set her head in her hands. "I'm so tired."

She wasn't making any sense. "You want to show me?" Issi repeated.

"Yes."

If nothing else, the girl had finally gotten her curiosity. Issi glanced at the forest, and at her own itching feet as she worried her lip. "Then show me."

"Are you sure?"

Issi gave the girl a weak smile as her heart thundered against her ribcage. "I'm never sure of anything anymore. But I'd like to see it anyway."

And everything went black.

Issi bolted upright, with a gasp. Outside her window the sun had climbed high in the sky. She grimaced as she lifted her hand from her plate. Honey and cream trailed from her fingers. She glanced around, half expecting her childhood etiquette teacher to appear in the corner before she licked her fingers clean.

Still sweet.

Vivid dreams.

She sat with the thought. There was no harm in checking...right?

Issi pulled a stack of reports she'd squirreled beneath her mattress. She spread the pages across her floor and started reading.

She skipped past the clinical information she'd once thought so important and started paying attention to the more fanciful aspects.

It was there. Nestled between the dreams and the pictures were small, almost unwilling, admissions of...loss. Quiet fears of incompleteness, hopeful notes on progress, longwinded passages on failures, and confessions of growing dissatisfaction, and sensations of emptiness.

Was that why the Grand Mage had chased the birds so fervently? It was certainly why she'd started following the vines.

Why she wandered about in her dreams.

This didn't *mean* anything. This wasn't a solution, or a cure, it was hardly even a direction.

Still.

They were all following *something*.

A knock at the door startled her. She shoved the papers beneath her bed and stood hurriedly. What was she supposed to have been doing? Certainly not staring at the wall for the last four bells or so.

"Come in." She ran her hands quickly through her hair. She hadn't tried to brush it since she'd gotten soaked and it had dried in odd little patches, one of which she had to tug down forcefully.

The green-eyed maid stood in the doorway. Her eyes darted nervously about the room. Her smile strained near the edges.

A few heartbeats passed. Issi tugged at her skirts. "Yes?"

The woman jumped. "Ah, yes, sorry, uhm, Miss Anders...you have a guest."

"A guest?" Issi repeated incredulously.

The maid nodded. "Yes, he's waiting for you in the main chamber."

What in Naya's hells was she supposed to do with a *visitor*? "Did master grant them permission?"

The woman shook her head.

"Did they send a letter?"

"He doesn't have to," the maid answered, shortly.

Issi's heart sank. "Yes, of course." She hadn't changed out of yesterday's clothes, and she looked a mess, but whoever had entered, by virtue of being more than a dog, vastly outranked her.

She couldn't make them wait.

The maid did not escort her, instead continuing down the long hall to the bathing room. And Issi for her part, tried to look prim and not at all like she'd just slept on a plate of sweets as she navigated the stairwell.

She wasn't in the mood for pretending.

As she reached the center of the main hall, her feet dragged to a stop, the rest of her nearly toppling over. She shut her eyes and hoped that when she opened them the figure lounging in her master's favorite chair would disappear.

Or at the very least, that the monster beside him would.

Hoten spared her no affections.

Issi forced herself to take a deep breath as she approached the chair and folded herself neatly before it, grinding her forehead into the stone floor. "My apologies for making you wait."

The third prince smirked. "Was I really so unanticipated?"

She hadn't really put much thought into anything. Least of all, how he was meant to contact her.

"You're a mess," he laughed, softly. Issi raised her head. Tiremalv looked well rested. And his guard felt as massive and suffocating as he had the night before, only marginally less intimidating when not lurking in hidden corridors.

"My prince, may I ask why you're here?"

"Well, ten days isn't long," he answered, "So, you have until tonight to get ready."

Issi blinked. That wasn't enough time, not for a proper enchantment. But what choice did she have? She nodded slightly, glancing about for a slip of servant's greys, but the floor seemed empty.

She darted a glance at the guard and began haltingly, "And the...escort?"

The prince grinned and gestured to the guard. "Is right here."

"No."

"No?" the prince echoed. "Del, you're in no position to be telling me—"

"Not him." She shook her head and sent a quiet prayer to Ipheoth, hoping the prince hadn't been stupid enough to tell the guard everything. "I won't make it, which means *you* won't make it."

Thanae fixed a glare on her that did its best to evaporate whatever courage she'd gathered. She swallowed uncomfortably.

"What I mean to say is, he's not a good...fit."

Annoyance flit across the prince's face. "In what way?"

A *royal guard* would never escort a magic wielding Pet anywhere other than the gallows. Was her life really this fragile? It felt like no matter how hard or fast or far she ran, she'd always end up right where she started.

What if you could be more than a tool?

Gods, what a fucking joke.

"My prince," she began, softly. "What am I?"

The prince blinked, his expression shifting through a thousand emotions in rapid succession only to be doused and buried. "You're Del, of course. I don't see what—"

"I didn't ask who," she pressed. "Nobody in this palace gives a damn about *who* I am. I asked *what*."

Thanae straightened, likely readying to cut her down, but Issi kept her attention on the prince.

His eyes were seas of confusion. "You're a mage," he answered.

So, the guard knew everything.

She paused, savoring the sound of it. *Mage.* How nice things could have been if that were the truth. "Wrong."

"Del, I don't have time—"

"Like you know *shit* about running out of time," she interrupted, "I am a *Pet*. A Pet who can wield magic. He is *a royal guard*, loyal to your family. Not you." She turned towards the guard. "How much of a reason do you need?"

He held her gaze, his eyes held nothing welcoming. They were cold and dead and flat as the grey of winter clouds.

She broke eye contact only when the prince began, "I trust him."

"And why in the nine-hells should that make a difference?"

"Because I'm demanding that you do too."

She opened her mouth to argue when an ache started on her arm, she could feel the magic shifting beneath the skin where the scar tissue circled. The blood drained from her face, *no no no no no.*

"Del, I've Promised you ten days of freedom, you Promised your loyalty. Now I know death doesn't scare you, but Shattering does, doesn't it?"

She searched his face for *anything*, humor, rage, annoyance, but he looked...bored. Like he wasn't threatening her with a fate worse than death.

The onyx eyes of the Shattered stared at nothing, and they couldn't *think*. Something about losing the only bit of freedom she'd trapped in her mind made her realize that dealing with the magic slowly leaching from her life was somehow the better alternative.

Issi turned her glare to the guard. Was there any way to actually trust him? Or was she already doomed?

Was trying enough?

The burning in her wrist faded, the magic beneath it settling back into a constant buzz. She frowned. *Loyalty.* Did that mean she just had to try?

Or was it something else?

"Thanae will accompany you to Egrea," the prince reiterated, "And he will make sure you come back. He already knows who you are, or...what you are, and what you can do."

Issi tried to keep the skepticism off her face. The knowledge did nothing to quiet the rage that sat in the pit of her stomach.

She smiled. "I'm sure he'll make a fine companion."

The prince stilled. "Don't do that."

"Do what?"

"Hide behind a blank smile and lie. I need you to be honest with me, Del, not please me."

Issi shifted, annoyance rolled off her in waves.

"Then he strikes me as a prick, my prince," she answered, blandly. "He doesn't like me, and he's nearly drawn his sword on me three times since we've met. If nothing else this trip will be deeply unpleasant."

"You think?"

Issi bit back a sharp retort. What was it the prince *wanted*? Was he dancing around just to infuriate her?

"Well, I'll have you know that I didn't just choose him for his winning personality." The prince waved, lazily, in the man's direction. "He is abrasive, but so are you. I think you'll get along fine. In terms of raw material, I trust you can make this work?"

Issi unfolded her legs, wincing as aches and bruises made themselves known. She hesitated only briefly in front of the guard before closing the distance between them. His breath smelled of sweets.

She arched her brows. He seemed the type who'd eat children for breakfast, but jam smothered tarts seemed to be his preference. She worked her way down his body. He was fitter than the Grand Mage had been, but it was nothing a well-placed pillow couldn't fix.

Maybe he was a finger or two shorter. Whatever the difference, it wasn't immediately noticeable. She glanced around the room, checking for servants, before reaching for his hand.

The guard stiffened, his head turning towards the prince. Whatever communication passed between them ended with his hand staying in hers. His fingers were long and surprisingly delicate, but his palms were rough from training.

His nose would be a problem too, it was wider than the Grand Mage's and the scar would make the expressions stiff.

He wasn't perfect, but Tiremalv was right. She bit the inside of her cheek, trying to keep the annoyance off her face.

"I can make him work," she answered, before addressing the guard, "How much do you know about illusions?"

Beats passed and his lips stayed stubbornly shut.

"Oh, yes, this'll be perfect," she muttered. He was going to be a hulking, silent mass of sunshine. "How much does he know about illusions?"

"I'd say nothing at all." The prince started picking at the trinkets that sat at the chair's side.

"What?"

"He's a palace guard, Del, not a mage."

"But defensive castings, armor, and—"

"He knows how to use them, not how they work. Is that right Thanae?"

Issi flinched as the mountain beside her huffed, "Yes, my prince."

Rumble and stone. She'd have to get used to that.

"Well." She shifted, casting another glance around the room. "I can't speak much on it at the moment, but—"

"The others have been dismissed," the prince added, as a figurine searched for stones in the palm of his hand, "The maid I sent to get you is just filling the washing tub."

Issi blinked. Gods, what were they imagining was going on between her and the prince? The rumors alone would send the Grand Mage into—

No, he was gone.

And the rumors were likely a good thing. It would look like the prince had started to favor her, and the Grand Mage was throwing a tantrum. It was believable, all but the prince having any interest in her at all, and it was interesting enough that nobody would bother looking any deeper.

Was that why he'd approached her the way he had at the king's dinner?

"Why the bath?" she asked finally.

"Because you'll be on the road for nearly a quarter moon without a bathing facility and I figured you might want to start clean."

Her brows lowered. She wasn't sure why he cared.

"Thank you," she offered, uncertainly, "I should...uhm..." What should she do? Bathe while the angry *huread* wandered about?

Or begin by shoving him into the workroom so she could start on the enchantment?

Issi froze as a thud sounded, the green-eyed maid picked herself up and scurried to the servant's corridor.

"We'll be around when you finish," the third prince provided.

"You really expect me to bathe?"

He snorted, "Del, you look awful."

She frowned. He really expected her to make herself pretty. She glanced at her wrist tempted to test exactly what she was permitted to do. Was loyalty synonymous with obedient? The prince seemed to think the guard was at least one of those things.

But the idea of failure scared her. And a bath seemed nice enough, she still smelled of the honey and cream she'd slept in.

Issi excused herself and winced her way up the stairs. She chose an outfit from her wardrobe, another ruffled monstrosity with an exceedingly low neckline, and folded it neatly over her arm.

She pinched the fabric and wondered about the trousers she wore in her dreams. If the Grand Mage were dead, could she start dressing as she wanted?

Because right now, she wanted a pair of trousers.

The hall was empty as she made her way to the bathing room. He really had dismissed everyone. She turned a gold engraved handle and pushed the door open.

Mosaiced floors spun geometric shapes to the tiled walls, while a series of arches led to shelves of soaps and lotions and a handful of windows covered in thick weighted curtains. The water itself sat in a pool set deep into the floor. Steam drifted gently from the surface. Her master had baths prepared for her every quarter moon, but today without his instruction, it didn't smell of roses and lavender, only of steam and water and the still damp air from outside.

Issi dropped her clothes into a heap and made her way to one of the windows. Her heart thrummed nervously as she pulled the fabric back. A deep breath rattled in her chest.

The Grand Mage had always insisted that the curtain stayed closed.

The view was spectacular. Vibrant flowers sat in neat rows beneath soft blooming trees that sent dazzling sun patterns bouncing against the walls and moss floors.

She almost wished the windows had been removed the way the ones in the ballroom had been. She'd be able to hear the brightly colored birds that called the gardens home beyond what came muffled through the panels.

She undressed efficiently and sank into the tub. The water nipped at her bruises and worked at the knot that'd formed between her shoulders.

A content sigh left her lips. For a moment, she felt quiet and still, like the world around her had righted itself in the first time since the Grand Mage had jumped from the roof.

Then a flash of silver caught her eye.

She grabbed a rough sponge and started to work over the silver stain that slid across her skin. The coin-colored vine now climbed from the center of her right cheek to the middle of her stomach.

She toyed briefly with the idea of hiding it.

It was supposed to be a burden. The Grand Mage had worn a shirt for the entire nine moons before his death. Looking at the mark had made him pale with disgust. Issi had always found the sprawling patterns beautiful. The prince, at least in that aspect, didn't seem to care either way.

She lingered in the bath until the water cooled. She loathed to use the soap her master had brought for her, so she scrubbed heartily until she was close enough to clean and massaged soft smelling oils into her skin. Her reflection showed her hair had snarled. Heavy bags sat beneath her mismatched eyes.

Ner was right, she did look tired.

But she also looked how she *felt* for the first time in ages, and maybe that was a good enough start.

A quarter bell went into convincing her hair into a lackluster braid that ended in the center of her spine and a couple beats into pulling on her dress. She rushed down to the main hall, feeling guilty that she'd taken so long. She was surprised to find the prince had actually waited.

Her legs froze in the entry to the main chamber beside a glass case filled with dun power stones begging to be struck or tossed into flame. How was she supposed to greet him? *Master* felt...wrong. And he wasn't *her* prince any more than she was his subject.

Did he expect her to walk up to him, or did he prefer that she waited to be addressed?

Issi coughed, and the prince glanced up from one of her master's older tomes. She stifled the urge to tell him that that book was fairly useless.

Her cheeks warmed as she gestured towards the workroom. "Do you want to...watch?" She couldn't imagine what he'd find interesting about it. But she couldn't imagine why else he might have lingered. Her eyes ticked nervously for the guard.

The prince nodded, closing the text and placing it on the table that sat by the chair he'd claimed. He stilled when he actually *looked* at her.

Issi's gaze dropped to the floor, had she gotten it wrong? She wrung her hands nervously. "Would you have preferred something closer to the Grand Mage's taste?"

Disgust rippled across his face. "No, I was just surprised."

He gestured to her cheek. Her fingers traced a path down the side of her face. They came away clean.

"The mark, Del, I didn't realize it was so large," he offered.

She shrugged, nodding to the workroom. "Is the huread already in there?"

"The huread?" the prince's voice tugged at the edges. Likely to the reference of the old, simple creature from children's stories tasked with protecting ill-prepared princes and princesses.

Issi's nose crinkled as she muttered, "What else could he be? He's large, he's silent, he's thought about ending my life at least three times to save your honor and—" The huread always carried out their instructions in the end. Even if it destroyed them. She didn't mention that part.

"He hasn't thought about killing you," the prince answered, dismissively, as he headed towards the door. He held it for her, and Issi's mind blanked. This was wrong, but was it worse to correct him?

Did he fly into rages too?

She hurried by before he started thinking about the meaning behind the gesture. Issi frowned when she found the guard, he seemed to be making a wonderful impression of an ominous cloud, or perhaps a petulant child, as he sorted through the tomes that had been stacked neatly on a large shelf.

Issi approached the desk sitting in the room's center and hesitated briefly before pulling her master's severed digit from the drawer. Her free hand moved to cover her nose, the smell of it was impressive, rot and blood. Despite having thawed, the flesh and bone had set curled like it was trying to beckon something closer.

She was searching for an engraving pen when Tiremalv settled behind her, peering over her shoulder.

Her stomach knotted. She didn't like people behind her, particularly not when she was about to do something that could easily have her hung, but the words to explain herself stuck in her throat. She swallowed and placed the pen against her master's finger, tugging at the magic pooled beneath the palace as she drew the first line, skirting the knuckle.

Oranges and greenery.

The world fell away as she wove magic into the fine lines she carved across her master's finger. It was an older spell, long forbidden, and all but forgotten. Hidden between the lines of an easily dismissed poem once sang by the followers of Mihr-Did and recorded before the gods had been banished. The book was left to gather dust on the upper shelves of the Grand Mage's library. A series of lines that spun about in an intricate, dizzying, dance.

Of course, this was all very...not legal. And crafting it in front of the prince, and his huread, felt wrong in more ways than Issi cared to articulate.

Impersonating a Grand Mage, or high nobility was a hanging offense, and the spell, by its nature, demanded a body part to work, which made the implications of success a bit darker.

To change the appearance of an object or person was one thing. To mimic somebody else, to get every line and wrinkle, the curve of a cheek, the nick they'd gotten on their finger when they were a child, was another thing entirely. The task was made easier by using their essence as a template of sorts, but it was still difficult.

And it felt *wonderful*.

The task consumed her. For the barest moment, there were no princes to obey, no moody guards to judge her, no masters to mourn or celebrate.

"What song is that?" She nearly cut too far as her attention split.

Breathe.

Had she been breathing?

"Song?" she echoed, trying desperately to hide her panic. Was this the fifth iteration, or the sixth? *Gods.*

"You were singing," the prince clarified. "What song was it?"

Her heart skipped. "I don't sing. Master doesn't like it."

"You did." He started a piss poor rendition of a lullaby. Her ears warmed.

"It's nothing." She finished the enchantment neatly, before nipping her thumb. Blood welled beside her nailbed. She smeared it across the finger's surface and grabbed a jar of dogwood oil she'd left on the table from the night before. She spent a moment daubing it carefully onto the finger's surface and felt the magic she'd wrangled lock into place.

She held the digit towards the prince. "Hold this."

"That's a bit—"

She wiggled the finger impatiently. The prince grabbed it.

A beat passed, then several. Nothing.

She let out a soft curse and took it back. She pulled a cloth from the desk drawer and wiped at the blood and oil.

Where had she gone wrong? The magic had locked, had she knotted it somewhere?

She set to it again.

The prince's interest waned around the third attempt, it took seven to get the illusion to cast, and five more to get it to stick to the scaffolding offered by the prince's body, rather than drift away like an errant shadow.

In the end, it was a clever thing, that required twelve iterations to work.

And every time it did, she felt a vice cinch around her lungs.

It was very much the Grand Mage in every way that mattered. His eyes, his hands, his scars.

Seeing him stand before her was difficult. It tied her thoughts, and made time slide away from her, like reality became less sure of itself in his presence.

Something dropped into her palm. Her fingers curled around it before she could make sense of what it was. "Uhm," *the enchantment*, "...ah, thanks, thank you."

"That's as far as you can get with me, isn't it?" the prince stated, pointedly.

Her mind stuttered. He'd been holding onto the enchantment for a while.

It'd been nearly perfect, hadn't it? She just had to make sure that it followed all of Thanae's movements. A second skin. Her head ticked about the room.

"Down." The prince pointed to a spot by her legs.

She stumbled backwards stifling a squeal. The guard sat cross-legged beside her. His eyes bore into hers.

"How...how long?"

Tiremalv shrugged. "A while. You don't notice much of anything when you work." He gestured towards her hair.

Issi ran a hand through it to find the braid had been redone, and that she'd a few petals and leaves woven in it.

"I just like magic," she muttered, petulantly. "It makes me feel more myself."

The prince didn't respond to that, instead he swiped twice at his shirt and cast a glance at the clock above the hearth. "I'll be taking my leave, take care of Thanae for me."

Issi glanced at the prince's huread who she suspected hadn't even had the decency to blink.

Chapter 15

The Grand Mage Gadna Niao was dead.

Issi tried to hold the idea in her mind, make it into something solid she could cling to. The image of the man himself standing before her was making the task considerably more complex.

Her heart fluttered nervously.

The Grand Mage Gadna Niao was dead.

But Issi reached up, to fix his collar anyway. The fabric beneath her palms was real, the body beneath it felt warm. Alive. Her master's muddied-green eyes tracked her just as they'd done in life.

She felt sick to her stomach. A tremor ran through her hands.

"You look..." Well, he looked like the Grand Mage, down to the clothes he wore, she'd secured a pillow about his middle so the illusion wouldn't collapse if anyone brushed against it. "I don't know, you look like him," she sighed.

The guard stayed quiet.

She checked him over one last time. It was a good illusion, not perfect, if he moved too quickly and one knew to look, the outline would trail behind like a fine mist, and, of course, he'd feel a chill for most of the time he wore it. Better people think the Grand Mage bloodless, than notice the air around him was permanently cold.

She sighed again, tugging her veil down with practiced efficiency. The world went muzzy and dull through the fabric. "Please, I need you to speak."

Nothing.

Maybe her huread observation hadn't been complete folly.

"What do you intend to do? Just glower at the driver?" she breathed softly, "The prince said you would help me. If you can't play the role properly, I can't get my family and your princeling Shatters."

His eyes narrowed. "Couldn't convince your master to buy another fuck toy?"

Her body went rigid as she fought the instinct to run. Her eyes darted over his form as she forced herself to find something that didn't fit.

It was Gadna's voice, but Thanae spoke too roughly, a little too slowly. Held himself too rigidly.

All she could manage was a whisper, "It didn't work that way."

"Looks like he let you do whatever you wanted," he grumbled.

"...how does talking feel?"

"Uncomfortable."

Issi took a deep breath and held it. Ipheoth grant her patience, this was difficult enough without him being obstinate. Surely, contemplating slaying the guard gifted to her by the prince wasn't *loyalty*.

"Is it *cold* or does it *hurt*?"

He shrugged. She bit her still aching lip. "Fine, if you insist on being an ass, it's your tissue damage, not mine."

Issi straightened as the grinding of carriage wheels neared, casting one last glance at Thanae and the small ornate trunk she'd hurriedly filled with what she imagined people who went outside would require.

Excitement was making her twitchy. It'd been three years since she'd left the palace gates without having to worry about getting rid of corpses and even before that her outings had been infrequent and had often stayed to the quieter parts of the island.

What if the enchantment failed before they even reached the gates? What if it worked?

The carriage came into view, a towering structure of oak and glass. It stopped neatly before the carriage house. The driver, a squat man with an infectious smile, skipped down from his perch, startling the two brightly colored birds hitched to the front.

Their feathers shifted colors, like waves of fire and water respectively, as he cooed at them.

As soon as they settled, he turned to the illusion of the Grand Mage and bowed. "Apologies. They weren't prepared, so they're a little skittish," he said.

Thanae frowned, and the driver shifted uncomfortably. His shoes ground against the pavers as he moved his weight. Beats passed, each one seeming to drag longer than the last as an unwelcome realization washed over Issi.

She pressed herself to the guard's side and searched his face. "Master...we might miss the boat, if we stay to discipline the driver."

There was no spark of understanding.

She swallowed a curse as she stood on her tiptoes, looking for all the world like she wanted to kiss his cheek and had been too dumb to remember the veil. "He needs the command to stand."

The guard's expression darkened. "...stand."

The driver straightened, looking relieved. He started towards her master's trunk, now filled with a dozen of the Grand Mage's outfits and even more of his books and reports, along with whatever Thanae thought to toss into it.

Issi tugged on the guard's clothes to stop him from opening the carriage door. Her heart was cannon fire.

Mihr-Did, bless her.

He didn't know *anything*.

She watched the driver pack their things. Did he suspect? He darted curious glances at the crates and Issi, but if he thought anything about the Grand Mage was off, he kept his opinion to himself.

The man returned at last to open the door and Issi nudged Thanae forward.

It was like hitting a wall.

He made a sound that was annoyingly similar to a scoff before pausing beside the driver. "Thank you."

Issi stopped. The driver looked at the Grand Mage with the same amazement he might have had if the sun had spawned a twin and the skies had dyed themselves purple.

A baffled grin tripped onto his face. "Ah, well, you're very welcome...sir." Issi stopped just short of physically shoving the guard into the carriage. The driver had an extra bounce in his step as he closed the door and returned to his seat.

The interior was as ornate as the exterior, filled with plush pillows and carvings of golden ravens with amethyst collars and eyes. Issi was nearly consumed by the decadence as she sat. She shifted to the edge of the seat and dared glance at Thanae.

Could he be pretending to make her nervous, or was he truly ignorant?

Which was worse?

She tugged uncomfortably at the ornate collar dripping down her neck, losing her fingers in the loops of silk that cascaded from the leather pressed against her skin. The collar for outdoors had always been ostentatious but today it was suffocating.

Outside, a whip cracked. One of the birds gave an angry high-pitched caw before the cart started forward and the carriage house drifted away.

Her eyes fixed on the palace gates that loomed before them. They grew larger by the moment, soaring, arching iron framework hanging open for morning traffic. Her fingers knotted together until the tips beneath her nails ran pale.

They stopped for the driver to hand the wall guard their papers. She cursed the veil that bled their shapes together.

Were they studying the papers for too long?

Had she somehow botched the Grand Mage's signature?

Tales of huread drifted between her ears as she waited for Thanae to stand and leave the carriage. Her imagination summoned the sound of him denouncing her in front of a makeshift audience.

She closed her eyes and counted the thundering beats of her heart. One, two, three, four, this was too long. Five, six, seven, she braced for a knock on the window, for Thanae to pull her out. Eight, nine, ten.

Laughter. Her eyes flew open, not that it was much help. The brown blob standing beside the carriage shifted before gaily waving the papers about and returning them to the driver.

And the carriage began to move.

Issi watched the walls. Surely the gate was about to snap shut or guards were to rain down from their posts and drag her to the gallows.

The driver led them beneath the arches and waved at someone she couldn't see. The palace began to shrink behind them.

It'd worked. She leaned back and shut her eyes, remembering to breathe.

Her hands trembled as some of the tension between her shoulders eased.

She opened her eyes as the carriage rumbled down a wide stone paved road. They were headed west, rather than south where the prince had taken her the night before and well around the plaza, much to her dismay.

In the late afternoon sun, the city seemed to glow. Pressed together houses basked in its warmth, while people hurried by. Issi tried not to gape.

There were so many people.

She'd never been this close to this many bodies *ever*. The clothes, the movement, the *noise*. Peals of laughter rang through the air mixing with shouts and chatter. People passed one another without even a wave, some pushed against throngs, others wove between them, others still were swept away.

Issi had read the histories, seen the reports and spent bells pouring over small, detailed pictures penned onto parchment. But none of that meant anything next to the reality that spread before her.

There was so much the books hadn't prepared her for. She hadn't realized commoners wouldn't prance about in highly organized groups, or that they wouldn't be marked by sashes of colors. In fact, nothing on them showed any sort of allegiance at all. They didn't even have the same types of fashion. Where the courts prized opulence and shape, the people outside seemed to prefer utility over everything else. She spied women wearing *pants*.

Was that common?

Issi set to fidgeting as excitement churned her stomach and curiosity set her throat aflame.

Something smacked her in the middle of her forehead. A dull thud rocked her skull. She cursed bitterly in Egrean as she righted herself. She'd forgotten about the window.

"Is there a festival today?" she managed breathlessly.

She turned to face her companion. Her joy dimmed as she met the Grand Mage's eyes.

No, the Grand Mage was dead, the *guard's* eyes.

Her nails dug into her palms, and she forced herself to keep his gaze. His brows furrowed in an expression the Grand Mage had never worn in life.

"Is it?" she pressed.

"It's always like this," he muttered, before turning away and killing any chance of conversation.

She flipped her veil up so she could see better.

Always.

It wasn't a festival.

Her breath fogged the window, and she propped herself on her knees to get a better view as the cushion worked to swallow her. Before she could think, she pressed against it, forcing the glass open. Noise leapt through the gap. Her ears burned as she tried to separate a thousand conversations, her nose twitched as the smells of roasted meat, fresh baked bread, and all sorts of magic rushed to greet her.

It wasn't a festival.

People got to live like this every day.

"Sit down." Thanae tugged, roughly, on the back of her dress. She fell hard on her ass.

The jostling knocked her veil into place. "What does it matter?"

"You look like a child," he grumbled.

"I—" She bit her tongue and settled herself. Was that so bad? What did people her age do? In the books, most were still in the midst of apprenticeships. Would they not press their noses against the window of a carriage?

Issi's fingers pressed against her collar. Her siblings would have to parse that particular mystery.

If she managed to get to them at all.

"What do you know of the Grand Mage?" she asked.

Thanae frowned. "Enough."

"It's not 'enough', you couldn't even handle the driver by yourself," she breathed, "I need this to work."

A growl rumbled in his throat and Issi fought the instinct to shrink away.

"You are my *guard*, the prince gifted you to me. You don't *scare* me." She prayed that she could make that feel true. "I need to know."

His jaw set, a distinctly unpleasant look passing across his face.

"His enchantments helped win the war against Repren. He trained hundreds of mages. He was smart, and respected. His only flaw was you."

"What of his temper?"

Thanae shrugged. "It's the reason he survived the war."

If Gadna had been a man before the war, he'd saved all the parts that hadn't mattered. "He wasn't kind to his subordinates, never *thank* anyone for anything. Ma—, the Grand Mage, had a volatile temper." The fingers on her left hand flexed, as a memory forced its way to the front of her mind. She continued, "...no one knew what would set him off. If people get noisy just look at them for a beat or two and they should fall into line. He was very protective of me—"

"Lot of good that did him."

"—he never struck me in public. You are not to strike me at all." She braced for an argument.

A beat passed and his head bobbed.

She studied him for a beat longer. "You won't hit me?"

He seemed confused by the question. "Not unless I have to?"

"Why would you have to?"

"To stop you from hurting anybody."

Hurt people? How would she even manage? It took time to craft enchantments. She'd have had to plan it, bring a myriad of oils she hadn't thought to bring, and all that aside, hurting the prince's people might doom her to Shattering.

Which meant Thanae wouldn't be hitting her. If she could trust his word.

The prince did.

"The way you speak is too rough. Keep your sentences short," she finished.

His nose crinkled.

She could fill a thousand books with her master's habits and ticks, but what could she tell him that mattered?

Thanae didn't need to be perfect, just close enough.

Market chatter was replaced by the abrasive dialect of the dock workers. Shouts reverberated through the air and people hurried about the riverside smelling of fish, and wood, and water.

Memories ignited at the smell of it, old ones. A quiet night and an even quieter shuffle past candlelit windows filled with soft laughter. When she'd first set foot on the dock, she'd the smallest hope that Kothen Palace might be better than where she'd come from.

The carriage stumbled to a stop. Issi was nearly thrown off the seat. She righted herself and heard the Grand Mage almost chuckle.

Thanae.

Not Gadna.

The structure swayed as the driver leapt from his seat. She counted the footsteps until he opened the door on her master's side. Thanae clambered down like a shoddy dock worker in fine silks.

Issi closed her eyes and sent one last prayer to Mihr-Did.

Please, just let this work.

Her heart sank as he walked away, surveying the ships with an intensity that was likely useful when keeping watch, but would be seen only as mounting paranoia in her master.

The driver observed him, confusion twisting his lips as he offered Del his hand. Gods, she stared at it a beat too long before taking it and tamped down viciously on the panic that spiked through her. The driver was just there to escort her down the step.

And he did. Her shoes set against the cobbles of the street, and he let her go. She pulled away too quickly, trying to forget the feel of him.

Worry tugged at her insides. The Grand Mage had never vacationed with her in this manner, so she wasn't entirely sure how this would have actually gone.

But he wouldn't have left her.

"He's weird today, isn't he?" the driver murmured. Issi's mind whirled as the sea of people swallowed them. It was like her senses were on fire, there were so many colors, and smells, and types of magic pushing up against her.

She wasn't sure where she was meant to look.

She tugged nervously at her sleeve, "The Grand Mage has been feeling unwell since dinner, the illness," she trailed off, it was a stupid excuse.

But the driver nodded sagely. "That bad, is it?"

"Uh…" Issi thought to her own growing mark, and ignored the urge to press against her cheek. "It's…interesting, the repor—, rumors, they don't do it justice."

"Poor thing," he mumbled softly as they reached the docks. He searched the blankness of her veil for something more.

Issi forced a smile, though he couldn't hope to see it. "Thank you."

His lips puckered as disappointment flashed in his eyes. The driver's mind was clearly elsewhere, he gave her a neat bow before trotting to her master's form.

It was eerie watching "Gadna" move. His steps were too rough, the way he held himself too…she wasn't sure. The Grand Mage had certainly walked confidently, but there was a comfort in Thanae's portrayal that hadn't existed in the original.

How well would someone have to have known him to recognize it?

She turned away, unwilling to watch the fiasco that was sure to happen.

The docks were busy, but what caught her eye wasn't the people, but the ships. They came in all shapes and sizes, the largest held masts that soared higher than the palace walls. Her mind tried and failed to make sense of something that *large* having the gall to move.

Gadna's laugh tolled. Issi's body reacted before she could stop it, her limbs locking, and her head bowing, a smile already pulling at her cheeks. She let out a long stream of curses, as she rolled her shoulders, startling someone who'd been trying to make their way around her.

The Grand Mage, Gadna Niao, was dead.

And the guard really hadn't known her master at all.

She gathered whatever sat beneath her skin that passed for courage these days and made her way to her master's side. His attention shifted to her and the warmth in his face bled away.

Thank the gods.

The man he was speaking to was a rugged type, thick about the middle with arms the size of her waist. His gaze pinned her to the spot.

"You're the one, eh?" his voice wasn't unkind, but there was no welcome in it either.

Issi's stomach dropped as she fell into a curtsy. "Nydelissi Anders, it's a pleasure to make your acquaintance..." She studied him, briefly, as she straightened. "...sir."

His eyes widened into pools of forest green. He smelled of magic, spring flowers, and something salty. Her nose twitched beneath her veil. Some of the kitchen workers had smelled of it too.

"She'll have to stay below deck."

"What?" Issi's complaint was drowned out by Thanae's. She turned to him in disbelief. She knew why *she* was upset, but what reason did he have?

"Pretty things need to be kept. What did you expect?"

"For you to control your crew," her master's voice was a low roll.

The captain looked nonplussed. "Well, for *people*, yes. But that's a *Pet*. I don't control what my crew does to animals."

A Pet.

She had nine full days until that was true again.

"I want to see us leave," she said, her voice had softened, like it knew that sounding was a mistake.

Nine days, she couldn't afford to be too afraid to make something of it.

The captain's lips pulled in disapproval. "Thought high class Pets were better trained."

"I'll go wherever I'm meant to be *after* nightfall," she continued. "I'll stay beside my master until then."

The man looked from her to Thanae. "Does it speak for you?"

The guard's mouth flattened into an irritated line. Issi's heart hammered between her ears.

"She does."

"Really?" The man shifted, his fingers brushing the stubble that came patchy across his chin. "I'd heard, but still—" He shrugged. "If you think the risk's worth it, I won't stop you. Just keep it locked below deck when you're not with it."

Her master's glare flared to life. "Control your crew."

The captain's boots slammed against the dock as he turned around. "I don't control what my men do with animals," he repeated, lightly, "I can tell them not to touch it. Won't mean they'll listen."

She grabbed Thanae's sleeve as he straightened beside her. "Don't."

"It's not—"

"I'll be fine," she insisted. The veil worked to hide the uncertainty that snaked across her face.

The guard frowned and turned to their driver. "Bring our things."

The man started at the command. His face was unreadable. Not a single part of that exchange had been normal.

Was it even worth trying anymore? How much of the Grand Mage could survive on image alone?

Her master's form dragged forward, she followed, ignoring the stares her attire was attracting, the way curiosity seemed to try to pick through the fabric of her veil.

The boat the prince had chartered was small compared to some of its counterparts, but meticulously kept and cared for. She spied no rust on the rigging and the castings she could see were kept tidy.

The salt smell she'd noticed on the captain drifted from the runes and seemed to breathe from the boat itself.

Curiosity led her to the bow.

Crowds passed beneath her. There were so many people, thousands upon thousands of lives.

Suddenly, the numbers listed in the illness reports meant something. What had it been? Two thousand mages this year alone? Two thousand people she'd never see walking along these docks, people who wouldn't go home, people who were buried, or burned, or drowned, or whatever it was this country had decided to do with its dead.

Hundreds, if not thousands more, were crossing borders and migrating eastward.

The king kept sending students to fill the voids they'd left behind, but they didn't last. So, land had gone unreplenished, domestic ware had broken down, and even if it didn't feel like it, she knew there were fewer ships too.

"You said you wanted to keep up appearances."

Issi flinched as her master's voice sounded by her ear. "I can't do that by myself," she answered, shortly, "And I wasn't going to miss *this*."

"Watching the docks?" Thanae responded disparagingly.

"Yes." Her own voice surprised her. It'd filled with warmth without her permission and curled comfortably around the word.

The guard grumbled and set to glowering by her side. Behind them, the sailors readied to launch.

It was a bell before the ship moved from the docks.

People became smears of color as the boat drifted away, buildings block impressions against the shoreline. The sound of everything faded until only the conversation and boot strikes of the sailors remained with the water that lapped against the boat's sides.

Issi wasn't sure what she was supposed to feel about any of this.

She'd never thought she'd make it off the island alive.

She watched until even the tallest towers of Kothen Palace were lost to the distance. Her eyes burned.

She'd left.

Somehow, impossibly, she'd escaped from the palace.

Tears streaked down her cheeks. She thanked Ipheoth for her veil and her mercy, before glancing to the guard to make sure he hadn't noticed. She stayed until the sun sank to the horizon, her vision blurry from tears that didn't seem to stop.

Chapter 16

Thanae glared at Issi from the door. She could *feel* it, despite the room's darkness and the fact that her back was towards him. She did her best to ignore him as she searched through her trunk.

The room they'd been granted was small, much smaller than her cage, having enough space for a single bit of fabric that hung suspended from two hooks on the wall and for her to take a single step away from it. If she stretched her arms, she'd be able to touch both walls.

And Thanae took a decent portion of it, large as he was.

Like a godsblessed tower.

She pushed past skirts and cosmetics and cast sealed documents until she reached the tin that'd sunk its way to the bottom. Tea was near impossible. She didn't trust the swaying of the boat and hadn't bothered with a kettle. Instead, she stuffed the leaves into her cheeks, chewing quickly as her face scrunched at the bitterness. They were somehow far worse without having been steeped in hot water.

She frowned at the cannister, there wasn't much left.

The lid squeaked as she twisted it shut and leapt back into her trunk. After some searching her left hand wrapped around the spine of a thin book.

She combed further for a quill and ink-well.

Thanae's gaze burned between her shoulder blades.

"Do you have anywhere else you need to be?" she breathed. "Perhaps someone needs you to stomp on some ill-intentioned rodents?"

She glanced at him as she pulled the tab to fill her quill. Thanae didn't respond. His face, now free of the enchantment, hadn't even twitched.

"I'm sorry, you'd rather boil them alive, wouldn't you?"

Nothing.

His non-reactions were getting to her. She was used to reading faces, but his never said much of anything except, perhaps, that he was extremely pissed.

She was beginning to think that was a permanent state.

The guard continued with his oppressive nothing as Issi clambered into the fabric swath. It folded and molded around her, until she found herself swinging in something that might have been a chair.

Her sketchbook fell open on her lap as her makeshift seat swung. It was going to take getting used to.

"No casting."

Issi's pen stopped. "Casting? On paper?"

The guard's gaze attempted to pin her. If it weren't for the sheer stupidity of his comment, he might have succeeded. He continued, "If you so much as draw a rune—"

She rolled her eyes. "You don't *draw* runes, you carve them, else the ink would run when you bled on it."

He still seemed ill at ease.

"If I wanted to cast, I wouldn't need the paper," she sighed and marked the air until a small orb appeared in her palm. She brought it to rest above her book.

"Don't."

Issi didn't bother looking at him. She wanted to draw the ship, and the docks, and the small brightly colored creatures that she'd spied in the clear waters of the Copros.

"Get rid of it," Thanae insisted.

"You're not really my master, you know." She'd start with the boat.

"Pet—"

She grimaced. "For the next nine days, I'm no such thing."

"Pet—"

"You don't know my name, do you?"

"Pet," he shouted. Issi's pen slipped, the ink scarring the page as her casting doused.

Her frown deepened. "What is it?"

"I said, 'don't cast'."

"So, you expect me to sit in the dark?"

The guard pointed to the unlit lamp that swung from the ceiling. The hair on her arms raised. "I don't like fire," she answered.

"Then dark it is."

Issi eyed the lantern, the flame would be dimmer than a torch, but still larger than anything she'd be comfortable with.

"And what will you do to me, if I cast anyway?"

The guard's expression went from flint to steel.

"Will you strike me? Burn me? Carve me?" Issi frowned. "If I disobey you, what will you do?"

Discomfort shifted onto his face. "I'll...stop you."

"How?"

"Just light the damn lantern."

"I don't like fire," she repeated. Her left hand twitched sending another stray arc across her paper.

He moved suddenly and Issi found herself shrinking away, trying to disappear into the fabric. The lantern rattled as he unhooked it from its perch. In a beat, a small flame flickered within its glass housing.

"Don't look at me like that," Thanae sighed. His shoulders slumped as he leaned against the door.

Issi sat completely still as she tried to convince her heart to slow.

"Please," his voice had dropped. She was half-sure she'd imagined it. What was that expression? Was he *pleading*?

"Uh, liking—" She swallowed and took a breath. "Like what?"

"I don't know." His arm flew in a frustrated arc, sending shadows limned by soft golden light dancing across the room "Like *that*, like I killed your family in front of you."

"I don't know what face I'd make if you did." She smiled, darkly, as her limbs decided to unfold. "It might have been a mercy."

"You're Pets, not prisoners."

"I *do* live in a cage, so it's not far off. I suppose the food's better."

"So is the jewelry, the clothes, the toys," he continued, coldly.

"I never asked for any of it," she muttered. "What would I need fine silks for when I can't even leave the wing? The nobles whisper about me because my clothes are out of style anyway."

She returned to her drawing. It looked like the ship had been struck down from the skies. Maybe things would be nicer if it had been.

A knock sent the lantern moving as Thanae moved, forcing the shadows into an awkward jig as he fished the Grand Mage's finger from his pocket.

The lock turned and the door swung open as Issi focused on the first few lines of what could very well be an omen, considering how fantastically this errand was going. A ship destined for sinking.

Maybe the train would have been better.

"Dinner," the voice outside the door announced in a gruff baritone.

Plates clattered and Thanae bit back a curse, followed by more clattering until the door finally closed. He set his burden on top of her master's trunk.

"Dinner," Gadna's voice gave to Thanae's in the middle of the word.

The food that'd been delivered boasted a smattering of seasonal fruit and some sort of stew filled the bowls. There wasn't much in the way of meat.

The guard held a bowl towards her. The liquid inside moved about with the gentle swaying of the ship.

He sighed. "Take it, it's not hot."

She closed her booklet and tucked it between the fabric and her hip, before grabbing the wooden vessel. He was right, it was just warm enough for her to feel the heat between her palms.

She studied him warily before grabbing the spoon and bringing it to her lips.

Her mouth filled with potatoes, onions, carrots, and what she suspected might have been a hint of some indistinguishable meat but wasn't entirely convinced. It was worlds worse than anything the chefs had cooked, but it was simple, and filling, and it reminded her of livelier dinners and a family she no longer bothered sketching.

Issi set the bowl in her lap after two spoonfuls.

"Not fancy enough?" Thanae grumbled.

She shook her head, her eyes glued to the vine that'd snaked over his shoulder. "No, it's...uhm...green. No, that being—." How much did he know of the mage's illness? She didn't think letting him know how bad it'd gotten would bring him anything other than joy.

"It's fine," she stated, softly. "The food's fine. It's been a busy day, and I just, I want it to be over." She set the bowl on her trunk. "Where are you going to sleep?"

Thanae scuffed his shoe across the floor. "Here."

She grimaced. "Are you—, would you prefer the, uh, this..." She patted the fabric. "This thing."

He frowned. "The hammock?"

"Hammock?" she echoed. "Hammock, yes, the...hammock."

"And you'd sleep on the floor?" His laughter was short lived and unkind.

"Fine, be an ass." She wriggled about until the hammock wrapped around her.

Then Thanae did something truly baffling. He dimmed the lantern.

She peeked above the fabric. He'd made a table of her master's trunk. The lantern sat in his lap as he ate with mechanical efficiency. If she cut him open, she was nearly convinced she'd find gears instead of organs. Or perhaps earth and spell work the huread held in legends.

Her imagination ran away from her. She conjured images of the odd prince summoning him, pulling, and shaping his form from malleable earth.

"Tani! Are you listening?"

Opening her eyes was like being struck, the world was loud and bright and noisy. She turned instinctively towards the voice, it belonged to a small woman with...

Brown, her eyes were brown. Pools of chocolate set into a simple face that people had told Tani was pretty.

Her head ached.

Tani, are you listening?

"I, I, uh, I need to go," her voice fell...off. Sharp, like she'd spent her whole life singing a different key.

Why? Trying to reach for the answer sent lightning through her skull.

The woman's, her mother's, lips turned downward. Tani nearly sighed before she caught herself. Was that disappointment or worry? They were so close to each other.

Well, whatever it was, she wasn't in the mood. "I'll see you at home?"

The sides of her mother's lips dug further down, disappointment then. "Can't you—"

"No."

"The neighbors will talk," she whispered. Why she cared so much what the neighbors' thought was beyond Tani, but answering as such was a good way to get into a shouting match. So, she waited.

Every beat that passed felt like an eternity.

Like she was a spring moments from snapping.

"Tani, *please*." Her mother shifted, her eyes searched Tani's face for an uncomfortable amount of time. "Just this once?"

The answer to that question was never yes. Tani's fingers drummed against her thigh. Waiting worked most days.

All she had to do was keep quiet. No questions, no fights. No fuss. Simple.

She stifled the urge to scream.

Her mother sighed. "Be home before nightfall."

Tani's heart leapt. She forced thoughts into words that landed like lead on her tongue. "Thank you, Mama." She pressed her lips to her mother's cheek and hurried off before she changed her mind.

Tani stuck to the edge of the market, ignoring the vendor's grating calls about fruit, and meats, and their gods awful colored scarves. The plaza was filled with people selling goods but never anything interesting. She'd always wanted to go to the capital where the news was sung while drumbeats rattled the air, and the markets were filled with goods from far off Erbos and Qasha.

Not the scarves, clothes, dolls, pots, and pans they were perpetually trading with the neighboring villages.

She kept her eyes on the ground, tracing the wagon tracks dug deep into the soil of the plaza.

Sometimes she liked to imagine they'd come from the capital, that someone had brought news of her father and the other warriors. But the vendors came from the south, not the north, which meant any news would have come from the Copros and Repren if she were lucky.

And, unfortunately, Reprenian politics had very little to do with her father these days.

Her legs carried her faster as she neared the forest's edge. The old warnings whispered in her ears: *Don't stray too far. Always stay within sight of the houses. Never go in alone.*

She heeded precisely none of them as she plunged between the trees and kept running. She tripped over roots and crashed through the undergrowth until the sounds of the market disappeared behind her.

Her chest heaved as she took stock of her surroundings. They were never quite right this far in. The sun that sent dappled light through the branches was a bit too high, the flowers that blossomed were meant for mid-summer, not late-spring, and the rabbits were always fat, even in the dead of winter.

But it was quiet. She tucked herself against a tree trunk, setting her head on her knees until the world decided that being so bright and loud and *awful* wasn't necessary.

She'd *told* her mother today just wasn't any good. She didn't even know why, but she'd been feeling off since she'd been forced to spend time with some of the village girls the day before. Talking with them was like trying to entertain ten of her mother at once.

She'd woken up feeling sluggish and had wanted nothing more than to disappear between her covers. But Mama had insisted. Tani shut her eyes, waiting for the pounding of her heart to slow and that stressed feeling to settle back to where it belonged.

When she felt more in control she groaned, shaking out her legs and unfurling before making her way to her feet. The forest was odd, and most of, well, Chousal, had come to the conclusion that it was haunted of sorts. Either that or that it was the realm of the gods. Really, it was an odd mixture of both, horror stories and gods wrapped and twined in one pristine, illogical package.

But to Tani, it had only felt the way home was supposed to.

"Good afternoon," she said, aloud. The forest didn't answer back, it never did. At least, not with words, but on the days she talked to it she'd find berries. She liked to imagine it wasn't a coincidence, but the forest answering her back.

"I went to the market today," she continued. "I'm hoping next week Papa comes home. Mama never listens."

She squinted, trying to determine the direction of the not-sun and put her back to it. "It's like she doesn't care what I have to say...no...it's more like we're supposed to be singing and we both have the same tune, but our lyrics never match. She's singing about oceans and I'm...not."

The forest still didn't answer.

Tani liked that about it. She also liked that it had its own set of rules completely different from everywhere else, it maybe even had its own *sun*.

It was completely possible that it *was* magical, not the way her Papa was, but the way things were in the old legends. The ones that mentioned the elder gods that nobody was meant to talk about anymore, that her father sometimes whispered about on quiet nights.

She grinned as she came upon the first bush filled with blackberries. She plucked one and popped it into her mouth. Perfectly sweet.

Don't cast.

The world shook violently. Ground and sky smeared together. The rules—

Issi's eyes flew open. A gasp sent her choking and sputtering as something clogged her mouth.

Her heart raced as she tried to take in her surroundings, but all she came up with was green, and more green. Her mind was hopelessly muddled.

Where was this? A wood or—

"I told you not to cast," Thanae's voice cut through the air.

She managed to sit up, sending bits of greenery cascading into her lap. She spat and a small oblong leaf deposited itself into her palm.

"Why?" the guard's annoyance forced the word to peak.

She cowered and hated herself for it. She'd set the hammock crinkling. It'd filled with leaves. Vines coiled around her legs and filled the spaces beside her body, before spilling over the fabric's edge and onto the floor. She willed them away.

Nothing happened.

"Why?" she repeated, softly. She pressed against the leaves; their thin bodies gave beneath her fingers.

They didn't disappear.

"Pet," Thanae snapped, "What were you doing?"

She frowned, trying to pull her thoughts together. "I was in a market, a forest, and...," she trailed off. Her head ached. It was almost as bad as the time her master had rammed it against a table.

The guard bared his teeth. "*In Qashan.*"

"Qashan," she echoed, distracted. She'd been so *sure* of where she'd been. "Where did you find the leaves?"

"You *cast* them," he spat.

She tore a leaf with her fingers. "That's not possible."

"*In Qashan.*"

"Maybe if your people weren't so closed off, you'd be able to understand me," she groused.

The guard straightened. Annoyance sat clear on his face. "*That* was Qashan."

"I know." Gods it was hard to think. "What you said, that isn't, that doesn't make any sense. I can't *cast* leaves."

"And the vines?"

"I don't," she muttered, her words strung together. "It's uh, I don't, I don't know. I can't make something from nothing. It's not how casting works."

"*You made an orb of light,*" he hissed.

"That's not *nothing*, it's the same with your enchantment, it steals heat. Besides that's *light* not..." Her fingers ran over the vines. "It's not matter. I don't—"

The leaves were real.

"Gods, my head." She pressed her forehead against her knees.

"Gods?"

"You have a thousand reasons to want me dead, what's one more? Unless this is the breaking point, in which case my answer is, 'no, the gods? I haven't heard about them since my violin instructor. I said, 'kings.'"

A snicker slipped from him. It seemed to startle him as much as it did her. He pressed himself against the far wall, like he suspected she'd drawn it from him through some nonsensical witchcraft.

"Are you going to kill me now?"

He hesitated before giving a minute shake of his head. "The prince wants you alive."

She wasn't sure what she'd wanted to hear, but that hadn't been it. "That's all it takes? I get to live so long as someone else wants it?" Maybe the mark crawling up her face was an act of defiance. It wasn't her decision to die, but it sure in Naya's hells hadn't been someone else's.

The guard breathed, "I was told to keep you alive."

"Then *act* like it."

Thanae deflated, like the argument wasn't something he had the energy to pursue. "What are we going to do about that?" He nodded towards the vines.

Issi frowned. "I...I don't know. I don't even know what they are."

"How do you not know what you cast?"

"I *didn't* cast them," she reiterated.

"I know what I saw."

Issi bit her lip and winced as the scab pulled. As impossible as the guard's story was, the vines had to have come from somewhere. And regardless of whether she had performed some stupidly impossible task, *in her sleep*, the vines were a problem.

She sighed and started working at her legs. The greenery had climbed to her knees, wrapping around her skirts and stockings.

She gave up after two ticks.

A cluster of buds sat in the palm of her hand. When they bloomed, they'd be delicate, white blossoms.

If they just tossed vines into the river, she wasn't sure the stupid things wouldn't take. What if it caused some sort of agricultural disaster?

Burning them was hardly an option either, at least, not in the room. Maybe the cook could manage something better, but she wasn't sure that setting them on fire wouldn't kill them all in a less fun way than the one Thanae offered.

Something brushed against her shoulder. Issi tensed, stilling at the sight of the knife by her head.

The guard was speaking. She had to listen. She shifted her gaze over to him and forced her breathing to slow, but she couldn't hear much of anything.

Was it an explanation? An apology?

He waved the knife in front of her face. The hilt, the hilt of it was towards her. People didn't stab with the hilt. If he meant to strike her with it, he was going about it all wrong.

The knife pulled away.

It was a pretty thing, simple in design, with a rune at the back that would, if he so desired, poison the blade. A nasty piece of work made by the Grand Mage a few years back.

He went for her legs. *Move.* She watched him as her heart thrashed about uselessly. The blade was going to reach her skin. What would he take away this time?

Her breast filled with denials that she caged behind her teeth. Pleading never helped, he never cared.

The blade cut through the first of the vines.

Then another.

The guard pulled a swath of leaves away and dumped them on floor. She waited as he worked, her body refusing to move, her thoughts cycling uselessly.

He said he wouldn't hurt her.

The knife was so close to her skin.

Beats passed and another vine was sent to the floor. When he nicked her, she didn't move, didn't breathe. He didn't even notice until the blood seeped through her stockings.

"What?" He pulled his hand away, the look he gave her was so full of concern she almost thought it was fake. "Why didn't you say anything?"

Issi opened her mouth. How was she to answer that? Her thoughts were a mess, he was too close, and the knife...

"I'm sorry."

His face shifted, the scar pulling as the right side insisted on confusion. "Shouldn't I be the one saying that?"

She shook her head, ignoring the ache screaming between her temples. "No, it's...uhm...it didn't hurting...*hurt* that much and I shouldn't have...you shouldn't feel...it's fine...the vines and—"

His expression scrunched like she was speaking nonsense.

This was Qashan, right?

It tasted like Qashan. Maybe she wasn't being clear. "I'm...uhm...I'm used..." The prince's concern flashed through her mind. "I...how am I supposed to react?"

"To being cut?"

To a lot of things. "Yes."

He paused and pulled the rest of the vines from her. The fabric of her skirts fell from the bundles they'd been bound in. The greenery took up a sizeable portion of their too small room.

"You have to change if you're going topside," he instructed. "Bloody clothes will bring attention."

Chapter 17

Issi stared at the sky trying futilely to coax the grey-blue into something more vibrant. The thrum of magic was so far beneath the land that trying to reach for it was like trying to dig to the earth's center with a spoon. Even the way the sun reflected off the water had become dull and foggy, even without the help of her veil.

She grasped at the tail ends of emotions, the fear when Thanae had woken her two days ago, the wonder that had struck her as they made their way down the river, the quiet joy that came from eating with someone, even if it *was* the ever-stolid huread.

But it was hard.

And it only became more difficult the nearer they grew to Egrea, the land of engines and metal and machines.

To her family.

She pressed her hand to her chest. Her heart gave a few tepid thrums, before settling back into a dirge-like rhythm.

Her nose twitched. Oranges and greenery. She searched for it before realizing what she was looking *for*. Castings, enchantments, *magic*. The world snapped into focus, or it tried to. The sky managed to drag itself to something further from grey.

"Time to go." The Grand Mage pointed over his shoulder. A wisp of dismay snaked through her.

"Five ticks," she began.

Her master's brow furrowed. "We already docked."

Issi blinked. He was right, the nonsensical clanging that'd been banging itself against her ears was the noise of a crowd. She looked down to find the docks sprawling beneath them.

Unlike in Kothen, there were no buildings in the immediate area. Instead, the Egreans had decided on a large open platform. Vendors were busy trying to solicit what she guessed might be a lunch crowd. Where there was space, she spied children playing with a small brown ball.

The sailors worked on loading the ship's cargo onto a small, almost trainlike, contraption upon a set of tracks. Something similar trundled along a paved road. Beside her the guard shifted uncomfortably.

"Come on," he ordered.

Issi followed him to the ramp that sat in the ship's center.

Even with so many people, the air was almost completely devoid of magic. Issi pressed herself to Thanae's side. He tensed, but she'd rather die than forfeit the only dregs of magic within three days' travelling distance.

Their bags had already been loaded into what seemed to be a small horseless carriage that smelled of smoke and charcoal. The driver greeted her master with a wide grin and broken Qashan.

"Hello, I being Lus, where taking you today?"

Thanae frowned. Beneath her veil Issi rolled her eyes.

"We need to go to Eizat's abode," she began, in Egrean.

The driver was already nodding. "Ah, the orchard near the island's center?"

"That's the one."

His smile grew. "Your friend looks very Qashan."

"He is."

"Do you mind if I increase the price?"

Issi smirked. "What would I care?"

"In *Qashan*," her master's voice boomed. Issi straightened abruptly and clasped her hands together to still them.

"Sorry, sorry," the driver began with theatric sincerity. He opened the door for them, "she telling me where going."

Thanae grumbled.

She dared to glance at her master's face. A tendril of discomfort chilled her, the best it could manage. It was the same expression he'd worn at the King's dinner all those days ago, the same he'd worn when he'd been lucid those final moments on the roof.

The Grand Mage was not meant to look afraid.

Thanae stepped up into the carriage's body. The driver had to help Issi reach the first step. She hesitated in the doorway. The entire structure purred and rumbled like some giant beast. It was hard not to imagine herself walking willingly into a gaping maw.

The interior was smaller than she was used to, sitting beside Thanae meant nearly pressing herself against him. As the driver shut the door, she made as much space as she could manage.

The carriage swayed as the driver clambered onto his perch. Enyemno's binding and a small metal version of Hoten's many petalled flower bounced against the glass that served to separate them from the small, hot, metal box the man was tending.

She stared at them uncomprehendingly, her eyes tracing the shapes.

"The driver's married," she murmured. The binding was decorative. Embroidery that'd been dirtied by soot. Beneath the grime, it'd been covered in neat little white petalled flowers that—

Issi leaned forward and banged on the window, the driver started.

He slid the glass to the side.

"Yes?"

"I, uhm, that is—" Gods, she'd lost the word. How could she speak three languages and be bad at all of them? "The, the string, rope, no, whatever, Enyemno's thingy. What flowers are those?"

"On the binding?"

That was the word. "The *binding*, yes. What flowers are on the binding?"

"Moonbriar blossoms?" Confusion made the skin around his eyes crinkle.

"Are you sure?" Issi pressed.

"Miss, I mean, yes, of course, it's tradition. Are you...okay?"

The question disrupted her thoughts. Was she alright? Gods, she hadn't the time to unpack that particular issue.

She was taking too long to respond.

"I'm fine," she answered, curtly. She settled back in her seat. The driver looked at her a moment longer before he shut the window and started shoveling coal into the box.

The Grand Mage glared at her, but Issi paid him little mind. She flipped her veil to get a better look at the binding as the carriage began to move forward.

"What was that about?" Gadna grumbled, as they made their way through the plaza. People split around the carriage like water. Issi pressed her ear to the glass.

The longer she was trapped with the guard, and his enchantment, the more real everything seemed to feel. After two days of fading colors and unintelligible noise, comprehensible conversation was music.

And it was *Egrean.*

She hadn't realized how much she'd missed hearing it. The tongue rose and fell in beautiful waves.

"What was that about?" her master's voice shook the carriage. Her blood turned to ice.

"I...uhm, do you see the cloth over there?"

Her master's eyes skipped towards the window and back. "The rag?"

"No, it's not a—." Her leg bounced her irritation against the floor. "It's a binding, for marriages. You wrap it around the pair's arms as they make their vows, but none of that matters because I saw the flowers."

The guard tilted his head and squinted, she was starting to suspect that whatever had given him that scar had either blinded him or partially blinded him on the left side.

"What about them?"

"The vines, the vines you think I made," the vines she saw in her waking dreams, "the ones climbing up the side of my face? Those are the flowers they make."

"So?"

"So?" she exclaimed and bit her lip, the still tender skin protested. She started again, quieter, "they're flowers from a legend and they're appearing on my *skin.*"

"And what does that *mean?*"

Issi opened her mouth to respond. What *did* it mean?

She mulled it over. "I don't know, I don't even know which tale they're from."

"Heretics," he muttered.

"You don't think that it's at least a little interesting that a disease ravaging your country leaves a mark that looks a lot like the symbol of a goddess, *after* you destroy the religious capital of the continent?"

"It's been twenty years." Thanae waved his hand dismissively. "If your so-called gods were going to do something, they'd have done it."

Issi refrained from pointing out that the disease had started spreading around that time, but the reports had been scattered and had gone largely ignored. That was around the time the war with Repren had started in earnest.

At least, according to what she'd gathered and what her mother had told her.

The beastless carriage left the market behind and began to trundle down neat dirt roads as the buildings grew to three and four stories tall. Many held giant walls of glass and ornate iron work that played with patches of fabric that kept Issi from looking inside.

They passed other carriages all moving slowly, like floating islands, through the waning crowds. In the town's small center sat a statue of Naya with her hands dug deep into the earth. Delicate metal herbs sprouted between her palms.

Issi shifted, unable to look away until it was just a patch in the distance.

Seeing religion expressed so freely was utterly terrifying. She'd seen people die for less, the cheers she'd heard as their legs started twitching had etched themselves into her memory.

Thanae seemed just as uncomfortable as she felt, his fingers drummed against the Grand Mage's robes and a frown tugged at the right side of his face.

He only relaxed when they'd passed the outskirts, when tall grasses reached tendrils to the windows and obscured their view. Issi tried to recall what she remembered about moonbriar, but eight years was a long time. Most of the tales her mother had spun had faded from memory. It wasn't like it'd been safe to whisper such things out loud.

After a bell, he spoke, "How long until we get there?"

Issi shook her head. "I've only made this trip once, and—" the Grand Mage had cast for her, and the world had come to life in a way it'd never done before. She had no idea, she'd been enamored the entire time. "It was different, everything was different."

Every tick that passed meant she was getting closer to her family, to her siblings and—

It wasn't good to think about things she couldn't change.

Worry circled, digging between her thoughts of legends and gods, and home.

Home was a funny word.

"Thanae—" She felt him startle beside her. "Oh, uhm, sorry, I didn't... you don't want to talk to me, do you?"

She stilled under her master's gaze; her heart leapt uncomfortably. Whispers of fear continued to feel through her mind.

"Have you ever done anything bad?" It was a stupid question. *Bad* wasn't the word for what she'd done.

"Like kill the man who gave me a life? Or continue as a heretic in a cleansed country?"

"Ruined someone who loved you," the rest of the words died in her throat.

Thanae studied her, she tried not to quail. "Gadna loved you."

The Grand Mage's voice had wrapped around the words with anger and sadness it'd no right to hold. Gods above, if it didn't sound like him.

Longing struck her.

Why did she *miss* him?

"Thanae, you're piece of shit."

The rattling of the carriage and sound of the engine filled the silence until they reached Eizat's estate.

Chapter 18

Lord Eizat's estate sprawled at the top of a hill, surrounded by nothing but neatly trimmed grasses and perfectly tended trees.

Issi's pulse bounded between her ears.

This had been a mistake.

Her fingers knotted together in her lap until they lost feeling. She was going to throw up.

Thanae shifted. "Del, is there anything I need to know?"

"Uhm," she worked to control her breathing as panic sent her thoughts scattering, "I'm sorry, what was the question?"

"Is there anything about this...that I should be aware of?"

Her laughter startled them both. "He's only met master once, I don't remember how it went, but I doubt he remembers much either."

"Anything else?"

She shook her head. "Just go through the steps, sign the papers, purchase my family."

The guard sighed, "Sounds easy enough."

Issi managed a weak nod as the carriage approached the front door. Eizat was already waiting for them.

His hair had been neatly braided and styled to frame his face. The driver stepped down from his perch and opened the door for her master, no, not her master, Thanae.

Focus.

Issi tugged her veil down, watching mutely as the driver charged Thanae triple what the trip was worth. If she hadn't been so gripped by fear, maybe she'd have gotten some enjoyment out of it.

"Come on," the Grand Mage's voice beckoned her forward.

She just had to do as she'd always done. She nearly tripped on her way down, the driver caught her before she made a complete fool of herself. It took all her strength not to leap away.

"Thank you," her voice warbled.

She saw the question in his eyes and answered before he had the chance to ask it. "I'm fine. I just, I don't do well in wagons." Her smile was brittle, but through the veil perhaps it'd be passable, even at this distance.

His expression informed her that it wasn't.

Breathe.

She was Issi, the Pet of the Grand Mage. The thought didn't sit well, despite its familiarity. She wasn't a Pet anymore.

She was Nydelissi Anders, a girl who had once dreamt of becoming a mage, the girl who'd once thought her leaving was worth the damage she'd caused. Del, the girl who, despite everything, had yet to die.

She wrapped the name around her as if it were a shield as she stepped behind the illusion of the Grand Mage.

Thanae seemed more at ease now that he was to be guided by someone who spoke a comfortable amount of Qashan. Lord Eizat, for his part, seemed just short of bouncing with joy. His hands painted wide arcs through the air as he spoke.

"—yes, we've been very excited to have you over, I apologize, my wife won't be back until the evening." Her former master's voice dipped, "I hope that isn't inconvenient, I'm not to close deals without her presence, so the paperwork will have to wait until evening to receive the seal."

"That's not a problem, we were supposed to stay a few nights anyway."

If the guard's bluntness bothered him, Eizat covered his discomfort neatly. "Well, of course, would you like to have dinner? I've just had th—"

"Take me to the…Pets first."

Eizat paused, his eyes ticking as if he could watch the words clatter through the air. His smile strained. "Are you sure? There's, there's been much prepared, and I know that the food from travel can be—"

"Did I ask?"

Eizat's gaze dropped to his feet, his wiry frame curved, crestfallen. It was quick, he started again like a wind-up, his enthusiasm somewhere closer to manic.

"Of course." He clapped, as he turned on his heel. "We'll eat later. There's always time for food and conversation, but you came here on business, didn't you?"

The servant by the door wasn't someone Del remembered. They only offered her a hand to help her climb the smattering of steps before the estate. She refused as politely as she could manage.

Walking through the house was like walking through a dream. Everything was just as she remembered it, the smell of oranges, the curves of the halls, Eizat's voice bouncing off the walls. But nothing had ever seemed this bright, the colors were off, the landmarks too close.

It was…small.

They passed through the dining hall, neatly skirting a table groaning beneath the weight of the decadent meal Eizat had prepared. The room claimed a wall of windows, at the base of which stood a set of doors that Eizat held open for the Grand Mage.

When Del passed through, he regarded her with an open curiosity that set her skin crawling.

"You're the girl, aren't you? Issi?"

Her mouth went dry as she dropped into a hurried curtsy. "Yes, sir."

"Ah, ah," he said as he circled in front of her. "I wonder how you turned out. You were such a pretty child."

His fingers pressed against the base of her veil. She wanted to step back or run. Her body went rigid.

Move.

She couldn't.

He flipped the fabric up. She felt it settle over her head as his eyes explored her face. His expression filled with discontent. "I wish I hadn't had to take such a loss on you. You're beautiful."

Del's stomach threatened to empty on his shoes.

Lord Eizat smiled. "What do you say when you receive a compliment?"

"Th-Thank you, sir."

He patted her cheek. "Good girl." It was only after he stepped away that Del was able to breathe again.

Thanae had already made progress on the pathway that led to the center of the orchard. Eizat hurried after him.

"Grand Mage, I'm afraid I can't sell you the others at the same price you got for this one. I hope you'll understand, without the defect, they hold higher value."

She felt Thanae's attention land on her.

Del wanted to disappear, for the ground to open and swallow her into Naya's hells. Instead, she rolled back her shoulders, hoping to project a confidence she did not feel, and started after them.

Each step wanted to drag, like stones had settled in her feet.

"You'll notice the others are far more cheerful than she was and, of course, they're older. So, we won't have to do what we did last time." He laughed until he met the Grand Mage's glare. "Ah, well, I'm sure you'll find the twins absolutely charming. Asha's the girl, Esca's the boy. They may not be quite as fetching as their sister, but they are by no means unattractive."

He started to dig through his pockets, searching his trousers before dipping into the many hiding spots tucked into his coat. "Honestly if I could have bred another like our Issi, I would have, but the one who fathered her had to be put down ages ago. Aggressive and stubborn, that one, thank the—" He coughed, uncomfortably. "Thank *goodness* none of that passed to the children."

He found his key and slid it into the lock.

Del had never known much about her father. She studied the neat embroidery that wrapped around the heels of her shoes.

He was dead. That was new.

When she finally looked up, she found the Grand Mage's illusion had started to look unwell. A sheen of sweat beaded along his brow.

The door opened easily, the interior was lit by half a dozen candles and the single window that faced eastward.

It smelled of her mother's perfume.

"Esca, Asha," Eizat's voice boomed, he continued in Egrean, "We've a buyer. He's very important, so behave yourselves."

Inside the room sat a large cage with metal bars the width of Issi's thumb and forefinger pressed together.

Eizat dug about for another key, before finding it hung neatly on a hook near the door.

Del's gaze dropped back to her shoes, and the stone floor she found herself on. There was movement within the cage, quiet steps on a carpeted floor.

"Ah, here we are." The key jangled, as the door swung open.

"As you can see, they're both fairly attractive. They'll be turning sixteen in the next moon. Unfortunately, they don't speak Qashan though I don't think that will present too much of a problem," he started in Qashan, before switching to Egrean, "Strip."

Del's nails dug into her palms.

She tried not to listen as Eizat spun out tales of submissive ideals, growing breasts, and instructions on how to keep her siblings well-behaved and compliant.

They were the same instructions he'd given the real Grand Mage so long ago.

It felt like an eternity passed before Eizat clapped his hands. "Alright, well, let's continue our discussion elsewhere. Would you like to discuss prices?" he asked jovially.

"Uh...," the Grand Mage's voice wavered. "...yes, I...would."

Eizat tapped her shoulder, and she nearly flinched. "Issi, get in the cage."

She moved to obey as the Grand Mage's voice rose, "Why does she—"

"Actually—. Sorry." Eizat looked flustered as he continued to usher her inside. "I shouldn't have interrupted you. It's bad for them to hear the price. Especially with the difference that's going to be involved. You don't want her getting jealous, jealousy can just ruin a well-behaved Pet."

Del jumped as the cage slammed shut behind her. The lock turned. She froze just beyond the threshold, unsure of how to proceed.

Thanae and Eizat left, locking the building behind them.

All she could hear was the too quick beating of her heart. This was a mistake. She shouldn't have come. All she'd had to do was purchase them and for that she wasn't needed, they didn't even have to know it was her but still—

"Nydelissi?" the voice came from her right.

She pressed herself against the bars. She didn't know what to say. What was there to say?

"I'm so sorry," she whispered.

"What did she say?" another, deeper voice, sounded from further away.

"She said she was sorry," the first voice answered.

"For what?"

"I don't know. Are you Nydelissi? Why are you sorry?"

Del opened her mouth and stalled. She didn't have the words.

"I...uhm, I left and Eizat," she trailed off. She was meant to be looking at them. She'd come all this way.

She'd brought herself all the way there simply because she'd wanted to see them.

"I missed you."

Del, the girl, had hidden a corpse, crafted an illegal enchantment, made a Promise with a prince, and traveled three days to see them. And still, tilting her head to look at their faces was somehow the hardest part.

"We missed you too," Asha said as she hugged her, and Del went rigid.

"I...I can't." She broke away as a tremor worked through her body. "I can't, please. I'm sorry."

Asha frowned. "No hugs?"

"No...no touching." Del swallowed. "Not unless you warn me and sometimes, not even then."

Her sister looked nothing like she remembered. It seemed obvious that she'd have grown considerably in the last eight years, but she'd been a child when Del had left. They'd all still been running through the orchard. And now her face had narrowed, she had their mother's eyes, two pools of dark brown.

"You look like Mama," Del murmured.

Asha's face lit up. "You think so? What about Esca?"

Del glanced at him, he did look like their mother, though she suspected the height had been something he'd gotten from his father. "Where's mama?"

The rest of the cage was empty. Or as empty as it could manage with gifts and trinkets piled along walls and shoved into corners to free up a path.

"Ataczi took her for a walk," Asha began. "But why are you here? Was that your master? What does he do?"

"Give her time to answer, you're scaring her," Esca interrupted.

"She doesn't get *scared*," Asha giggled. "It's *Nydelissi*, right?"

Del couldn't remember much of who she'd been while she was there. She hadn't *felt* fearless, just lost and far from everything that seemed well within reach of everyone else.

"I'm not used to being so close to," gods this was coming out all wrong. "Uhm, yes, you...it's a little...much, I can't."

Disappointment crossed Asha's face. "Really?"

"He's the Grand Mage of Qasha," Del changed the subject.

Her sister didn't hesitate. "The Grand Mage? Does that mean he can do magic and stuff? Like in the stories? Has it corrupted him?"

"I think that was the war, not the casting," she replied, smirking.

Asha seemed to think it over. She turned from Del and started moving further into the cage, leaving her sister to blink at the sudden space. "I bet that the magic didn't help, though."

"Do *you* know how to cast?" Esca asked. He'd settled on a thin mattress held up by a series of trunks.

Issi's heart skipped. She didn't want to lie. "Uh...a little."

She'd barely gotten the words out of her mouth before Asha was whirling around. "Can we see?"

The invitation was...tempting.

There were many reasons not to, not the least of which being the Egrean clergy had long ago declared casting a sacrilegious binding of the gods' powers.

Del found herself nodding. "Do you have anything in mind?"

Esca shifted, setting the mattress squeaking. "Asha, are you sure this is a good idea?"

"Shut up, there's no harm in looking," her eyes darted, uncertainly, to Del's, "is there?"

Del shook her head, "No, I don't know much of...anything combat based." Well, that wasn't *precisely* true, she'd read entire books of combat focused castings, but she'd been too afraid of getting caught to try them.

"So, what *can* you show us?"

"I'm good with..." *Illusions* escaped her, Del said it once in Qashan, and received a questioning look. "Uh...making things look...different?"

Asha squinted. "Can you show us?"

Del nodded, unable to keep her excitement from sending her fingers fluttering.

Pulling at the magic in Egrea was difficult. It took time for her to draw it to the surface, but Eizat was no saint. He had some sort of enchantment work done *somewhere*, because it was nowhere as deep as it was meant to be. Her vision bloomed as the smell of citrus filled the air. She worked quickly, her hands moving effortlessly in familiar patterns until an orb of light sat in the center of her palms.

It was a small enchantment, but seeing it there, feeling the light of it dust beneath her eyes and along her cheeks, made her smile.

Her sister stepped closer, her hands hovering over Del's until Del nodded. Asha plucked the orb tentatively from her hand.

"It's not hot," she whispered. She waved it around, "Esca! It's not hot!"

Esca tried his best to appear uninterested, but he gravitated towards the small light and soon had stolen it from Asha who fought against his outstretched hand to get it back.

"Is this all it can do?" he asked.

"Uh, no, I can change it." Del set a few dozen limits, trying to remember how she'd done this nightly all those years ago. She heard Asha gasp and watched as the enchantment drifted to the floor.

It'd taken the appearance of a small five petalled flower.

"It's a moonbriar blossom," Asha exclaimed.

"Moonbriar?" Del echoed. She hadn't meant to do that.

"Duh, ouch," Asha squealed, as Esca elbowed her. She took a step back before ramming herself into his side and sending him sprawling. "You're so *greedy*."

"If you'd *waited*—"

Del watched them tousle on the floor, unsure if she was meant to intervene. The fight was short lived. In a few beats Esca sat atop his sister and studied the image. Her siblings were...a lot.

"May you suffer through all of Naya's hells," Asha's muffled voice sounded from beneath him.

A laugh leapt unexpectedly from Del's lips. Her hands flew to cover her mouth as her casting doused.

"See, I told Ataczi I was funny," Asha groused. "Get off me."

Esca freed her before approaching Del. He was taller than she was, and he would one day be handsome, but all she saw now were the makings of a boy who had no business being sold off the way she'd been.

He opened his mouth and shut it, embarrassment heated his face before he asked with great difficulty, "Are you okay, Nydelissi? Nothing bad happened, right?"

If she did everything properly, they'd never have to know about the bad parts.

"It," she began. The door opened and saved her from finishing the lie.

Ataczi drew short, jostling their mother as she nearly tripped. "Nydelissi?" Del's name dripped from her lips like a prayer.

Guilt tightened around Del's throat as her eyes drifted to her mother. The woman she remembered as proud, and strong, who'd dared teach her children Chousalian, and how to read and write in flickering candlelight, regarded her with the same mild disinterest she'd had the day Del was sold to the Grand Mage.

"I'm sorry," Del whispered. And it was nowhere near enough.

Chapter 19

"Nydelissi!"

Ataczi gripped her mother's arm so tightly the skin beneath her nails turned white.

Del swallowed and tried to move. Her sister was staring at her as if she'd come straight from Naya's hells, and their mother...didn't seem to notice anything at all. Her gaze drifted over Del as if she were simply another chair.

"Gods above." Ataczi grabbed for the keys. They shook in her hands sending metallic notes scattering to the floor.

"She just got here," Asha supplied. "Her master was a big, tall type. He's just as handsome as you said."

"Come on, come on, come on." The eldest sister was a flurry of activity, her eyes darting from Asha, to Del, to her mother, to the keys still rattling around in the lock. The tumbler turned and the door opened on silent hinges as she ran fluttering fingers across her face. "Just a tick, I just have to..." She escorted their mother to a plush loveseat. The woman sank into the fabric, the dullness of her presence had her blending into the grey backdrop.

"I'm sorry," Del repeated.

"Didn't you hear me?" Asha griped. "I said, you were right."

"Uh-huh, sure." Ataczi waved the youngest away. She went for a hug and saw Del flinch. Her lips pursed as she settled for lifting an arm and tucking an errant strand behind Del's ear.

Del did her best to stand perfectly still. The touch was soft and brief, but when her sister allowed her palm to follow the curve of her cheek, her breathing hitched.

Her sister's hand sprung back. "You're bleeding."

The scab on her lip had split.

"Asha, bring the gauze," Ataczi breathed. "Less than a tick and you already need mending. Some things don't change, do they?"

A bundle of white fabric landed with a thump at Del's feet. Ataczi rolled her eyes, holding up a hand to stop her younger sister from moving to retrieve it.

"Don't, you'll get blood on the carpet."

A small pool had already formed in the center of Del's palm, a brilliant vibrant red, sinking its fingers into the delicate fabric of her glove.

She moved to take it off and stopped mid-motion. Would her family look at her the same way the prince had? She tried desperately to recall if her mother had been as scarred, but she couldn't remember. In all the lessons, and songs, the dark nights with charcoal clutched in her palm as she carefully traced the letters her mom had scrawled, she'd never thought to look.

She squeaked as Ataczi pressed the gauze to her lip.

"Sorry, did that hurt?"

Del shook her head and pulled the glove up to her elbow.

"You're quieter now," her sister whispered. Her eyes darted to where Del toyed with the fabric. "I want to say that's a good thing, that you grew up proper but...I don't think we're allowed to do that."

"I..." the words escaped her. She felt stripped bare, like her sister could see all of her, even the ugly bits she was trying so desperately to hide. "it was fine."

Skepticism blinked onto Ataczi's face.

"Did you know that Nydelissi can do magic?" Asha shouted.

The eldest froze. "She can do what now?"

"Can you show her?" Asha stared up at Del with bright eyes, ignoring Esca's look of warning.

Del took a step back and studied her shoes as if they might offer to carry her away. They didn't, damn useless things. She felt her sisters' gaze burning the top of her head.

"Is she telling the truth?"

The urge to lie struck her. She could smile and say exactly what Ataczi wanted to hear. *No,* it was just a trinket she'd picked up, some stupid trick she'd found at the markets in front of the palace.

But she had the feeling her sister would see right through it, like her mask didn't exist at all within these walls.

"It was only a small casting," she began, softly.

She knew it was a mistake as soon as she said it. She felt more than saw her sister stiffen. The gauze went away. Del wished she could eat the words, take them back and swallow them so they'd never existed.

Ataczi's voice was cold, "Have you forsaken the gods?"

Asha mouthed an apology, as Del searched for some answer her sister might find satisfactory. "I haven't."

"Then what's this about magic?"

"I—, I," what was there to say? "My master, he w—, he could cast and—"

Ataczi's face fell. "He forced you."

"*No,* he didn't *force* me," something about the idea of him having done so turned her stomach. "He, it was—, *Ataczi, it was magic,*" she couldn't keep the excitement from her voice any more than she could stop the way her lips curled upwards as she breathed the word. "He turned an apple from red to gold, right in front of my eyes. He made flowers with no mass, cleaved a stone in two using only air. And, *and*, the way it painted the world, Ataczi—"

"So, you *chose* to abandon the gods?" her sister's voice dripped with disappointment.

"No, I just let go of the silly superstitions that keep this damn country from moving forward—"

"Don't talk as if you know how the world works."

"What world?" Del snapped. "You mean these four little walls and the shit that's threatening to suffocate you?"

Her sister glanced around as if noticing her surroundings for the first time. "Magic isn't meant for us. Mama was very clear on that."

Del stopped, it felt as if someone else had slid into her limbs and held her still. "I'm sorry."

"I didn't..." Her sister ran a nervous hand through her hair. "Asha, Esca, leave."

Asha darted a nervous glance to Del. "But master wanted us to—"

"Just stay near, practice your dancing, the teacher seemed unimpressed."

"But—"

"We'll stay far from the main house." Esca grabbed Asha by her forearm and dragged her away, as she complained loudly about how the instructor couldn't tell a five-count from a four.

Ataczi watched the door until Asha's endless stream of complaints faded.

"*Nyde,*" her sister breathed. Her fingers nearly grazed Del's cheek. Del jerked away, cursing as she almost tumbled over a jewelry box brimming with necklaces.

Nyde, star.

She tried to cling to the name's meaning, but she couldn't grasp it. The more she tried to focus the quicker it slipped away.

"I can't, you can't touch me," her voice wavered, she paused to control it. "Please."

Ataczi frowned and dropped her hand. Without the twins there her motherly demeanor slipped. The beginning etchings of fear crept onto her face. "*Nyde, what's happened to you?*"

"Nothing." Del backed away, calming only when she'd managed to put an end table between them. "No, I mean. A lot. A lot has happened, and it was awful and scary and sometimes...Ataczi, I don't know. What do you want me to say?"

Her sister's brows lowered. "That you're happy and safe where you are. And that Asha and Esca have a chance at the same."

Del's heart stuttered. "I...I *can't*." Despite everything the prince had Promised her and the band that wrapped around her forearm, she wasn't convinced she could keep them safe and she sure as Naya's hells wasn't convinced she could keep them *happy*.

Ataczi's face crumpled. "Then how bad is it, Nyde? What am I sending them into?"

Del tugged at her glove, making sure her marks stayed hidden. "They will be cared for, and taught to read, and write, to speak Qashan."

"Qashan?" her sister interjected.

"My master is...the Grand Mage of Qasha," she breathed, tasting the bile that snuck beneath the words. "He is well funded."

"Qasha," her sister repeated.

Del paused. "Yes?"

"The same Qasha that razed our homeland to the ground?"

Could a land they'd never been to count as home? A small smile found its way onto Del's lips. "It's ironic, isn't it?"

"Troubling," Ataczi corrected. "Will they be safe?"

"They will be cared for."

Her sister ran her hands over her face. "But they won't be safe."

Del threw up her hands in frustration. "Are they safe here?"

Ataczi shook her head and sat heavily on the nearest bed. "No. But at least we're together...I..." Her sister swallowed, her eyes holding Del's gaze. "I know that's supposed to mean something."

Del's chest tightened. "I'm sorry I left you alone, Ataczi."

"Are you really?"

Silence filled the space between them.

Her sister's laugh came thick and bitter, "You've always said things you don't mean. Even when we were kids, I wasn't ever sure what you were thinking."

"I can tell you what I'm thinking now," Del tried, but the offer felt empty.

Her sister shook her head. "I just...why, Nyde?"

Del sat on the bed nearest her. Only two paces separated her from her sister, but it might as well have been the Great Ocean. "Are you asking why I sacrificed Mama? Or are you asking why I wanted to leave?"

Ataczi's features shifted from disbelief to disgust. "Gods above, just, why? I feel like if I had a reason, this would all make sense and I'd stop feeling like every day I'm being puppeted around like some child's—" She hummed, before starting anew, "I want the steps I take to have meaning, not to echo the snap decision made by a girl nearly a decade ago."

Del studied her gloves. There was no fixing this.

"Ataczi, I just had to leave."

Her sister turned towards her, searching her face, and all Del could do was offer a truth that'd leave nobody satisfied. "That's it. I woke one morning, and I knew that I had to go...I knew that Pets who could read or write were sold cheaper, sometimes early," she spread her palms, "So I told the young lady that I could read the names of the gods."

"But Mama—"

Del shook her head. At the time, it'd felt like a fair sacrifice.

"It was *suffocating*, here. Every breath was like trying to breathe water and...I couldn't do it anymore, I had to leave."

Ataczi studied her for a long moment. "And you'd do it again."

The knowledge sank between them. "I'm sorry."

"For what, Nyde?"

"That you're right," she paused, trying to pin the deeper sadness that moved through her, "And that I don't have a better reason for you."

Her sister fell onto the bed, as Del's eyes skipped back to their mother. She'd been lively once, animated to the point of absurdity, always bouncing a leg or twirling something between her hands.

She'd only fallen still at night, when she thought her children were asleep.

And now she hadn't moved at all.

"Can you tell me a story?" Del asked.

Her sister's brows furrowed, a small frown shaping her button lips as her nose scrunched. "Really, Nyde?"

"I know I'm asking a lot, but I..." Her hand pressed against her cheek, tracing the silver that lay hidden beneath a layer of flesh colored paint. "Please."

The silence that followed was heavy and awkward. Del wasn't sure how to press forward. A thousand lies circled in her head, while the truth loomed large, begging to be breathed to life.

Her sister heaved a weary sigh. "What kind of story?"

"The one about...Enyemno's binds."

Ataczi's eyes flicked to hers. "What?"

"Enyemno's promise bands," Del repeated, uncertainly. Had she gotten the tale wrong?

"*Nyde*, you hated that story. Every time Mama so much as hinted at it, you'd throw a fit."

Del couldn't remember anything of the sort. "Did I?"

"Every. Time," a small laugh twisted the edges of her words. "Gods, you were absolutely incorrigible...why now?"

"Because I can't remember it."

Ataczi frowned. "At all?"

"There are no gods in Qasha," she spoke the words with a practiced lilt, and upon seeing the horror on her sister's face added, "It's from the second Purging. It's not true, but—" She toyed with her hands, searching for comfort where there was none.

At the mention of the Purging, Ataczi's eyes widened. She shifted uncomfortably before breathing, "You know I'm not as good at this as Mama was."

Del studied their mother. "I know."

"Of course, you would," the words held a tint of bitterness. Ataczi closed her eyes.

She didn't speak for a few beats. When she began, her voice had taken a far off, almost dreamy quality.

"A long time ago, at the edge of the great woods, sat a village and in this village, there was a girl and a boy. The girl was as beautiful as the wild chovian vines that spanned the forest floors with a tongue as sharp as their thorns. The boy was every bit her opposite, ugly, but kind. Their mothers were friends, so it seemed only natural that they grew up as close as they did.

"Once their flaws became apparent, the families had dared to hope the children would fix each other, that the girl's roughness would soften and that the boy's softness would roughen. But nothing of the sort ever happened and as time went on, it became clear that each child simply had no desire to change the other.

"Well, no man would marry such a cruel woman and no woman would have held interest in such a weak man. As the children came of age, not a single marriage proposal was made.

"The families began to panic. The boy's sent proposals to every eligible girl in the surrounding villages. The girl's began to send her along the trails, draped in kaftans and golds, hoping to outrun rumors of her mercilessness.

"But the seasons wheeled by, and nothing worked.

"As the winter snows began to pile before their houses, the families grew desperate and at last looked to each other. Beneath the full shine of the sister moons, they struck a deal. Their children would be married on the first true day of spring.

"The children were unhappy with the arrangement, they were friends, nothing more. The boy asked his mother to reconsider, and wilted beneath her glare. 'No one will want a son as weak-willed as you,' she said, 'you should be grateful to marry someone so pretty.'

"When the girl asked her mother, the woman scoffed, 'No one will want a wife as cruel as you, you should be grateful to marry someone so kind.' And the girl wailed and raged, loud and wild as the spring rains, but to no avail.

"After her anger simmered, the girl left the warmth of her home and disappeared into the wood." Ataczi's eyes opened. "Do you remember the Chousalian woods, at least?" She shifted. "Nyde?"

It took Del a moment to respond. The tale her sister had been spinning still wound between her ears, dredging up memories of their mother's voice.

Del found herself fighting tears.

"The wood?" she echoed, softly. She recalled what Tani had said in her dreams but nothing else. "It...it was known for sweeping people away."

Her sister chuckled. "Well, it did that too, but the Chousalian forest is the in-between, a patch of land where both gods and humans can walk."

"I don't remember that," she admitted.

Ataczi paused. Del could feel her sister's attention running along the side of her head.

"Well, the girl walked into the forest, with a bow and arrows. She did not heed the elders' warnings against travelling too deep and ignored the stories of the poor souls lured there to be trapped wandering the trees for eternity. Instead, the girl walked until the snows melted and the trees grew green and lush with the summer sun that hung overhead.

"And she began to hunt.

"By her hand seven fat rabbits were felled, and it was during her hunt that the forest fell in love with her. She was beautiful and deadly, like the predators that travelled within it. Methodical and cold as the winter snows.

"The forest wished to keep her as it did all the things it loved, but the girl looked back, towards its edges, towards her home, and it did not wish to cage what did not want it. So, it hid a piece of itself into her hunting garb, a leaf no bigger than your smallest finger, so that it might watch over her.

"It watched as the girl went home, fascinated as she skinned the rabbits, and cracked their ribs to pluck hearts like ripe berries from their chests. It saw as she gathered them into the smallest of satchels and went to Enyemno's statue and set the bag at its feet.

"The forest heard the girl's prayer, and it felt the goddess's refusal.

"Dismayed, it gathered itself and sent an emissary to the goddess of love, a raven of pure magic, whose black wings held muted rainbows.

"'Please,' the forest begged, 'Answer her prayer.'

"The goddess was surprised, for the forest cared very little for what happened outside its boundaries. She waved the raven away.

"'I am the goddess of love,' she answered. 'This is a marriage of convenience, it has little to do with me.'

"'Please,' the forest begged.

"But the goddess sent the messenger away.

"The next day, the raven appeared with a crown of butterflies and asked again for the goddess's assistance. And once again it was sent away. On the third day, the raven returned with the seed of one of the great forest trees and on the third day the goddess sent it away. For seven days the raven returned, and each day, it was rejected.

"On the eighth day, it dropped a blossom by the goddess's feet, white petaled and so delicate, it looked to be made of moonlight.

"'What is this?' the goddess asked.

"'A moonbriar blossom,' the raven answered. 'It grows only in my heart, beneath the night sky.'

"The goddess sighed. 'You cannot have the girl,' she said, 'she is not of your world. She would die within you.'

"The forest had always known that to be the case and agreed to the goddess's terms.

"'Then I will offer her happiness. All she needs to do is find your heart, pick your flowers, and make a tea. Then everything will be as it should.'

"'And in exchange?' the raven asked.

"'You are not to help them. This is something they must do alone,' the goddess said. 'And I want you to give me moonbriar seeds, I'd like to grow some of my own,'

"The raven agreed, shocked at the forest's good fortune and the next evening laid a bundle with seven delicate seeds by the goddess's feet, one for each of its prior attempts.

"The goddess counted each in turn before heading to the mortal world in the guise of an old woman, stooped and wrinkled with age. She sat in the snows by the forest's edge and trembled and waited. The children passed her with arms full of firewood. The girl walked by without sparing her a glance. The boy who followed stopped, dropping the kindling before hurrying to the woman's side.

"The goddess stared at the wood settling in the snow. She knew the boy's house would run cold, that he'd set to shivering in the evening and night, and that he would blame her for none of it. The girl's house would keep warm and welcoming so her family might stay well. The goddess saw as the families had that the children needed one another.

"She shed her disguise and the boy fell to his knees begging forgiveness for his friend. The girl watched in horror, knowing that she'd been tested and found wanting.

"The goddess plucked a hair from her head and in her hands, it became a ribbon as thick as the children's wrists. 'I have been asked to offer you a way out of the loveless marriage you've been offered, all you must do is find the forest's heart and pluck the briar bare, make the flowers into a tea, once drunk, everything shall be as it should.'

"As she spoke, she placed the ribbon in the boy's hand. She instructed them to stay together, to bind themselves so they would not part and be forced to wander the wood with the other lost souls.

"Then the goddess was gone. Both children went home, and packed for the journey, they met at the forest's edge when the elder moon hung high.

"They wrapped their wrists together with the goddess's ribbon and went to find the heart of the forest. As they searched, winter snow melted, and spring blooms appeared, then the blooms scattered leaving nothing but the lush green of summer behind.

"The children stripped their winter clothes and pressed onwards. Days passed, their food ran low, and the forest did not provide. Despite the green there was no rain, despite the animals, there was no fruit, or mushrooms, or nuts. The children turned to eating leaves.

"They grew thin and tired, wondering if the goddess had tricked them, to watch them suffer and die in the forest's grip. They prayed for food, for rain, for some slow dumb animal to wander too close, but the gods never answered, and they went to bed hungry.

"The forest ached to help, but it kept to its word.

"They wandered until the binding ate away at the skin on their wrists and every morning, they began anew. On the twelfth day, the children found the forest's heart. Beneath the pale light of the elder moon, they spied the moonbriar and plucked it bare to brew their tea.

"They were nervous, after all this time, they were so close to the ending they'd seen for themselves. They poured two cups and drank together with their unbound hands.

"And nothing changed. There was no shift in the moon, no feeling of power, just a sweet-scented tea and the realization that everything they'd done had been for nothing.

"The children despaired. But what else was there to do but go home? The journey was long, and arduous, but the children were always there for each other. When the boy cried, the girl was there to comfort him, and when the girl raged, the boy would calm her. Together, they thought the marriage through.

"What they felt for each other was something cool and comforting. A feeling that allowed them to be themselves and feel accepted in a way that they'd felt nowhere else. They would not change each other, but together, they could become something greater than what they were apart.

"On the day they came across their winter coats, the girl planted her first kiss on the boy's lips, soft as a spring shower.

"And the binding holding them together unraveled. Enyemno having saved them from the loveless marriage they'd so loathed. Away from the forest's heart they began to find food. Fruits and nuts and animals. They regained their strength as they slowed on those last few days.

"They returned to their village surprised to find it was the first true day of spring.

Her sister stopped. Her gaze fixed far away, as if a tale of love was too much for her to handle. Del felt her lip curl.

"I see why I didn't like it," she murmured.

Ataczi blinked, her lips quirking before she laughed, "Of course you didn't, our little Nyde never cared for love."

"It's not that I didn't care—"

Her sister shook her head. "It's exactly that you don't care. You may have forgotten who you were, but I remember everything."

Chapter 20

Del paced the room. She felt her sister's eyes tracking her as she pivoted from corner to corner.

"Nyde, you're going to wear a hole in the carpet," she teased.

Del ignored her. Speaking with Ataczi about the story and what she'd wanted from it had little meaning if all her sister was going to do was lecture her on the wrongs she'd done. Del was well aware, and she simply didn't have it in her to care.

When the sun began to sink beyond the orchard's hills, dyeing the skies oranges that matched the orbs hiding in the branches of the trees, Esca and Asha returned.

Asha flashed Del an apologetic smile.

Neither of the twins asked what they might have talked about while they'd been away.

The servants knocked on the door soon after, and Del's family crammed around a too small table covered in what was obviously left over from one of the house meals. Del picked at her plate as her siblings chatted about things she couldn't hope to follow. Her eyes darted between the door and her mother, who ate whatever was placed in front of her with the same dull, quiet efficiency.

The door never opened, and a spark never appeared in her mother's eyes.

They stayed at the table until the stars had begun to trail overhead. Del resigned herself to the fact that she'd be sleeping there.

Her siblings were doing everything in their power to make her feel welcome, but there was a wall between them, and she couldn't for the life of her find a way around it.

She went through the motions.

Smile.

Don't flinch.

Laugh.

The glove is slipping.

They're staring.

Don't flinch.

Don't flinch.

Don't flinch.

Don't flinch.

She'd be hard pressed to recall what was being said. She was vaguely aware she was skirting questions about the Grand Mage, the rest of the conversation went between her ears and settled heavy in her stomach. Del sent a small prayer to Ipheoth when it became clear that everyone's excitement was finally flagging.

"Well, it's time for bed," Ataczi announced, as she helped their mother don a night slip. She walked her to the furthest cot and guided her beneath the covers.

The evening routine was an odd reflection of what Del remembered from her childhood.

Everyone's hair was combed and bound before being tucked neatly beneath silk scarves.

Ataczi sent her younger siblings to bed with practiced efficiency before approaching Del, comb in hand. "Would you like some help?"

Del shook her head. "I don't even have anything to sleep in, what's the point?"

Her sister frowned and marched over to a wardrobe. "We represent our masters, an unkempt Pet is a stain on their reputation."

She pulled a plain looking frock from its depths and threw it to her sister. Del leapt forward, falling short as the fabric fluttered neatly to the floor.

"Sorry." Ataczi shrugged in a way that indicated that she wasn't at all.

The dress bunched in Del's hand. "Uhm…"

"Go ahead."

"Could you…turn around?"

"Nyde, I'm not looking, besides, we've bathed together," she muttered, as she changed into her own nightgown.

"We were children."

Her sister glared at her. "You're still a child."

Del started towards the door. "I'll change outside."

"*Nyde*, you're being ridicu—"

"I'm not," she snapped. The stress of the dinner's conversation had soured her mood. "Ataczi, I *asked*, and I understand that you want things to be like they were, but they're not and I *can't* pretend like you do. So, please, let me change somewhere you can't see me."

A low growl came from Ataczi's throat as she spun dramatically. Del waited, and when it was clear she'd no plans on turning around, she stripped.

A small gasp sounded from Esca, who turned quickly in his bed. Shame heated her cheeks. Her scars had never felt so burdensome as they did when she was with other people.

Or had it been the silver that fell down her torso that'd gotten his attention?

She pulled the dress on quickly, fiddling with the close neckline. She'd nearly forgotten there were clothes that didn't plunge to expose her. It was uncomfortable, like a second collar, and the fabric was rougher than what she'd grown accustomed to.

The urge to scratch at it was something she stifled, as if doing so would somehow cement how *wrong* she was for being there. She longed for Thanae of all things, his cold rejection a thousand times more welcome than this soft refusal.

And there was the matter of the herbs.

"I'm done," she announced.

Her sister turned back towards her, brow furrowing. "The gloves?"

Del's eyes went to the floor. "I like them."

"They're covered in blood."

Del made no move to remove them. Ataczi sighed setting the comb down and pulling a brush from atop a pile of boxes. "Hair."

"I can do it myself."

Her sister sat heavily on the remaining bed and tapped her knee. "I've been wanting to do this for eight years. Humor me."

Del hesitated before crossing the room. She settled in the space her sister had left her on the floor. It was too close. She took a deep breath and forced her shoulders down.

Ataczi ran fingers through Del's hair and clicked her tongue. "What have they done?"

Del's heart thrummed, her nails dug into her thighs. "They don't like our hair in Qasha, they like it better this way."

"Dead?"

"I don't know, the Grand Mage liked it," she breathed. The memory of him flickered behind her eyes. She felt her sister straighten behind her.

"What kind of man is he?"

"...I don't know."

"Of course, you *know*. You've been with him for eight years."

Del closed her eyes. "Then maybe I just don't want to. He wa—, is a man Ataczi, he loves eating, and fucking, and...magic, I don't know what else there is to tell you."

"Is he kind?"

"...I don't want to answer that."

Ataczi started to braid her hair. "It's like trying to bind silk."

"I miss the way it was. Sometimes, I'll reach up and expect to touch something soft," hope fluttered in her chest, "Maybe, one day, I'll be able to cut it off and let it grow back the way it used to be." She wouldn't live long enough to do so, but the thought still warmed her.

"Masters don't change so easily, Del."

"I know, but don't you ever get tired of living for somebody else?" She tried to turn to see her sister's reaction, and Ataczi tutted, keeping her still. "I dress as he likes, speak as he likes, laugh as he likes, hold him as he likes, and none of it has brought me any closer to being happy or loved than I was when I started."

"That's how some things are."

"But if you *could* live for yourself, what would you want?"

Her sister finished the braid and bound the bottom with a ribbon. "That won't happen, Nyde."

"I'd want to be a mage," she whispered. Her sister's discomfort was palpable, "I'm very good at it. One of the best in the country."

"And you know that how?" Ataczi said, with a bitterness that took Del by surprise.

"I watched the best. I think I could cast circles around all of them. And still, nobody knows my name, *Issi the*

Grand Mage's Pet." Disgust curled her lips. "What a pretty little thing."

"You *are* beautiful, Nyde," her sister muttered.

"I know what I am, but I don't want that to be all I'm remembered for." She tilted her head forward as her sister slipped a scarf over her hair. "I didn't get to choose how I look, but I *chose* to cast, I *chose* to study, and I'm *good* Ataczi, I've published papers and—"

"It makes me sad hearing how you've thrown the gods away," her sister responded. She knotted the scarf in the front, leaving Del's hair housed safely beneath it.

"I didn't—"

"You speak of magic and your voice brightens, your face lights up...it's zealotry."

"Zealotry?" She turned to face her sister. "It's *passion.*"

"People who are truly lost are unable to tell the difference. Get up, it's my turn."

Del did as she was told, switching places with her sister. She couldn't remember how she'd done her hair before the thick, strong-smelling pastes had driven the life from it. Her fingers were instantly lost in the mass of curls.

"So, what would you like to do, Ataczi?"

Her sister sighed, her shoulders curling inwards. It made her look her age and so very small, "I don't know."

Del ran a wide toothed comb through her hair and started her first attempt of wrangling it. "Well, what do you like to do?"

"Do you think I have time for hobbies, Nyde? I have people to care for, Asha, Esca, Mama, *and* master. When I have time, I just *sleep.*"

Guilt twisted Del's stomach. If she'd stayed, the burden might have been shared. "...what do you think you'd like to do if you had the time?" she whispered.

Ataczi's spine went rigid. "What's the point of these questions? Nothing will come of them."

"Because we're not just meant to serve others," Del's voice rang too loud, she huffed, "I'm sorry, it's just...I mean, I can't believe that's all there is."

Her sister snorted. "Then you'll be disappointed."

Del's fingers knotted in vines, she paused, trying to think past the panic starting in her chest. "Ah, yes, I..."

She couldn't blink them away.

"Ataczi, are there...vines by your right hand?"

Her sister's hand curled through the stem. She glanced back at Del. "What are you talking about?"

Del stood abruptly. "Nothing, I...my master needs to..." Gods she couldn't hear above her pulse, she forced a breath. "He needs me."

"Nyde, you didn't even finish my hair."

"What? I need to, uhm, I'm sorry, Ataczi." She made a beeline for the door and thread her hand between the bars.

Her sister scrambled to her feet. "Where are you even trying to go?"

The keys jangled as Del's fingers brushed against them. "The guestroom."

"You don't know which one he's in."

"There's only one room where Eizat would put the Grand Mage," she snapped.

Del gasped as a shoulder rammed into the center of her back. The keys fell to the floor.

She sank to her knees trying to convince her heart to slow. "I'm," she began before recalling Thanae's confusion and cut her apology short. She wanted nothing more than to curl into a ball and let the world slip away.

Del convinced herself to stay, to feel the carpet beneath her, and the pain in her spine. "Gods Ataczi…that hurt."

"You can't leave, you'll get us in trouble."

"Just say my master came to pick me up in the middle of the night, I'm not Eizat's Pet, anymore," she wheezed. Her eyes burned, she wasn't going to cry, not here. "Did you really have to—"

"Nyde, what if he doesn't want you, you only go where your master—"

"He *always* wanted me, Ataczi." She unfolded herself and reached through the bars. "That's not a problem."

"He would send one of the servants-"

Del rolled her eyes as her fingers brushed against the ring. "Not everything is the same as it is here. I have to leave, because—" She closed her eyes as more vines started crawling along the bars of the cage.

Gods above, she wasn't going to be able to keep ignoring them. What was she meant to do if the vines wrapped around her come morning? It was bad enough her sister thought she'd turned away the gods. The last thing Del needed was Ataczi spinning her sickness into something to bolster her argument.

"Nyde, are you listening?"

"Ah." the keyring fell into her palm.

"*Nyde.*"

"Ataczi, why would I bother listening to you, when you don't listen to me? I said I had to go." She stood and slid the keys in the lock. "And you won't get in trouble, I swear on Ipheoth's roots."

Her sister's lips thinned as the door swung open, but she made no move to stop her.

"I'll see you tomorrow," Del tried, but no warmth entered her sister's eyes. She swallowed another apology as she returned the keys to their hook. She hurried through the second door and set across the orchard.

Memories pressed against her, good and bad, of nights spent running between the trees. Of the screams of her mother, of lessons and rapped knuckles and waltzing clumsily with her sister beneath the stars.

She tried to banish them by focusing on picking an orange from a low branch. Her eyes fixed on the fruit's surface.

Damned things were the reason any of this had started.

Del clutched the fruit as she circled the estate. Eizat's home was larger than her master's wing, but there was nothing special about it, no hidden gardens or climbing arches. She meandered past high windows and embroidered curtains. The kitchens had long gone dark. She stopped beneath the window she'd often peeked in as a child, hoping to catch sight of guests or imagine what it might be to have her own room.

She stuck the orange in her mouth, biting down until her teeth pierced the skin, eyeing the tree that reached to the second story. She'd grown considerably since she'd left, and there hadn't precisely been a long list of opportunities to climb trees while in the palace. Her hands hesitated before she gripped the branch. Climbing was familiar, like a song she knew the rhythm of. She only slipped once before she got close enough to the window to knock on it.

Candlelight danced on the other side. Painted flame and shade.

She spat the orange into her palm and took a deep breath. Her sister's worries dragged at her hand as she raised it and forced herself to rap twice on the glass.

A muffled curse sounded from inside, a large shadow limned by wavering light cast itself upon the curtains before the windows flew open.

Thanae blinked in the moonlight, searching the branches before finding her nestled in the leaves. He frowned, moving his hand away from his hip. "How'd you get up here?"

Del's nose crinkled. "...I climbed?"

He stalled, his eyes searching her face and the branches behind her as if he suspected she'd hidden someone nearby. He nodded shortly to himself before stepping back.

Del threaded herself through the window, her hand pressing through the vines that spilled over the sill. Her shoes were immediately swallowed by a carpet so lush it was almost comical.

The guard didn't move to help her, but he didn't rush to dismiss her either.

He rubbed his eyes. "You have no idea."

"What?"

"Kings..." He spun and ambled back to the bed, falling gracelessly atop the violet covers. "I forgot to get you."

Del frowned, could a guard really forget the thing he was meant to be *guarding*?

He stilled his eyes fixing on a patch of ceiling. "I hate it here."

Alcohol hung heavy in the air, mixing with the lighter scents of honey and oranges. He hadn't struck her as someone who drank to excess, but to be fair there was a lot about him she didn't know. She searched the room until she found her trunk, tucked in the corner closest to the door. She approached it, relieved.

"What's that leaf you're always eating?"

Del flipped the latch and dug through her belongings. "Does drinking make you talkative?"

"Wouldn't know, don't drink."

"Mhmm." Disbelief laced through her, as she grabbed her tea tin.

"The leaves, Del."

Her hands froze on the lid. "What did you call me?"

The guard huffed, "Del. You call yourself, Del."

"*Yes*, but you call me Pet. Or whore, or—"

"I'm calling you Del now." he waved his hand in her direction, as if fanning the concept over. "Or is Issi better?"

"No," the answer leapt from her throat before she'd the chance to stop it. The guard lifted his head so he could see her. Her cheeks warmed. "Del. Del's perfectly fine."

"Good." His head flopped back onto the bed. A moment later a snore ripped through the air.

"Thanae?"

He didn't move. She crept near him to find his jaw had gone slack.

"You're supposed to be guarding me."

The notion seemed to make him snore louder.

Had the prince really thought him the best he could offer? She opened the canister and wished for her kettle. In Egrea, for tea, she'd have to wake a servant and have them start the kitchen fire and gather water from the well.

Just to warm a kettle.

When she'd first gone to Qasha, she couldn't believe how soft the servants' hands were.

She found herself missing bits of the palace and the capital. She'd thought returning to Egrea would feel like home. There were things here, *people* here, that she cared for. But it wasn't what she'd wanted.

She settled on the floor feeling very far from everything that was supposed to matter.

Vines started to crawl up the tin and circle her fingers, the need to follow them warmed her. Del twisted her hand, watching the green cascade down her forearm as fragile white petals wafted onto the carpet.

Even as it killed her, magic was beautiful.

She stuffed a few leaves in her cheek, ignoring the bitterness as she forced her attention to the stars above.

Eight years she'd lived in the capital.

Eight years her nights had been filled with city torches, and light castings that had blocked out most of the stars. There were more than she remembered, she'd completely forgotten the bits of galaxy that hung between them. She watched the skies spelling out what she recalled of the tales her mother had told her so long ago.

She was so bad at it.

The nuances and names escaped her, she couldn't remember why the gods had acted as they had. Ataczi might be able to fill in the blanks, Asha and Esca too, but she didn't want to go back.

She fought through vines and green to find the orange in her hand and set to peeling it. Her mind tugged between memories of the prince and the desire to follow the plants to their source.

The first bite was sweet and tangy, the fruit perfectly ripe. Her eyes lit up as a few Egrean curses dropped from her mouth.

All the money in the kingdom at his disposal, and the prince had never even gotten close.

Chapter 21

"Tani, breathe. You're hurting me."

She nodded, dragging air into her lungs.

"Let go," Rua coaxed. "Or at least loosen your grip. I can't feel my fingers."

Tani glanced at their hands and willed her fingers to relax. As soon as Rua could manage to pull himself free, he did so. They were standing outside the largest building in the village, easily twice the size of the homes that petered out a hundred paces from its doors and thrice as ornate. All the gods' symbols adorned the arched doorway, while each of their prayers wound up the building's 14 pillars.

Tani had successfully avoided setting foot inside it for nearly two years.

And she wanted to keep that streak going.

"Mama said she needed me to bring some papers." She turned on her heel only to be caught at her collar and hauled back. As fat as he was, she suspected Rua was easily the strongest boy in the village.

"Rua, *please*," she begged, as he released her. "I don't want to go, and I can be so much more help if they just let me go on the—"

He cut her off, "Tani, you promised."

She had, but she'd been cornered when it happened. And this entire week, she'd been so sure she'd be able to make it. But this morning, even after she'd prepared herself, so little seemed to be working. It was going to be a disaster. She could *feel* it.

She wanted to go home.

"Tani, breathe."

"I *am breathing*, I just don't want to go inside."

"I'm going with you," he tried. It *was* a soothing thought, that at least she wouldn't screw up or stumble over her words and hurt *Rua's* feelings, even if she did so with nearly everyone else. Or that if she *did,* he wouldn't take it to mean she'd done it intentionally.

Still, she dug her heels into the earth. "I don't want to."

"The elders just need to see you, in and out," he assured her. "We step in, we greet them, that's it."

"The elders hate me Rua," she griped. She'd heard the way Nama Alyah had spoken about her at the market. The woman was out to get her.

"They don't hate you."

"Well, they don't *like* me."

"They don't like me either."

That was also the truth, and there was no guarantee that Rua would be able to squirm his way out of hunting duties in the next half-moon. If her mother caught her again, Tani might have to go alone.

"Can I have your hand back?"

She felt Rua relax, he reached for her. "Not so tightly."

"I'm not a child," she muttered.

"You're stronger than you think," he laughed, quietly. Softly. Everything about Rua was soft from his body to his voice to the way he seemed to float just above the ground.

He had to drag her to the doors. She tried to ignore the whispers that weighed on her.

"Doesn't it bother you?" she muttered.

"What?"

"All the...the *chattering*. It's stupid, they don't even talk to me and they still, somehow, all have opinions on how I do *everything*."

"I ignore it."

"It's not that easy, Rua," she griped.

His foot dragged along the bricks of the plaza. "I never said it was easy, it's just what I do."

The doors of the building loomed before them, ornate carvings spelling Naya's tale. She froze. She'd seen something like them before, another man, an ornate hall. Tani recoiled, pulling from Rua so quickly she managed to drag him a few steps back.

He turned to face her. "What was that?"

She blinked. "I...I don't know."

"Are you okay to go in?"

Tani's heart still pressed against her ribcage. "Ah, I...I need a tick."

Rua nodded and pulled a book from the satchel by his side, maneuvering deftly with his free hand. A few ticks passed before the sensation left her.

Rua had stayed Rua, and the door, when she'd finally managed to bring herself to look at it, was the same as it'd always had been.

"Ready?"

Tani nodded. "I don't know what that was."

Rua shrugged, and they made it the final few paces to the door. Tani opened it, and there were no weird memories, or feelings. Just a quiet wave of apprehension as she held it open for her friend.

The hall was quiet as they walked up the center.

Tani paused before the dais and tried not to wither beneath the attention directed her way.

"It's been too long, Tani," Nama Alyah creaked.

It hadn't been long enough, but Tani nodded her acknowledgment.

"And Rua too," Nama Illis laughed, clapping his hands together. "We'll be seeing you in the next half-moon, won't we?"

Rua stiffened beside her. "Of course."

"And no crying this time?"

"Of course not." His nails dug into Tani's palm, and she squeezed back. "I was a boy the last time that happened."

He still didn't like going on hunts.

Nama Fera let out a hacking cough, cutting the conversation short. "You're almost of age," she croaked, as she reached for a cup. She drained it and straightened. "It's almost time for you to be wed. Do you have anyone in mind?"

Tani paused trying to understand the direction the conversation had taken.

Rua shook his head. "No."

She'd never thought of marrying, it'd never interested her, and her father had promised to take her to the capital when he came back. She was meant to start training, learn a bit of casting, not become a wife.

She was so caught up in her own thoughts that she hardly heard Rua's answer.

"No?" she echoed in disbelief.

She frowned, thinking of the baker's daughter. His face had gone red beneath the brown of his skin. He gripped her hand tighter as Nama Fera coughed again.

"I see, I see. Your parents have expressed an interest in uniting your families. Do you have any opinions?"

"What?" Tani shouted. That couldn't be right. Her foot tapped against the floor. With great effort she lowered her voice. "Are you asking if I want to *marry*, Rua?"

"Lower your voice," Nama Illis warned.

"I already *did*," Tani snapped. Her foot tapped faster.

"Tani—" Nama Illis's voice was thick with disappointment.

"You have to know that's not going to work, right?" Tani continued.

The sides of Nama Fera's mouth ticked downwards. "Why not?"

"Because I don't *love* him that way. I—, I love him as *family*, not as some sort of, a, a *husband*."

"And you think yourself incapable of learning?" Nama Alyah interjected.

"I don't *want* to," she stressed. That was a mistake, her neighbors who'd already taken seats around the dais set to tittering. Gods, why were they so *loud*?

Nama Alyah leaned forward, her frail body perched against twig arms. "Stop acting like a child."

"You *asked* if I had an opinion, you don't just get to decide that you don't want it when it's not—"

Rua's hand covered her mouth. She panicked and bit down, hard. She glared at him as he pressed his hand more firmly against her. She could *feel* Nama Alyah's disapproval, the whispers of her neighbors were deafening.

Tani needed to leave, run. But Rua held her close. She struck at him, but he simply bore down, absorbing every blow.

This was wrong.

She wasn't meant to be hurting him. A whine built in her throat.

"We have objections," Rua's voice was so soft, there was no way anyone was going to hear him.

"Speak up, boy," Nama Alya's voice was thunder, and Tani's struggles doubled. Rua quailed, his grip on her tightening until it was hard to breathe.

"It's...we've just...we need time to think it over," he finished.

Nama Illis nodded. "This was sudden, though it was the obvious outcome. You handle her well."

It took time for the words to make sense. She wanted to be calm, like Rua. She wanted everyone to stop *staring* at her, to stop that incessant whispering that struck her ears like daggers.

Rua's blood filled her mouth as her jaw refused to unclench. She needed him to let go.

He couldn't.

To have her run out on a meeting with the elders was simply not an option.

The rest of the conversation fell between the notes of her keening. The stares of the council ate at her as she struggled, tears streaming down her face. She wanted to stop.

She just needed everything to *stop*.

"We'll be taking our leave." Rua bowed the best he could with her readying to flail in his arms. He carried her out—

—and shook her roughly. He *knew* not to do that.

But it wasn't Rua hoisting her off the ground.

Del blinked, taking in her surroundings, her breaths coming in short, panicked gasps. *Stars*, there were stars, and the faintest hint of grey at the horizon. Something hard dug into her stomach as the world rocked.

"Thanae," she croaked. The guard stopped short.

"Are you...here?"

She was too close to panic to understand what was happening. Her voice was a whisper, "Let me down, Thanae. Put me down."

He hesitated a fraction of a beat before setting her before him. His hands lingered on her shoulders.

"Let go," she insisted.

The guard shook his head. "Look down."

His words jumbled, tangling before landing nonsensically between her ears. She forced her lungs to cooperate and took a deep breath.

"Let go," she repeated. He frowned and a moment later, Del found herself back in his arms, having narrowly missed toppling onto her face.

Vines had bound her legs together, climbed up her arms and circled her waist. The flowers that bloomed between the leaves glowed softly in the moonlight. Moonbriar was a misnomer.

It wasn't a briar at all, she thought, dazed. It was a vine.

"You left the room," Thanae explained, slowly, as he hoisted her into his arms, "I found you here, the vines are too tight. I have to cut them. That will take time."

Del was too busy trying to get her bearings to respond. Her head ached and she wasn't entirely sure where she was in space. Every nerve seemed to exist solely to make her very, very aware that she was being touched.

The guard, for his part, moved quickly, going through Eizat's house as if he'd lived there his entire life. They passed no servants. Del tried her best to focus on breathing and not the sensation of being carried.

He dropped her on the bed and had the decency to look somewhat apologetic about it when she curled trying to keep the world from swimming. Had there been anything in her stomach, she'd have lost it.

"Do you remember leaving?"

Del squinted. "No, I...no."

"You, what?"

He studied the vines around her arms. She bit her lip, until the ache stopped her. "I don't..."

The guard didn't rush her. He pulled the knife from his belt and started cutting away at her bindings. Once he freed her arms, he ran his hand over her sleeve, searching for tears.

"I don't remember much about the nights anymore." The admission left her feeling vulnerable.

"And the vines?"

"I didn't make them," she answered, tersely.

The guard stilled and nodded, his eyes drifting to her left arm. She'd lost her gloves. Her skin, unmagicked and free of make-up, showed the burns and discoloration, the giant patch of missing skin on her palm. She hid it behind her back, feeling stupid.

The guard frowned. "Is there...a spell, that does that?"

"No."

Thanae turned back to the vines. Del relaxed only when it became apparent that he wasn't going to ask for clarification.

It took several ticks for him to finish. The pile of vines grew on the floor, until they were nearly half her height.

Moonbriar, the not briar.

The flower gifted by a forest that both was and wasn't a forest. The old stories nagged at her, passed down orally from generation to generation, surely something had to get lost.

But they'd remembered the flower.

"We were supposed to stay, for a few days," Del prompted.

Thanae stepped back. "Three."

"What if we go somewhere else, instead?"

"Our prince gave you ten days. You can do what you want with your time."

Del swallowed nervously. "Can you finish the paperwork today?"

The guard's lips pulled in annoyance. "I can, why?"

"I need you to charter a ship?"

"That's what we were supposed to do."

"Not to Kothen," she clarified, "To Chousal."

Chapter 22

Thanae's face was a mask of discontent, or, closer to one than usual. He seemed to be having a rough go at the morning, squinting at the sunlight that spread quietly through the room and hesitating at loud noises.

Del sat cross-legged on the bed, worrying a vine between her fingers as she watched him muck about. From what she could tell, despite their odd behavior, the plants were simply that. She felt no more magic in them than she felt in her master's garden.

They certainly didn't feel to be *made* of magic as Thanae seemed to think. Unravelling them was like trying to unmake her arm.

"Turn," the guard ordered.

Del sighed and faced her back towards him wondering, vaguely, if he had scars to hide too or if he was simply prudish. "Thanae?"

He didn't answer.

She sighed. Being alone was nothing new, but there'd always been some sort of reprieve. A quick conversation with Ner, or sneaking words with some of the students, or the palace guards.

She'd even settle for a conversation with Nalav. Vapid, unimportant, and wasteful as it would be, at least she'd be sure she'd spoken.

She started tearing at the vines until they piled broken beneath her hands.

"Don't do that."

Del rolled her eyes and swept the scraps off her dress. "Are you done?"

"Yes."

She turned back around to find the guard in one of her master's nicer shirts. The Grand Mage's raven winked at her from its perch on his breast.

He plucked the pendant from the night table. It swung between his fingers for a beat like he thought it poisonous, before he tied it around his neck.

The casting fell over him in a fine mist, the Grand Mage's visage coming in the form of a gentle rain rather than the hard here and gone she'd grown accustomed to.

She worried her lip.

The spell was beginning to unravel, and gods knew she hadn't the materials to fix it.

"It's king's damned freezing," her master's voice set her stomach twisting.

Del turned her attention to the green sitting atop her skirts and pressed her hands together to still them. Everything that had been her master still stood before her, and it didn't seem to be getting easier.

It was supposed to get easier, wasn't it?

A knock sounded at the door, surprising her.

The guard started towards it, and her heart moved to her throat. She scrambled off the bed.

"No," her voice came in a ragged whisper.

He hesitated long enough for her to reach the door first, she straightened and tried to hide her panic. One breath, two breaths.

The knocking started anew.

Three breaths.

She opened the door to reveal a small man positioned primly on the other side. "Good morning," she said.

A smile tugged briefly at his lips before it was replaced by a flat line of indifference.

"Welcome back, Nydelissi," he hesitated a beat, before continuing, "Lord Eizat would like to invite the Grand Mage to breakfast in one bell's time."

She tried to place him. Her childhood had been filled with faces at her periphery, but they'd blended into an amorphous mass as time passed. Picking one out was like trying to pluck clouds from the skies. She bowed. "I'll be sure to deliver the message."

Disappointment wore on the man's features.

"A wash basin will be delivered in a quarter bell." He was still staring at her like she was meant to do something. She wanted so badly to know what he wanted from her. If she could just please one damn person on this entire trip, maybe she'd start feeling *normal* again.

Things had been so much easier with Gadna. Simpler, if not happier.

She sighed. "Thank you, I will notify my master."

Pity flickered in the man's eyes as she slammed the door in his face.

"Del?"

She took a deep breath, then another, as she forced her fingers from the doorknob. Just a little longer. "A washbasin will be here in twenty ticks."

She ignored his questioning look, her gaze falling to the tree she'd climbed the night before.

"Would you like an orange for breakfast?" she asked suddenly.

"A what?"

"An orange." The guard didn't answer. His silence dug at her. "The fruit in all the trees...the *orange* ones?"

More silence.

She was moments from leaping through the glass to escape the quiet when a rumble sounded.

Thanae coughed a beat too late to cover it up. Her curiosity had her turning before she'd the time to think better of it. It was a small mercy that he'd removed the enchantment.

"I'd want one," he began, awkwardly. "If you can get it."

A smile twitched onto Del's lips. She stifled the urge to prod at him as she crossed the room and pushed the window open. The sun that leapt through it set the world in its softest hues.

Instinctively, she took a deep breath and tried to quell her disappointment. It didn't smell of magic. Just the vague scents of oranges and earth and the cleansing soaps that were the defining fragrance of Eizat's estate, but nothing more.

Bracing herself against the sill, she plucked four fruits from the tree's branches as Thanae did his best to shower her with disapproval, likely for the stealing. The growling of his stomach undermined any true attempt at menace.

She dropped her prizes onto the carpet where they settled and sank, before lowering herself beside them. She peeled the first fruit in silence. The guard didn't speak, didn't even breathe from what she could hear. When she couldn't stand it anymore, she glanced to make sure he hadn't slipped through the door.

He was watching her with an almost sheepish expression. No scowl.

Her hands stuttered in their work.

Del had known the king had been recruiting younger soldiers to help fill the ranks now that the mage's units were being plucked bare, but still. He wasn't much older than she was.

She thrust the fruit in his direction. "Here."

He took it from her, rotating it curiously before biting into it, like he would an apple or a pear.

"Uh..." She wasn't sure where to begin. She wasn't even sure he'd heard her. He was eating so quickly she worried he might bite off a finger by mistake.

She started on her own when he held his hand for another. In the end he ate three oranges while Del finished what she'd learned to protect.

The guard was eyeing the window.

How could he *still* be hungry?

A knock sounded. Del gathered the peels and tossed them through the window as Thanae donned the enchantment.

She opened the door and a smattering of servants pushed by her as if she didn't exist. They gathered around her guard, their voices a chorus of *good mornings,* and *welcomes,* that he returned well enough.

Two of the maids worked in tandem to haul in a water basin, maneuvering the load to the table intended for writing long winded letters about the charms of Eizat's estate. The basin hit the wood with a resounding thud and a slosh of water that hit one of the servant's hands, immediately dyeing the skin red.

The servant in question hid it quickly, shoving their hand behind their back before moving deftly to the back of the crowd fawning over the Grand Mage.

The small man from earlier brought in a second basin and a pitcher of cooler water, setting it on the other side of the table.

And then they were gone.

Del regarded the first basin warily as the Grand Mage's form absorbed the sudden quiet. The sheer amount of steam was concerning.

Thanae wasted no time dipping a towel in the basin and wiping briefly at his hands before discarding the fabric on the table with a heavy thwack.

She watched the wisps curling above the water with longing, as the guard tugged his sleeves into place.

"Do you need to wash?" her master's voice came gentle. She dug her nails into her palms.

Del wasn't sure if she *needed* to, but it'd been four days since she left the palace, and three days longer than she was used to not washing. She was fast learning that there was only so much perfumes could do.

Still disrobing before the guard made her pause.

It was stupid, he was a soldier, so he'd *seen* wounds and scars. He'd likely seen much worse than anything she'd on her body.

But the quiet horror that had sat in the prince's eyes made her wonder if that was the truth.

She tugged her clothes closer, as if the frock could protect her. "I'm fine."

"I'll leave," he said. He was trying to be kind. Or maybe, she really smelled that awful.

"Don't, I'm fine."

He sighed, and two beats later the door opened and shut.

Gadna was gone.

Thanae was gone.

Her ears strained and filled with the sounds of her heartbeat and breathing.

Del was alone.

She fought the urge to check, like some servant might have wedged themselves beneath the bed. She closed the curtains that ran along the second story window. The room lost its warm glow, without it, the edges of the furniture became sharp and unwelcoming.

She undressed, folding her sister's nightgown before setting it on the bed.

Beneath all the perfume she stank of the river, and sweat, and the smoke from the beastless carriage she'd ridden in the day before. She reached for the fresh cloth, fluffy and smelling of yesterday's sun.

It's not meant for you.

She flinched, her hand hovering above the fabric. Her heart sent out a panicked tattoo that begged her legs to move. In the mirror before her, the room was empty. No shadows twisted.

No Grand Mage. Just her own panicked expression reflected back at her.

She picked up the towel Thanae had abandoned, plunging both her hands in the scalding water with it. Pain drove her thoughts silent as she wrung the fabric.

She forced a breath between clenched teeth and risked turning around.

The room was empty.

She'd known that.

There'd been no one to speak the words that echoed between her ears. No one in the entire estate could have. It'd been perfect in cadence and poise, in a way Thanae's poor rendition would never be.

Del scrubbed at her arms, trying not to search the corners of the room as she drove the paint to oblivion. Small silver threads wove their way along her arms, and crept towards her temple, before climbing down the full expanse of her torso in a series of vines and flowers.

The water in the bowl stung every time she sank her hands in it. She worked until her skin was beyond raw and the water had turned a murky shade of flesh tone.

No more whispers reached her.

She dug through her trunk and picked out the plainest clothes she could. A shirt that stopped buttoning at her navel and a skirt that clung to her hips before flaring neatly at the bottom.

She could almost hear him, *you look beautiful.*

Her breakfast threatened to make a reappearance.

Breathe.

Her fingers worked her hair from its braid. She remembered the way Tani had worn hers, surrounded by forest and green. Even when the girl had looked quiet and small, she'd never looked *weak.*

Del fumbled, her fingers clumsy as she started the first braid. Her hair was lifeless beneath her touch, smooth and silken. She tied the braid off with a violet ribbon and started on the second, before wrapping them about her head like a crown and pinning them in place.

The styling was messier than she'd have liked, strands had escaped and a patch had sprung free to frame the left half of her face. She smiled, uncertainly, at the girl in the mirror, catching the flicker of the mage's mark in the deadened light from the window.

The Grand Mage would have loathed it.

It did, in fact, make her feel a bit more powerful. A little bit more in control.

Someone knocked at the door, as Del finished painting over the markings on her face and neck. She hurried to open it.

"We'll leave after—." The Grand Mage took in her outfit curiously and began anew, "We're leaving after breakfast."

"To Chousal?"

He heaved a sigh, annoyance clear on his face. "Yes."

Chapter 23

"As you can see, we purchased the glass from Surannie's territory, none of the magic, of course, but the work is the finest I've ever seen regardless," Eizat prattled. Thanae shifted in his seat, his hands balled into fists beneath the table like he was getting lectured.

Del had stopped listening ages ago, she'd heard the tales of the paneling in this room when she was a child, and it seemed Eizat hadn't seen a need to update it in the last decade or so.

She was watching his wife, Azel. She was a tall woman, dressed better than her husband, her fortune speaking in the cut and color of the material of her button down and slacks. Eizat had always been gaudy about his wealth, shiny things, and brightly colored over embroidered garments that drew the eye and hadn't the good sense to focus the attention it garnered. Azel's face twisted as Eizat said *something*.

Her delicate hand dug into her husband's arm. "None of that, dear."

Eizat paled and coughed briefly into a soaked handkerchief. "Ah, of course, that was a poor topic."

Azel returned to her meal and Del tried very hard to blend into the wall.

The air felt thick as Eizat continued his desperate attempts to wow an increasingly unimpressed Thanae. Ataczi's trying to bore a hole through Del's skull with her judgment certainly wasn't helping.

Del's eyes kept ticking over to the lady of the house. She looked too close to her daughter, the memory her face threatened to summon sent Del's heart skittering.

At the time, it'd felt the logical choice, telling Azel's daughter that she could read. But the way the girl's face had contorted, disgust mixed with a haughtiness only nobles had ever seemed to master, had stuck with her.

She was waiting for Azel's face to do the same.

The lady of the house picked politely at her food as Eizat wiped the sweat beading along his brow.

"I'm...that is—" He coughed again. The handkerchief smeared across his lips. "The food is truly the best, at least, on this side of the island."

"I bet it is," the Grand Mage's voice rang dully. Thanae made no move to touch his plate.

Eizat paled further. His handkerchief caught a drop of sweat rolling down his cheek.

Azel emptied her plate and Del sent a prayer to Mihr-Did that she would not move to refill it. She held her breath as the noblewoman studied the spread.

Gods above, just don't reach forward.

"Dear, I'm afraid I'll have to take my leave," the excuse fell flatter than the lady's expression. She gave Eizat a lackluster peck on the cheek before patting his head, like she might have done with a child, or a pet, and walking into the kitchen. Through the doorway, Del watched her gather more food.

Red tinted beneath the dusty brown of Eizat's cheeks. "My apologies, she must not be...feeling well."

Thanae's mouth twitched. "We should leave too."

Eizat's face went redder, like Mihr-Did had lit a candle beneath his flesh. "There's no need to—", he spluttered. His stupid handkerchief worked hard to catch the rivulet falling by his ear. He shriveled under the Grand Mage's glare. "Well, we can at least arrange for you to take some food for lunch...on the road as it were."

Gadna's form nodded. He stood before carefully guiding the chair beneath the table. "Prepare a carriage."

"Of course." Eizat stood abruptly, rattling the table. His handkerchief slipped from his hand and landed beside his plate with a wet thwack.

The room fell silent, as if the damned cloth had spoken. Del nearly laughed at the panic on Eizat's face as he rushed to pick it up, only to find it had left a pale-yellow mark on the tablecloth.

He placed his hand over the stain and forced cheer into his voice, "Two bells at the earliest."

Thanae made a sound somewhere between a bark and a snort, his shoulders tensing as they threatened to bounce, "Thank you."

Eizat looked positively scandalized. Even Ataczi had abandoned her new life's mission of willing a hole through Del's skull, in favor of schooling the amusement from her features.

Her old master's mouth opened and shut wordlessly as his cheeks approached the color of an overripe apple, he sat heavily in his chair as Thanae made his escape. Del hurried after him, closing the dining room door to her sister's soft assurances that Eizat hadn't made a complete ass of himself.

The guest room felt unbelievably far. Thanae walked quickly while Del struggled to keep pace. Her mind tried to wrap around Eizat's home, he, like her master, had enjoyed collecting baubles. But while the Grand Mage's wing had felt more like a museum, Eizat had somehow managed to fall short, perhaps at his wife's insistence, but his home felt *lived in.*

Thanae narrowly avoided walking headlong into the guestroom door. He wrenched it open and slipped inside with surprising grace. It was only after Del shut the door and the pendant sat on the bed, that he set to laughing.

If Thanae's anger was thunder, his laughter was the wind that swirled about in early autumn. Light and playful, accented with snorts and gasps, it was a sound that made Del want to lean closer.

Like she could catch bits of it and cage it in her chest for harder days.

He stopped when he caught her staring. The boyish grin that tilted his mouth disappeared. "Are you packed?" he asked.

Del studied him a beat longer, she wasn't sure why his laughter hadn't scared her the way the prince's and Gadna's had. "I'm not."

"Get it done."

There wasn't much for her to do. She tossed the vines into her trunk, though it was near to bursting with the godsblessed things. She locked it, trying to keep her mind on the task at hand.

She should say good-bye to her family.

Her nails dug against the wood, lodging in the carvings. She'd left her dress with them. She should at least go to retrieve it.

It felt impossibly daunting.

"You have time to see them," Thanae started. She'd been staring at the window despite the curtain that ran along it, facing the direction of the small building that had once been her home.

Gods, that felt stupid.

She turned to Thanae. "Are they really going to be purchased?"

"The paperwork still needs to go to the palace, and be approved," he grumbled.

"And then it's done?"

"Yes."

Del let out a breath, her hand running along the Promise band wrapped around her wrist. She'd done that right, at least.

It was nowhere near enough, not for all she'd done, but it'd get them away from this godsdamned orchard, get them away from Eizat. They'd have a chance at a freedom, she'd only get to brush against.

Enyemno's prayer sat on her lips. She glanced at Thanae and swallowed; the words turned to lead in the pit of her stomach.

I'll love you forever and always, the goddess's love flows through my veins, my heart is hers and everlasting.

"Stop doing that," Thanae snapped.

Del jumped; her eyes glued to the soldier.

Thanae sighed and ran a hand through the rough waves of hair atop his head. "Your wrist."

She peeled her fingers away, looking at the flesh she'd gathered beneath her nail. "Sorry," she muttered.

The guard rolled his eyes. "You're not sorry, you didn't even mean to do it."

She hadn't but that didn't change the fact that despite the grand delusions she'd been entertaining, she'd damaged the prince's property. Cuts, gashes, and carvings displeased him...or they seemed to. She didn't think he'd be as lenient about it as the Grand Mage had been.

"Sorry," she repeated. "It's nothing serious, I just..." The notion that her response to stress had led to her gaining, not one or two, but three distinct injuries in the last day, was not entirely healthy struck her.

It didn't seem to be *normal*.

"Are you going to patch it?"

Del stared blankly at the blood running along her skin. She'd never bothered patching something so small. She crossed the room and dunked her hand into the tepid basin water, watching ribbons of red drift towards the bottom.

"Good as new," she announced.

The guard huffed, "No."

Del frowned pulling her hand from the bowl. She still couldn't bring herself to reach for a clean towel. She cursed softly as she lifted the still wet one from earlier in the day, speckling it with small droplets of her blood.

Chapter 24

Del shut her eyes, feeling the sway of the carriage beneath her.

Thanae opened the box Eizat had gifted them. A wooden thing that sat just smaller than the guard's lap with hinges on the top and a hooked latch. Her former master had filled it with oranges, breads, tarts, and cured slabs of meat. The smell of it tickled her nose.

The scents were distant, an echo of an echo. She was still searching for magic, something beyond the orange and earth of Thanae's failing casting.

She opened her eyes and stilled.

It wasn't *wrong*, seeing her master curled over a box of food. But it wasn't something Gadna would have done. He'd thought the position he held required a degree of dignity that she was now beginning to realize, had bordered on the absurd.

She pressed her cheek against the carriage glass. Grasses swiped against the window, splitting shafts of light and scattering them through the meadow.

The guard started coughing, but imminent death wasn't going to stop him from finishing whatever he was eating. *That* was just patently wrong.

"Why didn't you eat at the house?" she asked.

Thanae paused briefly in his endeavors. "You're talking to me now?"

Del stopped short of biting into her lip. Her annoyance showed on her face before she could stop it.

He bit into a tart. "I didn't know how."

"To eat?"

"How to eat with nobles," he groused, the treat in his hand protested as his fingers threatened to clamp around it. "I don't know the rules."

"And the drinking?"

"He kept filling my glass." He made a face. "Bitter shit."

It was easy to imagine. Eizat's fluttering hospitality had been hard to watch. Del snickered, "do you remember the conversation we had last night?"

His hand stalled as he reached into the basket. "Was it important?"

Her smile faltered. She tried to hide her disappointment. "Not at all."

"I just remember you coming through the window."

"Why that?"

The guard shrugged and continued trying to devour everything within the basket and possibly moving onto the vessel itself.

They passed a small temple. A squat, dark building nestled in the grasses. Ipheoth's tree had been carved into the door, the pillars made of offshoots and roots. It still made her uncomfortable, the churches, the statues, the casual mentions of the gods.

She caught Thanae staring at the building, his lip curled in disgust. He was too young for Repren, but he might have been involved in the ensuing squabbles.

Had he made his name slaughtering believers? Or had it been something else?

She knotted her fingers together and shut her eyes.

She listened to the wind and grasses, the grinding of the wheels against the soft dirt roads. Then the voices, the Egrean her ears had starved for, the shouts of the market.

The carriage slowed by the plaza near the docks.

The driver opened the partition. "You going Qasha, right?"

"No," Del began in Egrean, relief settled on the driver's face. "Chousal."

"Chousal?" he echoed. His eyes skipped to the Grand Mage. "You going Chousal?" he asked in Qashan.

Thanae frowned. "Yes."

"I don't think there are any ships that stop there anymore," he informed Del. "It's cursed."

"How close can we get?"

He tapped his finger against a butterfly pendant hanging from the partition, knocking the blood-colored thing into the glass. "Maybe a half-day's travel south? Either that, or you'll have to cross into Athijan, and they don't take kindly to...*pro—*, mages, right now."

Del stiffened, darting a glance at Thanae, to see if he'd recognized the beginning of the slur.

He hadn't.

Del let out a breath. "Just, as close as we can get, then," she tried.

The man nodded before stepping down and disappearing into the crowd. What followed was a truly painful experience of him running from ship to ship, occasionally returning with crew members, who would take one look at Del and turn down the offer or haggle back and forth in broken Qashan with Thanae, only to storm off frustrated.

The sun ticked across the sky and Del did everything in her power to keep from bouncing or fiddling with her veil.

"I don't deal in flesh," a man said, in accented Egrean.

"You won't be *dealing* in it," the driver insisted. "She's been with him for years."

"She's a slave."

"She's a *Pet*. It's a life of luxury and treats."

Del's ears strained, attempting to catch the rest of the conversation as the noise around the carriage swelled. There was something about the man's voice that sent her searching, trying to pick him out from the crowd.

It wasn't hard to find him, he was a great deal darker than most anyone there. His clothes were bright and dozens of thin, colorful, rings sparkled across the fingers that remained on his right hand.

But most importantly, he was Chousalian.

Her heart hammered against her ribcage. How could he *be*? Did he know the merchant the prince had mentioned? Was there a community? Were there Chousalians *in* Chousal?

Was it possible that both her mother and the reports had been wrong?

Her gloved fingers dug into the fabric splayed across her lap.

When the driver knocked on the window, she did not look up. She didn't trust herself not to leap at the man, half-wild with desperation.

"I do not deal in flesh." The captain held himself with the quiet confidence of someone used to issuing commands, the fat ring on his left hand twinkled. His Qashan was crisp.

"I'm not dealing in anything, I just need a boat headed north," Thanae began.

"And that?" She felt him point at her. She swallowed and kept silent.

His ship was the one she had to take.

Beside her, Thanae flagged. "She's...my companion."

"By choice or by design?"

The guard stiffened and the man outside took a step back. "I don't deal in flesh," he repeated, in Egrean, to the driver.

Del turned towards him, cursing softly about the veil and all the rules and the fear that threatened to silence her when she needed so desperately to speak.

She flung the window open and nearly toppled through, her arms caught her and braced against the sill. "It's not what you think," she shouted, in Chousalian.

The captain stopped. Nearly tripped, really, as he hurried to whirl around knocking into a passerby. His eyes ran down the long slit in the front of her shirt. He grimaced.

"You sold yourself?"

"I'm eighteen," she answered.

He frowned. "What in Naya's hells?"

"Yes, exactly!" She steadied herself on the window frame. "I know what this looks like, but it's not what you think. *Please.*"

"Does he know how young you are?" He looked to the Grand Mage.

"Yes." Del shook her head. "I mean, no, not this one. I—"

She slid back into the carriage. "How old do you think I am?" she asked breathlessly.

The Grand Mage's brow lowered. "What does that have to do with anything?"

"Everything," she responded. "How old do you think I am?"

"Twenty...something?" The bafflement in his answer was enough to make even the driver pause. Thank Ose's infinite skies.

"I swear to you on Ipheoth's roots, I will explain everything on the ship, but it has to be *your* ship," she finished, in Chousalian.

The captain looked her over once again, his eyes fixing on the dark patch of exposed skin that gave her away.

"You speak like an Egrean," he spat, before switching to Qashan, "I'll take you, but I don't stop in Chousal. Nobody does. The nearest port is a ha'day's travel from the border."

The Grand Mage's eyes ticked from Del to the captain. "That's fine," he said.

They started discussing prices then, food, rooms, and services but none of it made it through the fog in her brain. He was *Chousalian.*

Living outside bars and cages wasn't just possible, it'd already been done. She watched everything about him, how he held himself, how he breathed, how his hands fluttered when he was annoyed and the light his rings bounced and toyed with.

Alive and living in a way neither Del nor her family had ever had a chance at.

"You're staring," Thanae warned.

The carriage rocked as a woman with skin the color of milk lifted the Grand Mage's crate.

"Sorry." Del peeled her eyes away, and grabbed the Grand Mages hand as he escorted her onto the plaza. She wanted to race for the captain, but she clung to Thanae's arm. Dangling herself like the perfect ornament she'd been bred to be.

The captain's judgement stung.

The man's ship was smaller than the one they'd arrived on, and so was his crew. Truthfully, it was only a smattering of people. A set of fraternal twins with eyes that seemed to change color with the light, a small stout man with a seemingly permanent snarl, and the milk-colored lady she'd seen before. Boxes upon boxes filled nearly every space that wasn't crucial to navigation.

As soon as she set foot on the deck the captain grabbed her. Del flinched, swallowing a yelp as he spun her to face him.

"Explain."

Her thoughts disintegrated.

He was still speaking. She stared at him unable to think past the feel of him. It was almost as if she would blink and slide through time and space, and land in the mage's quarters with everything having been a dream.

A beat passed. His hand was gone.

It took her a full tick to realize he was no longer touching her.

She struggled to piece together what had happened, the Grand Mage stood between her and the captain. "I said, don't touch her...she's jumpy."

The world stopped.

How had he said something so utterly stupid with such sincerity? How was he *real*?

"Jumpy?" she choked out. Thanae started and turned, she wasn't sure if it was worry that shone on his face or exasperation. "I...I guess? But that feels like an understatement don't you think?"

Her master's face warmed with embarrassment. She tried and failed to hold in a laugh.

"Girl?" the captain prompted impatiently.

She took a gasping breath, and tried to sober up. "Sorry, I'm not, I can't do the, uhm, I can't touch people...I...panic."

The captain's arms had crossed at some point, his ringed fingers tapped along his forearm. She wondered if they were a Chousalian thing. Some small bit of culture her mother had forgotten or hidden away.

"Can we go someplace more...private?" she asked, at last.

"What you say to me, you can say to my men."

Del looked to where they'd left the driver, the carriage was nowhere in sight. She shifted uncomfortably.

They were still in Egrea, but it wasn't as if they particularly cared that the *sailors* used magic. So long as they didn't bring it with them, else how would they get shipments from Athijan, or Erbos?

Del ticked through her options.

"Thanae, take the pendant off."

The guard opened his mouth.

"Please," she interrupted. "You're meant to guard me, not question my every move."

He stilled for a beat before untying the knot at the base of his neck. The pendant fell away from his skin.

The captain let out a string of curses, "That's—" his next words were lost on her. Whatever he'd spoken had been some form of Chousalian she'd never learned. The rest of the crew sent up a chorus of shouts that nearly drowned him out.

Thanae placed himself strategically between her and the crowd.

Gods it was loud. She locked her legs though they trembled with the effort of keeping herself upright.

"I don't want *that* magic on my ship," the captain snarled.

"It's not what you think," she reiterated, in Egrean. "Let me explain."

He looked between her and Thanae, his gaze lingering where he thought her eyes to be. "You have one tick."

Del sent up a quiet prayer to Mihr-Did. "I *am* a Pet, but I didn't sell myself, I was *born* into it. My master was a tyrant." She glanced to Thanae to gauge his reaction, even knowing there was no way for him to have understood. "He...he died, very suddenly, but he left behind a lot of money. So, I wanted to try to purchase and free the rest of my family, except the money isn't mine, it's his, and he didn't free me. I had to commission a mage to make the pendant so we could access his funds without raising too many questions."

The captain shut his eyes. His lips moved briefly whether in curse or in prayer, she wasn't sure. "And him?" He nodded to Thanae.

"I hired him, mercenary...I think, he's not very forthcoming," she answered, quickly.

The captain opened his eyes and looked between the two of them. Del's heart was in her throat, it beat so loudly she almost missed what he'd said next.

"I don't like that shit on my ship, get rid of it."

"You believe me?"

"I believe *enough*," he grumbled. "But that shit? Off my ship. It's bad luck."

"But we—"

"Off my ship, or you'll have to find another."

And give up her only chance of speaking with a Chousalian outside her family. She turned to the guard, and spoke in Qashan, "The pendant. Toss it."

He hesitated, though relief flooded his face. "Are you sure?"

She nodded with more certainty than she felt. "It was starting to fail anyway."

Thanae pulled back his arm, and the last bit of the Grand Mage went sailing through the air. It hit the water with a muffled thump, before sinking beneath the surface.

Del turned back to the captain. "It's done."

"Welcome aboard." There was no warmth in his greeting. He looked at Del a moment longer, like he was trying to decide if he'd made a mistake, before turning and barking orders to his crew.

Chapter 25

The wake the boat left behind it spread into an impossibly large funnel of rolling wave, reaching out to the shore that had been relegated to a line against the horizon. The vessel ran on a quiet sort of magic that pulled wind into the sails and filled the air with the scent of something sweet Del couldn't name.

It turned out the salt smell she'd gotten from all the boats when she'd left the capital had been the scent of the ocean. She'd read stories about it, how it swayed to and fro, a watered pendulum that spread for aeons. But nothing had prepared her for the vastness of it.

In one direction she could spy the shore, but in the other?

Nothing.

Just blue upon blue that bled to nonsense far in the distance where the sea and sky kissed.

Her boot brushed against Thanae who lay sprawled across the boards with a wet towel over his eyes.

He groaned softly.

"Is it any better?" she asked.

He shook his head before falling very still. To Del, he looked dead, his skin had gained an unhealthy pallor and he hardly dared move from the rear of the boat. Even when the waters were calm.

"And dinner?"

He nearly retched. The guard had been struck useless as soon as they'd hit the first true wave.

"Do you feel like you're going to die, or do you wish you were dead?" the captain shouted jovially as he approached.

The first thing Del had learned once they'd left the dock, was that the captain was *loud.* It still caught her by surprise, somehow. She'd never realized that people could make so much noise just by existing.

Thanae gathered the strength to send him a rude gesture. The captain laughed, twice, sharply, as if he didn't find the event funny at all but still felt the need to go through the motions. It still made Del stiffen. He was...something else.

She'd always imagined most Chousalians to be some sort of permutation of her mother, but the captain was nothing like her.

And he refused to speak much about Chousal at all. She'd been trying for days to get *anything* from him and had been shut out at every turn.

"Good evening," she offered.

He gave her a smile that landed somewhere south of warm. "I was just looking for you."

Panic flashed through her, setting her nerves alight. She waited for him to continue. A beat passed and he sighed.

"Come with me." He turned and headed towards the narrow set of stairs that led below deck.

Del hesitated by Thanae. He wouldn't be much help and he certainly wasn't going to offer her the protection he was meant to, but he was still the only person she knew in nearly five days' travel.

"I'll be back," she tried.

The guard lurched to his feet and ran to the rail. Whatever he'd managed to eat for dinner fell to the waves beneath them. He gave her a lackluster wave to send her off.

Del set after the captain. Below deck there were a handful of rooms, each just large enough to house a bed and a few artifacts. She passed two closed doors, and one that was left slightly ajar, that was filled with brightly colored embroidered fabrics and small trinkets bound to the walls. Del knew it to belong to the pale woman, whose boots she was currently borrowing.

She hadn't known that rooms could feel so cozy and safe.

The last room belonged to the captain, it was three times larger than the ones she'd just passed and held a desk as well as a bed and a set of chairs that for once looked to be for function rather than opulence. She was almost convinced she could sit on them without being swallowed alive.

"Take a seat." The captain rounded the desk and sat in his own little chair. A mewling sounded and a small beast that looked like a dog but was much too small leapt onto the table. The captain barely spared it a glance as it settled by his side.

She didn't move.

"Sit," he insisted.

She perched on the very edge of the seat opposite him. Her eyes drifted to the creature as the captain absently scratched behind its ears. It started to *rumble*. Del fought the urge to poke at it, to see if it might stop.

"Your friend isn't doing too well up there," he began.

Del frowned. "With all due respect, if you called me down here to speak of Thanae's circumstances, it was unnecessary. I don't know much more than you do."

The beast started kneading at the table, small claws pulsed in and out of existence, scraping against the wood.

Most definitely not a dog.

"No, that's not what I want to talk about," he said. The rumbling beast brushed its head against his arm, "I want to discuss…" He waved his hand in her general direction.

"That's all of me," Del pointed out mildly.

"Yes." She caught the tremor in his fingers, despite his effort to hide it. "I want to talk about...you."

She didn't like that question. It seemed the more people found out about her these days the more complicated it made things, "What do you wish to know?"

"How are you," he stopped abruptly, his eyes skipping from the tiny beast to Del before landing on the many rings of his left hand. He sighed and went beneath his desk, pulling a large glass bottle from its depths. "Do you drink?"

"My ma—," she began. Her cheeks heated. "No, I've never had the chance."

"Do you want to?" He popped the cork, and the air filled with the sharp tang of alcohol. Curiosity was a living thing in her breast, urging her to reach forward.

But she didn't know the captain, and the bond of their heritage wasn't something she understood.

She shook her head.

He shrugged and poured himself a glass, draining the contents before refilling it, only to empty it again.

"You were born after the Fall," he said, at last.

"...yes?"

"How?"

Del's face scrunched. "What?"

"How were you born? Conceived even?"

"Uh, when a man and a woman love, well, that isn't really true for several reasons." She liked to imagine there was love involved, but she wasn't naïve. "Well, when two individuals have sex—"

The captain slammed the bottle onto the table startling the beast and Del. "Not that, not that, not that," he muttered. He rubbed his temple with his free hand. "There aren't any children your age."

Del frowned. "I've seen plenty of children."

The look her gave her was so bland, she almost felt bad. "There are no Chousalian children your age," he clarified.

"I have a brother and sister who've almost turned sixteen."

He froze. "You have what?"

"Siblings? You're the first Chousalian I've met outside my family, but if you're looking for children born after the Fall...aren't you meant to make them?"

An annoyed smile curled his lips. "I can't."

Her face was fire. "I'm sorry."

He sighed and waved her away. "I can't, because no Chousalian children have been born since the—," he grumbled and rubbed his temple again. "Can't even call the damn thing a war. All children conceived before the Fall were born to Naya's arms, and after that, nothing. There are no children. We're barren."

His words dragged through the air.

The implications of his admission were worrying. There would be no rebuilding if the Chousalians couldn't have kids, no neighborhoods, no continuing of a society that could sustain them and her siblings, if they were just going to die out.

But that wasn't what kept her attention. *Survivors.* To know that they were barren, that would be more than a handful, wouldn't it?

"There's more than just you?"

He looked at her incredulously. "We didn't all just disappear off the Great Continent, this isn't some fairy story."

Any more embarrassment and she might actually die. "I wouldn't have had access to those reports."

"Access to reports?" he echoed, incredulously. "Most of your kind don't read."

"Well, I can."

"And you're close to reports about the war?"

She didn't answer.

He looked at her then, he'd been trying not to since he'd made the decision to let her stay aboard the ship. His face crumpled as if doing so caused him pain.

"What's it like in Qasha?" he asked.

"I wouldn't know," she answered, softly. "I was a Pet, not a citizen."

"A Pet with access to important documents," he spoke as if he were pointing out something of unseen import.

"Numbers don't replace experience," she snapped. She tried to tamp down on the rage that boiled in her stomach. "I can tell you how many people live in a particular district, but I cannot say what it means to walk down the street, if the buildings are sturdy, if the people are fed, or if a fire has wiped them out since the last census. But I can give you numbers and pretend that they matter."

He blinked and poured himself another glass.

"I didn't know there were any Chousalians still alive within the borders."

Her lips pulled into a smile, though she was sure no joy entered her expression. "I am, in any official sense, the only one."

"Are you sure you don't want a drink?"

"I—." She paused. She'd seen men drink together before and they'd grown sloppy and unkempt, but the secrets they spilled had always grown more interesting as the night worn on.

The captain had a great many secrets.

But so did she.

Mihr-Did bless her.

"Yes, I think I would like that a lot."

Chapter 26

The languages tangled.

Chousalian bled to Egrean bled to Qashan, one flowing into the next like they'd come from three great rivers that'd decided to dump their contents beneath her tongue and render it useless.

Qashan.

It always returned to Qashan.

She hated that.

The captain had passed out at his desk. His glass, less than half full, dangled precariously from his fingers. She plucked it from his hand and tried to figure out what to do with the contents. It was cheaper than anything she'd ever seen at the palace and gods knew she'd no desire to *taste* it again.

Awful stuff.

But having found no alternative, she finished it, and fought her body to keep it down before tucking the glass into its drawer.

It no longer burned going down.

As it turned out, being a Pet wasn't precisely good for much, but keeping company was the *one thing* she knew. And much like the Grand Mage, the captain was lonely.

Speaking with him had been like slipping into a warm bath. Familiar in ways she hadn't realized she'd missed. She'd gone down well-trod conversation paths, pushing and prodding when he offered the chance, but it had been a gentle thing. Unspooling him.

Simple.

The little beast watched her with eyes she swore reflected the lantern light. She closed the drawer.

It made no move to stop her as she left and shut the door quietly behind her.

Vines crept along the corridor, white blooms, delicate leaves. Moonbriar, or so she hoped. Gods, she wasn't even sure about what she was doing, where she was going. A helpless laugh bubbled in her throat as she tried and failed to blink them away.

She swayed at the top of the stairs and took a seat beside Thanae, or she'd tried to. Her leg went wrong. She ended sprawled somewhere nearby. Del huffed, her eyes fixing on the sky.

At sea, when the sun hit the horizon, everything became absurdly bright, like it was reaching fingers of light beneath the waves. In the evenings it felt as though everything was sky. Ose had outdone himself when he'd deigned to set the sun atop a body of water.

"You're back," Thanae offered, blandly.

"There are more like me," it came out stupid, jumbled. She'd started wrong. Thanae and his idiotic tongue. She blinked hard trying to focus.

"There are more like me," she tried again, "Chousalians."

He didn't answer. The wind smelled of the sea. It was cool against her skin. The only noise that passed between them was the lapping of the waves and the quiet breeze. By the time he spoke, Del had almost forgotten he was there. "What are you going to do?" he asked.

"About what?"

"The...Chousalians. You found them."

She wanted to laugh. He'd asked the question like she knew what she wanted from the world. She'd found them, yes. The captain had even been so loose lipped as to tell her how to contact them.

Small communities nestled into cities and towns all along the waterways. There were hundreds of survivors, perhaps even thousands. Chousal was *alive* and breathing, surviving through the existence of its people.

She tried to laugh.

The sob took her by surprise. It was such an ugly thing, it leapt from her ragged and raw, like the cry of a wounded animal. It was followed by a second, and a third as tears streamed down her face.

She tried to stop. Crying didn't help.

Nobody cared.

There was no one to rescue her.

But no matter how she wiped her cheeks, the tears kept coming. She couldn't even calm her godsdamned breathing. It was like she'd become a *child*. She felt stupid, and simple, and small.

Helpless.

"I wanted to see it," she managed.

The captain had described the ways in which the survivors had tried to emulate the land they'd left behind, how people had taken up fabric making, how they hung blessings by the doorways, and painted the walls inside their houses, crafting little bits of a home they'd been forced to flee.

"I wanted to see it and visit and look for the stories Mama used to tell. I wanted to feel like..." She wasn't sure, Gods what had she thought would happen? "Different? When I saw the captain, I was so sure that it meant *something*. I spend all my time looking for fucking signs Thanae, and there's nothing."

If the guard was listening, he didn't care, or she'd spoken wrong. She curled in on herself and glared at the sunset as if it were at fault for all her failings. It didn't stop her crying, and she suspected all it did was make her eyes burn.

Vines crawled around her. She refused to look at them, despite their constant nagging. It was the principle of the matter. Something that wasn't her wanted her to look, and she wasn't going to let it win today.

If she couldn't even control herself anymore, what did she have left?

Her sobs slowed as the sun sank beneath the waves, extinguishing to cast embers and clouds into the skies, painting Ose's heavens in violets before releasing pinpricks of lights that danced slowly as the bells ticked by.

She wasn't sure how long Thanae had been sitting by her side. She became aware of him slowly, the shape of him resting against the rail. He was trying very hard not to look at her. He'd placed some food by her side.

She picked up the bowl. The spoon scraped the bottom, leftovers. Whatever it was, was awful, but the bowl had been enchanted to keep it from getting too cold.

Shame warmed what the meal did not.

The bowl tinked against the wood of the deck as she set it down.

It seemed that making a fool of herself was becoming a habit.

"I miss the palace meals," the guard began, awkwardly. Del faced him, trying to get her mind to concentrate on his figure, rather than the green leaves and—

The palace meals?

"I miss them too," she answered, surprised to find it true and feeling silly for it.

He nodded and it was silent but for the sounds she'd grown to associate with the ship.

After a few ticks he picked up her bowl and stood. He was still unsteady as he went down the steps to return it to the kitchen. She wouldn't sleep, wouldn't let Tani dip her fingers into her mind. Wouldn't let the vines crawl along her flesh and claim her.

Nothing, she wouldn't do it. Not tonight.

Which meant that waking up in the forest was a particularly nasty sort of surprise. Tani stood before her, still quiet and pretty.

She rocked on her feet, her gaze skipping around the landscape.

"I'm sorry," she began, guiltily, after a few beats. "I...it's hard, controlling where I send you. I'm trying to choose the important bits, but stronger emotions pull harder, and I'm not used to—" She sighed, her hand tapping her side. "I'm not used to *trying* anymore. It's difficult. I have nicer memories to send you to, but it's just so much easier to remember the bad times. Isn't it?"

Del kept quiet. Part of her hoped that if she refused to speak, everything would start to feel less real.

"I asked you a question," the girl insisted.

Del's voice cracked, "It is."

"It just doesn't seem fair," Tani grumbled, "I think I have it, the memory...I think. I'm not too sure anymore."

And the world went black.

Del was too tired to fight it.

It was cold, the wind bit at Tani's nose. Her breath caught in the scarf wrapped around her mouth. She'd been told she looked like a chimney, puffing smoke straight up as the heat from her breath warmed her face and sent condensation dusting the air.

She turned around, searching through the winter bare trees. Picking out Rua's form was simple, he navigated the forest, the way young children walked through the hearth room. Ungainly steps.

"Rua, come on," she complained, "It's been *bells*, and I'm *cold*."

"If you'd charged your heating enchantment—"

"But I didn't, and I can't feel my fingers anymore," she griped. The crystal had gone dark, making the whole thing useless until she tossed it into the hearth fire to let it build. She flexed her hands she knew they'd gone red to the tips inside her gloves. She finished binding her firewood and kindling before securing it to her back.

Tani slipped her arms up her sleeves pressing them against her belly. Her feet crunched at the frozen ground as she danced from one foot to the next in the hopes of warming up, "Come on, come on, come on."

"I'm going as fast as I can."

That was a lie, but Tani let it be. "Please, Rua."

None of her whining convinced him to go any faster. By the time they'd reached the tree line all her thoughts had turned to home. She was ready to stoke the fire, change out of her clothes and wrap herself in the pelt her mother kept in the hearth room for precisely that purpose.

She was so lost in her anticipation, that she didn't notice the woman until she moved.

She was tucked against one of the trees at the tree line, curved against its base. She almost looked as if she'd been pulled from the bark itself.

The woman was old, very old. Possibly older than great-Anma Alra, the oldest woman in the village. Tani didn't know her, which was odd, but not unheard of. Strangers did pass through.

The odd bit was that the woman in question was dressed in a summer frock. Even her hair had been done in summer fashion, white strands caught in a scarf that swept braids from her shoulders to keep cool. And despite everything, she didn't shiver.

She shook. It was too regular to be called shivering.

"It's cold," the woman croaked.

"It is," Tani answered, uncomfortably.

"I would love to warm myself by a lovely fire," she continued.

Tani took a step away, she wanted to put as much distance between this woman and herself as humanly possible.

"Tani," Rua's panicked voice came from a dozen paces. His kindling fell soundlessly into the snow as he ran to the woman's side. "Can't you see she needs help?"

"Then she should have asked for it."

"Tani," his voice rang with disappointment. She bit her cheek as Rua snaked an arm around the old woman's waist and hoisted her to her feet.

A lump set itself in Tani's throat.

"I—"

"Not now," he grumbled. Tani's mouth sealed shut.

He didn't talk to her for the entire walk to his home.

Tani rushed forward to open the door for him in the hopes of starting some sort of conversation. Her heart sank as he passed by.

He didn't even look in her direction. She waffled about in the doorway before gathering the courage to follow him inside.

Rua set the woman in the rocking chair before the hearth. In the soft light of the fire's glow, Tani could see the tattoos that ran down the stranger's skin. She tried to make them out, but no matter how hard she tried to focus, she couldn't pin them. It was like they were shifting without moving.

She didn't like the woman.

She wanted to tell Rua, try to explain herself, but she could already hear his answer. He'd just go on about how Tani didn't like visitors and that she should "try to be more open minded". But this was *different*, she just didn't have the words to explain how.

Her stomach started to ache.

Rua set a blanket around the woman's shoulders before disappearing into the back to get the kettle.

She watched him and wished she were brave enough to follow.

If she'd thought to retrieve the wood he'd dropped, she'd have a reason to talk to him. A chance to make up.

She reached into her pack, taking half her wood and setting it in Rua's family's bin. It wouldn't be enough, it wouldn't even get them through the night, but it was better than nothing.

The old woman set the chair creaking. She laughed. The sound reminded Tani of the rustling of long dead leaves.

"I see, I see," the old woman spoke into the flames. "I heard tale of your arrangement." She twisted the words with obvious joy.

Tani didn't answer.

"Your marriage."

Embarrassment set Tani's heart thundering. Just remembering the meeting made her want to hide under her bed until next spring.

"Where's Rua?" He was taking too long for the kettle.

"Gone to get ingredients from the ice," the woman's mouth warped as she said it, it took Tani a moment to realize it was supposed to be a smile. "He's a good boy, that one. He's wasted on you, and you know it."

Tani winced. Everyone had been saying the same, despite Rua's insistence that it wasn't true. But if *everyone* was saying it...Tani rocked on her feet.

"I know that," she answered, softly.

"I know of a way to stop the marriage," the old woman said. "Free him so he can do what he wants instead of what people think is best. Let him love who he loves."

Tani looked at the old woman then, truly *looked* at her. She was beautiful in the way the statues in the square were. As if each wrinkle had been carved into her face with purpose. Even her clothes seemed to drape across her form with careful consideration.

She didn't make any effort to near the fire or clutch at the blanket Rua had set on her lap. And she didn't *move* like she'd been out in the cold for bells.

Tani kept her distance, but she wasn't going to miss a chance to set things right. "How?"

"The forest is capable of great magic," the woman said, "You of all the people know that best, don't you?"

Tani shifted uncomfortably. "How do you—"

The woman cut her off. "Go to the forest's heart and find the vine that gives flowers with petals the color of moonlight. You'll know it when you see it." An image formed in Tani's mind, the fluted shape of the blossom's body and the way the petals curled at the edges.

She didn't like that at all. She stilled and focused on the in and out of air in her lungs. "I...I don't...it's too easy."

The old woman cackled, "The best things are. Find the flower, come back home, and everything will be as it should."

"...how does it work?"

"Steep the petals until they run clear and drink the tea with the boy."

"That's it?"

The woman nodded. "That's all."

It felt too good to be true, Tani glanced at the doorway searching for Rua. "He...he won't hate me, will he?"

The woman shook her head, the patterns on her clothes seemed to shift the same ways the tattoos on her arms did. Motion without movement. The pang in Tani's stomach grew.

"He won't," the woman assured her.

There was nothing left to say. Tani set the rest of her wood in Rua's family's box and bundled herself up.

The woman made no move to stop her as she left the house, but Tani could feel her eyes following her. She shivered as she stepped into the cold.

Chapter 27

Del's eyes snapped open. Her head ached and her mouth was dry. She stilled as Thanae started working on the vines.

He didn't talk. And she didn't move. It didn't matter how often he did it, or how careful he was, seeing him with a knife drawn scattered her thoughts.

She shut her eyes, trying to sort what she'd seen in her dreams. But she was incredibly aware of the sound of the vines snapping and the tug of them against her and the imagined whisper of the knife blade against her skin.

"We've docked," Thanae's voice shocked her from her thoughts.

She watched as he cut the last bit of green from her ankles. Her toes wiggled. Pins and needles.

The vines were growing tighter.

He collected them from the floor. Del shifted, trying to find her voice. "When?"

The guard grimaced. "Yesterday."

"Evening?"

He shook his head. Del frowned, he wasn't making sense, surely, he had misspoken or—

She had to pee. She shot up from the bed, stiff legs be damned, and sprinted to the restroom. For once she didn't mind that the facilities on the ship were basically a bucket.

An entire day?

She washed her hands in something that looked worryingly like the first bucket before heading to the deck. The air still smelled of salt and sea, but there were heavier scents now. Food, alcohol, and smoke from the giant fires that sat outside, vied for attention.

And magic.

The air was heady with it. She leaned forward, the lifeline catching her in her stomach. Her head spun.

She tried to put the world straight, beating back a wave of euphoria as everything began to set itself right. Despite the flags that bore the royal family's insignia that flapped from nearly every window, she recognized none of the buildings. They weren't the practical many windowed designs of Egrean structures, nor were they the heavy, ornamental shapes of the buildings in the capital.

These homes were small, almost squat. They sat like brightly colored toads against the coastline. A Qasha that wasn't *Qashan.*

Reprenian, or what remained of it.

A smattering of people walked along the docks, moving quickly. It looked like they were trying to rush through a final bit of chores.

The guard's footsteps sounded behind her.

There was no Arn.

The signs that marked the stores held names in Qashan, but the pictographic language of the Reprenians was nowhere in sight.

"Are you ready?" Thanae asked.

Her fingers drummed against the lifeline's support. "Where are we going?"

To the forest.

"To the inn."

Her heart sank. "There's an inn?" The town seemed far too small. Even the dock that fed it felt like an afterthought.

"It's the top floor of a tavern, nothing fancy," he answered.

"Can't we call for a carriage or—"

"No carriage is leaving town this late."

"But if we paid them accordingly *and*—"

He didn't let her finish. "Tomorrow."

"Tomorrow?" she echoed.

"We'll head north, tomorrow."

It felt like a dismissal. She turned to face him, an argument on her lips, and stopped short. Dark bruise like bags sat beneath both of his eyes. Weariness had started dragging at his shoulders.

Guilt twisted Del's stomach.

He was exhausted.

She nodded, ignoring the impatience that set her legs itching and the disappointment that squirmed in her stomach.

Thanae shoved the vines into a leather satchel that she suspected was new. He struggled with the ties, pushing down tendrils of green that refused to behave and started off the boat.

She followed on his heels.

They passed two people. A child in a neatly sewn dress and a man dressed for dock work. Neither said a word, but the child took a long hard look at Thanae before laughing and racing between a gap in the houses.

The houses Del had seen from the ship all seemed to be empty. Not *quite* abandoned, but like all the owners had decided to leave at the same moment.

Vacant but still warm with the smoke of extinguished oil lamps.

Music tinted the air, so faint she might have imagined it. A stray note caught here and there as she peeked into the homes they continued to pass.

Notes coalesced into a song as they got closer to the inn. Drums set the ground vibrating and voices crooned.

It was worlds away from the dainty pieces the nobles waltzed to in the palace.

Del stopped short, a small "o" of surprise formed on her lips as the world brightened and focused in a way that it hadn't since the Grand Mage had dismissed his students.

"What's wrong?"

It was like *breathing*. She'd been struggling and hadn't even noticed.

"It's...nothing." She shook her head as a wave of giddiness washed over her. "It's nothing," she repeated.

The air was aflame with scents of cooked meats, and flowers, charred wood and deep, earthy broths. She felt the breeze acutely on her skin, the soft rays of the sun against her neck.

The music was so loud, it rattled the inn's door. Thanae frowned as he pressed his palm against it.

Del glanced to the small "inn" sign that hang from the boughs of a wild limbed tree. "What's going on?"

"Don't know."

How could he not *know*? From the smell of it, it seemed like they'd been cooking all day, someone must have—

"Get inside," he rumbled, as he opened the door.

The heat hit her first, the fires from the kitchens, the steam from the food, and the sweat from bodies packed close together. She turned to leave.

And bumped face first into Thanae, who hadn't even had the decency to move. She might as well have tried to shove a building.

"Can we, maybe, get in another way?"

"Why?"

"It's crowded," the words strung together, and she repeated herself, slower.

Thanae's lip lifted, making the skin of his scar crinkle as he tilted his head to better see her. "So?"

"I'm..." It was the moment with the prince all over again. The rest of the sentence caged behind her teeth. She studied the guard briefly, hoping she might find some better way to say she was afraid. That maybe he'd be able to see it on her face.

He didn't.

Bastard pushed her inside.

The inn was packed, tables had been pushed together and overflowed with both people and food. Fabric hung from the ceiling in thick ribbons of vibrant reds and deep violets, colors that had once sat on the Reprenian flag. A group of men in the corner started laughing and Del jumped.

The guard placed a hand on her back.

Everything in her wanted to run but she followed Thanae's lead like a stiff legged wind-up.

He sat her down at a table.

She blinked as the wood gave beneath her, "What?"

Thanae held a hand to his ear. Del tried again, "We were supposed to go to our room."

The guard leaned in. "Food's down here."

He disappeared into the crowd. Del's nails dug into her palms, her heart beat so loudly she was sure the drummers would pick it up and make a new song.

A tick passed.

Then another.

Her jaw unclenched as she took in her surroundings. It was crowded, dizzyingly so, but the man to her right had left her plenty of space and her back was towards the wall.

Del gathered her courage and tapped the man's arm. He spun, his hair a curly mass filled with ribbons, sagged to cover his eyes.

His smile was a wide, open thing, the likes of which she'd only seen a handful of times on the Grand Mage when he'd gone deep in his cups.

Her words died in her throat.

"Yes?" he prompted. His friendly demeanor didn't slip. She couldn't even find an undercurrent of annoyance.

"I...uhm." She dropped the Qashan and switched to Egrean. Most Reprenians spoke both, but Egrea hadn't been the one to take their country over and set most of its clergy hanging from gallows. "I wanted to know...what this party is about?"

He banged a fist against the table, and Del nearly bolted. The only thing keeping her in place was the knowledge that leaving would put her at the mercy of the crowd.

His face dropped as he gauged her reaction, his eyes shifting to his hand and back to her. "No, no, I didn't mean...don't be afraid."

I'm not afraid, she waited for the words to come.

Nothing.

She'd said them a thousand times before, even when they'd been lies, but somehow, they were out of reach. She gave the man a wary nod and bade her heart stop trying to escape at every loud noise.

His fingers flexed before he knocked a rhythm against the table. "Sorry, my friends tell me all the time, Dirg, you're an excitable one, they say. You move too much, too fast, the lasses will never come your way, they say." He frowned, briefly, before continuing, "Which is why I'm here, with them, instead of dancing, I guess. So, it goes."

She followed his gaze, and sure enough, there *was* dancing and truly awful singing. Brightly clad people swung about in pairs, ribbons fluttering behind them as they moved. There was no pattern to it, as far as she could tell, no neat turn or orderly lines.

It was chaos.

But it looked *fun*.

"Do you want to dance?"

Del turned to the man, Dirg, her cheeks warming. Had she been that obvious? But the very thought of him touching her—

Breathe.

She shook her head. "What are you celebrating?"

"It's the anniversary of the end of the war," he answered.

Del frowned. "And you *celebrate* that?"

He nodded, his smile faltering a fraction. Her unspoken acknowledgment hung between them. "We're still here. That's worth celebrating, isn't it?"

Something heavy hit the table in front of her. She scrambled away in time to see Thanae sit and set the other bowl of soup before himself. He held out a small loaf of sweet bread wrapped in a handkerchief.

"She's a twitchy one, isn't she?" Dirg began. He lifted his stein and took a long draught. "But who isn't these days, I suppose."

Thanae looked between them as she snatched the bread from his hand.

Del stood and whispered the translation in his ear.

His nose twitched. "I called you jumpy and you laugh me off the ship, but twitchy is fine?"

That earned him the barest of smiles. "Apparently."

He made a show of nodding at Dirg before descending onto his meal.

Del followed his example. Much like the food on the ship, it wasn't good. The vegetables were bland, and the sweet bread was hard. It was also just bread. She couldn't imagine them having the money for sugar.

Her eyes ticked from dancers, to feasters, before finally landing on the castings that ran along the walls to keep the noise from bothering those on the second floor. Another section set small orbs of light bumbling across the ceilings.

Castings still *working* this close to the border.

Del looked away.

For enchantments to still be running so close to the Chousalian border, some poor soul had either been sacrificed, which was unlikely, or the Reprenians still had a mage. And mages in Repren were an extension of the clergy.

She sent a prayer to Ose that the guard wouldn't notice, or that if he had, he'd fail to realize what it meant.

Del ate as fast as she reasonably could without choking. As soon as she finished, she made a show of pushing her plate away, earning a questioning look from Dirg. "Thanae, I'd like to go to our room now."

He stilled mid-chew.

"Now?" he asked.

She gave a vigorous nod. The guard's shoulders slumped. He heaved a heavy sigh before grabbing her plate and his own and heading towards the back of the tavern. Del followed behind him, sparing Dirg a tiny wave.

They passed through a set of wooden doors into the kitchens. The guard set their plates into a large half-filled basin before pausing in front of a stairwell.

He cleared his throat, "This way."

"I—" Her eyes were fixed to the back door. To the alley that ran beside the shop and let out in the street. "Sorry."

He grumbled as he set up the narrow set of stairs. The music deadened abruptly as they reached the top. *Magic.*

Jam and kitchen fires.

She studied the guard's exhaustion curved spine as he pulled a key from his satchel and unlocked the plain wooden door that sat at the end of the hall. He certainly didn't seem to be working himself up to slay any so-called "heretics".

He yawned as he pushed the door open. "This one's yours."

Hers? She scurried inside. A bed sat beneath a dusty window; a nightstand stood neatly beside it. Other than that, it was nearly barren. "Where are you staying?"

Thanae pointed to the wall. "Next door. Knock if you need help." He paused and added, "don't need help."

He closed the door before she could answer. Locked it.

Her trunk sat in the room's center, disgustingly opulent. She let out a curse and tried the door handle.

The lock held.

Del stopped short of banging her head against the wood. The room was meant to protect the belongings of its inhabitants while they were out. It only locked from the outside, which meant there was no way to reach the mechanism on her side.

She knocked her head against the wall.

The idea of sleeping didn't sit right. She'd slept an entire *day.* Her eyes fell upon the window.

She hesitated, trying to convince herself this wasn't a positively shit idea.

It was.

Gods above, she knew it was.

Del walked to her chest, and opened it, its lock giving with a satisfying pop. She dug through it until she found her small pouch of copper coins.

The bag weighed heavily in her hand.

This wasn't a betrayal. The quiet hum of the magic around her wrist was proof enough of that.

At least, that's what she hoped. Prayed, really, as she approached the window.

It opened easily, the latch leaping at the suggestion of a touch. The wooden panels opened outwards, letting in cool night air that set the skin on her arms prickling.

She climbed onto the sill. The fall wasn't far, so even if she messed up, she'd fair no worse than a broken bone. She'd experienced worse. Besides, it was only a small leap to the tree that stood before the inn.

Mihr-Did guide her feet.

Del took a breath and jumped. For a beat the world fell silent, she was weightless just moments above the ground. It really did almost feel like flying.

She landed haphazardly. Her heart was a drum in her chest as she struggled to find her balance. Her master broken, bloody, and wrong, flashed behind her eyelids as she scrabbled for purchase.

The branch bobbed and swayed. The rustling of leaves filled the air.

She let out a breath as the branch stilled.

"Is there a reason the front door wouldn't work?"

Beneath her, Dirg took a long drag from a pipe. Del tried to cobble together some sense of dignity as she shimmied toward the trunk in skirts that had torn somewhere between the window and the branch.

"I...uh..." She glanced at Thanae's window. It stood dim, and blessedly vacant. She continued, "My...friend is...overprotective?"

He let out a breath, dyeing the air with the sharp scent of whatever he was smoking. He watched dispassionately as she made her way down the trunk. "You seem used to that."

"Yes." She wiped at her dress and pulled a leaf from her hair. "Do you know anyone who can take me to the Chousalian forest?"

He frowned looking her over. "Should I get your friend?"

She shook her head. "No, but could you tell him where I went? Leave a note with the tavern owner or something?"

Dirg looked uncertain. Del shook her pouch. "Please, if you could just arrange for a carriage and tell him where I've gone, I'll give you everything I have."

Chapter 28

The wagon seat was small and cramped. With every bump Del came close to brushing against the woman beside her. It didn't help that the entire structure wobbled due to an errant wheel in desperate need of replacing. Still, despite everything, the structure lumbered determinedly down the dirt road as the sister moons sent down a lovely silver light that played off the leaves of the sparse trees that lined the roads.

A few barren fields shifted by, and once, the remains of a village that seemed to have been burned to the ground.

The road was new, else, Del imagined, she would have seen more.

"Are you alright there?" the woman spoke with a thick accent, but the Qashan was passable. She tilted the words in a way Del had never really had the chance to become familiar with. Low rumbling r's and swallowed vowels.

Del looked up. "I'm...," *fine* wasn't really the word. Her stomach buzzed with nerves and guilt as she ignored the implications of what she'd just done. What she was actively *doing*. "I'm fine," she lied.

Gods, that was getting harder.

"You don't look it."

Del turned to the cup she'd clasped in her hands. "Could I have another?"

The driver nodded and pulled a flask from her pocket. She was a stout, matronly type of woman, Del was almost sure she'd had to put her children to bed before taking her. She unscrewed the lid and filled Del's cup halfway before returning it.

Del took a long sip. It wasn't warm, and she wasn't thirsty, but the tea eased her nerves. Gave her something to do, something to think about.

It was *almost* the worst tea she'd ever drank.

"Thank you, for…taking me," she offered.

"You sure you want, that's," the woman huffed, her hands tightening around the reins. "If you need somewhere safe to go, my door is always open."

The world stopped.

Del's hands shook as she brought the cup back to her lips. She willed them still.

"I saw the scars," the woman continued.

The tea went down wrong, Del started coughing. Spluttering. The idea of leaping from the wagon and running off into the barren unknown was, for a brief moment, a very attractive option.

"Oh, sorry, I didn't mean—" the woman clucked. "You alright?"

Del shook her head as she tried to haul air into her lungs. Panicking, she was panicking. She should *have* . this.

"I'm fine," she repeated, unconvincingly. Gods, she could even hear it herself. This was awful.

The woman gave her a side eye and seemed ready to continue when Del insisted, "It wasn't Thanae, not, it's not my…companion. It was somebody else, and…I'm already as far from him as I need to be."

She recalled the way the Grand Mage's voice had echoed between her ears. It hadn't happened since, but maybe she could, in fact, afford to be a bit further.

"Alright then," the woman acquiesced. "Well, what do you like to do?"

The driver exuded nothing but warmth and good intentions. Motherly concern untouched by zealotry. It was, to Del, an unreal sort of encounter.

She reminded her of Ner, which is likely why Del answered honestly, "I like magic."

"Oh, castings and such?"

Del's hands went numb, her throat dry, but she was able to give the barest nod.

"You're not a mage, are you? No, sorry, that doesn't make sense. Mage headed for the forest." She laughed, softly, to herself. "We have a mage ourselves if you want to meet them when you get back."

"Are they...well?"

"Yup. They don't stay long. Just stop by, take our broken enchantments and return them the next moon. They're only spending the night on account of the festival."

The celebration had been in full swing when Del had scrambled into the wagon. The drummers had moved to the streets, the dancers having multiplied until the tavern could no longer contain them. Their songs, defiantly Reprenian, had been sung loudly to the heavens with a joy Del couldn't really comprehend.

Now, stars winked high overhead between heavy patches of cloud. She doubted the late hour would have slowed the celebration. If she'd been the mage, she might have risked death by staying too.

She swung her legs in her seat, hesitant. "...I...that's...what's it like living here?" she finished, shyly.

The driver's eyebrows shot up as a grin popped onto her lips.

The ride went by with quiet questions of magic, and life. Del liked the woman's answers about things the person in question apparently found very mundane. The process of chores, of work, and speaking with friends.

The woman answered with a bemused look on her face. She didn't ask Del *why* she didn't know anything. And Del tried not to feel simple when asking after conversion rates and how, precisely, money *worked*.

She suspected she had vastly overpaid for the ride.

It was nearly dawn when the forest finally came into view. Del realized, belatedly, that she hadn't seen a thing the entire night. There'd been no vines to send her crawling about the cart.

No Tani to whisk her to fairy stories or memories.

The carriage slowed as the last dredges of night slipped away.

Del slid from the wagon and stretched with relish as she took in where she was.

The tree line was...literally that. She could mark the start of the wood with a straight line for as far as the eye could see. Her brows knit together, that didn't seem proper.

"Are you sure this is, okay?" Del turned to find the woman looking around uncertainly, her hands were tight on the reins. "I can...wait for you or—"

"No." Del shook her head, before continuing, "you've done so much already. I'll be fine."

The woman seemed unconvinced, but having no better option, turned the forever rocking wagon around and trundled back the way they'd come. Del felt all the shortcomings of her plan fall into place as she watched her go.

Well, it hadn't really been a plan as much as a pressing need.

She hadn't even thought to bring water.

The thought came unbidden, and loud and clear as a bell, that the smart thing to do, would be to wait for Thanae. Her stomach knotted and Del shoved that particular thought to the back of her mind where it repeated itself on loop like an overwound music box. With effort, she managed to convince her attention to the forest.

Disappointment made itself known soon as she set eyes on it.

No feelings rose in her at the sight of it. There was no spark of magic, no pull as she'd felt in her dreams. It was simply, an admittedly vast, group of plants.

Just trees.

She walked past a few, expecting something to change. For her to feel *something* about it. This was the wood that had bordered the land her parents had come from, the world her mother had whispered about on quiet nights, the village Tani spelled out in her dreams. It was meant to be a part of Del; it was a piece of her heritage...and yet...

Nothing.

Nothing.

Even her feelings for her master's gardens held more definition.

Del walked past trees and patches of underbrush, up a hill and through a valley. The boots she'd stolen from the woman on the ship made quick work of twigs and protected her shins from branches and thorns. A few animals startled within the greenery, leaving trails of shuddering foliage, and twice birds let out frightened calls from the canopy.

After a bell, she leaned against the trunk of a flowering tree, staring at the variegated sunlight falling through the gaps between leaves.

She didn't know shit about forests.

Give her an enchantment and she could unravel land recreate it in a matter of bells, but a forest? Bestow upon her trees and growths unmarked by the small plaques that had denoted the species in her master's gardens, she might as well be trying to swim the Great Ocean. Del straightened and brushed absently at the dirt on her shirt, a frown on her lips. Her eyes darted from trees and vines to brambles and flowers.

Where had she come from?

There'd been a meadow and a valley, but she couldn't recall where they'd been or what order she'd crossed them in. She wandered in one direction for a tick, before giving up and trying another.

The truth tried to make itself known. She pushed it to the recesses of her mind until the fact was too obvious to ignore.

She'd gotten herself lost.

And Thanae would only have a vague idea of where she'd been dropped off.

Del rubbed her face. How could she have been so *stupid*? She knew very well the difference between books and reality, *fantasy* and reality. But she really had thought she'd just *know* when she got there. That something would click, and everything would settle, and it'd just feel *right*.

Stupid, stupid, stupid.

Anger set tears burning in her eyes as she gathered her skirts. The fabric protested as she tore it into long ragged strips. She stood on tiptoe and struggled to tie one around a low branch. When she finished, she stepped back and watched it ribbon in the wind, vibrant yellow against backdrop of green and brown.

She hoped Thanae would recognize it as hers if he ever came across it.

She wrapped the rest of the scraps around her wrist and continued forward. When the first ribbon was nearly out of sight, she set another. At least she could follow them back to *somewhere*.

After two bells, she started to get hungry and felt no closer to finding whatever she had deluded herself into thinking she'd find, than when she'd begun.

After a few ticks, she sank to the ground and stared vacantly at the sky above her.

She wondered if the gods could sense her now that she'd left the land they'd been banished from. Or had being in that country for so long severed whatever connection was meant to run between them?

She realized with a pang that she couldn't feel them at all.

Maybe Ataczi had been right.

She took a shuddering breath. It felt like Del was destined to disappoint everyone she met, the Grand Mage, her family, the *gods*...how much longer until Tiremalv realized his mistake as well? She couldn't imagine it would take long after this mess. She set her head in her hands despising the knot she felt in the throat.

Her fists clenched, she gave herself until the count of ten to feel sorry for herself, before she had to get up and find a solution. If she got out, she'd have all the time left until she died to wallow.

At "ten" she wiped her eyes and clambered to her aching feet.

And every plan she'd been in the midst of piecing together evaporated.

The trees had changed.

It was as if someone had taken their trunks and pulled them upwards, like stretched dough, until their branches rested just beneath the sky. She scrubbed her face against her sleeve. Maybe she was wrong.

Maybe she had somehow missed the giant fucking trees…that seemed to have clouds pressing against their branches.

Somehow.

She turned the way she'd come only to find her trail of ribbons had disappeared. She became aware of the magic in the air.

It was completely unlike the small eddies and pools she'd dredged sleepy little bits of magic from. Here, it was *awake* and so thick she felt she could sink into it.

"There you are," a voice came soft and sweet from the ether.

Soothing.

Del almost answered, but…that wasn't…right. Voices didn't just—. She blinked hard, trying to wrangle her thoughts.

"We've waited so *long*," it cooed. A breeze circled her neck, coaxing hair from her shoulders. "What took you?"

It was warm, and comfortable, and welcome. And Del realized distantly that this was precisely what she'd wanted to feel when she'd seen her family.

Her mind drifted.

"I know you can hear me," the voice chuckled. "Don't be rude."

Del shut her eyes and tried half-heartedly to pull the world into focus.

"That's not going to help," it informed her.

It was right, it didn't. And she wasn't sure if she wanted it to. For the first time in a very long time, there was no undercurrent of fear or worry to her thoughts. She could be everything she'd ever wanted to be, if she could just reach a little further, sink a little faster.

She could feel the magic running down every blade of grass, sluicing through the branches of every tree, sliding along the banks of a river.

You're stealing from the gods.

Ataczi's voice was a slap.

The world seemed to dim as reality slammed at its edges, seeping into the voids between her thoughts.

"Ah, *there* it is," the voice hummed.

She answered too muddled to remember her decision to keep quiet. "There what is?"

Delight filled the air and tried to slither beneath her skin. "Drowning in magic isn't a bad way to go, but everyone's put so much work into you, it'd be a shame."

Drowning.

Tani's warning spidered through her skull. And Del was suddenly unsure if the voice she was hearing was real. It didn't feel real. *Nothing* around her did. A soft, fantastic quality had tinted the air.

"Is this..." she began. She wasn't sure how to put it, she'd spoken to voices before, in her dreams, but...it'd been nothing this terrifying.

"Not a dream," the wind said, "Though I've seen you wandering here before, trailing behind the others. What stopped you?"

"Ta—" she stopped short as the air cooled around her.

"Ta—," it repeated, caustically.

Del's attention skittered across the landscape, searching for a form to bind the voice to. "That's, it's just, I wanted to...explore in my own time."

"You don't sound very convincing."

"You don't have a body," she said, as she tugged at dregs of indignation, trying to buy time to get her mind in order. "It's...making me uncomfortable."

Laughter filled her ears. "Fair enough," the voice ceased for a beat and when it started again, it'd filled with a hunger that made Del nervous. "Are you ready to become queen?" An image flashed before her eyes. A delicate silver crown dripping with jewels settled in her palms.

She blinked and it was gone.

Her hands looked bare without it.

"Queen?" Del echoed dully. The idea was so absurd the word barely consented to forming itself on her lips.

"Yes, 'queen'," the air said. It seemed to warm with the idea. "You're meant to be queen."

Gods, it was crazier the second time. Whatever the voice was, it was trying to mess with her, and Del didn't have time for that. She turned around and tried to walk in the direction she'd come from. Maybe she'd crossed some sort of barrier, been trapped by some malevolent spirit or *whatever* she'd forgotten from the stories of her childhood.

"How do I get out...to the regular forest?" she tried, without much hope.

"You haven't answered my question."

Del worried her lip. "...it's not something that needs answering, I'm a..." she paused. She wasn't sure what she was, neither Gadna's nor Tiremalv's, she hovered uncertainly above a title that no longer fit. "...I'm not...that."

"Why not?" The image flashed again and Del stopped short of walking into a tree.

"*Stop that*," she screeched. A wave of anger struck her with unfamiliar intensity. Her vision went red, as it coaxed her body into motion. Had the voice taken form, she was sure she'd have struck it.

"Answer me," the voice urged. "Are you ready to become queen?"

Del whirled searching high reaching branches for the voice's source, knowing she wouldn't find it. "Queen of what?"

"Chousal."

That was a joke if she'd ever heard one.

The crown flashed behind her eyelids. Her muscles ached to raise it to her head, to set it atop a bed of curls.

She shook herself, trying to escape a longing she didn't understand. "*Stop that.*"

"Not until you answer my question."

"I'm not ready, because it will never *happen*," she replied, sharply. She was reaching for anger, anything was better than the profound, empty sadness she'd found herself flailing in. "If you haven't noticed, Chousal is *gone*. And what's left of it is, apparently, dying."

"Is it because you don't know?" A small circle of leaves and grass lifted and swirled. Del grimaced.

She didn't like it placing images in her head, Tani, had asked permission. Whatever it was Del was speaking to had just assumed. It set her skin crawling. And the *feelings*...she'd been spiraling out of control since the Grand Mage had tumbled from the roof, but she'd hoped it was something that would fix itself. Her hands trembled and she clutched them to her chest.

"Where are you going?"

Del kept her mouth shut. Another vision filled her head, the same crown. Her gaze drifted to her reflection in a body length mirror. The eyes were wrong. Matching.

Pain exploded across her face. Del took a step back, reeling. Her hands caught a rivulet of blood.

She let out a slew of curses as the voice spread itself between her ears, laughing.

The remainder of her now useless rags went to staunch the bleeding.

"What are you?" she snapped.

The voice drifted lazily, "I'm myself, but I've been called many things, a spirit, a demon, a god—"

"You're not a god," Del spat.

"Oh, why not?"

Del frowned, trying to navigate her way around a pang of irritation as she readjusted her makeshift gauze to better catch her blood. Whatever that voice was, some sort of spirit or hallucination, it wasn't a *god*. It was too small. Gods were grand beings perched atop clouds that painted the skies in dazzling colors.

This was a dirty thing that set pictures between her ears.

Del probed her nose with her free hand. She hissed and let out every single curse she could think of. She couldn't even *breathe* through it. And she'd no knowledge of how to set it.

"Why not?" the voice prompted impatiently.

Her response came in irritated arcs, "Gods, why won't you just *leave me alone?*"

Leaves rose and fell in a rustling chuckle, "This is not the place for that."

Whatever *that* meant. Del started looking for an exit in earnest. Her teeth ground together as her own stupidity weighed on her.

You're impulsive Nyde, her mother's memory raised, and Del pushed it away. She didn't want to think of her empty eyes, or the things she'd done to hurt her. But child-like affection raised in response to the memory,

Enyemno's prayer spoke itself on her lips.

"So, you believe in that goddess, but not me?" the wind hissed and chilled.

Del shivered and refused to answer. She had a very tenuous control over what she thought and what she did. It was becoming deeply unnerving.

The image of her, the crown, her odd reflection, flashed rapidly in her mind. She stopped moving, lest she run into another tree. Curiosity was an unstoppable force, her lips peeled apart unbidden.

"Why that?" she muttered. "Why the crown? Why the reflection? It's *wrong*."

"To show what might have been and what may still come to pass," the voice announced, grandly.

"My mother is a *Pet*. Not a queen."

"And what was she before?"

That claimed her attention in a way she was sure nothing else would. Her mother had filled entire nights with tales of shops, festivals, churches, and stores, but she'd never spoken of herself.

Del spoke through grit teeth, "What do you know of my mother?"

"Oh dear," the wind chortled, "You really don't know anything, do you?"

It was trying to rile her. She took a breath, trying to divert irritation and anger with something less intense. Del took stock of her body, letting the pain in her nose and feet come to the forefront. The effort of it left her feeling off kilter and short of air.

"Your mother," the voice insisted, an image of her mother in finery that put Eizat's "gifts" to shame set itself in Del's mind.

She reminded herself fiercely that she'd dealt with worse. Gadna had—

"*Hasaq*, I knew her," it said. It summoned images of her mother laughing, raucously, in what seemed to be some sort of bar.

Gadna had never leveraged Del's mother.

And she wasn't convinced she wouldn't have tried to kill him if he had. "*Stop it*," her voice bounced off the trees. Her chest heaved as anger clawed its way from her belly to her throat.

The voice's glee slid against her skin.

"She was to be queen," it breathed.

Del plugged her ears. It didn't help, the voice snuck between the gaps in her fingers, the dips in her palms. It fed images straight to her mind.

She didn't want them.

Her mother donning a crown, her mother smiling at a grey eyed man, her mother dancing, grinning. As if she'd been so much more, before the collars and cages, before the bowing and scraping.

The sadness that struck her nearly brought her to her knees. She was crying, drowning in the feeling of complete and utter loss that she'd tasted on the ship after the captain had informed her of the Chousalian settlements. Except there was no one to talk to now, no sun to burn her eyes, no vines to sweep her away.

Del stood stock still as the visions continued to cycle. She spoke slowly as she wiped uselessly at her eyes, "These aren't real."

"They are," the kindness with which it spoke was some sort of insult she didn't understand.

Her mother in some armored dress, a crown atop her head, perched above a mass of people. She looked powerful. Del's thoughts failed. Her mother had been many things, but *powerful* had never been one of them.

"Stop it."

The forest came back into view. She didn't feel any better for it, the trees hadn't returned to normal, and she'd made no progress. Her chest heaved uselessly as she tried to control her breathing.

None of it had been real. But it hurt as if it were. Del picked up her thoughts slowly. If the *thing* messing with her could summon images, there was no guarantee that anything she was seeing was real. It could have her walking in circles for ages.

She pressed a bloody palm against the bark of a tree. Her hand passed through it.

She hiccupped a sob, "I *said,* stop it."

"What would it take for you to believe me?"

"I want you out of my head," her voice went high, as if she were still a child.

"What would it take for you to believe me?" it repeated.

"Get *out.*"

"What if I showed you?"

It was as if the lightest touch lifted from the inside of her skull. She swayed at the loss of a pressure she hadn't realized was there.

Before her the trees disappeared, petering out to the forest's edge that had been nestled into the bottom of a hill.

Del squinted trying to see past tears. "What is this?"

"The capital," the voice answered, faintly. She found herself struggling to make it out. "I can't bring you much closer than this."

It wasn't possible. The capital was in the center of the country and a three bell walk wouldn't have gotten Del anywhere close. Naya's hells it would take at least a week by carriage.

"This is fake too," she whispered.

"*Touch* it. You've seen what I can do, I make *pictures*," it seemed to sneer. "Nothing more."

"Nothing more," Del echoed. She wasn't sure she believed that, "Can you follow me there?"

A breeze pushed weakly at her back, "I can't."

Her stolen boots tacked against the cobblestone street as she left the safety of the forest's reach.

She followed the trail up a hill, to where a single building stood sentinel.

Its windows were dark.

She worked on controlling her emotions as she approached. It was a ramshackle structure that might have been at home in the Kothen slums. She spared a glance for the fallen sign half devoured by a swath of plants that marked it an eatery of some sort.

There wasn't much to see through the opening that served as the window: a smattering of tables, a few abandoned bottles with clouded glass. Some chairs had been overturned as if the occupants had left in a hurry or wildlife had gotten in and made a muck of things.

There was nothing that screamed *Chousalian*.

She mumbled unintelligibly as she wiped her eyes. She felt raw, like every emotion she'd ever tamped down had been forcibly scooped out of her. She wandered numbly along the road, her thoughts tumbling nonsensically in her skull.

The air chilled around her. She began to shiver, her breath painting wet, delicate clouds. Del pulled at her clothes, trying to keep herself warm as she crested the hill.

"*Voice?*"

She was greeted by nothing but the wind.

She *felt* alone, at least.

When she reached the top, she stopped, not quite believing her eyes. If it wasn't the capital, it was a very large town.

Chapter 29

A smattering of buildings started in the valley, before multiplying and climbing a slow rolling hill atop which perched a flat fortress of some sort. Del got the distinct feeling that she could have spent years wandering about, exploring homes and shops, and still wouldn't have scratched the surface.

She ran to the first houses, every step an echo of that night she'd caught herself racing across the Grand Mage's roof. She drove herself faster, ignoring the pain in her feet and the burning in her lungs. If only she could have been faster.

She'd still have let the bastard fall.

Del's feet slipped from beneath her and she hit the ground hard. A groan peeled from her lips as she made her way to her hands and knees.

Her palm sent a bone skittering across the pavers.

Del stifled a scream and scrambled to her feet.

The body had been neatly dressed before the elements had started to pick and peel away at its silks. The spear that'd pierced its back still remained, caught between its ribs.

She whispered a quiet prayer to Naya as she moved around it. Del had seen bodies, of course, *everyone* at the courts had and this one was very old. But that didn't stop the cheers of the crowd as the hangman cut the bodies down from echoing in her ears.

A pastel yellow kaftan, dirtied by prison grime.

She shook her head. One body, mostly bone, torn silks. She worked to convince herself that she could manage.

It wasn't long before she came across the second corpse, nestled against the wall of a bookshop. Arms frozen before its face as if it were warding off a blow.

This one wore a Qashan tunic.

Del sidled by it to reach the store entrance. The door moaned a protest and threatened to pitch off its hinges as a dull little bell gave out a half-hearted ring.

The building's roof had caved in, stone and clay tiles spilled into the center of the room, piled on fallen shelves and scattered books. The sunlight that plunged through the hole did nothing to warm the space.

She picked up the book closest to the door. Its pages had warped and melded together, so that she had to peel them apart. Sketches of flowers stamped pages filled with careful script.

All Chousalian. Her eyes wandered the lettering uncomprehendingly.

She couldn't understand most of it. Just words here and there, *flower, petals, vine.* Her mother had never had a *book* to teach them from, just scraps of parchment. And Del had been a child.

Her fingers traced the lettering, hesitating above swoops and curves.

The book shut softly between her palms, her nails digging into its spine as she clutched it to her chest. It was Chousalian, *actual* Chousalian. The strange house and the forest might not have meant anything, but this, *this* was something she could clutch and hold and point to with the absolute certainty that it was linked to the place her mother had once called home.

If she could somehow carry the entire store on her back and drag the building with her, she would have. She'd taken a handful of steps inside when the ceiling let out a low groan and a handful of pebbles rained from the sky.

The door fell off its hinges as Del backed through the entrance. She stared at it mutely, her heart in her throat as the dust it kicked up settled. Hoten's symbol winked back at her from the door's surface.

Its last offering, a smattering of coins and a ruined incense stick, sat in carved pockets.

She tried to imagine what it might have been to grow up without having to fear the symbols of the gods. To have made altars and offerings. Her mother had been far too cautious to have allowed any of those things, she'd barely even taught them the prayers.

The building let out another wail.

Del hurried away, leaving the structure to its settling, and wandered the streets.

The city had been designed around the fortress, every road intended to lead her there, like arteries to a still beating heart.

She tried to imagine what it looked like before the Fall, when the paths had to have been full of people who looked like her and the fabric that hung from windows and marked shop fronts had been vibrant and intact and the paints and decorations on the houses hadn't been sun bleached and worn.

But even Tani's village seemed to stretch the bounds of her imagination.

And there was the matter of the bodies.

The further from the forest she got, the more dead she encountered.

If whatever the voice was had the chance to create an entire city, why make one that was so profoundly sad?

The closer she got to the fortress the more it seemed to loom above the city, a tiny uncaring god.

Her heart shattered when she turned the last corner that left her in full sight of the building.

Corpses piled high against its gates. The desperate must have climbed over one another in an attempt to breach the wall. The carnage went along the gates and disappeared around the corner. She had a sinking feeling that it went around the entire building. There was no way for her to reach the fortress without picking her way through the dead.

Del's heart stuttered.

Her breath painted the air as she closed her eyes.

She didn't have to go.

Images of the bodies were already burning themselves into her memory and she had a feeling it was only going to get worse. She could just turn around and wander her way through all the houses in the area, peek into the lives that she might have lived, and make her way back to the relative safety of the forest.

But all the roads led towards the fortress and when danger struck everyone had run towards it...if this was Chousal or at least a memory of it. This was a part her mother had never mentioned, the story of the Fall told through the bodies left behind.

Del found herself moving forward, picking her way around the most disturbing bits of gore, trying to ignore the patches of dried skin and hair. A head rolled as her foot nudged against it and she fought the urge to retch.

The corpses reached her waist by the time she approached the wall, the smell finally reached past her broken nose and the cold. Rot and bone filled the air. Up close, she could see how they died, struck down from above. Many still had arrows in their backs, lodged in eye sockets, wedged between the vertebrae of their throats.

The arrows still bore the royal emblem her mother had sketched during lessons.

Del sized up the gate and felt her stomach twist.

It was ornate, the metal curved in complex winding patterns forming flowers and fields. A depiction of the forest that surrounded them.

And it was very much like the not-bars of her cage.

She tucked the book under her arm and wrapped her fingers around the stem of an oversized flower. The metal of the gate bit into her hands. Rust flaked beneath her palms and showered onto the bodies below as she worked her way up.

Patches of dried blood had solidified in the nooks and crannies of the designs. Being shot hadn't stopped people from climbing. If she looked closer at the bodies beneath her, she suspected she'd find broken arms and legs, fractured skulls.

Del's limbs shook as she reached the top, her hand scrabbled for the support wall, and she slowly hauled herself to its surface. Her body gave out as soon as her legs found purchase. It was all she could manage to roll over and stare at the sky as she tried to breathe.

There was something wrong about it.

Her eyes roved the heavens.

When it struck her, she sat up searching the sky for clouds or some large tree that might be blocking her view. There was nowhere for the sun to hide.

It simply wasn't there.

She'd been so preoccupied with the stores, the roads, and the stupid fortress, that she hadn't realized the skies hadn't changed for bells. They were an endless, unchanging and uncaring blue.

There were many problems with that, but she had neither the time nor the will to parse them out.

Del made her way to her feet.

From above, she could understand the shape of the carnage that'd slammed against the walls. She could even see where the last attack from the rear had cut through. They hadn't breached the gates, at least, not here.

On the other side of the wall, bodies were so tightly packed most were still in some iteration of standing.

She walked along the stone divide. The dead were here too, a smattering of soldiers, a few messengers, a bowman with a broken string sitting sentry. She tried not to stare at the blood that still stained its uniform.

The first set of stairs led to the overstuffed courtyard.

The second as well.

The wall led her around a series of smaller yards that might have been gardens. She'd nearly circled half the property before finding a stairwell that led to a sizeable overgrown yard, in the center of which sat a building that might have housed a number of servants or students or guards.

She hurried down the steps. After all the death that had surrounded her, the emptiness of the yard was eerie. She found herself searching for bodies hidden in the greenery, but if anything, this area had been evacuated before the attack. All that greeted her were tall grasses and a few determined trees.

The fortress had clearly been built for utility. Beneath new windows, gilded columns and sculptures, the structure was simple and practical. The hefty metal doors that led to its interior had been barricaded or locked. However, the window at its side sat broken.

She used the book to knock the rest of the glass from the paneling before hoisting herself inside.

She half-expected blood to appear on the sill. Her heart hammered as her hands lifted away.

It was clean.

Del swallowed and took a breath. She forced herself to stare at the sky, to recognize it was blue, instead of black and star filled.

It was fine. She was fine. The book protested in her hands. She turned away from the window, her boots sending echoes dancing down the soaring halls as she hurried along them.

This wasn't a servant corridor, at least, it wasn't in the way the ones in Kothen had been. These were large and had been made to be kept warm in the winter months and cool in the summer. Runes had been set into the walls, signs of light castings that had long since come unbound.

The hall was lit purely by the not-sunlight pouring through the windows.

Del wasn't sure what she was looking for.

The hall ended abruptly, the interior wall falling away in patches to reveal large open rooms. The smattering of bodies here, housed from the elements, had fared better. Their clothes still held bright patterns, jewels still dripped from their ears and necks.

The fortress was larger than she'd thought. She went about it methodically, working her way towards the interior, peering through broken doors, into bedrooms and meeting rooms, kitchens and healing chambers.

Nothing she saw seemed to tell her any more than she already knew.

And there was nothing of her mother.

The center of the building spun upwards in an addition that existed to let light in from the ceiling. Portraits hung on the walls beside a set of dubious looking stairs limned in gold. The railing held gaps where it'd given out unexpectedly, a few bodies lay where they'd landed on the floor.

The paintings Del could see were of battles, great beasts charging onto blood-soaked fields. She squinted trying to make out the enemy flags. Who had the Chousalians been fighting?

Any texts citing Chousal in Qasha had claimed the country hadn't had an army, but those certainly looked like warriors, and they most definitely had been armed.

None of the other paintings served to clarify.

Del pressed herself against the wall and started up the stairs. The first step set the entire structure swaying…she was going to get herself killed.

She sent quick prayers to Hoten and Mihr-Did before scurrying up. Her heart was thrumming faster than she'd thought possible by the time she reached the top and leapt to the relative safety of the floor.

The staircase let off to a large hall. It *felt* important, the portraits along the walls were filled with serious, dour looking people. She searched for her mother among them. The last portrait might have been her, if Del squinted and closed one eye.

The doors at the end of the hall were formed into a set of large, dark hands. The soil heaping between them and spilling from their borders served to smooth the doorway's edges. In neat carved letters it read: *We Rise And Fall In Naya's Hands.*

Perhaps her sister's claims of the gods abandoning their people weren't so far-fetched.

As Del neared the door, she gagged. The woman's tea splattered itself onto the marble floors. The stench that came with death was overpowering. She paused before the carved prayer and took a breath before pulling the handle.

Bodies collapsed through the doorway, shedding hair and skin and flecks of bone. Panic raised in her breast, she tried to breathe, but the air was thick with decay. Naya's prayer dropped from her lips in an endless loop.

Like the courtyard, the room was packed with bodies.

Their clothes varied from very ornate to incredibly simple. Tattered bows, stone jewelry, and pins still sat in the hair of those better preserved. Some bodies had the remains of tattered toys crushed to their ribs.

But Del processed none of that.

She started pulling the corpses down, forging a path. She didn't think about the desecration of bodies, the sound of bones crunching under foot, the feel of paper skin flaking beneath her touch.

She wasn't thinking at all.

She scrambled onto a high, complex stage, clutching to the book so tightly that her knuckles ran pale.

"Voice," she shouted loud enough to rattle the air. Her call ran high with rage and betrayal.

She waited for her echoes to die out before calling again, and again, and again, until her throat was sore.

The fortress stayed silent. Her audience of dead only fell in small smatterings where she'd left space for them to do so.

If the voice heard her, it didn't answer. Her mind felt to be her own. But she wasn't sure what that *meant* anymore.

This had to be some sort of joke.

Her mother was a Pet. And as far as Del was concerned, that's all she'd ever been.

A thin dirty being that set illusions between her ears, could not be a god. And her mother could never have been queen.

The portrait hanging before her was some sort of lie.

The woman in it looked remarkably like her mother.

Exactly like her, from the crinkling of her eyes to the quirk of her smile.

She sat on a throne beside a man with deep grey eyes. His mouth pulled in a suppressed smile. Their portrait was sillier than the others, like they hadn't been able to take it seriously, or hadn't wanted to.

Del's palm pressed against the paint. Pigment flaked onto her fingers. Gentle red, bleeding into orange. The colors of a dress that made even her mother look worthy of the title "queen".

Breathe.

Her lungs ached. She took a deep breath, her eyes ticking from the pigment to the portrait.

In gold letters stamped into the base spelled out her name, Queen Hasaq Andataz IV, the man's name was lettered beneath it, Ijetzan Andataz I.

It didn't make sense.

Her mother was the lively woman whose smile never quite reached her eyes, the woman who spun stories in the nights, and guided Del's hand as she traced letters across parchment. Hasaq was a woman who crafted small freedoms in caged rooms and thought that enough to sustain a child.

She wasn't a *queen* or *royalty*.

She was just the Pet of a very small man tucked into the Egrean countryside.

Del backed away until the ground disappeared. She yelped as she plummeted, and bones snapped beneath her. The gaping maw of a skeleton bent above her.

She screamed, scrambling backwards. Everywhere she moved, there were bones, and clothes, and rot.

Her pulse ripped through her body as her breathing sped. She bowled down more corpses, mothers, fathers, daughters, sons, children and parents, lovers and enemies, rich and poor.

They'd died here as if they hadn't tried to fight it.

As if they'd given in and accepted their fate with a half-smiling portrait there to mock them.

She ran as soon as she reached the door, tearing through the fortress, tracing past halls to the courtyard before scrambling up the wall and clambering down the fence. Her breath came in painful gasps as she waded through the last stretch of the dead before making her way back to the forest.

Chapter 30

"Oh, look at what you've found," the voice raised, weakly, a breeze wove around Del's arms, ending at her knuckles where she still clung to the book of flowers. "Did you find what you were looking for?"

Her shoulders hunched. "You lied."

"I didn't."

"You were in my head and made me see," her words petered out. It'd made her see what? Her mother, a barren city, the dead and their homes? The homes she'd *touched*, the buildings she'd *scaled*. Del finished uncertainly, "...what you wanted."

"I did not," the voice sneered. "I am bound to the forest."

Del moved further into the trees, trying in vain to outmaneuver the wind.

"Are you ready to become queen?"

Her feet dragged to a stop as she closed her eyes. "I'm no queen."

"Not yet."

"There's nothing to rule over," she insisted. "So even if..." The thought wasn't worth finishing. She continued weakly, "what does it matter?"

The air cooled. A hum zipped by her ears as she opened her eyes.

The voice was speaking, too soft and quick for Del to pick up. Then it fell silent for so long she thought it'd disappeared again.

She started walking hoping to at least find her way back to the tree where she'd gotten lost the second time.

"Ask me a question," the voice began.

Del jumped. "Gods, don't *do* that."

"Ask me a question only a god would know the answer to."

She bit her lip, thinking it over. "I'm not a god, so I won't know if you're just making it up."

"You're an alchemist," it continued, peevishly, "figure it out."

"I'm a *mage*."

The voice's laughter sent birds launching to the skies, "You are nothing like a mage."

For some reason *that* was what set her eyes burning. Not the death of her people, not the carnage, not the sheer incomprehensible loss she'd felt just walking around the empty streets, but the fact that a small voice had whispered she wasn't a mage.

"I am," her voice broke. She abandoned the sentence as and swallowed past the lump that'd made home in her throat. "I want to know about the mage's illness."

Nearly a tick passed before the voice answered, "the what?"

Del wiped her eyes and started walking faster. "I thought you said you were a god."

"And I said I am bound," the wind growled, "I may know it by another name, but the 'mage's illness'," It acknowledged the illness with the same disgust Eizat's maids held for cleaning the chamber pots, "means nothing to me."

"Excuses."

"Describe it."

"*Look* at me." Del let out a hopeless laugh as she raised her arm for inspection. "Colored pastes shouldn't be all it takes to fool a being that set moons in the heavens."

She *felt* its cool regard settle across her skin. It set gooseflesh raising along her arms.

"I see you are *untrained*," it scoffed, "But otherwise healthy."

She bridled, lowering her arm, "I've been *trained*."

The wind chilled. "Then whoever it was, had no idea what they were doing."

"He was the best mage in Qasha."

"A *Qashan* mage," it murmured, disapprovingly.

What in Naya's hells did it matter? "So, you *can't* help me. Is that what I'm hearing?" she snapped.

A tree appeared before her and she stopped short, a hand flying to cover her still tender nose.

"I cannot help if there is no problem," the voice explained slowly, as if it were speaking to a child.

"Is *dying* not an issue for you?"

A high-pitched giggle spun around her, setting dirt and twigs turning in little vortices.

"What about the marks on my skin?" Del tried. "The...nightmares?"

"Oh," the voice perked, as if it'd finally heard something worth responding to, "the marks? They're very pretty, aren't they?"

That was beside the point. "They're killing me."

"Hardly." The voice circled her. "They're *calling* you."

She couldn't fathom as to *where* other than Naya's eternal embrace. The voice didn't know, and it was going to string her along for as long as she allowed it. The air rose and fell beside her, a sigh.

"A protector needs something to protect," it drawled, "If it has nothing it will reach out and *find* something, though the strength of it was outside our calculations."

Del squinted. "What?"

"The *forest*, my queen—"

"I'm no queen."

"*Priestess* then," it continued, flatly. Del narrowed her eyes, somehow that was worse. "The forest was the protector of Chousal. Well, it *is* as you say. Chousal is a bit out of the running at the moment. And a protector needs something to protect, the forest needs a people, if it cannot find one it will call one. Such is the way of things."

"It's a forest, a *location*," Del exclaimed. "A patch of trees and animals, why are you talking like it's alive."

"It is, in a fashion."

"But that doesn't make any *sense*," her voice ran shrill, "Even if it *was* alive, nobody's coming if they're dead."

"As I said, the strength of it was unexpected," the voice repeated, blandly, "There was no way to know how much power this barbaric place wields."

"Some 'god' you are," she muttered, petulantly.

The wind stopped. A chill crawled down her spine as her heart sped. "I'm sorry, I didn't, I didn't mean that. I...I just would like to...is there a way to...," she gave up, "I'm dying."

"All you beings are dying, it's nothing new."

They were speaking past each other, a language barrier without the language.

"You said I got these marks because the forest is calling me," she tried, "So, is there a way to make it stop? I need to return to the prince."

"The Qashan?"

Del nodded.

"It's calling you closer, so grab something to approximate that," it responded, flippantly. "A twig, a plant, a seed. Keep it near, and when it calls, you will already be there."

"A twig," Del mumbled.

"So long as it's part of the forest, though it's better if it's something alive. Dead things only hold memories after all, and those are easy to lose."

"*A twig?*"

That couldn't be it, thousands of mages couldn't have died because they were too far from a piece of *foliage*. The cure she'd stumbled across had to have something to do with it being her mother's brew, a *Chousalian* brew.

There had to be some greater meaning.

"And the vines? The ones that grow on me, the ones on my skin?"

"Magic," the voice sighed. Its disinterest bore down on her, driving air from her lungs.

"What do you mean magic? I can't make something from nothing. I have to conserve mass, energy, there are rules."

"There *are* rules, but *conservation of mass* isn't one of them. Who cares if you pull flowers from the air, or guides from the ether? It's the energy that everyone is after. Stop getting caught in your little human antics."

This wasn't working. She couldn't make heads or tails of what it was saying. She was too busy trying to force air into her lungs, to keep the world steady beneath her.

"People have died," she whispered. They weren't *her* people but...they'd had families too. Someone had cared for them.

A twig?

None of this was real.

It couldn't be. The gods had rhyme and reason, the world they made was poetry. It was sunsets on the oceans, rainbow painted clouds, the steady rhythm of the seasons. This *voice* was trying to make it seem as if their actions might be some sort of *accident.*

But the only way to prove it a liar, was to prove it wrong. "How can I save the others?"

"Others?"

"Yes."

She waited for a response.

Waited.

And waited.

"Hello?"

Nothing.

She gathered herself, gulping at the air until breathing was less of a chore. Her hands brushed at the dirt and dust and whatever else she'd gotten on her clothes while in the city.

Going back to whatever that…place had been wasn't an option.

And neither was staying lost in this stupid wood.

Del tried to imagine some way to get her bearings and found herself staring at where the branches met the skies. It was too high to climb safely, and even if it wasn't, she doubted she had the stamina to reach the top.

She ran a hand through her hair, trying to imagine another option. Her fingers skimmed over tangles and patches that'd fallen loose at some point during the day, before brushing against something soft.

A ribbon the length of her forearm deposited itself in her palm. The royal insignia flickered a repeating pattern in delicate silver thread. Her eyes fixed on it blankly.

It was tucked between the pages of her book before she realized what she was doing.

"You need to be more," the voice announced.

Del squeaked. Her tome tumbled to the forest floor.

She dropped after it without thinking, half expecting the pages to erupt in blue flames. She only breathed once everything was in her hands, again. Unsinged.

"If I was meant to be more, the gods would have done a better job," she tried to laugh. It came out weak. Her hands still shook.

"We need you to be *more*," it repeated.

"Then *make* me more," she answered, wearily. "You say you're a god then you're supposed to have the answers. You're supposed to have the reason. If I'm meant to be stronger, then *make me stronger*. Otherwise, just leave me alone."

Her stomach growled as if to bleed the tension from the air.

She rolled her eyes and started walking. It didn't matter that she didn't know where she was going, so long as it was away.

The voice remained quiet, and her stomach insisted on making a ruckus to fill the silence it left behind.

She wandered until the pain in her feet forced her to break. She sank beneath the branches of one of the infinite trees.

Her fingers dug into what remained of her skirts as she tried to recall how Tani had seen the forest. She'd known how to navigate through it, there'd been patterns and logic.

But to Del's eyes there was no such thing to be found.

"Voice?" she called softly.

Nothing.

"Forest?" she tried. What had it been that Tani had noticed? If she talked to the forest, it would...something with fruit? It wasn't exactly what she needed, but it might take care of the hunger.

"I..." Her mouth shut, what was there to talk about? The city? How she'd gotten herself lost? How she'd watched the only person in the world who'd said they loved her in the last eight years tumble from a rooftop?

"I...I'm Nydelissi Anders," she began, uncomfortably. "I am the...I *was* the Pet of the Grand Mage of Qasha...and now I'm..."

Her nails burrowed into her thighs.

"It's just...Nydelissi...Del, now..." She ignored the blood rushing to her cheeks, she felt like an absolute ass. "I've had dreams about being here. It was different then. I didn't feel so...lost? But I think you like to be talked to."

There was no grand jostling of foliage, no sudden beam of light. No feeling of holiness or knowledge decided to conveniently flood her head.

It didn't even feel as if it were listening.

"It's a...pleasure to meet you?" she tried. "But if it's...possible...could you let me go?"

There was no response. She closed her eyes, the voice had said the forest was alive, not sentient.

Was it a question of faith?

She wondered if the people piled before the fortress prayed with faith run high on desperation, or had they felt it when the gods had left them to die?

Was that moment something she could sense?

Breathe.

Del opened her eyes, squinting at the foliage. The trees were still impossibly tall, but...

Stars.

She scrambled to her feet.

The sun was low, little more than a patch of brightness in the eastern corner of the sky. Delicate pinpricks of twinkling light scattered the heavens moving from the indigo fingers of morning.

If she was near the capital, she needed to head south.

She had a direction.

Del clasped her hands together, finding a new wave of energy. "Thank you."

There was no response.

Chapter 31

Del made it most of the morning before the headache that worked between her temples forced her to rest.

She cursed softly. In all her dreams and in Tani's memories, there had been clear running streams, grand pools, and waterfalls. Her ears strained for the sounds of trickling and met only wind and the rustling of leaves.

She knocked her head against a tree.

Her stomach grumbled. She needed water first, then food. She'd sweat while running through the city.

Move.

Her legs ached as she forced herself upright. Her head throbbed in time with the beating of her heart. The only reprieve came when the sun sank beneath the horizon and the forest bled dark.

But the pinpricks of light that wheeled overhead were senseless.

Del studied them, a frown etching itself onto her lips as her brows drew low. She muttered to herself as she waved away hordes of small insects that nipped at her skin.

Her mother had once spun the stars into stories of gods and goddesses and mortals who'd died valorously that now dotted the heavens. But she'd often been out at night and the stories had been few with many nights spanning between them.

And none that Del recalled had held anything that pointed in a cardinal direction.

She sat herself against a tree and waited for the day to come. Her nerves frayed steadily with every scuttle and whisper across the forest floor. When her eyes fluttered shut, her dreams held only nightmares. She woke twice with screams lodged in her throat before the sun rose.

Her muscles protested and cramped as she started her second day of travel. Her mind wavered listlessly between the need for food and water. Twice she caught herself looping in circles.

Prayers went unanswered.

The fear she'd been denying started picking at the edges of her thoughts. Del had imagined her death many times. When she was younger, she'd always thought Gadna would be at fault. That the last thing she'd see was his panicked face floating in the air above her. When she grew older, she imagined she'd die the way her music teacher had, on a platform before a swarm of people with jeering filling her ears. But she'd never once imagined she would die alone.

It scared her.

"Voice," she croaked, trying to drive away the images of her master's body. *Anything* was better than nothing, even the nasty little creature that claimed itself a god.

She stilled and held her breath.

Waited.

There was only the gentle rustling of leaves and the steady rhythm of her footsteps as she started walking again.

Del called for what felt like bells before she gave up and began talking to the forest. She talked about nothing. She told the forest how she used to love drawing her family, and running into Ner's arms so the maid would ruffle Del's hair. She prattled on about the importance of herbs in locking spells, and the difference in casting and how it changed from region to region. She explained how she'd taught herself to cast and the conversations she used to sneak with the students.

It made her feel less alone.

She slept just as poorly the second night, dozing fitfully until the sun forced her awake. Her thoughts jumbled and clinked together as she made her way to her feet. Her limbs shook, her head pounding as her blood forced itself through too dry arteries.

She whispered about her siblings as the day began, but her thoughts were so disorganized she found herself dropping into long stretches of silence. By midmorning, she'd run out of things to say.

The ground caught her feet, clutching at her rubber muscles until they locked, and she lurched forward like a drunkard. She didn't even know what she was looking for.

Anything really. A tree line, water, a campfire.

Something yellow flapped in the lowest branches of a tree.

She blinked, not believing her eyes. Yellow, *her skirts*. Her body ignored her insistence to move faster.

She cursed every branch and twig, along with every single span of distance that separated her from her goal. Distantly she worried that it might be an illusion, another image the voice might have put into her head, but godsdammit all to Naya's infinite hells that idea could suck the balls of her dead master and die.

It didn't matter if it wasn't real, she was going to reach it.

Her body gave out at the base of the tree. She groaned, shifting as she tried to clamber to her feet, but her arms refused to support her. Her legs were little more than string.

The strip of fabric flapped in the wind somewhere above her.

She sighed, accepting begrudgingly that she'd done all she could. Her thoughts listed drowsily, Tani's voice reached her half a memory. Chiding her really, *you don't sleep enough.* Del let out a hoarse chuckle.

Her eyelids drifted shut and she let the world go.

Del's stomach ached, a hunger pang that refused to go away. She was swaying. She groaned, her mind summoning images of rough seas and bloodied sheets.

Her eyes opened to a sky-blue swath of feathers. She'd been tossed over someone's shoulder.

Like a sack of flour.

She wriggled as fear shot through her. "I can't," her voice was dust and ash, speaking set her throat on fire. "Down. Put me down. Please."

The swaying stopped. A sob caught in her throat, but no tears came.

"I can't be touched, so, please," she begged.

The world twisted. Feather became sky as her feet pressed against the ground. Her eyes fixed on the hands clasped around her forearms.

Her breaths came fast and shallow. Her chest ached with the effort of it.

"I'll be good, I promise. So please let go," she whimpered, "I'm sorry. I'm so, so sorry."

The hands bore down on her a moment longer before lifting away.

And the world went black.

Chapter 32

Del dozed, somewhere between waking and dreaming, where the world stayed soft and kind.

It smelled of soup. The air was balmy with the scents of herbs and broth.

Someone was speaking. Their words sank into the background, a lullaby like the ones her mother once sang.

Something brushed her lips.

Memories of bitter tinctures sprang to life. The ghosts of healers' hands dug into her arms.

She pulled away instinctively.

Her body refused to cooperate. Her limbs dragged and something heavy bound her legs to the ground beneath her.

The speaker stopped.

Colors arced behind her eyelids as fresh pain stole her breath. Something pinched her nose. The cry she let out was pitiable, a single pleading wail that she managed to cut short. The earth cradled her as she tried to move away, her fingers dug into something soft.

Everything was soft.

Heavy.

She panted trying to catch her breath. A groan built in her throat as a headache ripped between her temples.

The thing pressed against her lips again. Something cold and sweet dribbled into her mouth before she'd the chance to close it.

She sputtered, shaking with racking coughs as she lurched forward.

Her eyes snapped open in time to watch the cup slip out of reach.

"Please," the word fell broken from her lips. She tried again, begging for water with a throat of flame that only seemed to make shattered sounds.

The voice spoke back to her. She couldn't make sense of it.

Noise.

The cup returned. This time she managed a few sips before it was pulled away. The cycle went on for what felt like an eternity. Drinking and waiting.

Drinking and waiting.

Until something small pressed against her lips. She opened her mouth more readily. unwilling to risk her nose a second time.

Sweet.

Her eyes widened as she bit down. It was like chewing a pebble. Candy?

Nobody gave Del candy. Sweet breads and cakes, tarts and desserts, but never candy. She'd spent nearly a decade watching the palace children with envy, and dutifully avoiding eye contact with sugar filled bowls.

Her master was against them. Something about caring for her teeth.

It was peppermint.

The smell cleared her nose, broke through the fog in her head and forced her more fully into a consciousness she found she did not want.

Being awake *hurt*.

The last bits the world shifted. Like a veil had been lifted. She blinked, taking in the room she'd left the nightstand and the window she'd leapt through the night of the festival. She was on the bed, propped up by a series of pillows. The boy before her looked toward the window, which he'd apparently had barred shut this time around.

He looked nearly as bad as she felt. The bruises beneath his eyes were massive, scratches and angry welts tore across his skin. The beginnings of a new scar traversed beneath his bad eye.

"Thanae?" her voice cracked; the end of the word trailed to nothing.

The guard turned suddenly, the speed of his movement put her ill at ease. "Are you with me?"

Del tried to laugh, and spikes sang through her lungs as her stomach clenched. Her chest heaved while she waited for the pain to pass. "What do you mean?" she asked.

He didn't answer.

Her candy dwindled to nothing.

Del sniffed. "You fixed my nose."

Nothing. There wasn't a single twitch of his mouth or crinkling about his eyes. His expression stayed utterly blank.

Her gaze dropped to her hands. "I'm sorry."

The guard heaved a sigh and set a dainty teacup onto the nightstand. He stood. She hadn't even realized he'd been on her travelling case.

"I had a book." She winced at her own desperation.

The guard didn't acknowledge her. He moved deliberately, lifting a small wooden bowl from the windowsill, and returning to his seat. His expression was ever unmoving.

"My book," she repeated.

He filled the spoon and held it towards her.

She was fast losing hope. "My book?"

The spoon wiggled.

"Thanae, I need the—"

The utensil bounced painfully against a tooth as he shoved it in her mouth. The soup was quite possibly the best thing she'd ever eaten.

"Gods, this is something the prince would make," she let out a half-hearted laugh.

Thanae frowned. The lines in his face settled, running deep down well-worn tracks. It was only a matter of time before they carved permanent divots.

"My book?" she tried.

"You almost died," he stated, plainly. She wasn't sure how to address that. There had been many times when she'd been hurt, but nobody had ever seemed to care. At some point she'd stopped thinking it was something to concern herself with.

A tick passed. He offered her another spoonful.

"I can feed myself," she pointed out.

"You can't."

Del glared at him. To her surprise, he spun the bowl to offer her the spoon. She reached out, ignoring her body's protests, the impossible weight of her fingers and wrist. Her hands shook too badly to even grasp the handle.

She spat out a curse that sent Thanae's brows arching as she let her hands fall into her lap.

Embarrassment heated her cheeks. Her eyes burned with unshed tears.

The guard's face held no judgement as he fixed his grip and continued feeding her as if nothing had happened. Which made her feel worse.

"I'm sorry," she repeated. "I didn't...it was supposed to be short." Del's face crumpled, she hadn't the energy to fix it. "Sorry, I'm, I—."

She wanted to disappear.

"I have a brother," the guard said, suddenly.

She looked at him, several obscenities clear on her face. "What?"

He continued, "He's eight years younger. Likes peppermints...it's why I had some."

He studied her, with...some sort of expectation.

What precisely, in Naya's hells, was going on? "Is...he...," she began, uncertainly, gods what was it normal kids did? "...enjoying school?"

Thanae nodded. "Good enough. He wants to cast."

"Oh."

"He doesn't have the mind for it, can't memorize runes, or the mixtures."

Her lip curled, as old annoyances rose. "He doesn't *need* to memorize, there are books for that and Qashan mages need to prepare their spells beforehand, regardless."

He smirked.

It reminded her of the way he'd looked at her after meeting her family. It wasn't unpleasant, but it was unexpected. There was no safe reaction to responding to it, so she looked away.

Her fingers twined together in her lap.

"My book...please."

The smile slipped from his face. He stood and set the lid of her travel case banged against the floor.

The guard set the book gently by her side along with the ribbon she'd caught in her hair, and a plant, which now sat somewhat haphazardly in a kitchen bowl filled with damp soil. She didn't remember grabbing it.

Her finger brushed tentatively against a leaf. "Did you do this?" she asked.

He grunted noncommittally as he returned to his seat.

"Why?" she wondered.

"It was going to die."

She shook her head and regretted it. Her eyes shut until the pain subsided. "That's not what I...," she sighed. "You're a mystery Thanae."

His gaze burned the top of her head.

She tugged nervously at her sleeve.

Del hadn't had sleeves in the forest. She tried to keep the panic from her eyes. "How much did you see?"

He shifted on the box, setting it creaking. "I had the innkeeper take care of you but, she called me in. She almost threw us out." The guard gestured to the silver that climbed up Del's fingers. "But she saw the scars and almost threw me out instead. It took a lot of convincing to get her to let me near you."

Del's entire face caught flame. The sheets bunched in her hands. "They're, uh..." She swallowed, unable to bring herself to look Thanae in the eye. "They're not as bad as they...look?"

The damned bed refused to sweep her away. Ose didn't summon lightning to dispatch her from the sky. The useless fucking voice didn't so much as whisper.

Was there even any point?

She squared her shoulders, summoning strength from some well she'd nearly drained and smiled. "I'm sorry to have shown you something unpleasant."

Chapter 33

The rest of the day, Del refused to say anything more. She was too afraid to see the pity in the guard's eyes, and she didn't want to have to explain. She was *fine*. What the Grand Mage had done had been what the Grand Mage had done, that was all.

She shouldn't have to defend herself from every godsblessed idiot who had the misfortune of catching sight of her bare skin. She waited for the guard to demand more of her, to give her orders or force her back to the capital, but he seemed happy enough to spend his days reading by her window.

It wasn't long before she caught herself dozing through most of the day and sleeping fitfully through the night.

She succumbed quietly to complete and utter exhaustion.

Eventually, Del woke to find herself back in the forest.

It was a dream, it had to be a dream. But her body didn't seem to care. Her heart pounded in her ears. The air went thin, she found herself struggling to drag it into her lungs. She shut her eyes and willed herself awake, and failing that, tried to focus on anything that wasn't *being there*.

She tried to guess what Thanae would bring her today. He'd taken to giving her small trinkets, not necklaces but stones and pebbles and breads from the bakery. Small promises of the outside world as they waited for her body to settle and heal.

And she'd never tell him, but she'd started looking forward to them.

Her nails dug into her thighs, as her thoughts of pebbles and sweets went up in smoke. This was *stupid*.

Breathe.

All she had to do was wake up.

Breathe.

Footsteps sounded near her. She glanced up to find Tani walking towards her.

A waking nightmare.

The girl studied her with a quiet detached interest. "You're having trouble."

Del's mind broke the sentence into fragments and tore the sounds into pieces that she couldn't hope to understand. She stared at the girl blankly, feeling helpless as the air in her lungs became solid.

Breathe.

It hurt.

"I'm bad at this," the girl said. The earth scuffed as she neared Del, "I don't know what to do."

Del couldn't hear her at all. Tani took a seat beside her and picked up one of her hands.

She almost pulled away, but she desperately wanted to be touched. To not be afraid. To be brave enough to take a hand when the world felt like it was falling apart. As the memories overlapped, Tani's hand with Ner's, the forest and the smell of blood, Del refused to let go.

"I'm here," the girl began, awkwardly. "My husband used to do this for me, sometimes. I didn't like it at first either."

Tani's hand was warm and delicate, but no matter how hard Del held on to it, it didn't give.

Breathe.

Del's lungs cooperated at last.

Breathe.

She managed to convince her hands still...let her shoulders down. There was no Gadna, no Ner, no blood, and the forest that surrounded her wasn't the one she'd been trapped in. The colors were warmer. More vibrant. Water ran somewhere she couldn't see.

Tani picked at a vine with her free hand. "Are you feeling better?"

"I'm sorry...," Del gasped, still focusing on the in and out of the air in her chest, "I...I didn't mean to." Her words caught, she struggled to track her thoughts. "I didn't mean to...show you something." She shook her head. That was the wrong apology. "Intrude. I didn't...mean to...intrude."

The girl shrugged. "It's okay. You aren't good with schedules anyway."

Del looked at their hands, her mind snagging on the way their fingers intertwined. She marveled at it.

She didn't think she'd ever be able to do this again.

"How did your...story end?" Del asked. "You're the girl...in Enyemno's tale, right? The one...with the binding cloth?"

"I...uh..." She shifted, uncomfortably. "Kind of?"

"What does that...mean?"

"Well...," Tani's said. Her fingers dug into the earth. "It's...my story? But that's not me in it."

"But you're the girl...the *sharp-tongued* girl," she insisted.

"I'm not sharp tongued," she muttered. "People just ask stupid questions."

"She's *you*," Del reiterated. "And the...the kind boy is Rua?"

"Sort of."

The girl was dancing around the topic, fluttering near it as if she were afraid to touch upon it. Irritation sharpened Del's voice, "What do you mean by sort of?"

"It's our *story*, but that's not us. It...chafes...I'm not the girl, but she's me. And Rua...Rua's not the boy."

Del shook her head. It still wasn't making any sense. Was it the difference between reputation and reality or were there two of each person?

Del squeezed Tani's hand. "Show me."

Tani knocked on Rua's window. Fog bloomed before her mouth and across the glass as she pressed her nose against it.

She knocked again, watching his bed waiting for the moment his blankets moved.

She knocked a third time and his brightly colored cocoon twisted and shifted upwards. A muzzy headed Rua squinted blearily at the window. She couldn't hear him curse through the glass but the way his head ticked back meant he was either praying or saying some very choice words.

He abandoned his covers and stumbled towards her on stiff legs. Tani was struck by a wave of warmth as he pushed the window open. Rua recoiled, crossing his arms over his chest.

"Do you know what time it is?"

Tani glanced at the moons. "About four bells after sundown."

He shivered. "And you're outside my window, why?"

"Because we have to go to the forest," she spoke, quickly, Rua was already moving to interrupt her. She'd been bringing it up every day since the old woman had disappeared. "I know that you're tired of hearing this, and you don't believe me, but *please* Rua. If I'm wrong, we'll be back before sunrise, and I'll never bring it up again."

She studied his room as she waited for his answer. A small stack of carved wooden flowers sat beneath his window and embroidered fabrics painted his walls in gentle animal portraits and poems. Soft cloth animals sat atop his bed, rabbits, deer, wolves, and birds brought to button eyed life.

A dozen beats passed before he heaved a sigh.

"Alright. Come in," he said, as he tottered inside. "Let me get dressed."

Tani hoisted herself through the window, watching his considerable frame curve to light a candle. She warmed herself near the heating enchantment by his bed as he gathered his clothes and changed.

He put on layer after layer, after layer, after layer and by the end, it was everything Tani could do not to laugh. He looked more like a child to be toted about than a boy on a mission.

"Okay." He looked out the window again, and grabbed a scarf before announcing, "I'm ready."

Tani didn't waste any time. She blew out his candle and had his window open a beat later. She tumbled gracelessly from his window, landing hard on her back before scrambling to her feet. "Come on."

Rua followed, crunching unhappily through the snow.

He mumbled something about sleep, but the simple fact was, they were running out of time. Their wedding was scheduled for the next moon, and nothing else had worked. Every time she'd tried to broach the subject, people spoke *over* her or *for* her, as if she hadn't the wits to come about her own decision. And she suspected Rua had suffered similar embarrassment.

So, this was all they had left.

Their village pressed right against the wood, carved from a patch of forest and lifted from the soil left behind.

People didn't like to speak of it, but she saw the way they eyed the greenery that always seemed to creep in on them, sending testing vines between the houses and trying to reclaim streets. She suspected everyone could tell that the forest wanted nothing more than to take the village in and eat it.

A trickle of learned fear trailed down her neck. She'd never tried to go this far into the forest with anyone before. Sure, she'd asked about obsessively, but it seemed like no one liked traveling beyond the sight of the houses. When it came to asking people where the heart of the forest might be located, they'd looked at her as if she'd gone stupid.

For his part, Rua didn't hesitate by the edge. He walked grumpy, with his legs doing that odd crouching they did whenever he was upset.

She followed behind him and tried to pretend she didn't notice his anger, but it tied her stomach in knots.

After a bell, the first hints of green started across the forest floor. Early spring buds formed on the branches of trees. Rua didn't notice until the flowers and leaves bloomed.

"Is this...normal?" he asked, as he studied a spring fresh blossom, running his fingers along pale yellow petals.

Tani nodded stiffly. She wasn't actually sure; she'd never gone this far in winter. But she was half-convinced that Rua would abandon her if she told him the truth.

She stopped abruptly, digging through her bag before finding a length of rope. She tied one end to Rua and the other to herself.

"You can't leave me, okay?" She tested the knots, she didn't know how the forest split people, but she wasn't going to risk him wandering off. "Promise me, you won't get lost."

He tugged at the rope. "I think that won't be a problem."

Tani glared at his chest. "Promise me."

His gaze heated the side of her face, probing. She didn't have any answers to give him. Only the words of an odd woman and the desperate hope that everything might turn out okay.

"I promise," he said, at last.

It made her feel better, at least he'd *try* even if he didn't understand her concern. He didn't even believe her about the old woman, not really. He didn't even like bringing her up, because she'd disappeared the next morning and Rua was sure they'd find her body in the spring thaw. So, how could Tani expect him to understand her rules? She couldn't hope to explain how she *knew* reality unraveled and rewove itself the longer they walked beneath the trees.

So, she just did what she always did. And she wasn't even sure how long that would work. There was a chance that everything could change due to some cue she couldn't hope to decipher.

Her heart fluttered uncomfortably at the thought.

After the second day, Rua asked if she knew where they were going. Tani lied, pointing in the direction the pattern provided but she didn't *know*. It ate at her.

The not knowing.

The lying.

The dwindling food supplies.

They were in no danger of going hungry, the forest was brimming with fruits and animals, but watching their reserves deplete had started to do something to Rua that made him quiet and thoughtful in a way she didn't understand.

When the days stopped wheeling overhead, he said nothing. He didn't even comment when the sun disappeared and refused to return. Rua welcomed eternal night with the same quiet acceptance he might have given a cut of rabbit.

She found that he had...started disappearing. It wasn't as though he'd *left* but...he wasn't precisely with her either.

And the longer they walked, the less of him there seemed to be.

Tani hurried them along. Get the plant, solve the problem, and when she got home Rua would come back.

Her Rua.

The one she loved.

It was during the endless night that she found them. Vines draping from the boughs of a tree that brushed the heavens. The small flowers that dripped from the greenery matched the image the woman had set in her head.

She picked them hurriedly as her mouth started moving. Her excitement seemed to set sparks in the air, making the world bright and new and beautiful, but it rolled off Rua.

He didn't congratulate her, he didn't offer any of his hugs, or laugh.

He simply stared at the vines as if they were the only thing left in the world.

Tani filled the kettle she'd been trudging around with, and with a small candle, she set it to boil. She bounced as she waited for it to finish.

Set the petals steeping.

They filled the air with a sweet scent that reminded her of the violet blossoms her mother filled the flower box with. She closed her eyes and took in the sound of the world while she waited.

Running water, rustling leaves, the quiet pulse of something deep and dark and endless that ran beneath the earth.

When she opened them, Rua was sitting across from her. She scrambled back, hand on her chest as she tried to piece together how, precisely, he'd gotten there.

He was quiet, but he'd never been…that was *too* quiet, wasn't it?

"Tani, are you alright?"

It sounded like Rua, the tones of his voice. The way he sounded her name.

She was just nervous. Tani didn't like trying new foods and while she'd been preparing herself for this moment since she walked into the forest, watching the flowers skim the surface of the water made her stomach clench. It wasn't any good to project her uncertainty onto her friend.

She emptied the kettle into two cups and handed one to Rua.

"I'm fine," she answered. "Just tired, maybe."

That was a lie.

Being in the forest felt *right*. It was easy.

It was breathing.

But Rua didn't seem to notice. He lifted his cup. "So, all we have to do is drink it?"

Tani nodded as she grabbed her own cup.

Now that they were there, it felt ridiculous to think that the small vessel of steaming water between her palms might make a difference.

Rua drank first.

And Tani found that she couldn't follow suit. Maybe it was the texture of the cup, or how the flowers crinkled and beat against the inside, but the idea of lifting it to her lips threatened to make her ill. A familiar, ugly panic surged through her.

She dumped the contents into the grass.

Gods, she'd try again. Gather more flowers, find more water. Sometimes, it took her time to do things. She still felt guilty.

"I'm sorry, Rua."

"Tani," he called. The ground gave as he shifted. He said her name wrong. Not the word, the word had been right, but the way he held it was...odd.

"Rua?"

"Tani," he repeated.

She shifted away from him. "Stop calling me like that."

"Tani, what's the matter?"

The sound of her name, the way he was saying it, set her skin twitching. It was *wrong*.

Not her Rua.

She glanced at the empty cup in his hands. "It's...do you feel any different?"

"Do you?"

Tani shook her head. Maybe the tea didn't matter. Maybe this had all been a cruel trick. Just her being too trusting of a stranger.

She made her way to her feet. A complicated mass of emotions settled in the pit of her stomach. "Let's go home."

Rua nodded and packed the kettle for her.

That was a very Rua gesture.

She felt him looking at her, and for the first time in her life, it made her uncomfortable. Her voice rang dull, "Come on, we'll...we'll figure something else out. Maybe I can convince Mama to let me become a disciple of Naya or I'll stall long enough for Papa to come back."

Rua didn't respond. His attention still seared her skin.

Tani shook her head, it had to be her imagination.

But she couldn't sleep beside him anymore.

Just standing near him while he was awake set her on edge. Like she was waiting for bad news or a tree to collapse.

At night, she waited for him to start snoring and undid the knot binding them together, preferring to sleep in the lower branches of a tree or on the other side of a bush instead of the makeshift shelters they crafted. And, even then, she slept poorly.

She was always up before Rua.

He was still gentle, still kind. For all her nerves, he still *acted* like Rua.

And it became more and more difficult to justify her discomfort.

Endless night became endless day, which soon became what felt to be an unnatural wheeling of the two. Summer faded to spring, but winter never brushed the forest's edges.

Soft blossoms and vibrant grasses appeared where there'd once been snow.

And then the tree line sat before them.

Rua's eyes were on her. She hid the tremor in her hands as she untied the knot at her waist.

"We're home," her voice broke, as the weight of everything to be done crashed into her. It was spring.

They were to be married.

"Tani," he said. She flinched, it was still wrong. She forced her legs still as he moved towards her.

She jerked and stopped when his hand moved to cup her cheek.

His lips pressed gently against hers.

Her eyes squeezed shut, her stomach twisting violently as she stumbled backwards.

"Rua?" Tani muttered more confused than upset, that hadn't felt like what anyone had described. "Why?"

"I love you," the words rang with the same hollow nothingness that'd bled into her name. She shook her head.

"You don't."

He took a step towards her, and she struggled to keep the distance between them. "Rua, you don't want this. You love Ira," she tried. Nothing in him suggested that he might have recognized the name. "The baker's daughter," she insisted.

That made him slow. Stop. A single worried note sang through the air, "*Tani?*"

And it was her name.

And for a brief beat, it was Rua. *Her* Rua.

Her friend.

Then his stance shifted, her name shuttered away so the next time he spoke, he said it wrong. Hollow, like the words of love he seemed to vomit unwillingly at her feet.

Was this what the woman had meant? To give them a flower that would rewrite their emotions? Make them choke empty affections at each other until Naya reclaimed them?

She'd never said they wouldn't marry, only that things would go the way they were meant to.

Rua was speaking, but none of the words reached her. She doubted they would have mattered.

Marriage wasn't an option. It never had been.

She took a step back and spun, sprinting through trees and slipping in patches wet from some spring rain she'd never gotten to feel. Rua lumbered behind her, calling her in that vast, empty way. But she was quick, and she knew the rules.

And she allowed the woods to steal her away.

Chapter 34

Del woke with the feeling of Tani's hand in hers.

Thanae peered at her above the pages of a small tome from his perch on the windowsill. "Are you awake?"

Del stared at her palms as if they were something foreign. Warmth still buzzed across her skin.

"You ask the oddest questions, Thanae," she croaked.

"Well, sometimes you open your eyes and talk, but it's not to me," he grumbled.

That was…a disturbing image and not something she was equipped to deal with. "My time is up, isn't it?"

The guard shrugged.

"Aren't we meant to be heading back? I only had ten days."

He snorted. "We're not leaving when you're like this."

"But my Promise," she trailed off. The band stayed stubbornly cool around her wrist, she frowned. She should be—

"The prince said he'll extend your…vacation, he needs you alive. He'd like healthy, but you have something against that."

Del glared at him, but the guard had turned to his reading and her annoyance alone wasn't enough to set the paper smoldering.

"So, what am I meant to do?"

"Rest."

"But…" She wasn't sure she could *do* that. She'd spent so much time just trying to get from one goal to the next, that she'd never had the chance to simply *be*. "Are you sure there isn't anything I'm supposed to do?"

"Besides sleep?"

"Yes."

"Eat, drink, and wash," he listed, blandly.

She fiddled nervously with her covers. That wasn't...a lot.

Her plant rested on her nightstand, freshly watered. The book she couldn't hope to read by its side, its fabric bookmark still nestled between its pages.

She reached for it.

The tome opened in her lap; a picture of a long-stemmed flower stared up at her. She ran her fingers over it, tracing the petals.

"Thanae?"

He grunted his acknowledgement.

"I'm bored," she breathed.

"Take a nap."

"I just woke up."

"Good for you." he didn't even look up from the romance book he thought she didn't recognize. She'd read it before, while trying to tailor herself. It was a truly wretched thing, all dewy eyes and long heart gushing proclamations.

Precisely the type of shit the Grand Mage had enjoyed.

She sighed flipping through a few pages before closing her tome. Gods, she needed something to *do*. Her mind, when unoccupied, liked to shift back to the forest, to the *portrait*, to her master...

Nothing had gone as it was supposed to, the Grand Mage was dead, and she still breathed, there was a future for her *outside* of his realm of influence. It may not be safer, but it was certainly...gentler. Kinder.

No.

She forced herself upright. She shouldn't mistake whatever the prince had been showing her for kindness.

He was trying to use her, which meant he'd only care for her for as long as she was *useful.*

So, she just had to ensure she remained useful.

Del started casting tentatively, her fingers hesitating as she reached for the magic in the earth beneath her. The memory of it having overwhelmed her sent her intentions scattering.

Magic had never been something she'd feared.

She grasped the tail ends before they drifted off, binding them into familiar runes and locking them until a small light rested above her. She held it, and started focusing on another, and another, placing them into the air in an approximation of a night sky.

Her body ran cool, sweat beading along her brow as she was forced to hold their shape and spacing while crafting new ones.

She set them twinkling, before she started to move them around, arranging them in the rough approximation of a box, then a circle, a tree...no, she pulled them apart into a senseless mass.

No trees.

It was better to focus on the task at hand. At proving she was useful, even after her ill-conceived foray.

She moved the orbs about, letting them drift out of reach before floating them over to Thanae. She arranged them into a halo around his head.

A shiver wracked her frame, but she held onto the lights stubbornly. The prince likely had no interest in this type of magic, but being able to cast, and control something at all meant she had at least some of the skill the prince demanded.

She could still be good for *something.*

"What's—," Thanae began. He glanced from his book, and spying the nearest orb, stilled, "I said no casting."

"It's light Thanae," she answered, breathlessly, "not a weapon."

He frowned turning his attention to her. "I said 'rest', too."

"That's all I've been doing," she griped, "I need to—"

When had he moved above her? The casting's doused as her focus shifted.

"I said, 'rest'" he reiterated.

Del shook her head against the pillow. "You can't really want me to do nothing."

She imagined the look he gave her was the precise expression he used when a child said something incredibly stupid. "Healing isn't nothing."

Another shiver took her even without the castings, the guard looked her over, taking in disheveled appearance and sweat soaked clothes.

"Close your eyes," he ordered, impatiently.

Del's eyes remained very open.

"I'll go to the window," he offered.

She mulled it over before nodding.

The guard ambled over and repeated his command, this time, she complied. A few beats passed.

"This feels silly," she muttered.

"Count to sixty."

"Why?"

"Because you should," he answered.

Del frowned and started counting, the words started losing shape around twenty, she switched tongues near thirty and finally, finally dozed off before reaching forty.

And for the first time, in a very long time, she had no dreams at all.

Chapter 35

The trick Thanae had pulled irked her, in no small part because it had worked. But after that, she'd stopped fighting the drowsiness that dragged at her and it seemed all she could do was sleep.

The next few days crawled by with infuriating slowness.

In her waking bells, she couldn't seem to settle. Doing *nothing* felt unnatural, but Thanae had taken her quills and papers and locked them away somewhere she couldn't find them. And he learned quickly that if he distracted her enough, she'd no hope of maintaining her castings.

So, she sat and tried to annoy Thanae into giving her her things. When she wasn't doing that, she bothered him for stories, or sweets, or souvenirs.

And in that manner five days wheeled past.

On the sixth Thanae studied her for a very long moment during breakfast. "Feeling better?"

She sighed, having long since set her head against the tiny table they'd taken to using as a dining area. Her hand flopped by her side.

"Is that a 'yes'?"

"It's *boring*, Thanae," she mumbled into the wood, "*Boring, boring, boring.*"

"You *sound* better," he answered, with infuriating calm. Nothing she did seemed to change whatever course he'd decided to set. She couldn't get *any* reaction most days and it was driving her insane.

"I feel like death might have been the kinder alternative."

He snorted as he gathered their plates into a pile and set them on the lip by the window. He'd take them down while she slept. She'd never said as much, but she suspected he'd realized being alone bothered her.

He never said anything about the nightmares either.

Why he didn't speak of it, or lord it over her was a mystery, much in the same vein as why he'd dimmed the lantern for her in the ship or why he'd saved and continued to care for her silly little plant.

"We leave in a bell," he announced.

"What?" the table shook as Del stood; her palms smacked against the surface.

"We leave in a bell," he repeated.

Her heart thrummed in her throat. "Really?"

"Yes."

Her entire body shook with anticipation. Part of the deal Thanae had struck with the innkeeper required Del to stay in her room to avoid "spreading" her illness. She hadn't even been able to go on walks once she'd felt well enough to do so.

She suspected she'd damn near wore a track in the floor.

The guard let out what might have been either a chuckle or a sneeze. Her ears heated. She shouldn't have made so much noise. She searched his face.

He looked back at her with honest curiosity. "What is it?"

"I don't...," she began. He simply wasn't making any sense. None of his reactions were right and she could *feel* herself responding to it, even if she wasn't entirely sure it was safe.

"It's nothing." She shook her head and returned to her seat. "Is everything packed?"

The guard nodded. "Mostly."

Del fidgeted with her sleeve. He'd even purchased new clothes. They weren't nearly as soft as what she was used to, but they were nice. Their fabric covered her body in a way the Grand Mage's gifted garments never did, and they didn't seek to strangle her as the frock she'd borrowed from her sister had.

A neckline that stopped mid chest rather than at her navel.

He'd seemed surprised when she'd asked for trousers, as well as several skirts, but he hadn't fought her on it.

Dressed the way she was felt *right*. Like she wasn't frowning at the girl she saw reflected in the mirror. Sometimes she even caught herself smiling, and that was...very new.

The sound of the bed scraping across the floor shook her from her thoughts. The guard bent down and pulled the handle of a small door set into the floor, wrenching it open.

Annoyance flashed through her as he pulled her travelling case from the crawlspace. Which explained why she couldn't seem to find it. Her fingers drummed her frustration against the table.

Thanae faced her, the beginnings of a cocky smile forming on his lips. "Ready?"

Del blinked. "Now?"

He nodded.

She shifted uncomfortably, her excitement waning. She'd known she couldn't stay in the tavern forever, she didn't *want* to, but...it was the first place that had started to feel like the home she'd always wished for.

Which was stupid, she shook her head and made her way to her feet. She grabbed her little plant from the windowsill and tried to ignore the niggling sensation that'd started in the back of her skull.

She waited for Thanae by the door as he packed the rest of their things away.

"It's right out front," he offered, as he pushed by her and started down the hall. She trailed behind him trying to make up the distance on the stairs and reached the bottom in time to see the kitchen door swing shut.

There were no "farewells", no "good-byes". The kitchen was empty, only the deep bellied pot that sat warming on a cooking tablet hinted that anyone had been there at all. Del wondered briefly about Dirg, and the woman who'd taken her to the border, about the captain, and Ner, and her siblings.

Maybe good-byes only existed in novels.

"Del?" Her name was muffled through the wood.

She pushed the door open, squinting in the mid-morning sun. Thanae waved from the end of the row of houses. She jogged to close the distance and was nearly winded by the time she reached him.

The carriage was already there. An ornate box set atop four giant wheels. It was about the same size as the horseless carriages in Egrea.

Their driver, a small man with laugh lines, held the door for her. She straightened and tried to keep her breathing from sounding like the final gasps of a drowning man.

His eyes searched her face, fixing on a patch of cheek. She reached up instinctively and found only skin.

A dull pulse of magic trilled beneath her fingers.

Her mage's mark. She'd forgotten to cover it.

She dropped her gaze and scurried up the stairs with a mumbled, "Thank you." The driver made no move to stop her.

She sat on the bench and tried to make herself small. Her hand pressed against her cheek as she tried in vain to cover the silver that now stretched across her forehead.

Her nails dug into her skin.

"What are you doing?" Thanae asked.

She flinched as the carriage door shut behind him. Her hands leapt into her lap and wrapped around her makeshift flowerpot. The guard didn't like it when she clawed at herself. "I'm sorry."

His brow furrowed. "For what?"

"I just...I was..." Her fingers pressed against the wood. "I didn't cover the mage's mark," she admitted.

The guard's face blanked. "Oh, shit. I forgot." The carriage jostled as he leapt down, offering excuses to the driver who had started to chide him.

She stared at the spot he left behind. He really was terrible at this. How could he possibly forget?

Thanae reappeared in the doorway and shoved her trunk onto the seat, forcing her flush against the carriage side as he squeezed in beside it. "I didn't know what you needed," he said.

"So...you brought the entire trunk?"

He nodded earnestly.

Gods, he was just...like Asha? Del squinted.

She knew all too well that people were nebulous. The Grand Mage had shifted from glib to violent in a matter of beats, and she'd *known* the Grand Mage.

She did not know Thanae.

"Thank you," she said, as she undid the clasp. Her pastes had fallen to the bottom, and she'd no water to start with. She made do, improvising with her reflection in the glass as the carriage began to move and left the village behind.

They rumbled down patches of high-grown weeds and memories of abandoned homes, burned temples, and ruined fields.

Once, they passed by a working farm, manned by Shattered. They moved with a quiet, eerie efficiency beneath the fading sunlight. The smell was so strong, she had to close the window and spent the next half-bell heaving violently into the sick bowl the driver provided.

They checked into an inn as night fell and started again at sunrise.

On the third day of travel, they rolled down a well paved street snaking between towering homes with flower boxes before glass windows and vines curling down walls. Everything had huddled together beneath a canopy of trees, so the light hit the ground like rain. At the end of the road a building sat patiently as people went in and out of its open doorways.

As the carriage moved closer, she realized how large it was. Its arches rivalled the height of the palace's atrium. The concrete lattice work spun and soared, dancing in a way only structures built before the war had. Vines grew along the frame, dripping flowers that spoke warm rainbows into the air.

It smelled of flowers and magic. Del received the latter with more trepidation than she liked. She did not revel in it, only touched upon it and felt the world sharpen as she tilted her head near the open window.

The carriage slowed behind a seemingly endless line of other, fancier traveling boxes. Many with colors she recognized as belonging to lady Surannie, or the royal family itself. A swarm of people approached the door dressed in uniforms that seemed to be a mixture of the knight's garb and servant greys.

Neat with the affectation of utility.

She steeled herself as Thanae opened the door.

"It's so lovely to see you," a man with a high reedy voice began, before barking orders to the rest of the attendants. Del scrambled behind the guard as skirts and searching hands picked around her.

Her hands clutched at her plant, her fingers digging into the bowl's surface.

It was like walking through a storm. All she could manage was to stick to the guard as attendants whipped around her some offering a hand, another complementing her clothes, another still swept their trunks away to somewhere she hoped they had been directed to go.

She nodded vaguely as they continued to brush against her, her pulse fluttering as she struggled to pull their sentences into words that held meaning instead of just sound. Her eyes darted through the crowd nervously as a woman with a blue pendant escorted them across the floors.

Del was able to pick up bits and pieces. "Built in...the vines are...as you know it's one of the...took the primitive and pulled it up to standard."

She craned her neck, peering through their bubble of servants to spy people milling about, buying trinkets and snacks from ornate stalls. Ladies dripping in finery drifted by as men in tailored suits or soft colored kaftans meandered. Smoke wafted from select pipes, sending wisps into the air that caught in petals and green.

Del felt silly in the midst of it all clutching a plant to her chest.

A deep earth-shaking rumble sounded, stealing what little breath she had. She backed into a kindly servant with wired braids.

"It's a lot, isn't it?" she said, and tried not to laugh as Del froze. A *building* thundered along a set of tracks dug into the floor.

The train was *huge*. It towered above her a giant metal creature glowing with deep red runes. Giant power stones the size of her body were set behind a metal grate placed onto the vehicles face. It smelled of the memories of fire and flame and scalding metal. If they'd been in Egrea, it would have belched smoke into the air.

"Come on." The woman pushed her, gently urging her forward. The trill that accompanied being touched overrode Del's fear. She pulled away too sharply, her cheeks warmed.

"Ah, sorry, I—, it's...very big." Del turned back to the train.

The woman chuckled and gave a small wave, "Have a nice trip, my lady." The protective bubble the servants had wrapped Del and Thanae in popped. The workers melted into a crowd of nobles clamoring a few paces away.

Thanae was talking to a man in a crisp uniform and a stiff brimmed hat, standing strategically before a set of winding metal stairs. She shrank under the ticket master's gaze. His attention rested on her for a beat too long, before shifting to Thanae with a beatific smile.

"You'll find your room up the steps, dinner is available upon request," he delivered, in a crisp Reprenian accent. He plucked the tickets Thanae handed him and sliced them deftly with a mage sized knife attached to his belt loop, before handing them back.

He stepped aside and Thanae started up the steps. Del picked her way after him, her footsteps were swallowed by the clamoring of the crowd below. They bottlenecked near the door, waving tickets in the man's face. His smile never faltered as he picked one ticket at a time and allowed passengers behind him, into the train's lower belly.

"Del."

She hurried down a narrow set of steps, her shoes met marble at the bottom. The entire top of the train was glass. Thin metal supports held the panels in place. Flowered vines draped themselves across the surface, moon briar among them, scattering petals across the surface.

That was something she was going to have to learn to live with.

The ground growled beneath her, sending tremors through her legs and settling in her stomach. She found Thanae lounging across a long chair. The interior was nearly another inn. A bed sat in a corner; a chandelier hung suspended from a metal rod attached to the ceiling.

A series of light castings sent warm beams scattering through a number of glass panels, giving the room an almost daylight glow, despite the way evening had started to creep in.

"Are all trains like this?" she asked hesitantly.

Thanae laughed, and she worried briefly if that had been a dumb assumption. The guard shook his head. "Didn't the—" He stopped himself, and coughed into his hand. "Only if you're very, very rich."

She wandered around the room, holding onto her plant like it was the only thing keeping her from drifting towards the ceiling. A moving inn.

She'd never imagined such a thing was possible, the pictures had always shown rows of seats, like those in the viewing boxes near the gallows.

As Del explored the bathing room and the bathroom, a high-pitched whistle sprang into the air. She jumped, rushing from her head deep exploration of the tub and reached the main room in time to nearly topple as the machinery lurched into action.

Vines ran their fingers over the glass as the train pulled away. She found her attention fixed on the skies. The chugging of the wheels picked up speed until they thrummed in a continuous loop beneath her. Ose's skies dipped from blue to violet, singing hues of reds and yellows.

"Are you hungry?" Thanae asked, after a few ticks. Del tilted her chin down and realized her neck had gone stiff. She shook her head as the guard yawned.

She squinted as the lights in the interior started reflecting off the glass too strongly to see beyond it. She worried her lip, glancing at the guard. "Can I turn off the lights?"

He nodded, already half-asleep.

Del dispelled the castings, feeling her skin twitch as they all unraveled at once. Even as the train rushed past the ghosts of trees and houses, the sky stayed the same. There was something comforting about that now that she knew it might disappear from above her.

She lay down on the floor, setting her plant by her side. It reminded her of when she'd done something similar in the orchards, but instead of the chirring of night insects she heard the steady *thrumthrumthrum* of the machinery far beneath her.

Thanae dozed off at some point, but she stayed awake.

Nights had always felt so short at the Grand Mage's wing, for the last several months she'd experiments to tend to, papers to write, a master to please, and even on those rare nights where there was nothing, she'd been too exhausted or wound to enjoy it.

But nights were long, she realized. They spooled out in quiet, dragging bells.

She raised her hand towards the sky as if she planned to catch the stars spanning above her. Her Promise band winked in the starlight. She frowned feeling the magic pulsing beneath her skin.

She brought it to her face, but it still just looked like another scar. There didn't seem to be anything special from the looks of it. Still bound her to Tiremalv all the same.

For the first time in nearly a decade, Del wondered what the future held.

If she'd be there in a year, and what she'd be doing.

She'd gone and Promised herself to a prince who snuck around, bedded all manner of nobility, and spoke to Shattered. A prince who'd spent half a year trying to get the attention of a Pet.

He reeked of trouble.

And being near him would make trying to fade into the background very difficult.

That wasn't going to be what he asked of her. So far, all her attempts to flatter and please had been met with annoyance. Her frown deepened.

If she wasn't meant to disappear, and she wasn't meant to preen...what precisely did the third prince of Qasha want from her? Just her knowledge? Was that really worth all this?

Thoughts pinged through her head until the sun rose, and her guard stirred.

She'd been trying to ignore it, but lights from the capital had seeped into the edge of her vision before the sun did. If she tilted her head, she knew with absolute certainty that she'd be able to spy the castle across the river, little more than a bright smear on the horizon.

Kothen Palace.

Chapter 36

The rising sun set the river in brilliant hues.

Del wondered what her master might have said if he'd been around to see it.

Surely, he'd slide his hand along her arm, and whisper something stupid in her ear. A shiver ran down her back at the imagining of it, some of her scars took the opportunity to remind her, unkindly, of their existence.

Thanae did not slide his hand down her arm, nor did he whisper in her ear. And if he'd been near her, she doubted he would have bothered with either.

She stood by the water's edge as he directed their things onto the boat. She'd found a place far from the crowd of servants waiting to be ferried in, to sulk.

It was sulking, she acknowledged with mild annoyance.

The distance didn't even stop the palace workers' conversation from hitting her in waves.

Questions about the "Chousalian girl" mixed with rumors about the third prince's latest tryst, the Athijans, the latest heretic hung in the square. The very same rumors she'd heard for nearly the last nine years, breathed to life.

Almost as though she'd never left at all.

It was far too easy to imagine returning to the Grand Mage's rooms. She could even hear Ner's worried tutting as she escorted Del to her cage.

She'd chide Del and strip her of her new clothes saying she smelled of travel, her nose doing that frustrated scrunch that happened whenever Del smelled wrong. Then the maid would order a bath run with the proper perfumes and soaps poured into the water and choose an outfit of deep violet ruffles and a neckline that stopped just short of Del's brands.

And Del would follow behind and prattle of nothing at all as her heart sank, and she'd cry alone in the warm waters of the bath.

And it would be as if this entire trip had all been in her imagination.

Her eyes fixed on the palace.

The Grand Mage wasn't there.

He wasn't waiting at his godsdamned desk, or pacing in his stupid rooms, or raging at her cage doorway waiting for her to return. He wasn't even drawing air.

The Grand Mage, Gadna Niao, was dead.

And she was not.

She took a deep breath, inhaling the smell of the docks and morning fires. Perfumes, and pastries. She stood at the bank of a river she'd not been allowed to cross for eight years; she breathed in the smell of fires that were never meant to reach her.

The Grand Mage Gadna Niao was dead.

"Del," her name cut through the chatter. She turned instinctively, her eyes searching the crowd until she found Thanae. He waved her over.

She forced her legs to move. Tried to hide how every motion seemed to drag behind her as if her body regretted every step that took her closer to the palace. Cutting through the crowd was still difficult, but with the servant greys, and the smell of palace soaps, it at least felt familiar.

Like trying to move to the kitchens before the king's dinner.

She latched onto Thanae as soon as she could, using him as a shield from the rest of the mob.

"That's a little—" he began.

She'd all but glued herself to his side, just a hair's breadth of actually touching him.

"I don't like crowds," she answered with more intensity than she'd intended, and promptly wished she'd kept her mouth shut.

The guard studied her the best he could, given the lack of space, before nodding. He handed a copper piece to the ferrywoman, possibly the tallest person Del had ever seen, who received it with a sly grin and let them onto the ship.

It was empty but for a few other ferry workers who shot them questioning glances. Del found a spot near the bow.

The river ran clear here, her gaze dragged to the palace which had grown large enough for her to see its towers soaring above the houses. The dread that came over her whenever she looked at it wasn't something she could explain or quantify. It was just...there, quietly waiting to be acknowledged.

"Thanae," she began, and stopped. She didn't really need him. She just wanted reassurance.

"What?"

She bit her lip, trying to swallow the question that sprang from her throat without permission, "The Grand Mage isn't waiting for me, is he?"

The way he looked at her made her wish she hadn't spoken at all.

She *knew* the Grand Mage was dead. She'd seen him. Cursed him. Felt his chest cold and still and she *still* couldn't make it feel real. Even now.

"He can't be there," the guard answered. He said it factually, the way one might spell numbers down a receipt.

She searched his face for the lie.

"He can't be there," he repeated, earnestly.

Somehow that was easier to grasp. She couldn't make sense of his dying, but his *leaving*. He'd done that before.

A horn rang out a low deep call that set her heart racing. The rest of the workers spilled onto the ship, flashing pendants and papers. Del found herself using Thanae as a shield again as nearly every free patch of the deck disappeared. It was the reason wealthier nobles usually chartered smaller, more private boats.

The type she'd half-expected the prince to arrange to retrieve her.

Thanae's bearing proved incredibly useful in keeping most people at bay as they made their slow way across the river. Kothen Palace grew closer with every passing moment.

The Grand Mage couldn't be there.

And he couldn't reach her, so long as the prince needed her. Her fingers ran over her Promise band as her eyes fixed on the growing blotch of the palace.

It took her a full tick to realize Thanae was talking to her and even longer to process what he was saying. From what she could piece together, it seemed to be a lot of nonsense, just a story about his home, his brother.

It threw off the anxious whirling of her thoughts.

She found herself unable to split her attention between the two.

And she realized that she'd rather be listening to Thanae's story.

She did a piss poor job of it. Most of his words passed uselessly between her ears. It seemed to be a soft story, something about running around the docks and making trouble for the sailors.

"You don't have to do that," she interrupted, abruptly.

The guard stopped midsentence and fixed his grey eyes on her. "Do what?"

Her thoughts churned slowly, as she tried to put her concerns into words, "I don't need you to...treat me...like a person."

"You *are* a person," he stated, blandly.

"But...I'm—" She shook her head. "Why? Why do you treat me the way you do? Even in the beginning, you turned off the lantern."

His brows arched. "Lantern?"

"On the *ship*, Thanae," she whined. "You don't make sense, and I don't understand why you do what you do."

"You don't like it?"

Her gaze shifted across the waters. "...that's not the *point*."

His expression went smug. "You *do* like it."

Del let out a breath, fighting the instinct to bang her head against the railing, she made do with setting her cheek against the bar. It was cold. "Both you and your prince are positively incorrigible."

"*My* prince?"

"He's my loyalty, not my fealty."

"Same thing."

A dry chuckle wound its way from her lips, "You think?" The band around her wrist stayed cool. Subservience was something she'd not thought too deeply about, but there was an air about the prince that made her think that wasn't what he desired.

What was the fantasy of the man who seemed to have everything?

The tick the boat docked, Thanae hurried her off. He cut through the sea of people with brutal efficiency as Del struggled to keep up with his loping strides.

He stopped short before a disgustingly opulent carriage. The body of it was made of wood so dark it bordered on black. Deep blue inlays formed a series of ornate swoops and swirls, that coalesced into an array of flowers and leaves that bled across the vehicle's brow. The royal serpent stretched beneath it all, azurite eyes sparkling in the light of the rising sun.

Her heart stuttered at the sight of it.

"We're riding in this?" she whispered, horrified. Thanae was already ushering her inside.

A small, neat package wrapped in delicate paper sat atop a royal blue cushion.

The guard muttered, as he shut the door, "That's yours, you need to change."

Del picked it up and sat in its place.

A cream-colored card peeked from one of the paper's folds. She plucked it out, and read:

To my darling Issi,

You captured my attention at the King's Dinner. You are by far the loveliest creature I have ever laid eyes on. Your beauty has reduced me to a man of wants. I find myself drunk on the very desire for your presence—

She rolled her eyes and flicked the note onto the floor. Pure drivel, the whole of it.

It was exactly the type of shit her master would mutter.

She opened the package to reveal a pile of blue fabric, slightly brighter than the carriage's interior. The trim had been completed in neat golden embroidery. She unfolded it and a patch of blue fell to the floor.

The dress was simple enough, long sleeves and a high collar with two slits starting at her upper thigh. The piece that had fallen turned out to be a pair of trousers with lacing that almost reminded her of a corset from the cuff to her knee. Matching silk slippers had been tucked into a pocket.

She set the fabric carefully atop her lap. "Thanae, there's been a mistake, these aren't mine."

He snorted. "It won't fit me."

Her cheeks heated. "But, this isn't, these aren't—"

"You need to get dressed," he interrupted.

Del bit the inside of her cheek, weighing whether or not this was something she was willing to argue. The carriage broke free of the dock side traffic and began to pick up speed.

She peeled her clothes away.

Thanae stared pointedly at his hands as she changed. The outfit fit loosely, leaving space around her wrists, stomach, and thighs, but she suspected that if she'd worn it when she'd left it might have been perfect.

She tied the lace and snuck her feet into the slippers as the carriage passed through the main gates. It slowed only for the driver to wave and for Thanae to pull back a curtain to show his face.

They continued unimpeded through the palace grounds, jostling through a number of gardens Del had never seen before, most with large blossoming trees and hidden alcoves.

It stopped when they neared the river. The driver climbed down from his seat and opened the door.

Thanae left from the other side as Del was escorted onto a section of pavers. The garden pressed against the edges, stopped only by the path they'd driven down and the platform she found herself on. The view of the river was obscured by a series of high growing bushes and a subtler set of magical barriers whose scents sang with the promise of flowers.

"Del," Thanae began, and coughed. "Miss Anders, we don't have all day."

Hearing her old title nearly made her wince. But the driver was watching, so she plastered a smile onto her face. "Oh, I'm sorry, I was lost in thought."

Thanae frowned as he watched her but said nothing when she joined him to pass through a large set of glass doors.

The prince's wing sprawled before them. The moonbriar vines she was growing used to snaked across the ground, spilling petals this way and that. Thanae followed them without comment.

She wondered if he could see them. If he'd deigned to follow them or if they were going to a predestined location. He gave no indication one way or the other.

The hall shrank to a corridor, and finally, Thanae stopped before a door. He knocked and let himself inside without invitation.

Del found herself rooted by the door.

It was just a step.

She swallowed nervously and waited.

Thanae reappeared a moment later. "Come on."

Del shuffled closer and peeked through the doorway. It was a sitting room. A series of chairs sat along the walls, facing a window that offered an unobscured view of the river. A chandelier suspended crystalline droplets from the ceiling above a heavy mahogany table brimming with sweets.

"Del, come in." Tiremalv's voice set her heart racing.

She tried to imagine what he might ask and how she was meant to respond as she entered the doorway. The prince lay on a couch facing the window. Her hands knotted in front of her to stop them from shaking.

"How was your trip?"

Every prepared response left her. "I...I...uhm," she struggled. The Grand Mage had very rarely asked for her opinion, her fingers bore down on themselves so heavily she worried they might snap.

"It was...unpleasant," she continued, quietly, "But I think it was something I had to do."

"And your little detour?"

She swallowed. "I'm sorry."

The prince scoffed, "Don't apologize. I can't *do* anything with that. What did you find?"

"What did I find?" she echoed.

The prince nodded. "Of course, you came back with a book and a plant so I'm assuming you found *something*."

Del darted a glance at Thanae who shrugged. "I...I found—."

"Del, please, sit down, and stop looking like I'm going to eat you. There's plenty else," he said, gesturing to the laden table. "You're fine."

She studied him for a moment. He wasn't Ardein...but he wasn't Gadna either. She set herself on the very edge of a chair. It was a spectacular view, here beyond the river, and days and days of travel, she saw the mountains.

"I found...Chousal," she began, softly. She waited for the prince to laugh or question. When he didn't, she continued, "I...it was the capital. The bodies are still there, as are the shops..." She trailed off, unsure of how to explain everything that had happened to her.

She felt like a child again, scolded for running off.

"Do you know how long you were gone?"

Del nodded. "It felt like days...two maybe three..."

"You were gone for nearly a quarter moon," he hummed, as he lifted a honey cake from a plate. "But the Promise Band didn't do anything, so I had Thanae wait."

"A quarter moon?" she echoed.

Tiremalv grinned. "It was very odd. But here you are, all together, in one piece. And healthy, though I think I remember your nose being a bit different."

Her hands flew up to cover it, Thanae had done his best, but it'd garnered a permanent crook. She was fond of it.

"Did you walk all the way there or—"

"No." She shifted, uncomfortably, in her chair as she tried to find a way to explain this that wouldn't leave the prince thinking her mad. "I...I didn't mean to go. Not to the forest, I meant that, but the capital. I didn't...I didn't have a choice."

The prince frowned as he bit into his sweet. "Meaning?"

"I..." She wasn't sure what he wanted to hear. "I'm very sorry to have caused you worry."

He sighed, "What else did you find, Del?"

"Just the capital and the things Thanae found with me."

His gaze heated her skin. Del's attention fixed on her left hand, her eyes tracing the dips in the flesh that'd never healed properly`.

"How are you still lucid?" he asked, at last.

"I...might have..." Naya's hells, she'd been trying to ignore that and the fact that she hadn't been getting worse since leaving the forest. "I might have found a..." She was hesitant to use the word *cure*. She shook her head and hurried on, trying to forget the feel of the Voice between her ears, "we might have been thinking about it wrong. There's a chance that it's not an illness at all but rather a—." She cut herself off abruptly, biting deep into the flesh of her cheek.

She tasted blood.

"Out with it, Del," his tone was thick with disappointment.

She winced. "It might not be a sickness...rather a...casting rebound...of sorts. Chousal might be...calling for its people...mages are sensitive to magic fluctuations, so...I think we're dying unintentionally because nobody knows what it's trying to do."

The prince's brows arched. "The *country*, the *dead* nation of Chousal, is calling people?"

Del's head bobbed in acknowledgment. She hated herself for it, for entertaining the very idea that the Voice, that'd haunted her might have been telling even a hint of truth.

"That makes no sense." The prince waved his free hand dismissively. "Then why are there no reports from the Northern Tribes or the Athijans?"

"Because they weren't at fault," Del snapped.

The prince stilled. Her hands clenched in her lap, the air in the room went thin. "I mean, I...that is, I've found something that *works* for me. I can't say that it will for anyone else," gods knew how much she hoped it would, and how desperately she needed it to fail, "but since trying it, I've had no dreams and the visions haven't gotten any worse."

"What is it?"

She looked away. "We just...need to be closer to the forest. It doesn't matter which form. Even a plant would work."

"The forest," he repeated. The princeling frowned as she sat there, her lungs laboring to pull air through her rapidly constricting throat.

He finished the rest of his treat and stood.

Del froze, hardly daring to breathe. The prince moved towards her. She steeled herself for whatever punishment he was readying to dole out.

"Come on." He waited in the doorway.

Del's heart sank, she had to convince her legs to work and followed him down the hallway. He was going to throw her out, she could feel it. She'd made no deal to ensure her own freedom or safety. She hadn't thought she'd live this long.

She walked right into the prince's back and let out a curse.

"Del, did you hear a single word I've said?"

Blood drained from her cheeks. She shook her head. The prince sighed and opened the door he'd stopped in front of.

"I said, we'll look into your...cure...once you feel more secure about your story. A lot of what you said doesn't make sense, but I can't have you fainting on me..." Annoyance flickered briefly across his face, and it was like taking a knife to her stomach. "So we'll try again later. I just wanted to show you this before taking you to your room."

He stepped inside and Del followed behind him before nearly tripping over nothing at all.

"I need you to—"

"It's a Transfer," she shouted, all thoughts of propriety and danger were shoved somewhere she couldn't reach. Gods above it was more beautiful than she'd imagined. The entire structure barely fit inside the room the prince had shoved it in. How he'd even managed to get it through the *door...*

She was already running her hands along the surface. None of the runes came to life beneath her touch, which meant this *beautiful* contraption didn't *work.*

"Ardein, do you...why do you, I mean." She bounced, nervously, trying not to let her excitement sweep her away so completely a second time. "A Transfer?"

Amusement was plain on the prince's features and for once Del found that she simply didn't care.

"Yes, it's a Transfer. Do you think you could fix it?"

Fix it?

"Prince, it's a *Transfer*," she stressed, a giant beast of a machine meant to send letters instantly to a partner that could be moons of travel away. It had taken the Grand Mage, half a dozen palace mages, fifteen Egrean metalsmiths, a scholar from the northern Tribes, and ten blacksmiths to craft the damn thing.

What hope did she have?

"Is that a 'no'?"

"I..." Her gaze followed the curves of the metal casing. She needed the prince to need her, she needed him to think her useful. She swallowed, nervously, feeling an uncertain future starting to sprawl before her.

Del had never meant to live this long.

She'd survived her family.

She'd survived the Grand Mage.

She could survive this too, she just had to bide her time until she figured out what was next.

"Yes," her voice rang with a confidence she didn't feel, "I can fix it."

Her eyes drifted to the prince's. They sparkled above his gap-toothed grin.

Ose's skies packed into two twin points.

Gods above, she hoped she hadn't just made the biggest mistake of her life. Because she had the sneaking suspicion that maybe, just maybe, she might have been better off perishing that night her master had leapt from the roof.